RAVE REVIEWS FOR DEBRA DIER'S OTHER ROMANCES!

"I ain't no gentleman, pretty lady," Ash said, his voice a harsh whisper.

Elizabeth trembled with the dark promise in his voice. "Are you warning me?"

"Guess maybe I am."

She stayed in his hold, knowing he would release her if she struggled. Yet she had no will to leave his warm embrace. She wanted to feel his arms around her. She wanted to taste the reality of his kiss that had lived in her dreams.

All her life she had daydreamed of a boy who had been lost in the wilderness, imagining how he would look as he grew older, wondering if one day they would meet. And now he was here, holding her, and he was more exciting than she had ever imagined.

Flickering flames flashed in the cool blue of his eyes. His fingers tensed on the nape of her neck, drawing her upward as he lowered his head. His breath felt warm and soft against her cheek, sweet as a meadow after a spring rain. He slid his lips over hers, taking possession, gliding slowly from one corner of her lips to the other, until he claimed her completely.

DEBRA DIER

Lord Savage

LSIEURE BOOKS **NEW YORK CITY**

For Faye and Corky. Thank you for all your love and support.

A LEISURE BOOK®

December 1996

Published by

Dorchester Publishing Co., Inc.
276 Fifth Avenue
New York, NY 10001

Printed in the United States of America.

Chapter One

Denver, 1889

Never in her life had Lady Elizabeth Barrington seen a more dangerous-looking man. Of course, never in her twenty-six years had she been given the opportunity to meet a man like Ash MacGregor. And now she stood in the hall of Miss Hattie's Fancy House, staring up at MacGregor, who filled the doorway of his bedroom.

Pure, undiluted power radiated from the man. It brushed against her like a hot wind, setting her pulse pounding against the high neck of her blue serge gown. Tall, broad shouldered, his lean body sheathed in a shirt and trousers of unrelieved black, his hair tumbling to his shoulders in untamed dark waves, MacGregor looked like some savage creature coaxed into the confines of this house, wary of what his unexpected visitor might want. He stared at her, his eyes narrowed beneath slanting dark brows.

Those eyes!

Even filled with suspicion his eyes were beautiful, mesmerizing, dangerous. Eyes the pale blue of a morning sky edged in the dark blue of midnight regarded her with unflinching scrutiny. He stripped away pretense with that intense blue stare. Penetrated her defenses. Perceived all of her secrets in a glance. Oh my, she couldn't breathe.

"So you say you're Hayward Trevelyan's *ward*."

There was a subtle shading in his deep voice, as though he doubted she had any connection with Hayward Emory Peyton Trevelyan, Duke of Marlow, or at least any of a legitimate nature. Elizabeth did her best to collect her scattered wits. She was confident she could control her emotions, as she had long ago learned to do, even if they were racing like a Thoroughbred out of control at the simple sight of the man. "Yes. And I must say it's very nice to meet you, Mr. MacGregor," she said, offering him her hand.

Ash hesitated a moment before he responded, his long fingers curving around her hand. His skin warmed her through her white kid glove. Instead of kissing her fingers, as she had expected, he squeezed her hand with a pressure that spoke of barely restrained power. Not at all like any gentleman who had ever held her hand in the past. But then, Ash MacGregor wasn't a gentleman. He was as wild and untamed as the mountains beyond this small oasis of civilization carved into the savage wilderness.

A smile tipped one corner of his lips, a decidedly masculine smile that told her he knew exactly how his touch had set her pulse racing. Heat flooded her cheeks. For heaven's sake, she was blushing. Like a schoolgirl at her first ball, or a fluttery spinster fascinated with an intriguing male.

Sunlight poured through the window at the end of the hall, exposing her fully to his scrutiny. Amusement glimmered in the startling blue depths of his eyes. Amusement purchased at her expense. She was certain her cheeks must be glowing as brightly as the huge red and gilt flowers splashed across the wallpaper lining the hall. She definitely had to get a rein on her emotions, before she made a complete fool of herself. She pulled her hand from his.

"I wonder if there might be a place we could talk." Her voice was too soft, far too breathy. But at the moment, looking up into his incredible eyes, she considered herself fortunate to find breath enough to speak.

"Me and Trevelyan said all that needed saying this morning."

Elizabeth swallowed hard against the tight knot in her throat. "Yes. He told me his interview with you was less than satisfactory."

MacGregor lifted one dark brow, regarding her as though she were one of the women she had noticed in the parlor downstairs—available for a price. Thick black lashes lowered as his gaze slid over her, from the top of her white straw hat to the tips of her blue kid shoes, peeking out from beneath her gown. Her skin tingled beneath that lazy perusal, as though he had stripped away her clothes and touched her bare flesh. A curious thrill hummed though her limbs. Never in her life had she been more aware of her own femininity.

"So he sent you over here to change my mind." An unspoken meaning shaded his deep voice, like dangerous currents rippling in a dark, uncharted sea.

Elizabeth lifted her chin, appalled at the heat shimmering across her skin. "My *guardian* doesn't know I'm here."

Ash grinned. "Hasn't anyone ever told you it's dangerous for little girls to go walkin' alone through the big bad woods?"

"It's the middle of the city, Mr. MacGregor. And I am hardly a little girl."

"All the more reason to bring a chaperone, Miss Barrington."

She refrained from telling him she was quite beyond the age when ladies required chaperones. Feminine laughter echoed through the door of the room behind her, the sound melding with deep male grunts and the rhythmic squeak of bed springs. Ash glanced toward the door, then looked down at her, a devilish grin curving his full lips.

Elizabeth shifted on her feet, regretting her all too hasty

decision to face the man in this dreadful place. "Mr. MacGregor, it's very important that I speak with you. Perhaps we could use the parlor."

Ash laughed. "The parlor wouldn't be a real good idea. One of Hattie's customers might take a shine to you."

Elizabeth touched her handkerchief to her upper lip, masking the scent of stale perfume hanging in the air with the delicate fragrance of lavender on the white linen. "I hadn't realized Miss Hattie's would be quite so . . . lively this time of day."

"It never stops being *lively* at Hattie's."

"I have a carriage."

"I know. I saw you come in, through the back door. I thought Hattie might've hired a new girl."

Elizabeth had a nagging suspicion the man was teasing her. She was quite certain no one would mistake her for an adventuress. "Perhaps we could have a cup of tea. There is a very nice tea room in the Hotel Windsor. If you . . ."

"Look, lady, I ain't goin' to no tea room. This is my home; you got something to say to me, come in and say it." He stepped aside, allowing her to look into the room behind him.

Although he sounded irritated, his eyes betrayed a certain vulnerability hiding beneath that terribly gruff facade. She sensed he was defensive about his home, and she had managed to step on his pride. Not at all what she had planned.

She glanced past him into his bedroom, knowing she would have to meet this man on his own terms. Still, it didn't ease her concern at all to realize she would be walking straight into the lion's lair.

He leaned toward her, his lips brushing the top of her ear as he spoke, sending shivers skittering across her shoulder. "I won't bite."

Elizabeth jumped, ramming his chin with the top of her

head. He grunted with the impact. She glanced up at him, cringing as she watched him rub his chin. She had waited most of her life to meet the man calling himself Ash MacGregor, and she was making a complete mess of things. "I'm terribly sorry. But you did startle me."

He frowned. "Remind me not to startle you again."

No doubt the man would make a habit of startling her, she thought as she crossed the threshold of his bedroom. It was a spacious corner room, with windows open on opposing walls. An early spring breeze drifted through the windows, a cool whisper fluttering plain white cotton curtains. That soft breeze rescued the room from the heavy, cloying scent of cheap perfume that pervaded the rest of the house. In fact, there was nothing cloying or sweet about this room. Nothing to betray the fact that this man had lived in this house of ill repute for the last fifteen years.

She glanced around, curious to discover more about this intriguing man. There was little to betray his tastes. Nothing adorned the white walls. The top of the oak bureau was bare, the wood polished to a glossy finish, the scent of lemon oil lingering.

A razor, shaving mug, and hairbrush sat on a shelf beside the washstand in one corner of the room. A single white linen towel was neatly draped on the rack beneath. Except for the redundant quilt of multicolored squares that lay neatly over the mattress of a big four-poster bed, the room had the clean, Spartan look of a monk's chambers.

She flinched at the soft thud of the door closing. She pivoted, finding him leaning against the door. Immediately she thought to ask him to keep the door open. But one look at his face froze the words in her throat. He was staring at her, his glorious azure eyes narrowed, his handsome face drawn into tight lines, as though he faced an enemy. The last thing she wanted was to antagonize this man. There was far too much at stake.

"You can relax. I ain't never had a reason to force a woman into anything."

She smiled, hoping to pry away some of the man's armor. "No, of course, I'm certain you haven't."

He regarded her a moment, as though she were a mystery that needed solving. Sunlight rushed through the windows behind her, eager to touch him, stroking every strong curve and line of a face that might have graced a knight of legend. A man bold in battle. A man fierce in loyalty. A man so blatantly handsome he could steal a woman's heart with a single glance.

Elizabeth forced air past the tightness in her throat and tried to disguise her fascination with this man behind a veneer of polite cordiality. She glanced at the only chair in the room, a wooden armchair positioned near one of the windows. "Perhaps I might sit."

He frowned, as though her voice had suddenly reminded him of something unpleasant. "You won't be stayin' that long."

"I see." She contained the disappointment at his desire to be rid of her. For most of her life she had been hoping for this moment. Yet, it was impossible to reconcile this man with the image she had carried with her all these years. Ash MacGregor certainly wasn't what she had expected.

No man she knew would dare go around in public with his shirt partially open, revealing the hollow of his neck and the intriguing shadow of dark curls beneath. But then, the only men she had to compare MacGregor with were English aristocrats like her guardian, and the American businessmen with whom he dealt. At the moment they seemed completely different species.

"What is it you got on your mind, Miss Barrington?"

She fought the urge to correct his form of address. She hadn't come here to dispense lessons in social etiquette. "I came to ask you to reconsider. Please come back with me to Mr. Radcliffe's home. Give Marlow a chance to speak with you again.''

''Marlow?''

''I had supposed he informed you of his title.''

One corner of his mouth tightened. ''I thought you'd call him uncle.''

''He isn't my uncle.''

Ash crossed his arms over his chest, his frown deepening as he studied her, staring at her as though he were searching for answers to mysteries in her eyes.

''Perhaps you're a bit confused because I address him by his title rather than his given name. It's customary for those very familiar with a peer to use his title as a form of address. That's why I call him Marlow.'' My goodness, she was babbling like a bedlamite.

''You ain't any bloodkin to him, are you?''

Elizabeth hesitated before she answered, startled by the turn in conversation. ''No.''

A muscle in his cheek flashed as he clenched his jaw. ''It seems Trevelyan makes a habit of buying people.''

''You think . . .'' She pressed her hand to the base of her neck, her fingers sliding against the cameo pinned to white lace. ''You certainly do look for the dark side of life, don't you, Mr. MacGregor?''

He tipped back his head, eyeing her like a sleepy lion bored with his prey. ''You don't usually have to look for the dark side.''

She resisted the urge to give the man a proper set-down. From what she knew of Ash MacGregor, the man had good reason to see only darkness in the world. ''I'm not certain you realize that Marlow's wife is still very much alive.''

''And she ain't with him.''

''She doesn't care much for long trips. Ships make her rather ill, and . . .'' She hesitated, thinking of the other reason the duchess had remained at home. Responsibilities that were truly more Elizabeth's own. If not for the duchess, Elizabeth would not have been free to make this trip. "Although the duchess was most anxious to see you, she decided it would be best if I came in her place."

"And I guess old Trevelyan didn't mind leaving the wife at home."

Elizabeth bristled under his gibe. "Hayward Trevelyan is an exceptional man. Honest. Kind. Compassionate. His reputation is beyond reproach."

Ash tilted his head, eyeing her with a measure of skepticism. "A real saint."

"In certain ways he is. My mother's parents died of cholera when she was very young. Marlow and my grandfather were business partners, and the closest of friends. They had both agreed that if anything happened to my grandparents, Marlow would become my mother's guardian. He raised my mother from the time she was three."

He held her steady gaze, betraying nothing in his eyes or expression. "So how is it he came to be your *guardian?*"

Elizabeth glanced away from his perceptive gaze, sensing he would see the sadness inside her. She stared at the book lying facedown on the nearby chair. "Since I'm only to be here a short time I would like to discuss your situation rather than mine."

"There's nothin' that needs to be said."

She looked at him, seeing the stubborn set of his jaw, taking comfort in knowing it was very familiar. "On the contrary, there is a great deal to be discussed. Marlow has been looking for you for twenty-three years. You simply can't turn away from him without giving him a chance."

"Look, lady, I ain't the man Trevelyan thinks I am."

"You can't be certain of that. There is a very good chance you are Peyton Emory Hayward Trevelyan."

Ash shook his head. "I realize how much the old man is hurting. I understand his loss. But I ain't his grandson."

"How do you know you aren't Peyton?"

He laughed, a harsh sound without a trace of warmth. "Do I really look like the grandson of some English duke?"

She pulled open her reticule and dragged out a photograph encased in an oval frame the size of her hand. Beneath the glass a man, woman, and child had been captured in a moment in time. Even in the stilted confines of the photograph they looked happy, satisfied, as though God had granted each of them all they had ever wanted on this earth. The payment for such contentment had been their lives.

Elizabeth studied their faces. Emory Trevelyan had been a handsome man, strong willed like his father. And his wife, Rebecca, had been beautiful, ethereal, like a fairy princess, fragile and mysterious. Yet it was the image of the boy that captured Elizabeth's imagination. Ever since she was a child she had wondered about Peyton. Had he grown to be as handsome as his father? Did he remember his home? Did he miss his family as much as they missed him? Like Hayward and the duchess, she had never given up hope of finding him.

Twenty-three years ago Emory, Rebecca, and Peyton had come to Denver on a trip that was both business and pleasure. They had come to visit Shelby Radcliffe, Rebecca's cousin and Emory's business associate. They had also come to witness the beauty of the Rocky Mountains. And it was there, in the savage surroundings of God's magnificent creation, they were attacked by renegade Indians.

She looked at the man standing with his back against the door, noting the sharply carved, high cheekbones, narrow straight nose, and square jaw that held more than a hint of a stubborn nature. "I assume Marlow told you about the circumstances surrounding the deaths of his son and daughter-in-law."

Ash nodded, his full lips drawn into a tight line.

"Although the bodies of Emory and Rebecca were recovered, Peyton was never found."

"Yeah. Trevelyan said as much. But it don't mean I'm his grandson."

"Please, look at this."

He hesitated a moment before he drew away from the door, stalking her in long, lazy strides, a predator—graceful in his power, deadly in his skill. She suddenly felt like a doe, in danger of being devoured by her own reckless attraction to this savage stranger.

He paused in front of her, so close she could feel the warmth of his skin radiate against her, so close she could catch the clean scent of him. He wore no cologne, yet there was a pleasant scent about him, a lemony citrus fragrance melding with the warm aroma of leather.

She stared up into his beautiful eyes, hoping he wouldn't notice how his nearness had set her legs trembling like leaves in a summer breeze. "This was taken in New York, a few days before they left for Denver. In the letter that accompanied it, Emory joked about it being the last photograph of them before they were swallowed by the wilderness. I'm certain he never realized how prophetic his words would be."

Ash frowned as he looked down at the photograph. She had the impression he was merely grazing the faces, glancing without acknowledging details of their features, as if he didn't want to remember anything about this lost family after she left. Perhaps he had more than enough memories of past tragedies. "They look like a real nice family."

"Do you notice anything about Emory?"

He slanted her a hooded glance. "What are you getting at?"

"The resemblance. You must see it. You bear a striking resemblance to him."

Ash looked down at the photograph. "The man had dark eyes."

"He did. But other than that, the resemblance can't be denied. You can see it in the shape of your face. In your nose, your mouth." She took the photograph from his hand, the silver frame warm from his touch, as warm as a living thing. "And look at Peyton. Even in the photograph you can see how light his eyes are. Peyton's eyes are like his mother's, a startling blue. It's obvious: You're their son."

He drew his lips into a tight line. "What's obvious is you see what you want to see."

"Mr. MacGregor, you can't ignore the facts. You were taken in by a group of Cheyenne who were traveling to the Black Hills when you were a child, right around the time Peyton was lost."

He glanced away from her, staring out the window behind her, but not before she caught a glimmer of uncertainty flicker in his eyes. "It don't mean nothin'. There were lots of families traveling in those mountains around the time those folks were killed. I expect my parents were out here to hunt for silver or gold when they got themselves killed in the mountains."

She smothered the frustration building inside her. "You're the right age."

A muscle flashed in his cheek as he clenched his jaw. "I don't even know for sure how old I am."

"Twenty-eight. You'll be twenty-nine on the fourteenth of December."

He looked at her, his expression as hard as chiseled granite. "You don't know that for sure."

Elizabeth sighed. "No. I don't know for certain who you are. But there is a very good possibility you are Peyton."

"The way I look at it, the odds ain't good."

Elizabeth squeezed the photograph. "I know you must

be stunned by all of this. It isn't every day you learn you could very well be the heir of the duke of Marlow.''

Ash turned away from her. He stalked to the farthest window and stood staring out into the small yard behind the big brick house. Sunlight slipped shimmering golden threads into his thick dark hair, and she wondered if that long, shaggy mane was as silky as it looked. Mentally she shook herself. This was hardly the time to be thinking of the texture of a man's hair.

''You don't know nothin' about me.''

Elizabeth knew a great deal about this man. The Pinkerton agents had been thorough in their report. In some subtle way, as she had listened to the details of this man's life, she had felt like a voyeur peeking into matters far too private to be shared. Yet it was necessary. Just as it was necessary for her to continue to pry. ''I know more than perhaps I should.''

He didn't look at her. ''Sometimes we think we know about more than we do.''

''I know six years after the Cheyennes took you in, the army attacked the village where you were living. Your Cheyenne family was killed, as were most of the other people living there. You were rescued by an army scout, a man named MacGregor. You lived with him for a year after the massacre, prospecting in the mountains outside of Denver, until he was killed in an altercation at a saloon in town. You lived on your own for nearly two years before Hattie Larsen took you into her house.''

Ash didn't react, except for a tensing of his broad shoulders, a subtle shifting of muscle she might have missed if she weren't so very much aware of him in every way. Much too aware of him. She had been courted by handsome men in the past, but she couldn't recall ever looking at one and mentally stripping away his clothes, as she had caught herself doing more than once since

MacGregor had opened that door. The man was dangerous.

She moistened her dry lips. "When you were fifteen you killed a man who was attacking one of the women who worked here. There was a reward for his apprehension. Since that day you've been tracking men wanted by the law, collecting rewards for their capture."

Ash glanced over his shoulder, blue eyes narrowed into an icy glare. "I don't know about England, but men around here ain't always real happy to find people been nosing around in their past."

Elizabeth glanced away from the anger shimmering in his eyes. She stared at the photograph she held, assuring herself that this was all necessary. "Marlow has had men looking for Peyton since the day he disappeared. I assure you, we never meant to pry into your life. We meant only to find the truth."

"Yeah, well, the way I see it, you're still a long way from finding it."

She looked up at him, braving the anger flaming in his incredible eyes. "I would think you might want to help us find that truth. If you were to come back to England . . ."

"I ain't got time to go traipsing all over tarnation, chasing after fool's gold. I told Trevelyan as much."

She slid her thumb over the smooth silver frame, studying her opponent the way she would study a chessboard when deciding on the strategy of her next move. "Do you remember anything of the time before you came to live with the Cheyenne?"

He studied her for a moment, as though he were deciding whether he should toss her out or answer her question. He turned away from her, lifting his face into the sunlight. "When the People found me I remembered nothing of my past. My *nibu*'—that's my Cheyenne father—was a medicine man. He said the shadows had drifted over my mind to protect me from what I'd seen. He believed in time the shadows would lift.''

''And have they?''

''There're times when I feel like the memories are there, just beyond my reach, teasing me with glimpses. But nothin' is clear.''

''Perhaps you need something to help chase away the shadows, Mr. MacGregor.''

Ash looked at her, his eyes filled with the wariness of a mountain lion facing a hunter. ''I ain't sure I understand what you mean.''

She smiled, hoping to win a small measure of trust. ''Often a certain scent has triggered a memory in me. Just as a shadow against the garden wall of my home, or a glimpse of an old photograph has done. Perhaps if you were surrounded by things from your past—if you could touch your old toys, see your home—you would remember.''

Ash laughed. ''Well, now, seein' as I don't know where I lived, I don't see how that would be possible. There ain't no old photographs or garden walls to trigger my memory.''

''If you would only agree to come to England with us, Mr. MacGregor. Perhaps if you returned to the place you were born and raised until the tragedy, you would remember something of your past.''

Ash shook his head. ''I got no place in England.''

''You could very well be Lord Peyton Emory Hayward Trevelyan, the Marquess of Angelstone, heir to the duke of Marlow. Do you understand what that means?''

Ash pivoted to face her. ''Yeah. It means a lot of folks would be real sorry to see someone like me go runnin' around pretendin' I'm something I ain't. If Trevelyan were smart, he'd pack up and get out of here before I decide to take him up on his little offer and shame him and his high-falutin name.''

She stared at him, noting his proud, defiant stance. He revealed more than he realized with his tense muscles, more than he intended in those expressive eyes. In those eyes she saw the shadow of a young boy who had lost nearly everyone he had ever cared about. A young boy who had struggled on his own for almost two years. A boy who had found a home in a brothel.

What was it like to grow up in this place, with the sights and sounds of depravity all around? What was it like to have all the children in school know you lived in a house of ill repute? How many nasty remarks had he endured? How many times had he felt not quite good enough? "I understand why you are apprehensive about going to England."

Ash shook his head, dismissing her attempt to reach him. "What do you suppose old Trevelyan will do if he can't find any proof of who I am?"

"We'll find proof."

"Not likely. You'd either find proof I'm not who you think I am, or you'd end up never really knowing. And all the while the old man would have this stranger under his roof, walkin' around with a name that might not be his. Every day he'd be lookin' at me, wondering if he made a mistake. Every time one of his high-and-mighty friends talked about me, the old man would wonder. And maybe one day he'd take a notion to send me packing. Well, I'm just goin' to save us both a lot of trouble."

Elizabeth held Ash's steady gaze. "You're frightened."

A muscle flashed in his cheek. "I think we both said all that needs saying."

"Not quite."

He moved toward her, in a slow stalk she was certain was meant to intimidate her. "It's time for you to be on your way."

"All I'm asking is that you talk with Marlow. Give him a chance to change your mind."

"The door's right behind you."

Elizabeth hugged the frame to her chest, staring up into the angry blue tempest of his eyes. "I think you're afraid, Mr. MacGregor. Afraid to face your past. Afraid to confront the truth."

Ash stared at her, his glance as harsh and bleak as the North Sea in December. She shivered under his glacial stare, but she refused to back down from her stance. This meant far too much to Marlow and the duchess. And if she were honest, finding Peyton had come to mean far too much to her.

"You got no call, comin' here and tellin' me how I feel. You got no call to go pokin' around in my life."

"You can't turn your back on your family. You must try to understand . . ."

"Now I'll ask you to go one more time, little lady. And then I'm gonna toss you out of here on your pretty little behind."

Elizabeth gasped. "You wouldn't dare."

He smiled, a generous description for that cold twisting of his lips. "If you knew me as well as you think you do, then you'd know there ain't much I wouldn't dare."

She turned and marched toward the door, trying to contain the anger surging inside her. Heaven forgive her, she truly wanted to shake the man until his teeth rattled. She threw open the door and turned to face him.

"It's a pity you can't demonstrate as much courage with my guardian, Mr. MacGregor. But then, only a truly brave man would be willing to risk his pride for a chance to regain his destiny. I hope you are well and truly satisfied with chasing outlaws and living in your little room. Because you shall certainly never amount to more than what you are today. Not without courage."

Chapter Two

The door closed with a soft click. Ash curled his hands into fists at his sides, trying to corral the emotions Elizabeth Barrington had unleashed within him. Any other woman he knew would have slammed the door. Not Elizabeth Barrington. Truth was, she wasn't like any woman he had ever known.

He stood staring at the door, listening to the soft taps of her shoes against the wood floor as she marched away from his room. Her words echoed in his brain, awakening doubts he couldn't ignore. Deep within him, he perceived a trembling, a stirring in a part of him where dreams long ago forgotten lay buried. He forced the lid down over those dreams. He had learned a long time ago that some dreams were better off buried and forgotten.

He turned and walked to the window overlooking the yard and the alley behind the house. Beyond the neat square of closely clipped grass and carefully tended flower beds, Elizabeth Barrington's shiny black carriage was tied to a post near the stables. A pair of bays stood with heads bowed, long necks stretched, nibbling on the fringe of grass just beyond the gravel alleyway.

He stiffened at a soft knock on the door. He turned, stunned by the sudden surge of excitement flooding his veins. Excitement at the prospect of seeing that bossy little lady again. He molded his features into a look that had put the fear of God into more than a few desperate men.

25

If Miss Barrington wanted to go another round, he was ready for her. "Come in."

The door opened, revealing a short, plump woman dressed in a pink satin gown. Hattie Larsen frowned when she saw him. "Good God, Ash, you look angry enough to split someone in two. Whatever that girl wanted, it don't look like you were real happy about it."

Ash leaned back against the window casement, aware of a curious disappointment filling him. "That *girl* was Hayward Trevelyan's ward."

The white feathers stuck into the pale blond curls piled high on Hattie's head bobbed as she sauntered toward him. "Ward, is it? Sounds like that rich English duke's got a pretty way to keep a mistress."

"I don't think so." Ash glanced out the window, watching Elizabeth Barrington as she marched down the brick-lined path toward her carriage. The lace and bows on her fancy blue gown twitched with each angry step she took.

"Naw; I expect your right." Hattie paused beside him, the small white feathers edging the low neckline of her gown fluttering in the breeze. "She ain't the kind men pay to keep close. She's too skinny."

Miss Barrington was slender. Her waist didn't look much bigger than his thigh. But as she turned to step up into the carriage, she presented him a profile with nicely rounded curves he would bet weren't padding.

"Too stiff."

Stiff enough to snap in a strong wind, Ash thought. But he couldn't help wonder what it would take to turn all that ice into warm, sweet honey in his hands.

"Too plain."

At first glance he might have agreed with Hattie. But he had taken more than a glance at the lady. He had looked straight down into eyes as deep and gray as San Francisco Bay, and nearly drowned.

True, Elizabeth Barrington didn't have the sparkling beauty a man would pay to possess. She didn't have lush curves or perfect features, or hair the color of sunlight or midnight or a red sunset. No, she didn't have the kind of looks to stop a man in his tracks. With her honey-colored hair and her big gray eyes, what little Miss Prim and Proper did have were the looks of a pretty schoolmarm. The kind a boy mooned over from the back of the schoolroom.

And when she smiled the simple curve of her lips transformed those pretty features into a far more potent feminine weapon. That woman had a smile that could light up the darkest room, or a heart that had lived a life in shadows.

Yet she wasn't smiling now. Elizabeth glanced up at him, her lips drawn into a pout, her huge gray eyes conveying all her disappointment. She had expected more from him. More than he knew how to give.

"She don't look real happy with you neither." Hattie wiggled her fingers at Elizabeth, lifting her voice to carry across the yard. "You come on back if you ever want a job, sweetie."

Elizabeth lifted her chin, sending Hattie a look cold enough to freeze scalding coffee in July. She slapped the ribbons across the bays' rumps, sending the carriage rattling down the alley. Ash watched until her carriage disappeared behind a row of houses.

"God save us from respectable woman," Hattie muttered.

"Amen." A woman like Elizabeth Barrington got a man thinking about things he shouldn't, things beyond his reach. A man like him had no business thinking about holding her, or pulling all the pins from that yellow-brown hair and feeling the soft tumble of silky strands against his bare chest.

But Peyton Trevelyan, he would have every right to

touch her. Was it possible? Could he be the grandson of some fancy English duke? He didn't want to think of that possibility. A man could set himself up for one hell of a fall with that kind of thinking.

"What'd she want with you?" Hattie asked.

Ash sat on the window sill and propped his foot against the casement. "She wanted to talk me into taking the old man up on his offer."

Hattie nodded. "Now that skinny spinster just might have one damn good idea. I tell you, you're a fool if you let all that money pass you by."

Ash clasped his hands on his raised knee, smiling as he looked up at Hattie. Her brown eyes shimmered with thoughts of gold. Twenty years ago she had left a farm in Kentucky to come out west, a young bride with her new husband, looking for gold. Her husband had found an early grave; Hattie had found there were easier ways to make gold than by digging in the dirt.

Aside from being a shrewd businesswoman, Hattie looked after everyone under her roof like a mama hen. Only this mama liked the idea of renting out her chicks by the hour. She treated you well enough, as long as you worked for your keep—and that included skinny kids she took in off the streets.

"There's more to this life than money, Hattie."

"Sugar, what I can't get with money I don't need. I always say, people come and go. There's only one thing in this world you can count on, and that's gold."

Ash shook his head. "We never did see things the same."

She cupped Ash's face between her hands. "You tell me you don't wanna get out of this place. You tell me you don't wanna get out of this business of huntin' down men for a livin'. You tell me you don't wanna buy some of that pretty California land you're always talking about, and raise yourself some horses."

Ash drew in his breath, filling his nostrils with the cloying scent of Hattie's perfume. "In a few years I'll have enough money to buy that land."

Hattie dropped her hands, her smooth brow tugged into a frown as she stared down at him. "You might be one of the fastest men I ever did see with a gun. You might have the guts to keep tracking down one outlaw after another. But in time it's gonna catch up with you. Maybe it'll be some friend or relative of Ned Waller will get you. I hear they ain't real happy to hear you put old Ned behind bars."

Ash frowned when he thought of the bank robber he had put in prison last week. "I can handle Ned's men."

"Maybe. But time has a way of catchin' up with you. It might be a bushwhack, or someone just lucky enough to get the drop on you. But sure enough, you're gonna end up dead before you ever get a chance to buy a pebble on that California beach."

"Dammit, Hattie, what do you expect me to do? I ain't who they think I am."

"You don't know that. You don't know who you are."

He turned his head, staring down at the roses that spread in a star-shaped pattern from a corner of the back porch. The newly awakened canes lifted dark green leaves toward the sky, inviting the lingering kiss of sunlight.

Taking care of the yard and garden had been one of his chores when he had first come to live here. Few people knew he still tended the gardens. Not because he had to, but because he got satisfaction out of watching things grow. It was the one place in his life where he helped things live rather than die.

"I don't understand, Ash," Hattie said softly. "You used to tell me you wondered if you had family somewhere, wonderin' about you. Now you got someone wantin' to claim you as kin, and you don't wanna give him as much as the dust off your hat."

He stared at the gardens, trying to find a way to explain how he felt. "I always thought my ma and pa were farmers. Simple folks just looking for a better life, hoping to find it out here. I never dreamed some English duke would want to claim me."

Hattie slid her fingers into his hair, giving the shaggy mane a gentle tug. "The way I look at it, sugar, give me an English duke over some dirt farmer any day."

Ash smiled. "It ain't that easy."

She shrugged. "He wants a grandson, you want a family. Seems mighty easy to me."

Ash shook his head, trying to dismiss the doubts that wouldn't go away. "I can't go pretendin' to be someone I ain't."

"Hell, sugar, how do you think the girls and me make a livin'? Why, if a girl couldn't go on pretendin' to like every ole boy that slammed into her, she wouldn't have no customers."

Ash rubbed his palm over his raised knee. "It ain't the same."

"What's bothering you about this? It's more than just thinking this Englishman ain't your kin. 'Cause you know damn well he could be."

Ash leaned his head back against the window frame. The sun had burned away every cloud from the sky, stripping away every defense against that bright light. The sunlight touched his face, warming him, like the hope he had seen shining in Elizabeth Barrington's eyes. She wanted him to be someone he wasn't. It had nothing at all to do with whose blood ran through his veins. Nothing at all to do with the truth of his name. It had everything to do with the man inside. "Maybe he could be."

Hattie studied him a moment, in that unsettling way she had of stripping a man down to his bare essentials. "If I didn't know you for havin' more guts than sense,

I'd say that old man and his skinny ward make you nervous.''

He stared at the roses, watching the green canes sway in the breeze, avoiding Hattie's direct stare.

''Maybe you think Miss Fancy Pants is prettier than I thought. Maybe you're afraid of gettin' to like her too much, only to find yourself kicked out of the big house when they find out you ain't who they think you are.''

Ash glanced up at her. ''I got no place in some fancy house. It'd be like taking a wolf out of the mountains and tryin' to turn him into a puppy dog. It just don't work.''

''Maybe.'' She smiled. ''And maybe that old wolf would take a real shine to sittin' by a warm fire and eatin' steak every night.''

''Maybe he would.'' He'd been searching for a home and a family all his life. Now, he might be within spitting distance of his grandfather. He wasn't sure he could walk away, even if his gut told him it was the smart thing to do.

''So what you gonna do?''

''Trevelyan invited me to come have dinner tonight at Shelby Radcliffe's.''

Hattie whistled. ''Dinner on Brown's Bluff. Fancy.''

''Yeah.''

''You gonna go?''

He could face a dozen outlaws ready to fill him full of lead without so much as flinching, but the thought of having dinner in Shelby Radcliffe's big white castle with that pretty English lady made his palms damp. Still, he had never been one to tuck his tail and hide. He wasn't going to start now. ''Guess I better get over to Henderson's and buy myself a fancy coat.''

As the butler served the soup, Elizabeth glanced across the table to where Ash MacGregor sat beside the eldest of Shelby Radcliffe's four daughters. The younger girls had taken supper earlier and been sent to their rooms. Mrs. Radcliffe didn't want them exposed to a man like MacGregor. If not for Shelby's insistence, eighteen-year-old Nancy would have shared her younger siblings' fate. As it was, he had insisted the young woman not only attend dinner but sit beside Ash, which in turn delighted Nancy and infuriated her mother.

What did Mrs. Radcliffe expect of the man? Elizabeth wondered. Did she honestly expect Mr. MacGregor to accost the girl at the dinner table? Ash MacGregor was hardly an animal slavering to ravish any unsuspecting female. Elizabeth could well testify to that fact. If she were willing to reveal her all too inappropriate visit to his room. But she wasn't. And, thankfully, neither was Mr. MacGregor.

"My husband tells me you are in law enforcement, Mr. MacGregor," Lillian said, looking at Ash down the length of her slim nose.

Ash glanced at her. Candlelight from the ornately carved silver candelabra flickered against a face that might have been carved from marble, so cold was his expression. "In a way."

Lillian lifted one dark brow, her expression as haughty as that of a queen addressing a peasant. "And what exactly do you do?"

A smile lifted one corner of his lips as Ash held her condescending look. "I hunt down outlaws and turn them over to the law for the reward."

"I see." Lillian drew herself up in her chair, like a cat arching her back. She cast a dark look at her husband, who sat at the opposite end of the long expanse of white linen.

Shelby didn't notice his wife's angry glance. His attention was focused on Ash. He studied the younger man, as though he were trying to fit together pieces of a puzzle.

"You're a bounty hunter," Nancy said, her voice filled

with the same excitement that was glowing in her dark eyes.

Ash slanted the girl a hooded glance. "That's right."

Nancy toyed with one dark curl lying across her shoulder. "And do you bring them in dead or alive?"

"I always let them make that choice," Ash said.

Nancy stared at Ash, as though he were some wild animal brought into her home for her amusement—beautiful, fascinating, and quite removed from the human race. "How very dangerous your life must be."

Elizabeth shifted in her chair. She had never been one to tolerate snobbery of any kind, especially not from people whose only claim to polite Society was the money in their pockets. These women had no right to look at Mr. MacGregor as though he weren't fit to clean their stables.

Perhaps his black coat and trousers weren't quite appropriate for formal evening wear. And perhaps his hair was much too long. But it wasn't as though he had many occasions to attend a formal dinner. With his hair trimmed, and dressed in elegant formal attire, he would rival any gentleman of her acquaintance. She only wished one day she had the chance to see him dressed and groomed as befitted a man of his rank. She only wished she could see him take his rightful place as the Marquess of Angelstone.

But at the moment he didn't look like a marquess. He didn't look like the dangerous young man she had met this afternoon either. He looked like a man awaiting a trip to the gallows.

Elizabeth studied Ash a moment, seeing the tension in the tight line of his mouth, in the narrowed stare of his beautiful eyes. He was looking down at the array of china, glasses, and silver spread out before him, as though each were a trap set to ensnare any unsuspecting mountain lion who made a wrong move. She had never really considered it before, but she suspected a well-dressed table could prove bewildering to someone not initiated into the customs of polite Society.

She lifted the proper spoon from the silver laid out before her, staring at MacGregor, wondering how to catch his eye without drawing attention to what she was doing. She cleared her throat. He glanced up, staring straight at her. The stunning beauty of his eyes startled her, even though she carried the memory of those eyes seared across her memory.

She drew a breath that tangled in her tight throat. She rolled the handle of the spoon in her fingers, hoping the gesture was both obvious to him and inconspicuous to the others. She lifted her brows, glancing down at the silver laid out before him, hoping he understood her meaning. If he would only follow her lead, she would guide him through the confusing twists and turns of the meal.

One corner of his lips tipped upward, the smile draining some of the tension from his handsome face. He lifted the correct spoon and winked at her.

Her spoon slipped from her shaky fingers, striking the side of her crystal water goblet. Crystal sang like a bell on Sunday morning, drawing the attention of the other five people seated at the table. Ash MacGregor grinned, amusement glittering in the depths of those stunning eyes. Amusement at her expense. Once again.

Good heavens, the man must think she had never before been winked at by a man. Come to think of it, she never had.

"Do you remember anything of how you came to be wandering the mountains as a child, Mr. MacGregor?" Shelby asked.

Ash took a sip of water before he responded. "No."

In spite of Shelby's smile, Elizabeth perceived a wariness within him. There was a tightness about his mouth, a shuttered look in his brown eyes. And she wondered if he were perhaps anxious to discover if this unorthodox young man was actually one of his relatives.

Shelby stroked his long dark mustache, as though it were a favorite cat. "Was it an accident, do you think? Or perhaps an Indian attack?"

"You're mighty curious," Ash said.

Shelby drew in his breath and released it slowly, as though he was trying to relax the tension Elizabeth could see on his face. "I was very close to my cousin, Rebecca, Peyton's mother. We lived next to each other in New York. We played together every day as children. I guess I just want to know whether or not you're truly her son."

Ash twisted the stem of the water goblet in his fingers, the crystal catching the candlelight, spinning the golden light into a rainbow of color. "I guess I can understand that."

"Do you have any recollection at all?" Shelby asked.

Ash shook his head. "There's times when I feel like the memories are there, just beyond my reach, teasing me with glimpses. But nothin' is clear."

"I believe once you're in familiar surroundings your memories will return." Hayward regarded Ash from across the table. "The question remains, when will you decide to face your past?"

Ash clenched his jaw. "I ain't all that certain it's my past to face."

Shelby dabbed his napkin against his lips. "You surprise me, Mr. MacGregor. Peyton Trevelyan is a very wealthy young man. In addition to the Trevelyan title and fortune, my cousin Rebecca was my uncle's only surviving child. She inherited a fortune when he died, which went to Emory in turn, and upon his death to Peyton. Most men would kill for that kind of money."

Ash shrugged. "Guess I ain't like most men."

Elizabeth was beginning to understand the truth of that statement more each time she saw the man. Ash MacGregor might be rough around the edges. Indeed, he might

be savage. But he had a quality about him that quit
ply stole her breath away.

She hoped he truly was Peyton Trevelyan. A futur
might be possible with Peyton. But she and Ash
Gregor would forever be banished to different worl
matter how much she might wish the contrary.

She glanced at the man sitting beside her, notin
way Hayward was regarding Mr. MacGregor, as the
he were preparing to do battle with an opponent who
already won the first round. The next engagement w
take place after dinner. She only prayed Hayward w
emerge the victor.

Chapter Three

Ash glanced at Trevelyan and Radcliffe, who were standing near the door of the library. He had known this little meeting was coming all night. Still, he wasn't looking forward to it, or the decision he had to make.

"I hope you don't mind, but I would like to speak with Mr. MacGregor alone," Hayward said.

"Of course," Shelby said. "I have a few things to attend to in my study. Just step in when you're ready to join the ladies."

The door closed, leaving Ash alone with the man who might be his grandfather. The possibility was enough to make his chest tighten. He stared into one of the glass-lined bookcases built into the walls of Shelby Radcliffe's library, ignoring the old man who stood staring at him, studying him as though he were some freak in a sideshow.

Behind the glass panes, leather-bound volumes stood shoulder-to-shoulder on walnut shelves, gold letters proclaiming the titles of old friends as well as those Ash had never met. When he was a boy he had learned the secret about books: You could open the covers and escape all the ugliness in the world around you. At least for a little while.

Ash stiffened as he sensed Trevelyan approaching him. The old man paused beside him, his image reflected in the glass beside Ash's own, mirror images of youth and maturity, disturbingly familiar in their sharply defined features. The old man was smiling, looking at Ash as though he had learned a secret he was eager to share.

"My son started collecting rare editions when he was eighteen. He had a particular fancy for medieval manuscripts. You should see his collection."

Ash turned, regarding the old man for a moment before he spoke. "Seems like a long way to go just to look at a few old books."

Trevelyan smiled, deep lines flaring out from his dark blue eyes. "Ah, but there is so much more to see. Such as the stream where you caught your first trout."

Ash swirled the brandy in his snifter, gaslight twisting in the amber liquid. "Seems you're dead set on me goin' to England with you."

"You've been away a long time. It's time for you to come home."

Ash squeezed the glass, his fingers sliding against the deep bevels cut into the crystal. "I don't know how you can be so sure of who I am."

"All I need do is look at you and I know who you are."

Ash looked at the old man. Beneath thick white brows determination glittered in his dark blue eyes. "I believe you see what you want to see, Mr. Trevelyan."

"And I believe you are far too reluctant to see what is right before your eyes," Hayward said. "I wonder why."

Elizabeth Barrington's words echoed in Ash's mind— *Only a truly brave man would be willing to risk his pride for a chance to regain his destiny.* Maybe he *was* afraid. Afraid he really was Peyton Trevelyan, and everyone would see he could never live up to the name.

Hayward smiled, as though he had glimpsed Ash's doubts and liked what he saw. "My offer stands. I'm willing to pay you sixty thousand dollars for six months of your time."

Ash stared into the man's eyes and tried not to think

of all the things he could buy with that kind of money—
like a brand-new start in life. "You think you can buy
anything and anyone with your money."

Trevelyan shook his head, smiling at Ash as though he
found him amusing. "I have a great deal of money. But
you must know it means nothing compared to having my
grandson return to me. Your grandmother and I have
waited a very long time for your return. I've offered you
money to compensate you for your time. And have no
doubt about it, Mr. MacGregor, you shall earn your
keep."

"What do you expect me to do to earn my keep?"

"I expect you to keep an open mind. Search for clues
to your identity. And I also expect you to become my
grandson. For six months you shall be Peyton Emory
Hayward Trevelyan, Marquess of Angelstone."

"How the hell am I supposed to become someone I
ain't?"

Trevelyan sipped his brandy, studying Ash over the rim
of his glass. "You are Peyton. You shall eventually come
to realize the truth."

Ash felt as though he had been sucked up by a whirl-
wind. None of this made sense. All his life he had wondered about his family, searched for clues, found nothing.
Now this man was talking about a miracle. He had learned
a long time ago that miracles didn't happen to men like
him.

Ash turned away from the old man and all the temptation he offered. He crossed the room, seeking the chilly
breeze drifting through open doors leading to the terrace.
He stepped into the moonlight, taking deep breaths. He
wanted to run, to get as far away from this man and his
pretty ward as he could. Yet he knew a man couldn't
outrun his own doubts.

A few yards away golden light spilled from a pair of
open doors, cutting a wedge of light in the darkness. Ash

paused against the balustrade before reaching the yellow light. Yet there was no place to hide. Moonlight exposed him and all of his doubts. Without looking he knew the old man was standing in the doorway, watching him.

Then Trevelyan moved toward him, his footsteps falling softly against the granite terrace. "I imagine this all seems a little overwhelming."

Ash laughed softly. "You might say that."

Trevelyan rested his hands on the balustrade and stared out toward the mountains that rose like ragged black diamonds piercing the moonlit sky. "I often think of things I wish I had told my son before he left that day in June. I like to think he knew how much I loved him. But I wish I had told him, one last time. I wish I had told him how proud I was of him."

Ash glanced at Trevelyan. Moonlight fell across the old man's face, illuminating every line time had carved into it. Traces of pain lingered there, and pain was one thing Ash understood. "Something tells me he knew."

Trevelyan drew in his breath as he turned and looked at Ash. "You're a remarkable young man, Rises from the Ashes."

Ash stiffened, the name conjuring memories within him. "Seems like the Pinkertons did a pretty good job of digging up everything about me."

Trevelyan nodded. "The Cheyenne gave you that name because they sensed the strength in you. You've managed to grow strong and straight where others would have withered and died. I want you to come back to England, to claim everything that is rightfully yours."

Ash shook his head. "You got this need inside you, a need to save part of your son, part of yourself. But you can't be takin' a stranger into your house and tryin' to turn him into something he ain't."

"You aren't a stranger to me." Trevelyan gripped Ash's arm. "I knew the first moment I saw you who you were. You are my grandson. And you can't deny the possibility, even to yourself.''

Ash stared down at the long, slender hand gripping his arm as though the old man were afraid Ash might disappear in the night. ''No sir, I can't.''

''It won't be easy; nothing worth having ever is. But I have faith in you. I know you can take your proper place in the world. All I ask is that you come back to England with me. Give me six months of your life, six months to prove you really are Peyton.''

''And what happens if you can't find any proof?''

''Then the decision is yours.'' He released Ash's arm. ''You can return here, with your sixty thousand dollars, or you can stay where you belong.''

Ash's arm tingled with the imprint of Trevelyan's fingers. ''All you want me to do is turn myself inside out.''

''I want you to become the man you were meant to be.'' Hayward looked straight into his eyes. ''Say you'll agree to come home with me.''

Ash rested his hands on the balustrade, his palms damp against the stone. ''Six months, that's the deal.''

''That's right.''

Ash curled his hand into a fist against the stone. He stared at the mountains, listening to the whisper of the wind through alder and aspen trees. ''I suppose I ain't got a lot to lose.''

''And a whole new world to gain.''

Ash felt as though he were making a deal with the devil for six months' time in hell. But he couldn't forget what sixty thousand dollars could buy. And he couldn't deny the fact that he wanted a chance to see the place where Peyton was born. Maybe he wanted to see if there was a place for him in Elizabeth Barrington's world. ''All right. You got a deal.''

Trevelyan didn't move for a moment, but stood staring at Ash, a smile drawing up one corner of his lips. ''You

shall never regret this, my dear young man. I promise
you.''

Ash looked straight into Trevelyan's eyes. ''Yeah, well,
I guess we'll both see if that's true.''

Elizabeth clasped her hands in her lap, resisting the
urge to pace the length of Mrs. Radcliffe's parlor. She sat
on the edge of a stiff armchair, staring at the wall across
from her, wishing she could look past the clutter of paintings, beyond the green and pink flowers splashed across
the wallpaper, into the room next door. Marlow and Mr.
MacGregor were in the library next door, discussing matters that concerned them all. There was so very much at
stake. Marlow's happiness. Peyton's future. Her own
hopes.

Would Mr. MacGregor agree?

Would he return to England with them?

As much as she wanted him to see reason, she had the
uneasy feeling that Mr. MacGregor was a very stubborn
man. With each passing moment the anxiety grew within
her, like steam building in a kettle. Still, she contained
her emotions as she had long ago learned to do, presenting
a calm facade to the two other women in this slavishly
fashionable room. She didn't want to upset anyone by
revealing her anxiety.

''Is the duke really going to make Ash MacGregor a
marquess?'' Nancy asked.

Elizabeth looked to where Nancy sat beside her mother
on a sofa near the open French doors. ''There is every
reason to believe Mr. MacGregor is Peyton Trevelyan,
which would make him the Marquess of Angelstone.''

Nancy's lips curved into a smug smile. ''He looks more
like the Marquess of *Devilstone,* if you ask me.''

Elizabeth refrained from telling the girl she hadn't requested her opinion. ''Given the fact that he was raised
in the west, one would hardly expect Mr. MacGregor to

look the part of an English marquess.''

Nancy fiddled with a long dark curl resting against the white satin covering her shoulder. ''I have to admit, he is handsome, in a dangerous sort of way.''

Lillian shook her head. ''Nancy, really! Only a base-born woman would consider that vulgar masculinity handsome.''

Elizabeth squeezed her hands in her lap, fighting to retain control over her rising irritation. ''I would think most women would find Mr. MacGregor attractive.''

Lillian titled her head, her dark eyes filling with surprise as she stared at Elizabeth. ''Lady Elizabeth, certainly *you* don't find the man attractive.''

Elizabeth managed to force her lips into a smile. ''He resembles his father. And Emory Trevelyan was considered a remarkably handsome man.''

Nancy eyed Elizabeth in that deprecating way a haughty young woman certain of her beauty looks at a woman past her prime. ''Will the duke force you to marry MacGregor?''

Hayward had often told Elizabeth how very much he wished to see her married to Peyton. Still, she saw no reason to share that confidence with these women. ''Marlow would never force me to marry anyone.''

''Well, no one could force me to marry that savage.'' Nancy shuddered. ''Can you imagine what horrible things a man like that would force upon a helpless woman?''

More than once since meeting Ash MacGregor, Elizabeth had wondered what it might be like to be held in his strong arms, to experience the singular thrill of tasting his kiss. These women, with their aspirations to some artificial form of royalty, certainly had no right to speak of the man as though he were an animal.

Elizabeth squeezed her hands together until her fingers ached. ''I should like to remind you, Miss Radcliffe, that you are speaking of your cousin,'' she said, her voice carrying every ounce of her displeasure.

Nancy leaned against the tufted back of the sofa, color rising in her cheeks, as though Elizabeth had slapped her. She looked to her mother, a wounded sparrow seeking shelter from a hawk. "Mama?"

Lillian twisted her sherry glass in her fingers, gaslight rippling along the rim of the crystal. "I beg your pardon, Lady Elizabeth, but I certainly don't believe that man is any relation to my husband."

"I see," Elizabeth said, maintaining the ice in her voice. "You choose to ignore the evidence."

"Evidence?" Lillian frowned as though she had bitten into a lemon. "Did you see the way he was dressed? The man hasn't an ounce of fashion sense."

Nancy giggled. "He looks more like a gunfighter than a marquess."

Elizabeth's back stiffened with her rising anger. "Given his situation, I believe his appearance is understandable."

Lillian sipped her sherry. "I kept expecting him to skewer the roast beef with his knife and gnaw on it as though it was a bone."

"I thought he did very well," Elizabeth said. "Considering he has never been taught which fork or knife to use with each course."

Lillian looked at her guest as though Elizabeth were some poor bewildered child in need of guidance. "I understand how much His Grace would like to find his grandson, but honestly, Ash MacGregor cannot possibly be that man. He is obviously of much inferior stock."

Elizabeth lifted one brow, fixing Lillian with a cold stare. "It is my understanding, Mrs. Radcliffe, that gentleman are raised, not born."

Lillian shifted beneath the icy chill of Elizabeth's steady regard. "I'm quite certain that savage young man could never be made a gentleman."

"And I'm quite certain that, given the proper opportunities, Ash MacGregor would rival any gentleman of my acquaintance," Elizabeth said.

Lillian shook her head. "I'm afraid money cannot buy good breeding."

"There are many things money cannot buy, Mrs. Radcliffe." Elizabeth surveyed the room, sliding a critical glance over the paintings of landscapes and horses and family portraits crowding the large pink and green flowers of the wallpaper, every frame elaborately carved and so heavy with gilt they looked in danger of falling from the weight. With three sofas and more than a dozen chairs, the room was stuffed with furniture. Dark wood, heavily carved with vines and clumps of grapes, lined each piece, and the upholstery was a peculiar shade of green velvet. She looked straight at Mrs. Radcliffe, revealing every ounce of her disdain. "Money certainly cannot buy a sense of style. Nor can it buy a sensibility to the feelings of others."

Lillian's dark eyes grew wide, twin points of red coloring her cheeks. "I assure you, Lady Elizabeth, I never meant to injure your feelings. I only meant to demonstrate the impossibility of that man being Rebecca and Emory's son. Please, I hope you won't take offense."

"I've taken no offense." The rose silk of her gown rustled softly as Elizabeth stood, her muscles shimmering with the strain of containing her anger. She forced her lips into a smile. "It is obvious we share differing opinions, Mrs. Radcliffe. Now, if you will excuse me, I would like a breath of air."

"Yes. Yes, of course."

Elizabeth marched to the French doors, which stood ajar to allow a cool breeze to enter the room. She left the room with all the dignity of a queen, closing the doors behind her. Her footsteps tapped against granite, echoing the anger tightly coiled inside her as she crossed the terrace, seeking shelter in the moonlight. Never in her life had she met anyone more bigoted. She rested her hands on the balustrade, pressing hard against the cold granite, allowing the anger bottled up inside her to break free.

It was all so unfair. How could they judge the man without truly knowing him? Yet she wondered if she would be given the chance to know the man calling himself Ash MacGregor. The man was no doubt too stubborn to listen to reason. She lifted her face to the moonlight and released her breath in a sharp exhalation. Oh, she wanted to scream.

"You look mad enough to scare a full-grown grizzly."

Elizabeth jumped at the sound of Ash MacGregor's deep voice. She pivoted, her hand pressed to her racing heart, her eyes wide as she took in the sight of him. He stood with one broad shoulder braced against the white bricks shaping the wall between the library and the parlor, beyond the golden light spilling from both rooms. A dark phantom from her fondest hopes and dreams.

She drew a trembling breath. "You startled me."

He shifted, stepping away from the wall, moving toward her in long, lazy strides. "I seem to be makin' a habit of that."

"So it seems."

A chilly breeze swept across the gardens, rustling the leaves of aspen and alder trees standing like forgotten chess pieces on the dark lawn as it rushed to touch him. It slipped into his thick hair, sweeping silky strands back from his shoulders, tossing a dark lock over his forehead. Elizabeth curled her fingers against her palms, fighting the insane urge to brush that dark wave back from his brow. She shivered with more than the chill of the evening air.

"I thought you were in the library with Marlow."

"I was." He paused beside her, so close the warmth of his body chased away the coolness of the night. Far too close for propriety. Yet propriety was hardly a staple in his life. While the other men she knew were governed by strict rules of behavior, Ash MacGregor did what he pleased.

Wild.

Untamed.

Beautiful.

He was the type of man a lady should avoid at all costs. Still, she stayed within reach of his warmth, intrigued by the raw power radiating from him. "Did you reach an agreement?"

He rested one hip against the balustrade, cocking his knee at a blatantly masculine angle. "Yeah."

She moistened her dry lips. "Does this mean you will be returning with us to England?"

He studied her for a moment, with that cool, direct stare that penetrated the best of her defenses. "You seem mighty interested in having this Peyton come waltzin' back to life. Any of it personal?"

She glanced away from him, staring at the white marble pavilion that rose in the shape of a small Greek temple at the far end of the garden path. "I simply want to see Marlow reunited with his grandson."

"That the only reason?"

In the corner of her eye she saw him watching her, his intense regard coaxing heat into her cheeks. "Of course."

"And here I thought maybe you had ideas about this Peyton. Maybe you were plannin' to marry into the family."

Elizabeth turned toward him, anger flaring at his far too perceptive comments.

"From what I hear, this guy Peyton is worth a fortune," Ash said.

"I will have you know, Mr. MacGregor, my father was the Marquess of Wakefield. I certainly have never contemplated marrying any man for the coin in his purse."

He grinned at her anger. "You aren't exactly what you

seem, are you, Miss Barrington?''

The sudden turn of the conversation startled her. "I'm not sure what you mean.''

"I mean, you look like this fancy, highfalutin lady.''

Elizabeth touched her hair, assuring herself that all her pins were in place.

"Don't fret." He eyed her for a moment, smiling as though he found her amusing. "Every hair is in place.''

She lowered her hand, wishing she could cover her face with it. She felt so exposed with this man, as though he could look deep inside her to the place where she hid all her secrets.

"Outside you're all smooth and cold. Carved like one of those statues." He inclined his head toward the gardens, where Greek gods of white marble stood on pedestals, peering at the mortals in their midst from clumps of evergreen bushes. "But inside . . .''

He touched her cheek, a warm slide of the back of his long fingers against her skin. She stared up into the stunning beauty of his eyes, all the air evaporating from her lungs. She should step away from him, but she couldn't move. She didn't really want to. His touch was so very warm. The heat of him tingled along her every nerve.

"Inside you're all fire." He slipped his fingers along her jaw, supporting her chin on the heel of his palm. "I've seen your anger from both sides. And I gotta say, I like it a whole lot more when you're on my side.''

"You heard," she whispered.

"Yeah, I heard," he said, his voice revealing the flicker of anger beneath his smile. "You sure got a way of flaying the skin right off a body with that English voice of yours. Gets colder than a December wind coming off the mountains.''

"I suppose I was a bit harsh.''

"Here I thought you didn't like me. And then you go sticking up for me." He stroked his thumb over her lower lip, the moonlight in his eyes turning to flames.

She melted beneath the fire, her muscles dissolving, her body flowing into his heat. "They had no right to say those things about you."

He slid his hand into her hair, long fingers moving against her scalp, cradling her head. "They're right about me."

"No they aren't." She rested her hands on his chest, her gloved fingers curling against the soft white cotton of his shirt, seeking the warmth of his skin. He slid one strong arm around her, holding her close, as though he thought she might run away from him. Impossible. Her legs scarcely had the strength to hold her, even if she wanted to escape. She didn't. A part of her had waited for this moment all her life.

"I ain't no gentleman, pretty lady," he said, his voice a harsh whisper.

Elizabeth trembled with the dark promise in his voice. "Are you warning me?"

"Guess maybe I am."

She stayed in his hold, knowing he would release her if she struggled. Yet she had no will to leave his warm embrace. She wanted to feel his arms around her. She wanted to taste the reality of a kiss that had lived in her dreams.

All her life she had daydreamed of a boy who had been lost in the wilderness, imagining how he would look as he grew older, wondering if one day they would meet. And now he was here, holding her, and he was more exciting than she had ever imagined.

Flickering flames flashed in the cool blue of his eyes. His fingers tensed on the nape of her neck, drawing her upward as he lowered his head. His breath fell warm and soft against her cheek, sweet as a meadow after a spring rain. He slid his lips over hers, taking possession, gliding slowly from one corner of her mouth to the other, until he claimed her completely.

Elizabeth groaned deep in her throat, stunned by the pure pleasure filling her, surging through every vessel, like liquid sunlight. Excitement tingled along her every nerve, until she was trembling in his arms. She hesitated a moment, shocked by her own forward thoughts, before she followed her instinct and slid her arms around his shoulders, holding him close the way she had always imagined holding him.

She slipped her hand into the thick dark waves at his neck, wishing she had tossed away her gloves. She wanted the softness of his hair sliding against her bare fingers. He parted his lips over hers, growling deep in his throat, as though he wanted to devour her. The primal sound whispered to a secret element buried deep inside her, awakening a part of her untouched by rules and restrictions.

Emotions she had never suspected existed stirred from their slumber, stretching inside her, like tender blossoms reaching for the heat of the sun, coaxing her to open to him, to receive the slick thrust of his tongue into her mouth. She leaned closer to this intoxicating male, her breath catching as her breasts nestled against his hard chest. A pulse flickered low in her belly, a moist ache fluttering to the rhythm of his tongue, thrusting, withdrawing, thrusting past her trembling lips.

He groaned, the sound of a man in pain. He pulled away and stared down at her, his beautiful eyes burning with desire and doubt.

Deprived of his strong embrace, Elizabeth sagged against the balustrade. She stared at him in stunned silence, awed by the feelings he had awakened in her.

He stepped back, putting three feet of cool night air between them, his breath coming as sharp and ragged as her own. "You got no business bein' alone with a man like me."

Elizabeth flinched at the anger in his voice. "I seem to recall you saying you had never in your life forced a woman to do anything."

He drew in his breath. "Lady, a few more minutes of that and I'd have you on your back, in the grass, with me between your legs."

Elizabeth gasped. "Really, Mr. MacGregor, I believe you hold your skills of seduction in much too high a regard."

"I ain't one of your fancy gentleman, Beth." He leaned toward her, trapping her, his hands positioned on the stone balustrade on either side of her, his hard body pressed against her, his lips a whisper away. "Don't play games with me. You'll get hurt."

Elizabeth looked up into his eyes, hiding her injured feelings behind an angry mask. "You don't frighten me, Mr. MacGregor."

"I sure as hell should frighten you."

She lifted her chin, ignoring the trembling in her legs. "If you were truly the blackguard you want me to believe you are, you would never stop to warn me of your intentions."

"Look, lady, you'd be smart to remember just who and what I am."

"You're a man who has been lost for a long time. A man who can finally find his way home. If you are only willing to risk your pride. Are you a brave man, Mr. MacGregor? Or a coward?"

A muscle flashed beneath his smooth cheek as he clenched his jaw. "There ain't no need for any more speeches. I already told Trevelyan I'd go to England."

Elizabeth pressed her hand to her heart, silently giving thanks for the answer to her prayers. "Oh, that's wonderful."

"Don't pin your hopes on me, Beth. I ain't got no place in England. I'm givin' the old man six months, that's all. Six months and then I'm gone."

"Six months? But that's hardly enough time to become acquainted." She toyed with the pearls of her necklace, realizing she had revealed too much of her hopes in her careless response. "I mean, you and Marlow, of course."

Ash drew his lips into a tight line. "Let's get this straight right here and now. I'm goin' for the money, not for anything or anyone else."

Elizabeth stared up into his eyes, hoping to find a contradiction there to his harsh words and finding nothing but ice in the blue depths. The kiss they had shared might have left her breathless, it might have been straight out of her dreams, but it meant less than nothing to him.

She stared at the narrow black tie dangling from the collar of his white shirt, hoping he wouldn't see the disappointment rising inside her. "I'm not certain how you can say such things, when you have Marlow to consider."

"He's just some crazy old man as far as I'm concerned."

Her back stiffened. To insult her was one thing; to insult Marlow was quite another. "How dare you speak of him that way?"

"He might be your saint, lady, but to me he's just some old man with more money then sense."

She glared at him. "He is your grandfather."

Ash laughed, the deep rumble mocking her indignation. "You're a bigger fool than he is if you believe that."

She stared up into his eyes, seeing the harsh reality her foolish hopes had overlooked. Where she had imagined vulnerability she saw only polished steel. Where she had imagined desire she saw only mockery for a woman's weakness. Her hopes and dreams withered beneath the burning light of reality. "You're right, Mr. MacGregor, I was a fool."

He stepped back, his eyes narrowing as though he were facing an opponent who might strike at any moment.

"Only a fool would look at you and see sensitivity where there is only callousness. Only a fool would ever believe a man with your ignoble spirit could ever become a gentleman worthy of the Trevelyan name."

"Guess you're beginnin' to doubt ever thinkin' I could be Peyton Trevelyan."

She swallowed against the band of regret tightening around her throat. "No. Unfortunately, I still believe you are Peyton Trevelyan. I only wish the blood in your veins was enough to make you half the man Marlow is. You, sir, are a complete knave."

He glanced past her, staring for a moment over her left shoulder, his jaw tightly clenched. When he looked at her a corner of his lips drew upward in a chilling imitation of a smile. "Keep that in mind next time you have the notion to go sparkin' in the moonlight. If you're real smart, Beth, you'll stay away from me."

She leaned back against the balustrade, watching as he marched away from her. She shivered, the involuntary trembling having more to do with Ash MacGregor's words than the chill of the evening breeze.

Oh, he was the most selfish, arrogant . . . "Oooo."

She hugged her arms to her waist, staring at the shadows where he had disappeared. The man hadn't a care for Marlow's feelings. Not to mention her own. He had toyed with her as though she were one of Miss Hattie's girls. And she had allowed it. No, to be completely truthful, she had welcomed his attentions. More to the point, she had thrown herself into his arms.

She turned away from the shadows, resting her hands on the balustrade. The mountains rose like dark phantoms in the distance, a solid reminder of the boy who had been lost so many years ago. No matter how much she wished to the contrary, the man calling himself Ash MacGregor was nothing at all like the one she had imagined he would be. Oh, he was handsome; undeniably so. But he was also cruel. Heartless enough to destroy an elderly man's hopes for the future. And one foolish woman's dreams.

Most of her life she had wished for Peyton Trevelyan to come home. Now she wished she had never met him.

Chapter Four

"Mr. Dibell, please. I'm certain Lord Angelstone had no intention of snapping your neck like a dried twig." Elizabeth hurried down the winding staircase, her hand skimming the smooth mahogany banister as she tried to keep up with the fleeing tailor. The sound of the front door slamming ricocheted through the hall, heralding the escape of Dibell's two assistants. "Do come back. I'm certain His Grace would make it well worth your trouble."

Mr. Dibell paused at the foot of the stairs, casting a nervous glance upward, as though he expected the devil breathing fire in hot pursuit. He passed a trembling hand across his brow, smoothing down the oiled strands poking up like dark spikes. "Lady Elizabeth, there is not enough money in Denver to persuade me to return to that room."

Elizabeth pursued him as the short man rushed across the entry hall, their footsteps tapping a quick staccato against squares of white marble veined in gold. "Mr. Dibell, I'm certain this has all been a misunderstanding."

Dibell paused at the front door, breathing hard, his thin cheeks brushed with color. "Lady Elizabeth." He tucked his crumpled dark green cravat into his gray waistcoat. "I believe the only misunderstanding here is on your part. That savage cannot possibly be the missing heir of the duke of Marlow."

Elizabeth bristled at the distant slur on her guardian's name, but she managed to conceal her irritation behind a smile. "Mr. Dibell, I assure you Mr. MacGregor is the marquess of Angelstone. If you would only return with me, I'm certain . . ."

"Never." His fingers trembled as he tried to tug his twisted collar back into place. "And if I were you, Lady Elizabeth, I would lock my door at night. A man like that is capable of anything. Why, he might strangle you in your sleep."

Elizabeth lifted one brow, pinning the man with an icy glare. "I realize you are upset, Mr. Dibell, but . . ."

"Upset! That man nearly killed me." He rubbed his neck.

Elizabeth eased a deep breath into her tight chest. Oh, she wanted to strangle MacGregor for causing this disaster. "Lord Angelstone simply took offense at your . . ."

"If that man MacGregor is an English marquis, than I'm the king of England."

"In England the title is Marquess, Mr. Dibell. Lord Angelstone is not French."

He rolled his eyes. "He isn't all human, if you ask me."

She folded her hands at her waist, giving the man a glance that had put many an overly familiar aristocrat in his place. "I believe on further consideration His Grace will not require your services. Good day."

Dibell swallowed hard. "I meant no disrespect to the duke."

"No. You simply insulted his grandson."

"The man lifted me up off the floor by my collar," Dibell said.

Elizabeth allowed a smile to curve her lips. "I trust a certain amount of discretion is required for a man in your business, Mr. Dibell. Especially if he wishes to remain in business."

Dibell's dark eyes grew wide. "Of course."

"Good day, Mr. Dibell. A check shall be sent to cover

your time for this morning.'' Dibell pulled open the door
and scrambled out of the house. Elizabeth caught a
glimpse of the man scurrying to his carriage as she closed
the door. She had little doubt all of Denver would hear
of his near extinction at the hands of Marlow's savage
grandson by this afternoon. She had never in her life contemplated doing physical injury to anyone or anything,
but she was seriously considering pushing Ash Mac-
Gregor out a window.

''Having a little trouble this morning?''

Elizabeth stiffened at the sound of Lillian Radcliffe's
smug-sounding voice. She drew in her breath and forced
her features into a calm mask before she turned away from
the front door. Lillian stood in the doorway of the parlor,
stiff as a lamppost in a bright yellow poplin gown, her
lips pulled into a tight smile. Nancy stood a little behind
her mother, regarding Elizabeth with a look of satisfaction
on her pretty face.

''I'm afraid we've had a minor misunderstanding,''
Elizabeth said, keeping her voice even and cool.

Lillian lifted her brows. ''From what I heard, Mr. Dibell was quite certain of what had happened.''

Elizabeth smiled. ''Mr. Dibell was a bit overwrought.''

''With seemingly good reason.''

''Things are not always what they seem, Mrs. Radcliffe. Now you must excuse me; we are expecting a barber at any moment.'' Elizabeth intended to make certain
the man would not be risking his life in an attempt to
shear the beast.

She headed for the stairs, her limbs trembling with the
effort to control her fury. If MacGregor were left to his
own devices, the barbarian would utterly destroy the
proud Trevelyan name. Heaven help her, she wanted to
strangle the man.

*   *   *

Ash stood staring at the open door where Beth had disappeared, chasing after Mr. Dibell. God, the look she'd given him. He had felt that glance like a slap across the face. It wasn't so much the anger in her eyes that got to him, as the damnable disappointment, as though he had let her down.

What the hell did she expect of him? And why the hell should he care? But he did care. Dammit, he didn't like having little Miss Prim and Proper think he was some snarling beast. And he sure as hell didn't like the fact that he cared what she thought of him.

He wasn't a man quick to temper. A man in his line of work couldn't be. Not if he wanted to stay alive. He had managed to keep a tight rein on his anger for a time, while that little weasel of a tailor had sidled around him, as though Ash were a wolf about to bite. He had managed to ignore most of Dibell's snide comments, but the weasel had taken one step too far when he mentioned the fact that proper clothes could transform even a bloody savage into a gentleman.

Ash clenched his hands into fists, aware of Trevelyan standing by the fireplace, watching him. He glanced at the old man, feeling like a kid caught stealing candy. "I didn't mean to send him running off that way."

Hayward rubbed his right eyebrow, studying Ash for a moment before he spoke. "I take it Mr. Dibell annoyed you in some way?"

Ash opened his hands, stretching his fingers close to his thighs. "I didn't want his hands on me."

"Ah, I see. Hummm, I suppose it's the first time you've been measured by a tailor."

"Ain't never had the need."

Hayward nodded. "Well, I'm afraid having a tailor measure one is the only way to have one's clothes properly made."

"I don't see why a man can't just buy his clothes ready made."

Hayward stared at him. "Buy one's clothes ready made?"

"That's right. They got suits and shirts and everything else a body needs at the dry goods store."

Hayward pursed his lips, as though considering Ash's statement. "I rather suspect the fit isn't quite as precise."

"It's always been good enough for me."

Hayward smiled. "Yes, well, things have changed. Most gentlemen have their clothes custom made."

Things had changed, all right. It was as though Ash had stepped into one side of a tunnel and come out the other straight into a whole different world. A place where he fit as well as a bear in a hat shop. He glanced toward the doorway as Elizabeth marched through it.

She paused in the middle of the room, looking at Ash as though he had just crawled out from beneath the nearest rock. "Mr. Dibell has left." Her crisp English voice dripped icicles.

"Yes, well, I rather suspected you wouldn't be able to persuade him to return. Not to worry. The man made note of the measurements." Hayward retrieved the black note book Dibell's assistant had left on a table by the fireplace. "I'll telegraph a set to a tailor I've used in New York. We can pick up the clothing when we arrive. I'll also send them to my tailor in London. You'll be well on your way to a proper wardrobe by the time we reach home. In the meantime we'll purchase a few essentials from the *dry goods store.*"

Elizabeth cast her guardian a censuring look. "A proper wardrobe shall make little difference if the man wearing the clothes is a barbarian who believes in solving problems with brawn rather than wits."

Ash tilted his head, glancing at her from beneath half-lowered lids. She held herself as stiff as a frozen aspen, yet there was nothing frozen about the anger burning in her eyes. "I ain't never pretended to be anything I ain't."

Elizabeth clasped her hands at her waist, as though she were trying to contain all the emotions that simmered within her. "I believe you take a certain pleasure in demonstrating your lack of manners, Mr. MacGregor."

He refused to glance away from her angry glare, though he suspected that's what she expected him to do. She wanted him to turn away from the anger with the embarrassment of a wayward child. Instead, he smiled, a slow arrogant grin that brought color high in her cheeks.

"I believe it's time we begin addressing Peyton by his proper name, Elizabeth," Hayward said, smiling at his ward.

"And I believe it's time Mr. MacGregor began to behave in a manner befitting the Trevelyan name," she replied.

"Look, I didn't like having that little bootlicker puttin' his hands on me."

Elizabeth raised a finely arched brow. "A gentleman is more interested in the proper cut of his clothing than he is in some ridiculous aversion to having a servant touch him."

Ash frowned. "I ain't gonna have no . . ."

"Listen to me, Mr. MacGregor. You have agreed to become Peyton Emory Hayward Trevelyan, Marquess of Angelstone, for the next six months. That means you will dress properly, you will speak properly, you will behave properly in all situations. You will not cause any embarrassment to the Trevelyan name." She moved toward him as she spoke until she was so close he could catch the scent of lavender warm from her skin. "In short, Mr. MacGregor, you will become civilized."

Sunlight streamed through the windows behind him, touching her face, mining gold in the yellow brown curls piled high at the back of her head. Ash stared down into the turbulent gray depths of her eyes, his muscles tensing with an excitement he couldn't control. Through the haze of his rising anger, he recognized the pure, undiluted lust pumping hard and fast through his veins. It was as if his body had a hidden trigger that went off each time she was within a hundred yards of him. "Last time I looked you weren't my boss, Miss Barrington."

Her eyes narrowed. Yet her voice remained level and cool when she spoke. "The last time I looked you had agreed to become Peyton Trevelyan. That involves more than pinning on a name."

Although she didn't quite reach his chin, she faced him with all the cool fury of a gunslinger. He didn't flinch beneath her icy regard, but inside he cringed from the contempt burning in her eyes. Last night he had seen something else in her eyes—warmth and acceptance, a desire that had startled him as much as it had her. It might be damn stupid, but he wanted to see those beckoning flames once more.

Hayward cleared his throat. "Elizabeth does have a point."

Ash clenched his jaw. He thought back on all the names he'd been called, all the times people had made him feel he was nothing but dirt under their feet. He had no intention of going through that again. "If I ain't good enough as I am, then I guess we got no deal."

"My dear young man, don't raise your hackles. If you are to function in England as my grandson, you must learn proper social protocol. It will save you untold embarrassment."

"And you . . ." Ash glanced over Beth's head, meeting Trevelyan's gentle blue gaze. "It wouldn't do to have some rough-edged bounty hunter prowlin' around one of your fancy balls. Would it?"

Hayward tilted back his head, laughing softly, as though he found the image amusing rather than frightening. "My goodness, we would start some tongues wagging, wouldn't we?"

Elizabeth cast her guardian a dark glance.

Hayward cleared his throat. "But I'm afraid it would be better for you in the long run if you didn't give people any more gossip to chew. Believe me, your background will be enough to cause a stir for months. Can you imagine, the marquess of Angelstone, heir of the duke of Marlow, was actually raised by Indians."

A bead of sweat trickled down Ash's spine. "And the owner of Denver's finest whorehouse. Don't forget Hattie."

Hayward grinned. "You will be the talk of London for months. Perhaps years. London is frightfully boring these days."

"Yeah, well, nothing like a gunfighter to liven things up a bit," Ash said.

Hayward nodded, smiling broadly. "That's the spirit."

Ash shook his head. "I ain't some fancy man, and I ain't interested in becomin' one."

"Afraid you aren't up to the challenge, Mr. MacGregor?" Elizabeth smiled, a tight curve of her lips that left her eyes shimmering with fury. "Afraid you really aren't as good as all of those fancy-dressed gentlemen you so disdain?"

He looked into her eyes and realized he wanted to see respect in those stormy depths. When she looked at him, he wanted her to see a man every bit as good as any she had ever met. "You go about judging all men by the way they dress, Miss Barrington? By the way they talk?"

"I judge a man by his deeds, Mr. MacGregor."

"Yet you stand here lookin' at me like I ain't fit to clean your shoes."

"And what have you done to earn my respect? You put money before family. You go about bullying a poor little man who is only doing his job. And now you refuse to even attempt to better yourself.''

Ash curled his hands into tight fists at his sides, his only concession to the anxiety tying his insides into knots. ''The world ain't all fancy dressin' and fancy talkin'.''

''Your world isn't, Mr. MacGregor, but the world of Peyton Trevelyan is quite different.'' She drew in a long, slow breath, some of the anger easing from her. ''You must understand. The society in which Marlow and I live judges a man by his appearance, his deportment, his wit. Unless you wish to hold yourself and Marlow up to ridicule, you must learn to function properly in that society.''

''And what the hell do you expect me to do? Go back to school?''

''Of course not,'' Hayward said. ''Elizabeth can teach you everything you need to know.''

Elizabeth pivoted to face her guardian. ''You expect me to tutor him?''

Hayward rested his arm on the carved back of a narrow armchair set before the fire, smiling at his ward. ''I think it's an excellent solution to our problem.''

''But I assumed you would hire a tutor for him.''

With the tip of his finger, Hayward traced the wing of the black and yellow bird printed on the bright blue upholstery covering the chair. ''I'm certain Peyton would feel much more comfortable with someone he knows.''

She glanced up at Ash as though she expected him to bite her. Ash smiled down into her wide, wary eyes, thinking of a few things he would like to teach his pretty tutor. ''What's the matter, Miss Barrington, afraid you ain't up to the challenge?''

She stiffened. ''It's *Lady* Elizabeth.''

He laughed softly, for no other reason than to watch an angry blush rise in her cheeks. ''So what's it gonna be, Lady Beth? You think you're up to teaching me how to be one of your highfalutin gentlemen?''

A corner of her lips twitched. ''That depends.''

The back of his neck prickled as he held her furious stare. Growing up at Miss Hattie's had given him a real good appreciation of how dangerous a woman could be when you got her back up. And right now Lady Beth looked like a cat about to tear a mouse to pieces. "Depends on what?"

She smiled. "On whether or not you're willing to try, Mr. MacGregor."

"What do you say, my lad?" Hayward asked. "Are you up to the challenge?"

Ash didn't look away from Beth's pretty face. He stared down into her eyes, wondering just how hard it would be to teach little Miss Prim and Proper how to act like a woman instead of a walking, talking statue. "You're on."

She stepped back, some of the bravura draining from her features. "I shall expect your complete cooperation."

Ash lowered his eyes, following the emerald velvet ribbon that wound in and out of white eyelet, the fancy work plunging in a vee between her breasts. If Hattie had been wearing the gown, her breasts would be rising smooth and pale above that fancy lace. Lady Beth's gown was all filled in with a soft-looking mint green cloth clear up to her chin, letting a man wonder what lay beneath. He watched the lace flutter with the soft rise and fall of her breasts, his blood pumping slow and hot, low in his belly. "Don't fret. I'm gonna give you all my attention."

She pressed her hand to her neck, her long fingers brushing the lace at the high neckline, as though she meant to prevent him from unfastening the buttons lining the front of her gown, the way he was doing in his mind.

"I'm afraid there are a few measurements that still must be taken." Hayward frowned as he studied the open notebook in his hands. "I doubt the tailors can do anything without them. Fortunately Mr. Dibell dropped his measuring tape in his rather hasty retreat."

Ash clenched his jaw. He suspected the old man intended to have one of his servants finish the job. Another little weasel who looked at Ash as though he was some freak on display, mincing around him, touching him as though he were afraid Ash would somehow contaminate his clean hands. Dibell had expected Ash to act like an uncivilized animal. And dammit, he had obliged. Well, he'd be damned before he put on another show. He'd be damned before he'd give little Miss Prim and Proper another reason to look at him with scorn and contempt in her pretty gray eyes.

"I'm certain you wouldn't mind if Elizabeth completed taking the remaining measurements. Would you, Peyton?"

The tension in his muscles eased; here was a man who had been expecting the lash of a whip across his back only to find the blow a soft brush of silk. On the other hand, the little lady looked as though she had taken a big bite of a green apple. He had a feeling she would rather cross the desert barefoot than measure him for a new suit. Ash grinned, wondering if the lady was up to the challenge. "Lady Beth can measure anything she wants."

Chapter Five

Elizabeth glared at the rogue. He was looking at her as though he expected her to run, as though she were a dried-up spinster all a flutter at the thought of touching a man. Well, she might be unmarried, but it was by choice. There had been many men interested in marrying her. There were those who still thought to coax her to the altar. Handsome men. Sophisticated gentlemen. All with the good sense to see her best qualities, even if she was a trifle past the age when women were considered on the shelf.

No matter what the beast might think, she certainly was not a fluttery old spinster who had never before been in the company of a man. Still, she wasn't at all interested in getting close to MacGregor. She was too honest to deny an unfortunate infatuation with the man, a fascination that had her hands trembling at the thought of touching him. She looked at Hayward, wondering how best to point out the impropriety of the situation. "Wouldn't it be more appropriate if you completed taking the measurements?"

Hayward dismissed her protest with a wave of his hand. "Nothing indecent about taking a few measurements, my girl."

Elizabeth fiddled with the emerald satin ribbon at her waist. "But I . . ."

"You call out each measurement and I'll record it in Dibell's notebook." Hayward retrieved a pencil from the table. "There's nothing to it."

Nothing to it, except she would be forced to stand near Ash MacGregor. Obliged to touch him. Which, unfortunately, was hardly a disagreeable task. It was much too tempting. Which was, in fact, the problem.

Hayward glanced up from the notebook, his eyes filled with curiosity. "Is something wrong?"

Elizabeth twisted the ribbon in her fingers. "I've never taken measurements before."

"Just imagine it's a fitting for one of your gowns," Hayward said.

Still she hesitated. It was hardly proper for a lady to touch a gentleman in the manner a fitting required. Still, she had long ago realized that Hayward had little respect for many of the niceties of polite society. If he thought a rule silly, he ignored it, doing precisely what he wanted.

Hayward frowned. "I would really appreciate this, Elizabeth, but if you feel it somehow demeaning to take a few measurements, I believe I could manage."

"I promise not to bite," Ash said, his voice filled with arrogant mockery.

She turned toward MacGregor. He was dangling the measuring tape from his fingers, like a lion teasing a mouse. Infuriating rogue! He expected her to lift her skirts and run screaming from the room.

It seemed she had two options. She could refuse, by reason of the terribly improper nature of Hayward's request, thus insulting her guardian and looking like a snob. If not entirely too much like a frightened mouse. Or she could crush the unfortunate infatuation she had for the man and take the measurements without so much as batting an eye. Thus proving to the arrogant barbarian that she was quite immune to his primitive male charms. That choice had a definite appeal.

She crossed the distance in two quick strides and slipped the measuring tape from his hand. "I believe Mr.

Dibell was measuring your waist when you turned into a snarling beast.''

Ash chuckled softly as he held out his hands at his sides. "Be my guest."

She stared at the rogue, trying not to notice the way his black shirt stretched tautly across his broad chest. Memories tumbled uninvited into her mind—his strong arms closing around her, as though she were something very special to be held close to his heart. His lips, warm and demanding, sliding against hers, as though she were some exotic spice and he couldn't get enough of her. For one insane moment she entertained the ridiculous notion of stepping straight into his inviting embrace.

"Lady Beth?" Ash asked, his dark voice taunting her with her own weakness.

Hen-witted fool.

He was a man.

Only a man.

Hardly a rare species, even if he was one of the most splendid specimens she had ever seen. It didn't matter to her. He didn't matter to her. He was an arrogant, heartless, thoroughly contemptuous barbarian. Still, she couldn't quite convince her limbs to stop trembling. She glanced up into his glorious eyes, saw the humor shimmering there, and took a deep breath. She could do this, she assured herself.

She slipped her arms around him, solely for the purpose of bringing the twill tape around his waist, she assured herself. The warmth of his skin radiated through the black cotton of his shirt, bathing her cheek. The scent of him swirled through her head—lemony citrus and leather and potent masculinity. Heat unfurled like a banner low in her belly, curling upward until her breasts tingled.

"Thirty-four," she murmured, painfully aware of the breathless quality of her voice.

"Right," Hayward said, noting the measurement in Dibell's book. "We'll take some off for the clothes he's wearing."

She stepped back, forcing her face into a composed mask, aware that MacGregor was watching her. Not for the world would she allow the rogue the satisfaction of knowing the power he held over her impossibly foolish senses. She glanced at Hayward, hoping he had filled in all the necessary numbers on the page.

Hayward looked up from the book. "We need his inseam."

Elizabeth swallowed hard. "His *inseam?*"

"Yes." Hayward continued, apparently unaware of her true reason for hesitating. "That's the length of the inside of his leg."

She was all too aware of the required measurement. She looked at MacGregor, watching as he shifted his feet, separating his legs in a blatantly masculine manner. Her lips were dry, and her mouth had turned to parchment. She held one end of the tape out to him, hoping he wouldn't notice the way the twill twitched like the tail of a cat in her nervous fingers. "Hold this against the top of your . . . limb."

He took the tape, grinning at her as he pressed one end of the tape high against his inner thigh. For some unforgivable reason her gaze fixed on that white twill tape pressed against the black cloth. An image came to mind of all the statues of male perfection one so often sees in museums. Sharply defined muscles. Long limbs carved from white marble. Bare, except for a strategically placed fig leaf. She suspected Mr. MacGregor would require a particularly large leaf. A curious tingle rippled through her at the image that thought triggered. Yet, even as it formed she chastised herself for having such wicked notions. Particularly about this barbarian.

He tugged on the measuring tape she still held, like a master steering a mare, dragging her gaze from a place it never should have wandered to the dark, savage beauty of his handsome face. The humor in his eyes told her he knew exactly the path her thoughts had taken. Infuriating rogue!

She knelt before him, the rustling of merino wool against linen crashing with the blood pounding in her ears. This little exercise was meant to teach him that she was completely immune to him, she reminded herself as she pressed the tape against his ankle.

Through the stiff black cotton trousers, his leather boot eased against her fingers. The black boot was polished to a shine in spite of the scratches she could see in the leather. She had the strange urge to run her fingers over the curve of his instep. The insane notion to press her cheek against his leg, trace the curve of his calf with her fingertips. She shivered inside, but not from fear. Oh no, she recognized desire when she felt it, even though she had never in her life experienced it before.

She stared at the tape, trying to decipher the number above her thumb through the tangled mess that had once been a fully functioning brain. "Thirty-five," she said, appalled at the tremor in her voice, hoping no one noticed.

"Excellent!" Hayward said. "I believe we have all we need."

She had far more than she needed. This infatuation was truly inconvenient. Not to mention dangerous. Ash gripped her arms as she struggled with her gown in an attempt to stand. His long fingers curved around her upper arms as he lifted her from the floor, as though she were no heavier than the rag doll she felt herself to be. She stumbled as her unsteady feet took her weight. He slipped his arms around her, imposing balance, holding her far too close.

She rested her hand on his chest. For balance. Certainly not because she wanted to touch him. Unfortunately, she couldn't convince herself of that lie. She kept her gaze fixed on the top button of his shirt, or at least the upper-most one that was fastened. Above that button stretched an intriguing expanse of golden skin and dark masculine curls. Above that was a handsome face she felt certain currently wore a very smug expression. "Thank you," she murmured.

"My pleasure."

There was something in his deep voice that coaxed her to look up at him, a husky note that stroked her like a warm caress. She looked up, expecting to see amusement along with her own humiliation mirrored in his eyes. What she saw instead stole the last wisps of breath from her lungs.

Hunger.

She had seen desire before, in the eyes of men intent on courting her with pretty words and trinkets and all the trifles available to a gentleman of polite society. Yet that desire had always been shielded by propriety. There was nothing proper about the look in MacGregor's eyes.

Never in her life had she seen the raw hunger that blazed in this man's eyes. Primal. Primitive. Lust in all its animal glory. The power of it thrummed through him, into her, arcing along her every nerve.

"I'll have a carriage brought 'round. Elizabeth can take you on a shopping expedition."

Ash released her. He stepped back, glancing at Hayward as though he had only just remembered the man was there. He turned away and stalked to a window, where he braced his hand against the casement and lifted his face to the breeze.

Elizabeth looked at her guardian, stunned at his complacent expression. He obviously had no idea the havoc Ash MacGregor wrecked on her composure, or he wouldn't want her within a mile of the man. "Wouldn't you prefer to take him shopping?"

"Not at all. I'm certain I would only be in the way."

Hayward smiled at her. ''And you have such a marvelous sense of fashion. I'm certain Radcliffe will be able to tell you where you might find the things Peyton requires.''

''I'll ask him straight away.'' She took the opportunity to escape before she did something shocking, such as throw her arms around Ash MacGregor's neck and kiss him until she fainted. She forced her strides into a dignified pace as she crossed the room, resisting the urge to lift her skirts and run.

Once she reached the safety of the hall she leaned against an oak-paneled wall and drew deep drafts of air into her tight lungs. She was a fool. A silly spinster who trembled at the touch of a man. At least at the touch of Ash MacGregor.

He was a rogue, she reminded herself. Heartless. Without a conscience. The man no doubt believed women had been placed on earth to satisfy men's most basic hunger. And she was appalled to find she very much wanted to satisfy that hunger. She drew away from the wall and squared her shoulders. No more of this nonsense.

It was an infatuation. Lust. Nothing more. She refused to play the role of lovesick spinster for any man. Especially a savage like Ash MacGregor. She marched away from the room, determined to crush the misguided fascination she had for the barbarian.

The rustle of her skirts whispered as Elizabeth left the room. Ash clenched his hand into a fist against the window frame, fighting the insane urge to follow her. Blood pounded through his veins, hot and stinging, melting his brain and stiffening another part of his anatomy. All because one sharp-tongued little prude had touched him, had placed her hand against his ankle.

Only she wasn't a prude. No, little Miss Prim and Proper might look as though she could freeze a man with a glance at a hundred paces, but beneath that icy exterior burned the soul of a temptress. While she had stood there, staring at him, he had felt as though she were stripping him bare, removing every last stitch of his clothes, until he was as naked as Adam before the fall. And the look in her eyes—as though he was the most fascinating man she had ever set eyes on before.

God, it had taken every scrap of his will power to keep from doing something insane, like crushing her in his arms and kissing that bossy little mouth of hers until she couldn't think straight.

"Elizabeth has wonderful taste. I hope you will trust her judgment in choosing the proper apparel."

Ash glanced back at the old man. If Hayward had any idea of the way that woman could set fire to his blood, he wouldn't want Ash within a mile of his pretty ward. "Guess she knows better than me."

Hayward smiled. "You can rest assured, you're in excellent hands with Elizabeth."

In Elizabeth's hands. Now that conjured an image. One that had no business sneaking into his head—her slender white hands roaming over his skin, touching him as though she loved the feel of him.

Damn, he really was going insane. Little Miss Prim and Proper wasn't his type. No, his type came fast and loose and didn't bother a man about what might come with the morning. His type didn't try trapping a man,

He had never gotten himself tangled up with a respectable woman, and he didn't intend to start with Elizabeth Barrington. They wanted different things from life. They lived in two different worlds. He intended to keep it that way.

"There is something I want you to have," Hayward said.

Ash turned to face the old man, frowning as he approached. "What?"

Hayward slipped his hand into his coat pocket and

withdrew a ring. "This belonged to your father. I gave it to him when he was sixteen."

Ash stared down at the thick gold ring lying in Hayward's palm. Sunlight slipped through the window behind him, winking on a single square-cut emerald embedded in a fancy crest carved into the gold. An odd feeling gripped him as he stared down at the ring, a flicker of familiarity that brushed his skin like an icy breath.

"Take it, my lad," Hayward said. "It belongs to you now."

Ash had to swallow hard before he could use his voice. "I wouldn't feel right wearing it. It don't belong to me."

Hayward hesitated a moment before closing his fingers over the ring. "When you do feel comfortable about wearing it let me know," he said softly. "It will be waiting for you."

Instincts that had kept him alive all his life screamed inside Ash's head. He should walk out of here and not look back. These people wanted more from him than he could give. They expected him to be something he wasn't.

Yet, he had made a deal. And he wasn't going anywhere until he had enough money to buy a new life. Even if it meant giving little Miss Prim and Proper the chance to rip him inside out. He could handle the lady, he assured himself.

"I buy my clothes at Henderson's Dry Goods," Ash said.

Elizabeth glanced up at the man walking beside her down a wide corridor leading to the gentleman's department of Mansfield's. "I believe we will find what we need here."

He frowned as he looked at her. "I ain't gonna wear no fancy red plaid suit."

"Rest assured, Mr. MacGregor, I shall make certain you don't wear a fancy red plaid suit." She had taken leave of her senses. It was the only explanation for her agreeing to tackle the task of turning this barbarian into a gentleman. She had doubts anyone could manage the job.

From the corner of her eye she watched MacGregor. He was glancing around, frowning as though he didn't approve of the walnut-paneled walls, the white marble floors, the glass-lined cases displaying an assortment of ladies' gloves and fans. Perhaps Mansfield's wasn't his idea of an appropriate place to shop, but according to Shelby Radcliffe it was one of the most fashionable stores in Denver. One of the few places where they had a reasonable chance of procuring decent apparel for the rogue.

Sunlight poured through the skylight rotunda six stories overhead, glinting on the silver handle of the revolver Ash wore strapped on his narrow hips. He wore the revolver in spite of her request that he leave the weapon at Radcliffe's house. Dressed entirely in black, with that weapon at his side, he looked like a dark, avenging angel. Hardly the appearance the marquess of Angelstone should wish to cultivate. Even if she had to admit that she found the image somewhat . . . extraordinary.

An image teased her mind as she looked at him. She kept seeing a knight dressed entirely in black. A man ready to charge into battle. A man so powerful in his masculinity, he could steal a lady's heart with a single touch.

Oh my, she really must stop thinking of him in this way. He was hardly a knight. She doubted he had the least knowledge of chivalry. No doubt his interest in a woman wouldn't extend beyond the time he took for him to unbutton his trousers and tumble her.

She must definitely stop thinking of Ash MacGregor as anything but a casual acquaintance. A student she must teach for the sake of her guardian. Unless, of course, she wished for her maidenhead to be dispatched with the same gentleness as a hawk ripping apart a mouse.

Following the direction of a clerk, she turned from the main corridor into a large room that might have graced a country house. Leather upholstered armchairs sat upon a Persian carpet in shades of ivory, burgundy, and green, before a white marble fireplace. Ties and various other items of apparel were displayed like precious artwork on polished mahogany tables. Hats, coats, and trousers stood like suits of armor on narrow walnut stands around the room. Shoes and boots lined walnut shelves like volumes in a library.

Elizabeth paused near a table covered with neatly folded, crisp white linen handkerchiefs, glancing around the room for assistance. She was definitely going to need help where MacGregor was concerned. The rogue left her side, prowling the room like a wary warrior, looking at the suits as though each were a foe about to draw a sword and strike. This was not going to be easy.

A clerk who had been arranging an assortment of braces on a round pedestal table beside the fireplace paused in his task and immediately moved in her direction. She noticed the way the short, thin man glanced at MacGregor as he passed him, his brown eyes growing wide and wary behind the round lenses of his glasses.

"I'm Harvey. How may I be of service to you, madame?" the clerk asked, glancing toward MacGregor, like a mouse keeping his eyes on a prowling cat.

"I was told you might have ready-to-wear garments for a gentleman," Elizabeth said.

"We have a wide variety of accessories." Harvey saw MacGregor pause beside a table of neckties of various colors. "And we can make to order any of the suits you see displayed."

Although she understood the clerk's uneasiness at the sight of MacGregor, at the same time it pricked Elizabeth's anger. Mr. MacGregor had done nothing except walk around the room, and here was this man looking at him as though Ash had crawled out from under a rock. "Do you have garments already completed?"

The clerk smiled. "Most gentlemen prefer to purchase a suit that fits properly."

She didn't care much for the patronizing tone of his voice. "Yes. I'm quite aware of that. If I wish to purchase a suit, how long does it take to have it completed?"

"A week to ten days, depending on the garment." Harvey slid MacGregor a sidelong glance, frowning as though he was wondering how best to get rid of him.

Elizabeth looked past the mouse of a clerk to MacGregor. He was standing beside a suit of dark gray cashmere, watching her, and from the look in his hooded eyes he knew exactly what the snobbish little man was thinking. Oh, dear; she only hoped he wouldn't decide to drag the man up by his collar and threaten to snap his neck like a dried twig. It really wouldn't do a thing for his reputation. "Is there any possibility of having at least one suit available by the end of the week?"

"Impossible. Our tailors are really quite precise about their work."

And quite inflexible. Mr. Dibell had promised two suits by the time they had planned to leave. "What about the suits you have on display? Are there any that might fit the gentleman in black standing by the ties?"

The clerk glanced at Ash, then turned his indignant gaze on Elizabeth. "You're with *him?*"

Elizabeth bristled at the tone and the insult it implied. "Yes. Now if you would kindly tell me whether any of the suits you have on display would fit the gentleman . . ."

One light brown brow lifted above the shiny rim of his glasses. He stared at her as though she weren't quite fit to stand beneath the roof of Mansfield's. "I'm quite certain nothing we have would fit the *gentleman.*"

Her skin prickled beneath the contempt in his eyes.

How dare the man! "Pity. I shall have to tell Mr. Radcliffe he was quite wrong in recommending Mansfield's. It seems the store is not quite up to the standards he believed it was."

Harvey frowned. "Mr. Shelby Radcliffe?"

"That's right," she said, noticing that Ash was walking toward them, with the slow prowl of a predator with the scent of his prey. She pinned the little clerk with an icy glare. "The gentleman in black is Mr. Radcliffe's cousin, the marquess of Angelstone."

"Him?" The clerk glanced back and flinched, obviously startled to find MacGregor stalking him.

"Yes." She didn't like the way MacGregor's eyes had narrowed into icy blue glints. As she recalled, they had looked just that way when he had hoisted Dibell from the floor. "Now if you will excuse me, His Lordship and I really must be going."

"Ah . . . I . . . ah—" Harvey backpedaled as MacGregor drew near, keeping his eyes on the tall man in black.

MacGregor's lips curved upward into a a chilling imitation of a smile as he stared down at the snobbish clerk. "Is there any problem?"

"No. Not at all." Harvey stepped back, straight into a small pedestal table covered with handkerchiefs. He hit one edge of the table. It tipped. He tripped. He tumbled backward, his arms windmilling, then smacking the handkerchiefs. The handkerchiefs flew in all directions. The table whacked the floor. Harvey smacked the carpet. He sat, as if frozen with shock, handkerchiefs drifting around him.

Elizabeth bit her lower lip, stifling a giggle as one square of white linen settled on the clerk's head. Harvey sat there flat on his bottom, staring up at MacGregor with wide eyes. Stunned and frightened and so very deserving of his fate.

"Was there anything else you wanted to see, Lady Elizabeth?" Ash asked, mimicking her English accent to perfection.

She glanced up at him, startled. The glint of mischief in his eyes told her the act was all for the sake of the man shivering at their feet. She slipped her arm through his. "I'm afraid this store really doesn't have anything we want, Angelstone."

Ash looked down at her, a smile curving his lips, a glimmer of warmth touching his eyes. Oh, my, he certainly had a nice smile.

"Please, I'm certain we can provide anything you want," the clerk whispered. "I didn't realize you were related to Mr. Radcliffe."

Elizabeth glanced at the little man, as though he was no more than an annoyance. "Perhaps in the future you will not be so quick to judge by appearances. Good day."

Chapter Six

Ash grinned down at the lady walking like a queen beside him, her head high, her shoulders back. Except for the defiant tilt to her chin and the tightness about her pretty mouth, she hid all the anger stewing inside her. But it was there. He had heard it in her voice as she had skinned the little weasel of a clerk with that sharp-edged tongue of hers. He had seen it flash like silver lightning in her stormy gray eyes. He had to admit he was glad for once it wasn't directed at him.

From a distance all that fury was a sight to behold. With the color high in her cheeks and her eyes turning all silvery, she could rival the prettiest women he'd ever seen. It made a man wonder what it would be like to tame all that fury, to hold her, to feel the fire streaking through her body. His blood kicked into a gallop at the thought.

Her skirts rustled softly, brushing his leg, triggering the image of long pale legs sliding against soft white sheets. He glanced down at her as they stepped out of the store, wrestling with the urge to pull the pins and combs from hair that turned to gold in the sunlight. His muscles tightened with the picture of that soft-looking hair spilling across his bare chest.

"The impertinence of the man." She kept her voice just above a whisper. She didn't need to scream; that crisp English accent stung like a December blast off the mountains. She halted as they reached the carriage and the pair of bays he had tied to the brass hitching post in front of the store. ''And you certainly didn't help matters.''

''Me?'' He frowned, wondering how all that fury had managed to get pointed back at him. ''What the hell did I do?''

She pursed her lips in that angry schoolmarm way of hers. ''You scared him half to death.''

''I never touched him.''

''You didn't need to. You stalked him as though you were going to murder him. Staring at him with that icy glare of yours.''

He shrugged. ''What if I did? You can't say the little weasel didn't deserve to be scared half out of his skin.''

''Going about menacing people is hardly appropriate behavior for an English nobleman. Even if the little toad deserved it.'' She released her breath in a huff. ''Did you see the way he looked at me? As though I were some guttersnipe unfit to set foot in that second-class establishment.''

The lady didn't know what it was like to feel dirty, to see contempt in the eyes of those lucky enough to have been born with a home and a family. The little lady went through life as though walking on clouds far above the real world.

''As though I were . . .''

''One of Miss Hattie's girls?'' he asked, readily supplying a dry log to the fire of her anger.

She looked up at him, fury flashing like lightning in her stormy gray eyes. ''I seriously doubt anyone would ever imagine I was one of Miss Hattie's girls, Mr. MacGregor.''

Her indignant glare pricked his anger. He'd seen that look too many times in the eyes of men and women who thought he wasn't fit to share the same sidewalk with them. And here it was, in her pretty eyes.

In her eyes he saw the same condemning look that all

the fine ladies had given him as they walked past him on the street—those that didn't cross to the other side to avoid him—holding their skirts aside to keep from being contaminated by him. They called him a half-breed because he'd been raised by the Cheyenne. And after a time he stopped trying to make them believe otherwise. After a time he cultivated their fear. With fear came some measure of respect. But he didn't see fear in Lady Beth; he saw only contempt.

He looked her over slowly, feigning a thoughtful expression. As though he needed to examine the goods to determine if she was good enough to sell. As though he didn't already see every feature of her face in his dreams. As though he hadn't already explored every lush curve of her slender body with his mind. "You're right. Hattie would want to put some meat on your bones before she allowed you to take care of any customers. She's got the reputation of her establishment to think of."

Her mouth dropped open. "How dare you imply I'm not good enough to work for that woman!"

"Well now, Lady Beth, I didn't know you was so interested in becomin' one of Hattie's girls. I'm sure if I talked to her, she might take you on. Provided you was willin' to take some lessons in how to act like a real woman."

Her eyes narrowed like a cat about to strike, yet she kept her voice so low he could scarcely hear her over the clatter of carriage wheels rumbling against the busy brick-lined street, as though she were afraid the men and women strolling by might overhear what she had to say. "Contrary to what you might believe, Mr. MacGregor, women were not placed on this earth for the sole purpose of entertaining the base urges of barbarians like you."

He shrugged, as though her words hadn't raked like razors across his pride. "Guess fancy gentlemen don't ever spend time at a place like Hattie's, is that what you're saying?''

"I'm not as naive as you believe. I'm well aware of the fact that gentlemen are not immune to the attractions of a place such as Miss Hattie's."

"But they ain't barbarians for doing it?"

"The difference is, a gentleman would never suggest anything so base as to compare a lady to a woman of easy virtue."

Pale green feathers fluttered in the breeze amid the dark green velvet ribbons on her fancy bonnet. The piece of fluff probably cost more than he made in a month. The little prude had been raised like a princess. She'd never been dirty in her life. She'd never felt so hungry she'd sell her soul for a piece of bread. She'd never lived in an alley, burrowing into garbage just to keep warm. She'd never awakened to the dull pain of rats gnawing on her leg. She'd never known the humiliation of it all.

He swallowed back the bile etching a burning path upward in his throat, pushing down the memories with the acid. "There ain't nothin' easy about workin' at Hattie's."

She lifted her chin. "There are alternatives if one should choose to look for them."

"Are there?" He looked down into her pretty face, resisting the urge to grab her and kiss her until he crushed that smug little smile right off. Damnation! He should be keeping his distance from the spoiled little wench instead of thinking about dragging up her skirts and teaching her all the dirty little secrets a savage had to teach a fine lady like her. "Guess maybe you know more about tryin' to make a livin' on your own than I do."

Some of the confidence faded from her eyes. Although her voice was soft, her determination was as hard as steel when she spoke. "I can assure you, Mr. MacGregor, I would find an alternative to selling myself at a place like Miss Hattie's.''

''Maybe. But maybe after you'd tried to get a job at a store or a restaurant or some other place and found they didn't need no one, you might just find yourself with nothin' in your pocket or your belly, and nowhere to go.'' No one had a place for a boy they thought was half Indian. No one cared if he lived or died. No one, except a whore who knew what it meant to be an outcast. A whore who saw the value of a skinny little kid who would work his fingers raw for a chance to live under her roof. ''Maybe if that happened, you wouldn't be so quick to judge folks for doing what they got to do to survive.''

She frowned. ''You make it sound as though I'm a bigoted bore for insisting I would never entertain the thought of working in a bordello.''

He shrugged, glancing away from her, unwilling to risk the chance she might see something that would betray him in his eyes. He didn't want her to know how stupid he felt at the moment, standing here arguing about her becoming a whore. He didn't want her to see what lay beneath it. Maybe because he wasn't sure he wanted to know everything that lay beneath it. The reasons he wanted to pull her down from her clouds and turn her into a woman of easy virtue. At least easy with one man.

He stared at a mannequin in one of the picture windows of Mansfield's, the figure of a woman dressed in a fancy pink and black gown. She stared through the window at him with her painted blue eyes, removed from the world around her, above the touch of man. In a way Beth was like that mannequin in the window. Sheltered from men like him by a pane of glass. Problem was, he had the urge to take a brick and throw it against that glass.

''I got some business to take care of this afternoon. Guess you can find your way back to Radcliffe's.'' Later he'd get a ride back up to Brown's Bluff to get his horse.

Now, he just wanted some time away from one confusing little lady.

She rested her hand on his arm when he turned to leave. He glared at her slender hand, her white glove stark against his black sleeve. When he looked into her face she was frowning beneath the slim brim of her fancy little bonnet, firmly refusing to flinch beneath a glare that had put the fear of God into more than a few cold-blooded murderers.

"Mr. MacGregor, a gentleman does not abandon a lady to find her way back home."

He clenched his jaw. "It seems to me you didn't have any trouble gettin' back home from Hattie's the other day."

She shoved back her shoulders. "I've been charged with the rather Herculean task of turning you into a gentleman."

"Look, lady, I ain't . . ."

"Mr. MacGregor, I recall hearing you agree to cooperate fully with me."

His deal with the devil. He released his breath. He had too much to lose to let one bossy little female ambush his chances for his ranch. "Fine. I'll take you to Radcliffe's. Then get my business taken care of."

She looked unhappy with that idea. She glanced at the small gold watch pinned to her bodice. "Marlow is expecting you to join us for tea at five. Will your business take more than an hour?"

"Shouldn't."

"In that case I would like you to escort me to the nearest bookshop, then continue on with your business. When you are finished you can come by to collect me. In that way we will arrive in time for tea." She smiled, obviously satisfied with her plan.

"Are all ladies as bossy as you?"

"Only when dealing with men who believe a lady

should run away and join a bordello.''

He cocked back his hat and molded his lips into a taunting smile. ''You mean us barbarians?''

''Exactly.'' She offered him her arm, her eyes flashing a fiery challenge as she stared up at him. ''A gentleman always helps a lady into a carriage. You should place your left hand . . .''

He slipped his hands around her waist and lifted her straight up off the ground, until he could look straight into her wide, startled eyes, her parted lips so close he could have kissed her. He smiled as he realized how horrified little Miss Prim and Proper would be if a barbarian kissed her, right here in the middle of the afternoon. Right in front of everyone. She would probably faint from embarrassment. Made him almost crazy enough to do it.

She grabbed his shoulders, as though she expected him to drop her. ''What are you doing?''

''Helping you into the carriage.'' He held her a few moments longer than necessary, absorbing the unexpected warmth of her hands against his shoulders, a warmth her proper white gloves and his improper black shirt couldn't prevent him from feeling. That warmth seeped into his blood, sluicing like fire through his veins, gathering in a pool low in his belly. He lifted her to the carriage and dropped her on the black leather seat.

She pressed her hand to the base of her neck as he stepped back. ''That isn't exactly what I meant.''

He frowned. ''What did you mean?''

She cleared her throat. ''A gentleman places his left hand beneath a lady's elbow while he holds the horses steady by keeping the ribbons in his right hand. He provides her balance.''

He shrugged, as though he didn't care what was proper, hiding the fact that he felt like a stupid clod for not even knowing how to help a lady into a carriage. ''Seems easier my way.''

"Yes." She fiddled with the cameo pinned to the high neck of her gown while staring at the horses. "But it isn't at all polite to put one's hands on a lady's waist."

And it wasn't at all smart getting close to this particular lady, he reminded himself. "Guess I've got a few things to learn." Like keeping his distance from one fiery temptress masquerading as a prudish old maid. He didn't intend to get burned.

Infuriating rogue! Elizabeth fixed her gaze on the fluttering black manes of the horses, trying to ignore the man sitting beside her on the carriage seat. Unfortunately, the seat wasn't large enough to promote independence. She was squeezed as far to one side as she could manage, and still she couldn't escape contact with the beast of a man. With every sway of the carriage his thigh brushed against her limb. The heat of the soft, rhythmic caress penetrated the layers of her gown and petticoat, tingling against her skin.

She caught herself wondering what it might be like to have his strong arm around her shoulders, holding her close. She imagined him smiling at her as though he believed she was the prettiest woman he had ever seen. It was frightening to realize how much she wanted this man to think she was in some way desirable.

Idiot!

She should not permit any wayward thoughts of what might have been invade her mind. The man had made it quite clear what he thought of her. He didn't think she was half the woman of any of the poor creatures working at Miss Hattie's. He found her lacking. In every respect.

Contemptible blackguard!

She glanced at him through her lashes. Sunlight poured against the brim of his flat-crowned black hat, casting his face in shadow. He looked hard and cold and angry—his full lips pulled into a tight line, a muscle in his lean cheek bunched from the clenching of his jaw. And she knew the object of his anger.

This wasn't at all the way she had hoped it would be, she thought. All of her life she had imagined what it would be like when she met Peyton. They would become friends when first they met. And after a short time they would both realize that friendship was a pale reflection of what they actually felt for one another. Peyton would of course fall head over heals in love with her. And she in turn would admit that she had always harbored a secret desire for him.

Silly hen-witted fool!

She swallowed against the tightening in her throat, refusing to give in to the tears that threatened. She certainly would not weep because one infuriating rogue found her unattractive. Oh, he really would find it amusing if he knew how she trembled at his touch. He would laugh in her face if he realized how very much his biting comments had wounded her pride.

She had to accept the fact that Ash MacGregor was not the Peyton Trevelyan she had imagined he would be. What she found much more difficult to accept was the fact that Ash MacGregor was even more fascinating than the well-mannered gentleman who had lived in her imagination. *Fascination.* Even that word seemed tepid for the fierce reaction she had toward the man. Mesmerized. Captivated. Besotted. Demented!

He pulled the ribbons, halting the carriage close to the sidewalk in front of a bookshop. For the entire length of the block, on both sides of the street, shops and restaurants and public rooms—or saloons, as they were called there—lined the first floor of red brick buildings standing shoulder to shoulder two and three stories high. The carriage swayed as MacGregor jumped down from the seat. As he walked around the carriage to help her alight, Elizabeth resisted the impulse to bolt from the carriage. He had the most unsettling way of shredding her defenses with a single touch of his hand.

He tipped back his hat, frowning as he looked at her. "Guess you don't want me just lifting you out of the carriage."

"No. That isn't at all the way it's done." She refrained from telling him that many gentlemen would find it impossible to go about lifting ladies from carriages. Thus, it couldn't possibly be proper. Even if she had found it singularly exciting to have him lift her. For one brief moment she had felt as small and delicate as a Dresden-china doll.

She rested her hands on his shoulders, all too aware of the solid muscles beneath her gloved palms. The intriguing scent of citrus and leather and man curled around her with the cool breeze. He didn't move, but stood like a statue beneath her touch. Completely unmoved by the contact that had her trembling.

With the advantage of the high carriage seat, she was nearly eye to eye with him. She looked straight into those stunning blue eyes and acknowledged how very much she wanted to see more than cool detachment or heated anger there. She wanted to see a glimmer of warmth, a flicker of desire. For all the impropriety of the notion, she wanted him to slip his arms around her and kiss her. Right here in the middle of the street. Oh, my; what was happening to her?

"A gentleman always places his palms under a lady's elbows and leads her balance as she alights," she said, fighting to keep her voice cool and composed.

He did as she requested, placing big, bare hands beneath her elbows. "Like this?"

"Yes." She jumped from the carriage, attempting to look light and graceful in a body that had grown all jittery. When her feet touched the sidewalk she snatched her hands from his shoulders, afraid any prolonged contact would cause her to do something horribly foolish.

His mouth flattened into an angry line as he glared at her. "I'll be back in forty minutes."

Inwardly she cringed at the anger in his beautiful eyes. Outwardly she forced a polite smile to her lips. "I will be ready."

He nodded and walked around the carriage, leaving her alone in front of the store. She drew a deep breath, told herself it really didn't matter what Ash MacGregor thought of her, and marched into the store.

Chapter Seven

He sure as hell didn't care what that little old maid thought about him, Ash assured himself. So what if she thought he was a no-account, half-civilized savage. He didn't care. No, sir; she didn't mean one damn thing to him. Not one. And maybe if he repeated the sentiment in his head long enough, he would convince himself it was true.

He rubbed the taut muscles at the nape of his neck, studying the wanted posters tacked to a board in Sheriff Hogan's office. From habit he evaluated the men who stared back at him from each sheet of paper. Any one of the men sketched here could kill a man without a moment's pause. More than once he had wondered if the prey would manage to kill the hunter.

Yet the job had suited him—a man with nothing to lose but a life that wasn't much use to anyone in particular. For the past thirteen years he had forged himself into the type of man who could risk his life to bring in an outlaw for reward. And he had long ago realized money was only part of what he sought.

"I was thinking you might take out after old Jack Keelen. He's been hitting the banks in the territory real hard." Hogan chuckled softly. "But I guess the grandson of an English duke ain't got no cause for chasing outlaws."

His stomach clenched at Hogan's words. "Guess not." Problem was, Ash wasn't sure what the grandson of a duke was supposed to do, or say, or think.

"Maybe it's for the best, you gettin' out of town for a time. Old Ned Waller's got a pack of kin who ain't real happy to know you put him behind bars."

Ash glanced over his shoulder. Hogan was leaning back in the black leather chair behind his big oak desk, his polished brown boots propped on the paper littering the desktop. He was grinning at Ash, like a rooster that had just serviced a whole chicken coop. "I've handled worse."

Hogan nodded, the humor in his dark eyes fading into a healthy look of respect. "I've got to admit you're one of the best manhunters I ever seen. Quick with a gun. Even quicker with your head."

Praise from Sam Hogan didn't come easy. Earning Hogan's respect had taken a lot of years. But he'd earned it. And he was damn proud of it. Yet Lady Beth's scorn twisted along the edge of his pride, like a cougar's claws.

For the past thirteen years he had scraped together a life that demanded some measure of respect from the men he met. No one could say he was dishonest. No one could say he ever took a man with a bullet in the back. No one could say he ever backed away from a challenge. But all that didn't matter. The lady thought he was a half-civilized savage. Problem was, in her world that's just what he was.

"You sure lasted longer than I thought you would." Hogan plowed his hand through his graying brown hair. "You were nothing but a skinny kid when you walked into my office for the first time, all hell bent on becoming a bounty hunter. I got to admit, back then I bet you'd be dead inside a week."

Ash grinned. "I'm real glad you lost that bet."

Hogan nodded, a smile twitching one corner of his thick mustache. "Got to admit, I would've liked to have seen you pin on a badge."

"Ain't enough money in it."

"Ain't that the truth. But a man tends to live longer if he ain't out chasing outlaws all by himself, like a lone wolf. Someday it's gotta catch up with him."

Ash shrugged. The truth was he'd always felt isolated, a man who didn't quite fit in, no matter where he was. Being a lone wolf suited him just fine. "I best get going. Got a lady waitin' on me."

Hogan swung his feet off the desk and stood, the chair legs thumping with the thud of his boots against the pine floor. "I wish you all the luck in the world, Ash. Can't think of a better man I'd like to see wind up landin' in a honey pot."

"Thanks." Ash shook the callused hand Hogan held out to him, keeping his thoughts to himself. There wasn't any need to let anyone know he felt close to drowning in that pot of honey.

Elizabeth wandered through the aisles of oak bookcases, allowing the warm scent of the leather-bound books curl around her, seeking a short respite from the storm that was Ash MacGregor. She perused the shop for her allotted time, careful not to keep the beast waiting for her, choosing several novels to read while on the trip back to England, as well as a book of etiquette to help in the task of transforming MacGregor into Lord Angelstone. She wondered if anyone or anything could actually transform that cold-hearted barbarian into a sensitive human being. For the sake of Hayward and the duchess, she hoped for a miracle.

Elizabeth stood outside the bookshop, waiting. Horses and carriages crowded both sides of the thoroughfare. The black carriage and the team of bays Marlow had brought with him from England stood near the sidewalk a short distance down the street. But MacGregor was nowhere in sight. She hugged her books to her chest, feeling conspicuous standing alone while people strolled past her, cowboys in dusty clothes prowling amid ladies and gentlemen dressed in the height of fashion. She refused to acknowledge the leering stares of a few of the cowboys as they sauntered past her. Yet as the seconds expanded into minutes, her patience grew thin.

How long did he intend to keep her waiting? She glanced at her watch. If they didn't leave soon, they would be late for tea.

Where was the man? The tinny sound of a piano poured into the street from the saloon a few doors away, as if a clue to the mystery of the missing beast. She hesitated a moment before venturing toward the saloon. The stench of spilled whiskey, stale beer, and cigar smoke drifted into the street. She paused beside one of the large, square windows that flanked the open double doors and looked through the glass.

Through the smoke hanging in gray swags in the crowded room, Elizabeth could see several men standing at the bar. There were others, sitting at round tables, playing cards and drinking. Intent on locating MacGregor in the crowd, she scarcely noticed two men as they left the saloon, until one of them stepped close behind her.

"Ain't that a purty sight," the man said, his breath a damp scrape against her neck. "Are you lookin' fer me, honey?"

She pivoted, turning to face two rough-looking young men dressed in dusty clothes. They each wore sweat-stained, broad-brimmed, flat-crowned hats perched on hair that hadn't been trimmed in months. And, from the smell of them, they hadn't been near a cake of soap in as many days.

"You sure are a purty one." The man who had spoken earlier looked her over, as though she were a purchase he intended to make.

She glared at the man, concealing her uneasiness behind a facade of icy contempt.

"Looks like a lady to me, Hank," his companion said. "Best leave 'er alone."

"Since when do ladies go around lookin' in saloon winders?" Hank grinned at her, revealing stained teeth clotted with bits of tobacco. " 'Less of course she's lookin' fer customers."

She was going to strangle MacGregor, she decided. "I'm looking for my escort."

Hank planted one dirty hand on her shoulder. "You found 'im."

She looked at the hand he held against her shoulder, then stared straight up into his bloodshot brown eyes. "Take your hand off me."

"Ain't you a fancy talker." Hank rubbed his fingers against her shoulder.

"Hank, best leave 'er be," his friend said.

Hank leaned close to her, his whiskey-soaked breath pouring over her face as he spoke. "Bet yer one of Miss Hattie's girls. She's always got the purtiest gals in town."

She pulled away from the blackguard, but before she could put any distance between them, he grabbed her arm, dropping her books. The leather-bound volumes plopped against the wooden sidewalk. She fixed the drunken fool in a chilling stare. "Get away from me." She kept her voice level and as cold as ice, in spite of the panic rising inside her.

"Hank, best do as the lady says," his friend said, a note of urgency in his voice.

Hank ignored his friend's warning. "You and me'll go on back to Hattie's and have us a real good . . ."

"The lady is with me."

The tension inside her released like a spent bow string at the sound of Ash MacGregor's voice. She glanced past the dirty red plaid covering Hank's shoulder, her breath tangling in her throat at the sight of MacGregor. Tall, broad shouldered, dressed entirely in black, his face cast in shadows beneath his hat, he looked a dark, beautiful warrior. He stood as still as a sculpted piece of marble, a masterpiece of barely restrained masculine power.

"I saw the lady first," Hank said, smiling down at Elizabeth. "You go on and find yerself another gal."

"I said the lady was with me."

Heat simmered through her at the dark possessive tone of MacGregor's voice. He had charged to her rescue, just like a knight in shining armor. It was almost enough to make her forgive him for putting her in this situation in the first place.

"Step away from her," Ash said, his voice as dark and smooth as a river at midnight. And just as dangerous. "Now."

Elizabeth shivered, but not from fear. The power of the man was as intoxicating as brandy.

"Hank, I think you better do as the man asks," his friend said, his voice betraying his fear. "Best leave the lady alone."

Hank frowned as he turned away from Elizabeth. "Now, look here. I . . ." He paused, as if one look at MacGregor had chased all thoughts from his head. He stared at the man in black as though he faced a devil come to claim his unworthy soul.

Ash smiled, a chilling twist of his lips that left his blue eyes glittering with icy intent. "Make yourself scarce."

Hank swallowed so hard, Elizabeth could hear his throat click. "Yes, sir. Weren't meanin' no disrespect to the lady."

Ash didn't move. "Leave."

Hank bobbed his head as he backed away from MacGregor. "Yes, sir."

Elizabeth sagged back against the window, watching as Hank and his friend hurried down the street and around the corner, as though they wanted to put as much distance between them and the dark-haired devil as possible. MacGregor hadn't lifted a hand. He'd chased off two men with nothing more than a look. It wasn't at all what she had expected.

Ash looked her over, a frown creasing his brow. "They hurt you?"

"No," she said, appalled at the breathless sound of her voice. "I'm fine. Thank you for interceding."

He accepted her gratitude with a curt nod of his head, then bent to retrieve the books she had spilled across the sidewalk.

She watched him, still mesmerized by the display of restrained power he had used against the man. "You didn't hit him."

He glanced up at her, his hand poised on the book near her left shoe. "You wanted me to hit him?"

"No. I'm surprised, that's all."

His frown deepened, carving lines between the dark wings of his brows. He stood, cradling three of the books in the crook of his arm. The fourth he held in his right hand, frowning as he stared at the gold letters tooled against dark brown leather. "You figure all barbarians settle disputes with fists? Or do they use clubs?"

"I didn't mean to imply . . ."

"Guess you figure everything a man needs to know is in this book." He waved the book of etiquette under her nose.

"Not at all. But proper etiquette is certainly important. It's what helps keep society functioning."

"Does it tell you in here the proper way to get rid of a man bent on forcing his way with a woman?"

She resisted the impulse to moisten her dry lips. "No. But I must say you did an excel—"

"What the hell were you doing in front of the saloon?"

She bristled at the anger in his voice. "Looking for you."

His lips flattened into a tight line. "And you figured the only place you'd find a man like me is in the saloon."

She lifted her chin, meeting his anger with defiance. "It certainly seemed a possibility."

He turned and started walking back toward the carriage. "Never found much call for hangin' around saloons."

She hurried after him, racing to keep up with his long strides. "And I seldom find it necessary to keep people waiting."

"I got back early. I figured you'd be like most females—late. So I stepped into a shop down the street. Only took a couple of minutes."

She refrained from asking him precisely what he had purchased, even though she was curious. "I try to be on time whenever possible. It's really quite impolite to keep someone waiting."

Muscles bunched in his sun-darkened cheek as he clenched his jaw. "I keep forgettin', you ain't like most women."

The words pricked her wounded pride. Yet she fought to crush her rising anger. It certainly didn't matter if the man thought she was less of a woman than any of the females of his acquaintance. But it certainly hurt. "It would seem not every man believes I'm not good enough to work for Miss Hattie. The man you chased away had mistaken me for one of 'Hattie's gals.' "

He glanced at her, a corner of his lips tipping upward into a devilish grin. The glint of humor in his stunning eyes made her wish she had never mentioned the subject. "Now Lady Beth, you got to understand, when a man gets enough licker in him he don't see straight."

"I see." Heat prickled across her neck.

"Of course, it's possible he just has a hankerin' for skinny women. I hear some men do."

She fixed her gaze on the carriage, hoping the well-dressed lady and gentleman passing them hadn't heard the rogue's words. He was merely trying to provoke her, she assured herself. She should ignore him. Show him she didn't care. She certainly shouldn't continue the discussion. She halted when they reached the carriage, glaring up at him. "In spite of what you might believe, Mr. MacGregor, more than a few men prefer a trim figure over one more overblown."

"That so?" He considered this a moment, tilting his head as he examined her figure, his look cool, dispassionate, that of a connoisseur appraising a particularly unattractive piece of art. "Seems to me a man would get all bruised cuddling up to a woman who was more bone than meat."

For the first time in her life she wanted to punch someone. She forced her lips into a smile. "I suppose a man accustomed to the charms of ladies who ply their trade by *pretending* to enjoy intimate liaisons with any man who can pay their price would lack the ability to discern quality over quantity."

"That might be true for men who pay for the company of a woman." He tossed her books into the small leather boot behind the seat, then turned to face her, his lips curved into that infuriating, mocking grin. "But, I ain't never paid a woman to do anything."

She should retreat. Now. "You're very certain of yourself, Mr. MacGregor."

"I ain't never had any complaints."

"Perhaps because the women with whom you consort don't expect much from a man."

He tipped back his hat, allowing the sun to kiss the grin curving his finely molded lips. Thick black lashes lowered as he studied her bodice, his gaze caressing her, conjuring a warmth that spread like heated honey across her breasts. "Well, now, the girls at Miss Hattie's can be real demandin'."

She stepped closer, clenching her hands into fists at her

sides, anger chasing away all thoughts of the people who might be watching from the crowded street. "Do they demand respect and caring? Mutual affection?"

"No, ma'am. All they demand is a real good time."

She tried to push aside the images flickering to life in her mind—this man surrounded by women, all buxom and pretty, touching him in ways she didn't wish to know. But that image remained, bright and vivid as an oil painting. Taunting her with a completely inappropriate, absolutely insane, positively white-hot streak of jealousy. "A lady demands more than lust, Mr. MacGregor. A lady demands sensitivity and honest affection, and . . . a desire to build a home and raise a family. A lady demands more than a fleeting moment's pleasure."

All of the humor in his eyes faded with his smile. "From what I've heard, ladies are real good at demandin'. But they ain't willin' to give much in return."

"Perhaps you are a trifle too quick to judge."

"Yes, ma'am." He touched her arm, sliding his big bare hand under her elbow, the warmth of his palm searing her through the merino wool of her gown. "Maybe I am. Since I ain't got any close-up experience of my own."

He lowered his eyes, staring at her lips in a way that stole the breath from her lungs. He was going to kiss her. He was going to pull her into his arms and kiss her. Right here in the middle of the street. And for all the world she couldn't find the words to stop him.

"Am I doing it right this time, Lady Beth?" he asked, his voice a soft brush against her cheek.

The question swirled around in her befuddled brain. "What?"

He smiled, a lazy curving of his lips that filled his eyes with light and made her knees wobble. He pressed his fingertips against her arm, her elbow resting in the warm cradle of his palm. "Is this the proper way for a man to help a lady into a carriage?"

With his words came a torrent of reality. They were standing in a public place. And she had managed to engage in a debate about the most indelicate of subjects.

"Yes." She stepped up into the carriage and sank against the seat, leaving an unfortunate amount of her pride on the sidewalk behind her.

Chapter Eight

Ash glanced at the lady sitting next to him on the narrow carriage seat. She was staring straight ahead, her chin tilted at a damn-the-world angle, as stiff and cold as an icicle. But then, he figured going around like an icicle was all part of being a *lady*.

True, he didn't know any ladies up close, but he knew enough men who were married to the creatures. To hear them tell it, all ladies were taught to be blocks of ice from the time they were born. Those unfortunate men lived their lives with ladies who had been taught it was scandalous to enjoy the marriage act. From what they said a lady refused to undress in front of her husband, leaving the husband to lift a nightgown in the dark and rut between lily white thighs that might as well be connected to a dead woman.

No wonder there was a whole pack of *gentlemen* who left their lady wives at home to find pleasure at Hattie's. Still, he had to wonder at men who married all that ice in the first place. A man should know whether a woman had a spark inside her before he agreed to spend the rest of his life with her. And if there was a spark, a man with any sense could coax that spark into a blaze.

And there was a spark in Lady Beth. Hell, there was fire simmering beneath that ice. He had glimpsed it in her eyes as she came flying at him like a hen with her feathers ruffled. He had heard it in that crisp English voice that

102

never rose to a shout, even though she was angry enough to roast him over an open fire. And he had tasted it in that one kiss they had shared. Fire and passion simmering just beneath her cool surface. So hot she set his blood on fire.

The lady was sure a strange little thing. She believed in love. She believed in devotion. She believed a lady could keep a man satisfied in bed. Sure did make a man curious. It made him want to strip away all those fancy clothes and touch all that smooth white skin. It made him want to see if there really was as much fire in her as he had glimpsed.

Easy, boy. The last thing he needed was to get all tangled up with some highfalutin female who thought he had only recently crawled out of a cave. Yet he couldn't deny the swift surge of protectiveness he had felt when he had seen that cowboy with his dirty hand on her shoulder. Lord in heaven, it had taken every ounce of willpower to keep from breaking the bastard's neck. Of course, that was what the lady had expected him to do: attack like a rabid dog.

The little snob thought he was some half-civilized savage, unfit to share the same breathing space with her. And here he was feeling about as low as a rattler's belly because he'd managed to wound her pride. He'd taken aim right where he figured it would hurt. And he'd hit the mark.

He was only lashing back, hitting her where she had hit him, he assured himself. Still, it didn't make him feel any better. Even though he was sure he was completely justified in his actions.

He shifted on the seat and reached back into the carriage boot, his hand brushing her arm in the process. She flinched, as though he had slapped her. She cast him one icy glance, then proceeded to stare straight ahead.

His hand curled into a fist against the soft leather of

the compartment as he resisted the urge to grab her slender shoulder, pull her straight across his lap, and kiss her the way he'd been wanting to kiss her from the first moment she had barged into his life. What would her little book of etiquette say about that? He knew what his little book of common sense would say about it—*damn stupid.* Even if the lady was begging him for it. And the lady was begging for a kiss, if not more. He knew enough about women to know she might think he was a wild beast, but she also had a healthy curiosity about untamed stallions.

He grabbed the bag he had tossed in the boot before he had noticed her in front of the saloon and set it on the seat between them. "Want some?" He flipped open the top of the small white bag.

She glanced at him, her stormy gray eyes narrowed with suspicion. "What?"

He plucked a small chunk of dark chocolate from the bag and wiggled it in front of her, like an angler tempting a wary trout. "Larson makes some of the best chocolate in Denver." He took a deep breath, savoring the scent of chocolate before popping the rich confection into his mouth.

She frowned as she glanced into the bag. "You were in the confectionery while I was in the bookshop?" she asked, her voice revealing her shock.

He rolled the chocolate against the inside of his cheek, allowing the heat of his mouth to melt the candy, a slow drizzle of chocolate spilling across his tongue. "What's the matter? Ain't a man supposed to like chocolate?"

"Of course there are men who like chocolate." A few wisps of hair had escaped the pile of curls Elizabeth had stacked beneath her bonnet. They fluttered in the breeze, the honey gold strands framing the look of surprise on her pretty face. "I just didn't expect *you* to like it."

He frowned. "Because I'm a half-civilized savage?"

The corners of her lips turned down. "Because I don't associate anything remotely sweet with you."

He grinned at that. One thing he could say about her, she sure didn't dance around the truth. He rattled the bag on the seat, admitting to himself that he was hoping the sweets would be a kind of peace offering. "Take some."

"Thank you."

He stared past the horses to the street that stretched out in front of him. From the corner of his eye he watched her unfasten two small pearl buttons attached to her glove just above her wrist. None of the women he knew wore gloves, while this one wore them nearly all the time, as though her hands were something to hide, the way she hid the curves of her breasts. The truth was, except for her pretty face, most of the time she was covered all the way up to her chin. Maybe that was the reason the simple act of her peeling off that glove grabbed his attention.

He tilted his head, staring as she tugged the white kid from her hand, exposing her wrist, the pale mound at the base of her thumb, her smooth white palm. Heat skittered across his belly.

Strange; it seemed more revealing than when one of Hattie's girls took off her dress. He imagined nuzzling his lips against that smooth white palm, feeling her long fingers curve against his cheek. Truth was, the sight of that slender white hand exposed in the sunlight did something hot and aching to his insides.

"Look out!" she shouted, gripping his arm.

He glanced up just in time to steer the horses clear of a stagecoach that was barreling toward them on the opposite side of the road. The side he had veered into while staring at her bare hand. The stagecoach thundered past them, wheels clattering on the cobblestones, the driver sending him a black look that screamed—*Idiot!*

He was more than an idiot, Ash thought; he was a damn fool. He couldn't imagine why the sight of a lady's naked hand could start his blood pumping like a stallion near a mare in season. But then, nothing about the lady made any sense. He drew in his breath and glanced toward the woman who was gripping his arm as though he was all that kept her from falling off a cliff. "Sorry."

She managed a smile. "He did take quite a large portion of the roadway," she said, lifting her hand from his arm.

His skin tingled where she had touched him. "Not as much as I was taking."

She smoothed her bare hand over her skirt. "Well, there was no harm done."

No thanks to the damn idiot holding the reins, he thought. His heart was pounding, keeping time with the quick clip-clop of horseshoes against cobblestones. And it had nothing to do with their near collision.

He stared at the road, trying to ignore the strange female sitting beside him. In spite of his best intention to ignore her, he was aware of every move she made. The way her skirts brushed his leg with the steady sway of the carriage. The way she eased her slim white hand into the bag, as though she didn't want to disturb it. The way she lifted a plump little dark brown nugget to her soft pink lips. She touched the chocolate with her tongue, a quick graze, like a kitten dabbing at cream. And in his mind the most erotic image bloomed.

"Do you practice looking dangerous?"

He glanced at her, stunned by her question. "Beg pardon?"

"I was just wondering whether that fierce glare of yours came naturally, or whether you had to practice looking dangerous."

He pulled his lips into a flat line. "Lady, I *am* dangerous."

She considered this a moment, studying him as though

he were an interesting puzzle. "Yes. I have little doubt you are."

There was a tone in her voice that made him uneasy. It was as though she could peel back the edges of his defenses and look at the naked boy inside him. She nibbled her chocolate, chewed it, ate it like a person who took the sweet confection for granted. Of course she wasn't like him. She had probably had her first taste of chocolate long before she was fifteen.

"Did you have to practice in front of a mirror to perfect that look you use to frighten people?"

He frowned. "I don't know what you're talkin' about."

"When you want to frighten people you look at them like this." She looked at him, narrowing her eyes and drawing her lips into a tight line. "Do you practice it?"

He felt his lips tipping into a smile. He immediately set his jaw. "Are you thinkin' of tryin' your hand at bein' a gunfighter?"

She shrugged her slender shoulders. "I was simply curious; that's all."

She moistened her lips, a quick slide of the tip of her tongue that left her lips damp and the inside of his mouth as dry as a desert. For some unholy reason all he could think about was sliding his tongue over the curve of her lips and licking the taste of chocolate from the tempting curves. He fixed his gaze on the road in front of him, determined to stamp out the fire this woman set in his blood.

"I get the impression you enjoy frightening people." She nibbled her chocolate. He glared at her. "You're doing it now. You're looking at me as though you want to pick me up and toss me from the carriage."

He wanted to pick her up, all right. Pick her up, slide her long legs around his waist, and sample the hot honey hidden beneath those prim skirts. He turned his gaze toward the horses, resisting the urge to slap the reins across their rumps and coax them into a run. The less time he spent alone with the lady, the better for both of them.

"I think I should warn you, that menacing glare of yours could prove lethal if you use it without prudence."

He slanted her a glance, wondering what the odd little female was getting at. "Lethal?"

She nodded, her expression much too severe for the glitter in her eyes. "You will be meeting many elderly ladies and gentlemen when we arrive in London. You must remember they have lived rather sheltered lives. I'm afraid you could easily scare one of them straight to the grave if you should flash that scorching look. One could easily believe an avenging angel has been turned loose among us."

He grinned. "Avenging angel?"

She lifted one arched brow. "Perhaps devil would be a more appropriate term."

"Yeah, maybe it would." He looked at her, watching as she slipped the remaining morsel of chocolate into her mouth. "I don't seem to frighten you."

She licked the tip of her finger, and he wondered if she had any idea the thoughts that action conjured in his head. "I see that look for what it is."

He frowned, an uneasy prickle teasing the base of his spine. "And just what is it?"

She smiled, obviously pleased with herself. "Distilled defiance."

He steered the horses through Radcliffe's open wrought-iron gates, wishing he could jump on his horse and get the hell away from the confusing little female.

"I think you use that look to keep people at a distance. Like one of your American rattlesnakes shaking his tail. You want people to fear you."

He pulled up on the reins, halting the horses under the roof beside the carriage entrance to the big white house. For a few beats of his pounding heart he stared at the brown leather reins in his hands, resisting the urge to toss them down and grab the lady's slender shoulders. She had no right to go poking into his life. No right to make him want to strangle her one minute and make love to her the next. "Lady, I don't have to try to make people fear me. They've been doing that most of my life."

She was quiet for a moment. He could feel her watching him, studying him as though she were trying to pick him apart, as though he were some tangled piece of yarn. "It must have been very difficult for you, growing up without a proper family."

He squeezed the reins between his fingers. The horses stepped uneasily, harnesses jangling. "I doubt you can even begin to understand. So don't try."

She drew in her breath, a long, slow inhalation, as though she were drawing strength from the air. "I have to."

He gave her a hard look, one designed to put her back in her place, right behind that pane of glass that separated their two worlds. "Like hell you do."

She smiled, a generous curve of her lips that filled her eyes with light. "I have to try to help you find your way home. Your grandparents have been waiting for you for a very long time."

He turned on the seat, staring straight into her eyes, fighting against the beguiling warmth he saw there. "I can't be somethin' I ain't."

"No. You can't."

He caught himself staring at a tiny smudge of chocolate at the right corner of her lips.

"But you can be the man you were born to be," she said, in that crisp English voice. "If you only try."

That bit of chocolate teased him, tempted him to flick the tip of his tongue against that tiny smudge, taste the sweetness of her lips. He lifted his hand, feeling her startle beneath his touch as he brushed his fingertip over the corner of her lips. "Can't have you going inside with chocolate on your face."

"Oh." She frowned, and he could see her collecting the composure he had momentarily shattered. "You're ignoring me."

He only wished he could. He lifted his finger and licked the tip, tasting chocolate sweetened by her skin, watching her lips part, her eyes grow wide and bewildered and filled with the same bitter longing twisting in his gut.

She moistened her lips. "I'm certain, if you only give yourself some time, you will realize you were meant to live your life in England, with your family."

"Don't pin any hopes on me. I promised the old man I'd stay six months. I ain't gonna stay any longer."

She straightened, her soft mouth pulling into a hard line. "You have a remarkably stubborn nature, Mr. MacGregor."

He smiled, yet he wasn't feeling at all amusing or amused. "Maybe I just know who I am, what I am, and where I belong."

She studied him for a moment, her gray eyes as serious as a judge about to deliver a verdict. "I doubt you're certain of any of those things, Mr. MacGregor."

He held her look a moment, then turned away and stepped from the carriage. The lady had the most infuriating way of getting under his skin. The problem was, she seemed to look straight into his soul with those pretty gray eyes, see things even he didn't want to see.

He helped her from the carriage, determined to ignore the startling effect touching the woman had on his pulse. He followed her into the big white house, knowing deep in his soul he would never feel at home in her world.

Elizabeth stood at a window of Marlow's sitting room, watching Ash MacGregor walk along the brick-lined path toward the horse waiting for him beneath an alder tree

near the porte cochere at the side of the house. His every
move was filled with a fluid grace. Long, easy strides. A
slow shift of muscles beneath close-fitting black cloth.
Even from a distance the man had the uncanny ability to
turn her all fluttery. Her skin tingled with an excitement
she had never felt before meeting him. Never in her life
had she felt more alive.

Beneath a flat-crowned black hat his dark waves of hair
grazed the collar of his black shirt. Once they got him
into a proper suit he would at least look respectable. Yet
she knew it would take much more than a haircut and
clothes to turn the savage into a tamed gentleman. And
she wondered if she had any chance of taming him.

"I'm afraid this morning with Dibell was entirely my
fault," Hayward said. "I really should have warned him
about everything a fitting entailed."

Hayward's voice was little more than a distant buzz in
her ears, her attention focused on MacGregor. His gray
stallion tossed his head as he drew near, long silvery mane
swaying in the breeze. He paused beside the horse, speaking softly, rubbing his hand across the horse's long neck,
his lips curving into a smile as the animal nickered in
response.

Elizabeth watched, transfixed by the gentleness of his
touch. A gentleness coupled with raw power. She touched
the corner of her lips, remembering his gentleness. He
swung up into the saddle, leather creaking softly beneath
him.

"I must say, I was pleased with what the barber was
able to accomplish," Hayward said. "The lad is a handsome cub."

MacGregor glanced toward the house, trapping her with
his gaze. Elizabeth flinched. Too late to move, even if her
legs weren't shaking like aspic. Too late to pretend a casual pose. Even if her wits were capable of functioning.

He had caught her staring at him like a lovesick spinster. Again.

A slow smile curved his lips, assuring her that he knew exactly how fascinating she found him. He touched the brim of his hat in a casual salute before easing his horse into a canter, leading the animal down the brick-lined drive. She stared until he disappeared around the corner of the house. And she had a horrible vision of her standing at this window, like a lost waif, waiting for him to return tomorrow morning.

"Elizabeth?" Hayward touched her arm.

She jumped, startled by the sudden contact. "What is it?"

Hayward frowned. "Elizabeth, you aren't still at daggers with me, are you?"

Elizabeth toyed with the cameo pinned to the lace in the center of her high collar, hoping Marlow wouldn't realize the real reason for her agitation. "At daggers with you?"

He nodded. "I know you weren't particularly pleased with acting as Peyton's tutor. But I'm disinclined to hire someone."

"I can certainly see where it might be difficult to find someone who would survive his rather volatile temper."

Hayward chuckled softly. "Yes, but more than that, I keep thinking it would hurt his pride terribly to be tutored like a boy in knee pants. I believe he would be much more comfortable with you."

"I'm not certain why you would think such a thing. I'm hardly on cordial terms with Mr. MacGregor."

Hayward studied her, a faint smile curving his lips. "I don't believe I've ever seen you as vexed with anyone as I did this morning. You're normally so very reserved."

The heat of shame tingled in her cheeks. "I apologize for my behavior."

"There is no need." He touched the tip of her nose

with his fingertip, the way he had from the time she was a child. "I've indulged a time or two in venting my feelings. I suspect telling the young man exactly what you thought of him felt very gratifying."

Elizabeth shook her head, appalled at her lack of control. "I'm afraid he has a way of provoking me as no one else has ever done."

"Yes." He smiled, as though he found her humiliating display more than a little amusing. "I noticed."

Elizabeth frowned. "Yet you want me to tutor him in the rules of propriety?"

"I suspect the two of you will get on famously, once you have a chance to get to know one another."

She wasn't certain it was wise at all to become better acquainted with Ash MacGregor. The man was going to walk out of her life in six months. She intended to make certain he didn't take her heart with him.

Hayward stood beside her, staring at the mountains, a deep-seated satisfaction radiating from him, as though he were facing an opponent he had finally beaten. "Have you ever met a man with more spirit than my grandson? He reminds me so very much of his father."

"I don't recall ever hearing tales of your son sending a tailor scurrying for the woods." Or frightening a pair of rough-looking men with a glance, she thought.

"No, but there was that time he filled his tutor's bed with snakes." Hayward chuckled low in his throat. "And there was a particularly interesting incident with a trained bear when he was at Cambridge. Ah, he had spirit. Just as Peyton does."

Hayward had waited so long for the return of his grandson, placing all his hopes in a boy who had managed to grow into a heartless blackguard. A tight knot of apprehension pressed against her heart when she thought of how terribly this dear man would be hurt by the callousness of his grandson. "Is he really what you expected?"

Hayward took a deep breath of the early evening air. He was quiet a moment, gathering his thoughts as he stared out at the mountains. "I expected him to be strong-willed. This may surprise you, but we Trevelyans have a stubborn streak."

Elizabeth smiled. "Really? I never would have suspected."

He slanted her a glance, a smile tipping one corner of his lips. "Keep it under your hat, my girl."

She gave him a look filled with exaggerated sincerity. "You can rely on me to keep your secret."

He chuckled, lifting his face into the breeze sweeping through the trees lining the drive. He was quiet for a long moment, and when he spoke his voice held a soft note of disappointment. "I suppose I expected him to welcome me with open arms. I imagined he would be just as eager to find me as I was to find him."

"He isn't convinced he is Peyton."

Hayward nodded. "It's that stubborn streak. But we'll change his mind. Lord, it will be good to have him home once again. Where he belongs. Of course, we really must teach him to enjoy tea. I was rather startled when he said he preferred coffee."

"At least he didn't spill anything. Mrs. Radcliffe kept staring at him as though she expected him to hurl his teacup against the wall."

Hayward nodded, his lips growing tight. "I don't care for the way she looks at him. I'm quite certain that young man has suffered that kind of prejudice all his life. Especially with people thinking he was half Indian. Of all things."

"People are quick to judge on appearances."

"Yes. I don't care to subject him to any more of Mrs. Radcliffe's scornful looks; that's the reason I didn't press him when Peyton declined to stay for dinner. I must say I never noticed she was such a bore until this trip. She was pleasant enough when they came to visit at Chatswyck last year. Pity; Radcliffe is an amiable fellow. He was genuinely disappointed when I told him we would be leaving tomorrow morning.''

Elizabeth rubbed her finger over her cameo. ''I had hoped we would have sufficient time to civilize MacGregor before we reached England.''

''You shall have three days to New York. And another eight while we make the crossing.''

''Less than a fortnight.'' Elizabeth sighed at the difficult task laid out for her.

Hayward patted her shoulder. ''All you need do is chip away the first layer of granite, my girl. Start to see the shape of the man beneath. You'll have time once we reach Chatswyck to complete the job. In time we'll wipe away all the ugliness from his past. With your help he'll feel right at home in society. Ah, it will be good to have him back where he belongs.''

Elizabeth looked away from the hope in his eyes, staring at the brass hitching post where MacGregor's horse had stood. ''I wonder if it's wise to grow very accustomed to the idea of Mr. MacGregor remaining in England.''

''Of course he'll remain in England.''

She drew in her breath. ''Marlow, he doesn't intend to stay.''

Hayward chuckled softly. ''I know. He thinks he will stay for six months, collect my money, and be on his way.''

''You don't seem to take him very seriously.''

''Oh, I take my grandson very seriously. I'm certain he means to leave in six months.''

''You're very calm about it.''

''That young man is clinging to the only way of life he has ever known. He's confused, unsure of his emotions, and of me. In time he will come to realize his rightful place.'' Hayward grinned. ''I shall make certain of it.''

Elizabeth brushed her hand over the silk brocade of the drape hanging beside her, where small yellow and black birds flew in a bright blue sky. Ash MacGregor was as wild and untamed as a soaring hawk. She didn't have a great deal of faith that the man would ever truly be comfortable in England.

"I know you've looked forward to meeting my grandson for a long time. Are you terribly disappointed by Peyton, my girl?"

She took a moment, composing her words carefully. "He isn't at all what I expected."

"What did you expect?"

Elizabeth smoothed her fingertip over a fold of the drape, tracing the raised image of a bird. "I suppose I expected him to care about his family. He seems more interested in money than he does in anything, or anyone."

"He lost his mother and father when he was five. By the time he was eleven he lost the Indian family that had raised him, watched helplessly as they were massacred around him. A year later the man who had rescued him from death, who had taken him in as a son, was killed. He lived on his own, God only knows how, for nearly two years. I would imagine that would make a man cautious in giving his affection to anyone."

Elizabeth frowned. "I would think it would make a man anxious for a home and people to care for him."

"He will. In time. We simply have to help him in every way we can." Hayward rested his hand on her shoulder. "I know this is a great favor to ask of you, but I would feel much better knowing you were looking to his transformation."

Elizabeth fiddled with her cameo, wondering how she could keep her composure if she were forced to be in MacGregor's company day in, day out, from morning till night. He had the most infuriating way of stirring her emotions, making her nervous and anxious, and . . . terribly restless. She thought of that one moment when he had held her in his arms, his lips warm against hers. With the memory came a delicious thrill that tingled through her entire body. Oh my goodness, she really had to keep her distance from the man.

"Elizabeth, I don't want to force you into anything. If you wish, I'll find someone else to help my grandson."

She looked up into Hayward's dark blue eyes, knowing she owed him more than she could repay in one lifetime.

Hayward smiled. "What shall it be?"

She smiled. "Of course I'll do it."

Hayward squeezed her shoulder, a smile curving his lips. "That's my girl. I know you'll turn that rough-cut diamond into a polished gem."

Elizabeth wished she felt as confident as Hayward. She had the uncomfortable feeling that Mr. MacGregor would be a most difficult student.

Chapter Nine

The player piano in the parlor pounded out the notes to "Oh Dem Golden Slippers," invading the quiet of Ash's room. It was half past midnight and the party at Hattie's was still going strong. The place was full of gentleman escaping their wives. Strange, but for the first time he wondered if any of those fine gentlemen had ever tried to melt the ice in their beds. He wondered if they had ever attempted to lift their pretty little lady wives from the shelf where they kept them.

His thoughts went back to Lady Beth. Images from that one moment he had held her flickered in his mind. Her lips, so soft and innocently eager beneath his. Her breasts burning him through the layers of clothing he wanted to strip away. What would the lady say if she knew how much he wanted her? What would she say if she knew how much he wanted her to look at him, to see some value in the man he was, not the man she wanted him to become?

A knock on the door interrupted his thoughts. For one crazy moment, after he'd invited his caller to come in, he wondered if Lady Beth would step into the room, anxious to continue pounding on him, forging him into a man he didn't even understand. And what was worse, he couldn't understand the reason the skinny little old maid kept haunting his thoughts.

Hattie sauntered into the room and closed the door behind her. She strolled toward him, the emerald satin of her gown swishing with the sway of her rounded hips. "The girls wanna know when you're gonna come back to the party."

In spite of all his talk about preferring Hattie's girls over *ladies,* he found himself wishing the woman in his room was a slender lady with big gray eyes. "Maybe later." He lifted a necklace of wooden beads from the top drawer of his bureau.

"Looks like you're almost packed."

"Yeah." He glanced at the carpetbag that sat alongside his saddlebags on the quilt covering his bed. In the past few years he hadn't spent much time here at Hattie's. Most of his time he spent on the trail of some outlaw, sleeping out under the stars or in some cheap room above a saloon. Still, it was real settling to realize most of what you owned could be stuffed into an old carpetbag and a pair of saddlebags. "The old man wants to leave after breakfast tomorrow."

"Me and Millie went out to the train station this afternoon to take a look at that private train he come in on." Hattie whistled softly. "Sure is fancy."

"Most things about old Trevelyan are fancy." *Especially his ward.* Mentally he shook himself. He had to stop thinking of the little snob.

"You know, a few of the girls are anxious to give you a real proper send-off." She winked at him. "Guess they figure they're gonna get one last taste of you before you go runnin' off and become a gentleman."

Ash thought of the seven ladies who worked here at Hattie's. Over the past few years he'd had occasion to bed down with most of them. Not for money. Not because there were any pledges of love and devotion. But for the simple truth that everyone needed to hold someone from time to time. Everyone needed to know he wasn't alone in the world, that he could hold and touch and give pleasure for no other reason than that it felt good.

"What do you say?" Hattie slid her fingers across his shoulder and down his arm. "Want to have a little celebration up here?"

The heavy spice of her perfume crept through his senses, and he caught himself longing for the delicate fragrance of lavender. He looked into Hattie's brown eyes, saw the desire burning there, and realized he wanted none of it. He didn't want to prove to himself what his instincts were telling him. He didn't want to prove that a tumble with Hattie or one of the gals wouldn't take the edge off his hunger. "Tell 'em thanks, but not tonight."

Hattie frowned. "The girls are gonna be real disappointed, Ash. They even drew straws to see who'd be the first one to say good-bye."

Ash grinned. "It won't take long for them to get over it."

She pouted. "It's gonna be a long trip, with no one except an old man and a skinny old maid to keep you company."

A skinny old maid who could tempt the devil to find his way back to heaven. "I'll manage."

"I bet it'll be a while before you can hook up with some willin' gal over there in England."

He shrugged. "I figure I can survive."

She plucked at his sleeve. "I guess maybe I understand how you feel. You're all set to start a new life. Time to let go of the old one."

It seemed he was always letting go of part of his life, leaving pieces of himself behind. He slid the smooth brown beads of the necklace through his fingers, trying to recall the face of the medicine man who had given it to him so many years ago. Lightning Walker and his wife, Summer Raven, had saved his life. Now they were no more than faded memories. Distant. Indistinct. Like images reflected on the surface of a rippling lake.

He stared at the beads lying across his palm, dragging the images of Lightning Walker and Summer Raven from the coffin that stored the remains of his life with the Cheyenne. He'd been happy with them, as happy as a child could be when he knew he was different. Even though they had raised him as one of their own, he had never really belonged. There were those in the village who had looked at him with suspicion because he was white. Even though he had tried as hard as he could to be one of them, he couldn't change the color of his skin, the color of his eyes, the blood in his veins.

When John MacGregor had rescued him, Ash had tried as hard as he could to learn the ways of the whites. But there wasn't any place for him in this world either. The whites looked at his dark hair and where he had come from and assumed he was part Cheyenne. They shunned him for being a half-breed. Hated him on sight.

"You ain't had it easy. I know. I seen how people treated you, like you was worse than a whore." She stroked his arm. "But now you got a chance to show all of 'em. You got a chance to really belong somewhere. To make somethin' of yourself."

He had spent his whole life trying to belong someplace, hammering on himself like a blacksmith pounding hot metal and finally shaping himself into Ash MacGregor. Hell, he'd even made up his own name. But at least he felt comfortable in this skin, satisfied with the notion of buying a ranch, raising horses, making a decent life for himself. He closed his hand into a fist, squeezing the beads in his palm. Here he was again, plunging back into the fire. Only this time it was a pretty gray-eyed lady who was holding the hammer. "I don't belong in some fancy house in England."

"If you're real smart, you'll find some way to belong."

Ash laid the necklace on top of the clothes packed in his carpetbag. "I'm tired of having my life turned inside

out. I know what I want, and it ain't runnin' around in
fancy clothes tryin' to be something I ain't.''

Hattie shook her head. "One thing about you, Ash
MacGregor, you sure are a stubborn man."

He clenched his jaw, hearing Lady Beth's words echo
in his brain. "I'm just a man who knows what he wants."

"Maybe you do." She shrugged, as if it really didn't
matter one way or another. "I just hope you don't end up
throwin' away something better than what you think you
want."

He watched as she sauntered from his room, uneasy
with the thoughts her words sparked in his mind. He knew
what he wanted from life, even if women kept telling him
he didn't. In spite of his resolve not to think of her, his
thoughts kept running back to Elizabeth Barrington. He
wanted her; he couldn't deny it. But he'd be damned before he let the pretty little prude turn him inside out. Not
again.

Elizabeth had always found the soft sway of a railroad
car relaxing. Yet, the gentle rock of Hayward's private
train failed to ease her tension this morning. For the last
hour she had been sitting in the parlor car, waiting for her
guardian to complete the tour he was giving to Mac-
Gregor, while inwardly she tried to convince herself she
could keep her wayward emotions under lock and key.
She simply would not entertain any ridiculous attraction
to the man.

Now, as Hayward showed MacGregor into the parlor
car, she assured herself she was quite prepared to deal
with the situation. MacGregor was, after all, only a man.

A man who could fill the entire room with his powerful
presence. She sat on the emerald silk velvet of a high-
backed armchair that stood against one of the walnut-
paneled walls, clenching her hands in her lap, watching
as MacGregor strolled into the car. He paused in a shaft

of sunlight streaming through one of the windows. Dressed entirely in black, he seemed a dark, fallen angel teasing heaven.

He looked at her, a direct shot from those stunning blue eyes. The air crackled around her, like the clashing of electricity in a summer storm. Her heart hammered. Her pulse was so loud, she feared he could hear it. In spite of all the arguments she had presented to herself, in spite of how foolish she knew it was, she couldn't suppress the sudden rush of excitement sluicing through her veins.

And he knew it. She could see the recognition of her unfortunate reaction in the glitter of his eyes. He removed his black hat in a silent salute, one corner of his lips tipping upward into the very essence of male arrogance. She rose from her chair, appalled at the shaking of her legs.

As he and Hayward engaged in conversation, Elizabeth tugged on the reins of her runaway emotions. She would not, could not, allow herself to be overwhelmed by the man. After a few moments Hayward left, saying they didn't need him to get in the way of Peyton's lessons. She resisted the urge to call him back. She wasn't at all comfortable alone with Ash MacGregor and the way he made her feel.

Ash slid his startling blue gaze over her, from the curls piled high on her head to the black kid slippers peeking out from under her garnet wool gown, taking time to examine all the more intimate places in between. He seemed especially intrigued by the black plaited silk that formed a vee down the front of her bodice, running from her shoulders over her breasts to the center of her waist. Heat simmered in the wake of his gaze, as though he could conjure fire with a glance. When he lifted his eyes and looked straight into her own, she only prayed he couldn't see the full extent of his power over her.

"What do you want to teach me first?" he asked, his dark voice filled with dangerous currents.

She needed desperately to moisten her dry lips, but she resisted, knowing the gesture would betray her. "I suppose we should start with the proper way for a gentleman to greet a lady. And I assure you, Mr. MacGregor, it isn't by staring at her as though she were on the auction block."

He laughed, a dark rumble deep in his chest. "Is that what I was doing, Lady Beth?"

"You know perfectly well what you were doing." She lifted her chin. "And it's unacceptable."

He sauntered toward her, smiling, as though he found her amusing. He paused a foot in front of her, far too close, smiling down at her. "So tell me, how does a gentleman greet a lady?"

She stared up into those incredible eyes and realized what he was doing. He was trying to intimidate her, the way he intimidated most people. She suspected it was his way of keeping the world at a distance. Well, she couldn't allow him to continue keeping society at a distance. "You will greet a lady differently depending on where you encounter her."

"What if she shows up at my bedroom door?"

She clenched her teeth at the reminder of their regrettable encounter at Miss Hattie's. "Mr. MacGregor, a lady will not come to your bedroom door unless it is under quite extraordinary circumstances."

"Yeah. Quite extraordinary." He grinned, the glint in his eyes pure mischief. "So tell me, how should I greet a lady when she knocks on my door?"

She clasped her hands at her waist, refusing to allow the man to spur her to anger or anything else. "I believe we will concentrate on salutations you will use more often."

"Now, Lady Beth, you're assuming I won't often have the need to welcome a lady into my bedroom."

She suddenly had a vision of this man seducing half

the women in London, all the besotted females swooning over the untamed male in their midst. She squeezed her hands together. "A gentleman does not go about seducing ladies and inviting them into his bedroom."

He considered this for a moment, his face a study in feigned confusion. "What about a lady who just knocks on my bedroom door?"

She lifted her chin. "I came on business. Not because I was captivated by you."

He grinned, his eyes sparkling with devilment. "Ah, now, Lady Beth, you're breakin' my heart."

"I doubt you have one," she said, forcing the words past her clenched teeth.

" 'Cause I ain't civilized?"

"You aren't taking this seriously."

He shook his head. "There are things a man needs to know. Even gentlemen. Like the proper way to handle a lady." He lifted one end of the black silk sash that wrapped twice around her waist before falling over her hip. "Could it be you aren't sure how a gentleman should greet a lady at his bedroom door?"

She felt the slow slide of his fingers against the black silk, as though he were caressing her skin. The man was absolutely infuriating. "Mr. MacGregor, we have only a short time to attempt to civilize you before we reach England. I suggest we not waste a minute on attempts to distract me."

"Is that what I'm tryin' to do?"

"You know perfectly well that's what you're attempting." She jerked the sash from his fingers and turned away from him. She marched to the windows across from her, seeking the breeze to cool her warm cheeks. The air touched her face with a wisp of cedar and pine laced with the pungent scent of burning coal. Jagged slopes covered with pine and aspen slid past her eyes. She took a moment to compose her features into a calm mask before turning to face him.

He was watching her with the self-assured look of a male who understands his prowess over the female of the species. He thought he could waltz in here and fracture her composure. Show nothing but contempt for the rules by which she had lived her entire life. The fact that he could set her a flutter with a glance didn't help her mood. "I assume you have no desire to be humiliated once you enter society."

One dark brow lifted. "No, ma'am. I ain't got any desire to ever be humiliated."

Again. Although he didn't say it, she heard it just the same. He had been right when he'd said she could never fully understand how he had felt growing up the way he had. The clerk at Mansfield's had given her only a taste of the bitter scorn this man had lived with all his life. Prejudice. Humiliation. In spite of the fact that she wanted to strangle him at times, she was determined he would never experience those things again.

The only way to spare him and his family from society's contempt was to teach him proper decorum. Even if she had to force those rules down his throat. "Now then, if you are ready to take our lessons seriously, we can begin."

"Oh, I'm ready." He sat on the arm of the chair she had recently occupied, stretching his long legs as though he didn't have a smidgeon of tension in his entire body.

She stared at him, searching her mind for a thread of logic amid the tumble of thoughts he sparked. What had they been discussing before the man had turned her normally functioning brain to jelly?

"So tell me, how am I supposed to do it?"

She blinked. "What?"

He grinned. "Greet a lady properly."

"Oh. Yes." She moistened her dry lips. "If you should

see a lady with whom you are not well acquainted while you are walking, you should wait for her to recognize you before you greet her. If she should choose not to recognize your acquaintance and pass without speaking, you must not try to press her.''

''If she's the type to walk on by without saying hello, then I ain't got any need to talk to her.''

''Simply because a lady fails to acknowledge you doesn't mean she is being rude.''

He lifted one dark brow. ''Oh, yeah? So tell me what it does mean when someone I know puts her little nose in the air and walks on by as though I ain't good enough to waste her breath on a simple hello.''

She hesitated a moment. She had never quite thought of the lack of acknowledgment in quite that light. ''In general it doesn't present a problem. If you are well acquainted, there is no need to wait for her to acknowledge you.''

He smoothed the brim of his hat, holding the hat against his thigh. ''Would you say we're well acquainted?''

The dark, husky tone in his voice stirred memories of that one kiss they had shared. They were far better acquainted than they should be, and the rogue knew it. ''Yes, of course. It's only if your acquaintance is not well established. Or if you haven't been properly introduced, although you've met.''

He frowned. ''I've met the lady. But we haven't been introduced?''

Oh, dear, she was bungling this. ''Let's say the introduction was made at a house party or dinner or some other private entertainment. In which case the fact that you have all been accepted under your host's roof gives everyone gathered the sanction to speak with anyone. But no one should expect the obligation of an acquaintance to carry beyond the doors of their host.''

''So if I met you at a party, you could turn around and

pretend you ain't never set eyes on me?''

She dearly wished she could. "You must understand, great care is taken in giving introductions.''

He flicked his finger against the crown of his hat. "Wouldn't want to expose some fragile lady to the likes of a man like me, now would we?''

In spite of the cool breeze drifting through the windows behind her, she was growing warm under his direct stare. "It isn't as snobbish as you make it sound.''

"No? You mean to say if old man Trevelyan hadn't taken this notion that I'm his kin, you'd even look at me if we passed on the street?''

She would have noticed the man. Ash MacGregor was impossible not to notice. But she also knew she would never have entertained the idea of speaking to him. And somehow that admission made her uneasy.

His lips drew into a tight line as he stared at her, seeming to read every thought in her head. "Lady, if you didn't think I was this Peyton Trevelyan, you wouldn't come within a mile of me.''

She saw it then: a glimpse past a crack in his defenses—the vulnerability hidden beneath the gruff voice and the fierce expression. The vulnerability of a child who had been taunted and humiliated. The vulnerability of a man who carried those wounds carved deep in his soul. Society had wounded him. She had to make him understand that society was not his enemy. "Would you expect me to speak to every dangerous-looking man who passed me on the street?''

He held her steady gaze, a steely edge of defiance glittering in his eyes. "No, ma'am.''

"I know some of the rules of proper decorum may seem snobbish. But proper behavior is what maintains the very fabric of society.''

"Your society.''

She held his icy look without flinching from his con-

demnation of her and the rules by which she lived, clinging to her convictions like a lifeline. "I believe a true
gentleman can be found in any level of society. He is a
man who cares for the feelings of others. He has a kind
heart."

A corner of his mouth pulled a little tighter, the only
hint her barb had hit home.

"As for all the rest, the customs and manners, they
change with the times. Perhaps it isn't right, but we are
all judged by the way we present ourselves. Proper manners can only be acquired by learning the rules. By prac-
ticing. By caring about what others think of us. Without
proper manners, no matter what a man's title may be, he
will be regarded as a clod."

His lips twitched, as though there was a smile hidden
there, struggling to break free. "And you're worried all
those fancy folks back in England will think old man Trevelyan is out of his mind for bringing a half-civilized
'clod' into his house."

"I would prefer not to have anyone humiliated, Mr.
MacGregor."

He rubbed his chin. "Don't guess I care much to give
anyone a reason to look down their noses at me, or the
old man."

Some of the weight lifted from her shoulders. "Right.
Then we must concentrate on the essentials. We have very
little time. You can begin by not sitting on the arm of that
chair."

He hesitated a moment before he stood, as though he
didn't care for taking orders of any kind. She searched
her befuddled mind for a safe topic to broach, one that
would skirt the issue of men and women by a mile.

He tossed his hat on the seat of the chair and lifted the
book of etiquette she had left on the black walnut pedestal
table beside the chair. He began flipping through the pages
as he spoke. "So tell me, why do ladies sometimes walk

right past a gentleman they've met? Even if it was at a party or dinner or . . ." he glanced at her, his smile growing wicked, "some private entertainment."

She tried not to dwell on the images his words conjured in her mind, tried not to remember the excitement of having his arms around her. She had the distinct impression that that was exactly what he wanted her to remember. "I think perhaps we should start with visiting cards, and how they should properly be presented."

"Does she ignore him to play hard to get?" he asked, ignoring her attempt to shift the conversation. "Is that the reason she pretends not to see him?"

"There are various reasons why a lady would not wish to encourage an acquaintance with a particular gentleman." *Especially if that man is as dangerous as you.*

"He might not have enough money."

She pursed her lips. "He might be exceedingly rude."

He grinned. "We're talking about saying hello, not getting married."

"It's important for a lady to be careful not to encourage a gentleman unless she is inclined to favor his friendship, or his courtship."

"Courtship." He tipped back his head as he studied her, making her wish she had never blundered into this particular topic. "Does every lady think a man wants to marry her just because he says hello on the street?"

"No, of course not. But she shouldn't invite unwanted attention."

He glanced down at the open book he held, studying a page for a moment before he continued. "What does a lady do if she is interested in his attention? How does she let him know?"

He was baiting her. And she certainly didn't intend to fall into his snare. "I'm certain I don't need to enlighten you on the ways a lady encourages a gentleman's attentions. You are hardly a naive schoolboy."

He closed the book, smiling slowly. "No, ma'am, I ain't. I know women, but from what I can tell, women and ladies ain't got much in common."

"If you are basing all your knowledge concerning women on the 'gals' at Miss Hattie's, then I'm afraid you have a rather distorted view of the subject."

One corner of his lips tightened, his eyes glittering with a glint of anger that sent a ripple of dread spiraling along her spine. "Guess that's true."

She didn't like the easy capitulation. She suspected this man never surrendered without bloodshed.

"Unless you want me stumbling around with all those *ladies* in England, looks like you're gonna have to teach me all I need to know."

Her skin prickled when she thought of turning this beast loose among the ladies of England. He could slay far too many hearts, beginning with her own. "Since you're planning to spend only six months in England, I doubt you will have time to cultivate more than a few casual acquaintances."

"Six months is a long time." He set the book on the table and advanced toward her as he continued. "Who knows, maybe I'll find a very special lady, a lady I can't resist."

Warning bells sounded the retreat in her head. She suddenly felt as though she were trapped in a cage with a hungry lion. Yet her anger and pride wouldn't allow her to withdraw from the battle. She held her ground, even when he stepped so close, she could feel the heat of his body radiate against her.

"So tell me, Lady Beth, what does a gentleman do when he wants a lady?"

She swallowed hard. "Wants?"

"That's right." He lifted the sash from her side. "What does a gentleman do when he desires a lady? When he wants to take her to his bed and make love to her all night long?''

Shivers swirled across her breasts. ''A gentleman would not entertain such thoughts about a lady.''

His smile left a hard glitter in his eyes. ''Come now, Lady Beth, you don't mean to say all those fancy gentleman who've courted you never had a spark of desire for you?''

She felt as though she were stepping away from the shore, walking into the sea, with the water lapping closer and closer to her neck. ''A gentleman feels respect toward a lady. Admiration. Perhaps even affection. But he certainly never entertains base thoughts about her.''

''So a gentleman keeps a lady up high, like a pretty doll kept on a shelf. Nice to look at, too delicate to touch.'' He tugged on her sash, drawing her farther away from shore, closer to the heat of his body.

She stared up into the stunning blue depths of his eyes and fought to keep from drowning. Longing curled around her, a heated current drawing her toward him. He touched her cheek, a soft brush of the back of his long fingers against her skin. She sighed at the gentleness of his touch. She couldn't prevent it.

''And when he wants a real woman, he has to go lookin' in a place like Miss Hattie's.'' He dropped her sash and stepped back, looking at her as though, after taking a close inspection of her, he found nothing he wanted.

Elizabeth stared at him, emotions whirling like a pinwheel inside her, anger and humiliation and a misguided hurt stealing her voice for all of a dozen quick beats of her heart. ''It's obvious a man of your character cannot possibly understand the complexities of a proper courtship between a civilized man and woman.''

''What's obvious, Lady Beth, is that you don't have any idea what a man wants from a woman.''

"I can assure you, a *gentleman* wants more than a fleeting moment's pleasure. He wants a wife he can be proud of. A woman he respects. Someone to share his hopes and dreams." She searched for words. "A companion. A helpmate."

He studied her, as though he found her terribly amusing. "Maybe he does. Maybe he wants his pretty little doll sitting up on a shelf in his proper house, while he takes his pleasure with a woman who can warm his bed, not turn the sheets to ice. Maybe that's why all those married gentlemen leave home and come runnin' to Miss Hattie and her gals. 'Cause their lady wives don't give 'em what they want."

She should end this battle. Step away while she still had some measure of her dignity. Step away before this depraved discussion plummeted into even murkier depths. Oh, the arrogant beast! She stepped right up to him, halting so close, her skirt was flattened against his legs. "It seems to me, Mr. MacGregor, if a man is worth the trousers he wears, he should be able to melt a little ice in his own bed."

He lifted one brow, his expression revealing a flicker of surprise as he held her challenging stare. "Think so?"

She tipped her chin and gave him an icy smile. "A woman needn't sell herself to have a spark of fire within her. She needn't be plump and experienced to please a man. Simply because a lady is taught to contain her emotions in public certainly does not mean she is a block of ice in private."

Flames flickered to life in the dazzling blue depths of his eyes, burning away mockery and scorn, leaving something all the more scorching in its stead. "Guess maybe I should wait until I get some experience with the breed, before I start deciding I know all about 'em."

Elizabeth reached for her anger, seeking a shield against this devastating male. He really was the most infuriating creature. One moment she wanted to throttle the man; the next she wanted to throw her arms around his broad shoulders and kiss him until he crumbled at her feet. Of course, the crumbling was something that would only happen should she also decided to strike him over the head with a mallet while she kissed him. While she was thinking of it, that would serve her wayward, often jumbled, far too volatile emotions just fine.

She stepped back, retreating to a respectable distance. "Before you go about acquiring your knowledge of my species, perhaps you should consider learning the rules by which we live."

He nodded. "Never go trailing after an outlaw till you learn all you can about him."

Outlaw. It wasn't exactly the way she had hoped he would view a lady. She studied him a moment, searching for a place to begin, trying not to think of all the reasons she should throw up her hands and run for her life.

He smiled at her. "I'm ready when you are."

Elizabeth looked into his eyes and wondered if she would ever truly be prepared to deal with this potent male. Still, she had to find a way to civilize the man. Or, at the very least, trim his claws. She didn't intend to release a lion among the sheep of London. "I believe we should start with the proper etiquette for visiting."

Chapter Ten

Ash had been on a train before, but he had never seen anything like Hayward Trevelyan's private train. Six cars, and all of them for three people and a fistful of servants. A man could eat, sleep, take a bath, and never even slow down. It sure was a different way to live. He couldn't help feeling as though he was in a whole new world. And he felt about as awkward as a newborn colt.

"You should never be in a hurry to seat yourself when you enter a reception room." Elizabeth strolled from the door leading to the back of the train to the center of the parlor car. "After you are announced you should enter at a leisurely pace."

Ash leaned back against the soft emerald velvet covering his chair. He propped his chin on the steeple of his fingers, watching little Miss Prim and Proper demonstrate the proper way to enter a room. The lady had been lecturing him for an hour, and all she had talked about was fancy name cards and the different rules for leaving them at people's houses and receiving the ones people left at your own.

"You should take a few moments to speak with the hostess before taking your seat," she said.

He gave her a look filled with mock surprise. "You mean to say you society folks really do get around to seeing each other, face-to-face?"

She paused near the sofa across from him. "I've spent

135

a great deal of time explaining the etiquette of calling cards, Mr. MacGregor. Haven't you been listening?''

"I've been listening, all right. I figured you folks spent so much time sendin' and leavin' cards, you never did get around to visitin' with anyone."

She folded her hands at her waist, pinning him with her disapproving schoolmarm stare. ''There would be little sense in leaving a calling card if one didn't have an intention of calling.''

Ash shook his head. ''From what I can see there ain't much about your rules that makes sense.''

"There *isn't* much that makes sense."

He grinned. ''I didn't realize you thought that way too.''

She pursed her pretty lips. "I assure you, there is a reason for every rule.''

Ash figured all those rules were invented by rich people who wanted more reasons for looking down their noses at the poor peasants. He had seen those looks too many times. ''I've managed pretty well without ever seein' one of those fancy name cards you seem to think are so damn important.''

"Please do not swear."

Ash rubbed his fingertips against his chin. Every time he opened his mouth she managed to make him feel like a stupid ox.

''Circumstances have changed,'' she said softly, as though speaking to a frightened child. Her gentle tone managed to make him feel even more awkward. ''People will expect more from you when they discover you're Marlow's grandson.''

People expected him to be something he wasn't. Ash came to his feet and paced the length of the car, feeling like a trapped cougar testing the limits of his cage. He threw open the door and stalked out onto the platform at the back of the train. There was no escape. The wrought iron was cold against his hands as he gripped the railing and stared back along the curving tracks, watching the Colorado countryside slip away from him.

The door opened and closed softly behind him. He squeezed the cold iron, tensing as Elizabeth joined him at the railing. She rested one white gloved hand on the railing, steadying herself against the rocking motion of the train, her gown brushing his leg with each sway of the platform. She was quiet, staring out at the mountains, sharing the beauty of the day. And he caught himself staring at her, admiring a beauty that grew each time he saw her.

"I realize all of these rules must seem somewhat confusing to you." She glanced up at him, her eyes revealing the gentleness he had often glimpsed in her. "Once you're more familiar with proper etiquette I'm certain you will feel much more confident about everything."

"Do you really think fillin' my head with all your rules will change who I am?"

"I think it will give you a better perspective of the life you were meant to live."

"I've lived my life here." He swept his hand toward the vista of granite cliffs and tree-covered slopes. "I don't belong in your fancy little world."

"You don't know that for certain. You can't. Not until you give yourself a chance to understand the people, their way of life. You belong in England, with your family."

He watched a hawk soar from an aspen tree growing on the rocky cliff that rose from the edge of the tracks. The granite was scarred by men who had carved this railway out of the wilderness. But the hawk still soared free. "Learning a bunch of rules some rich people made up because they didn't have nothin' better to do won't change who I am."

"What are you afraid of? Why are you so reluctant to acknowledge your family?"

Ash clenched his jaw. "I ain't afraid. I just ain't interested in all the fancy talkin' and fancy ways. It sure don't make a man better than anybody else." All it did was make a man feel small and stupid. Well, he'd had a belly full of feeling no good.

Her lips flattened into a tight line. "I never realized you were so bigoted."

"Just what the hell do you mean by that?"

"If Marlow was an American rancher, I doubt you would have quite this amount of resistance to admitting your identity."

"Look, lady, I . . ."

"How do you think he feels every time you deny you're his grandson?"

How the hell did she think he felt? Clawing his way through the shadows of his memory. Not knowing the truth from fantasy. Wondering if he could ever meet the expectations he saw in her eyes. That was the hell of it. Wanting her respect. Knowing she didn't think he deserved it.

He stared down into her eyes, anger and frustration churning in his gut. Silently, he tried to frighten her. She didn't flinch. She stood her ground with her chin lifted, her eyes flashing with fury.

He wanted to grab her shoulders and shake her. He wanted to shout his rage. He wanted to slam his mouth over hers, kiss her like the beast he was, make her see what years of hard living did to a man. "Guess you should know all about bigotry. You wouldn't be on the same train with me if you didn't think I was some fancy English marquess. And as for Marlow, if he didn't think I was Peyton, he wouldn't come within a mile of me."

She released her breath in an indignant huff that brushed his chin with heat. "You can't possibly compare the two situations."

"Why the hell can't I?"

"Because . . . because . . . Oh, they aren't at all the same."

He grinned. "Look, lady, you live in a precious little world where the doors are carefully barred against men like me."

"And you live in a world where men do nothing but find fault with women like me."

The sudden turn of the conversation stunned him. She glared at him, her eyes a startling shade of silver, her cheeks high with color. Damn, if she wasn't the prettiest woman he'd ever seen. "What the hell do you care what a man like me thinks of you? According to you, I'm a half-civilized barbarian. You're a damn princess."

"I'm not a princess. Even though you seem to think I'm some kind of different species, I'm a woman, with feelings like anyone else. I'm every bit as much of a woman as any you might have known at Miss Hattie's."

He tipped back his head and laughed; he couldn't help it. Here was this beautiful, untouchable princess comparing herself to a poor little peasant who could be purchased for a few dollars. God, the woman had no idea of what life was like outside of her fancy kingdom.

"How dare you laugh at me! I'm every bit as good as any of Miss Hattie's gals." She thumped his chest with her dainty little fist. "You insufferable . . ."

He whipped his arm around her, pulled her close, and trapped her startled gasp beneath his lips. She had pushed him one step too far. If the strange little female wanted to pretend she was on the same level as a whore, he would damn well give her a taste of it.

He cupped the back of her head, holding her as he devoured her sweet mouth, slanting his lips across hers with a passion that startled him with its intensity. God she tasted sweet, like the clean fresh rain that fell high in the mountains. He sipped from her mouth, like a man long parched finding the sweet solace of nectar.

She struggled in his arms, pounding her small fists against his shoulders—the indignant princess. Yet he didn't care. He was a beast. He was a man who had learned all about passion at the hands of pretty whores. He was a peasant who could teach this princess all the dirty truths of life outside the palace.

She squirmed in his arms, trying to free herself. But the firm feel of her breasts brushing his chest only inflamed him. The gentle rocking of the platform brushed his body against hers in a rhythm that triggered heat. He opened his hand, massaging her back with his fingers, kissing her with all the desire humming through his veins.

She moaned against his lips. In the next heartbeat she threw her arms around his neck, all of her outrage dissolving in the rising flames of a desire he could feel rippling through her. She parted her lips and kissed him back with an eager innocence that was more than anything he had imagined possible. Ash staggered with the impact.

He leaned back against the door, pulling her between his thighs. She followed without hesitation, keeping her arms tight around his neck, her lips moving sweetly beneath his. A growl issued from deep in his chest, surprising him with his own need as she snuggled against his loins.

This had to stop. Of course it had to stop. He couldn't touch her in all the ways he wanted to touch her. He couldn't strip away her clothes, kiss her, taste her, savor every delicious inch of her. He slid his hands up and down her back, resisting the urge to unfasten all the small fabric-covered buttons. He should pull away. Now.

Yet he couldn't release her. Not yet. He wanted to tell her how he had dreamed of this moment. He wanted to tell her this was sweeter than his dreams. Never in his life had he felt anything as sweet as having Elizabeth in his arms. She smelled of sunlight and lavender and woman. So clean. So innocent. So damned tempting.

He slipped the tip of his tongue past her lips, tasting her. She stiffened with a shock that dissolved in a hasty beat of his heart. A tremor rippled through him as she plunged with all her innocence into the sensual pleasure of dipping and tasting and exploring the depths of the kiss.

He slid his hands over the curve of her hips, searching in vain for the woman beneath the layers of wool and petticoats. What would he find if he lifted her skirts and touched her, slipped his fingers into that lush nest between her thighs? Would she be warm and wet and aching for the slow slide of his body into hers?

Lust knifed through him with every beat of his heart. He trembled with need. He couldn't remember ever wanting a woman as much as he wanted this one.

A soft moan slipped from her lips as he pulled away from her. She opened her eyes, like someone jolted from a pleasant slumber. She blinked twice, then stared up at him, her gray eyes revealing her bewilderment. Ash smiled in spite of the torture of having her soft and supple against the hard plane of his body. He brushed his knuckles over the curve of her cheek. "You do surprise me, Lady Beth."

She pulled away from him, tottered back several steps, and bumped into the railing.

He grabbed her arm, imposing balance. "Careful. I wouldn't want to explain to the old man how you ended up on the tracks."

She stood with her gown pressed flat against the railing, gripping the wrought iron with both hands, staring at him with wide eyes. "Why did you do that?"

"Do what?" he asked, deliberately trying to provoke her. He understood her anger, felt safe with it, much safer than with the other emotions that flared between them.

"Why did you kiss me?" she asked again, sounding more bewildered than angry.

He shrugged, refusing to acknowledge what was really

behind that kiss—his need. It went far too deep, far beyond the physical ache that throbbed low in his belly. His need for her lay in the dark places deep in his soul where dreams were buried beneath the ugliness of his life. "That's what uncivilized savages do when they get a chance. They kiss pretty women."

"I see." She glanced away from him, staring for a moment at the swift shift of the countryside whipping past them before fixing him in an angry glare. "Even though you seem compelled to wallow in your barbarism, I feel I must remind you that allowing one's more primitive instincts to run wild is really quite unacceptable in this society."

The smoke-tinged air left bitterness on his tongue as he took a deep breath. He should turn away from her, leave her here, standing alone. But something trapped him here—the lure of her, the warmth he had felt in her arms. He wanted more from her, an affirmation that what he had felt was real. "Is that what you were doing, Lady Beth? Allowing your more primitive instincts to run wild?"

She glanced away from him, staring down at the wooden planks of the platform. "I find you have the most infuriating capacity for teasing my emotions," she said, the icy edge of her voice melting with a soft note of confusion.

Ash pressed his back against the door, anchoring himself in a safe position, resisting the lure of her. His pulse was still pumping hard from having her in his arms, and he wanted nothing more than to grab her and hold her, until her warmth melted all his doubts. "If it makes you feel better, you bring out the beast in me."

She slanted him a glance. "I can assure you, that gives me no consolation at all."

God help him, he wanted to fall on his knees before her and beg for a smile, a touch, an encouraging word. He hated this weakness inside him, hated her for making him want her as he had never wanted anything in his life. She would trap him with her smiles, trap him with the affection he imagined glowing in her eyes, trap him with his own weakness. Trap him in a world where he didn't belong, no matter what the hell his name might be.

He didn't have a future as Peyton Trevelyan. He didn't have a future with the lady. He only prayed to God he could remember that the next time he looked into her pretty gray eyes.

"I suggest we continue with your lessons." She marched toward the door. "You obviously have a great deal to learn."

Ash opened the door and stood aside for her to pass. With her head held high and her shoulders thrust back, she was once again the prim little schoolteacher. Except for the blush high on her cheeks. It was better for both of them if he didn't think about what had put the color in her cheeks.

Elizabeth marched past MacGregor, hoping she at least looked dignified. Of course, she wasn't at all certain how a woman could look dignified after behaving with all the wanton abandon of an adventuress.

Idiot. Fool. Lunatic!

She marched across the room and snatched the book of etiquette from the pedestal table that stood between a pair of upholstered armchairs against one wall. She had allowed the man to toy with her. No, if she was going to be completely honest, she had invited his attentions. In fact she had pushed him, prodded him, poked him, hoping he might assault her. For the last two days she had dreamed of being held in his arms once more. She had longed for his kisses.

Idiot!

That type of longing would get her flat on her back. And, as intriguing as she found that possibility, she was not insane enough to think for an instant that her surrender would lead to anything but ruin.

MacGregor was hardly a man who realized the importance of a kiss, let alone anything of a more intimate nature. To him, kissing a woman was natural. He indulged in intimate liaisons without thought of lasting commitments. Without indulging in sentiment. She must keep that in mind. Oh, my, yes, she must certainly keep that in mind. Before she did something unforgivably foolish.

She leafed through the book, trying to concentrate on the pages, rather than the man who had taken a place in the chair to her left. This foolish infatuation had to end. She refused to be turned into a silly, simpering spinster all for the amusement of one infuriating male. She would show Mr. Ash MacGregor that she was made of stronger stuff.

Chapter Eleven

Ash pressed his fingertips together and rested his chin on the steeple of his fingers. Little Miss Prim and Proper sat across from him, reading from the etiquette book she held propped open on her lap. Just like a pretty schoolmarm, reciting lessons.

"For success in society one must cultivate one's mind," she said in her crisp, no-nonsense voice.

She had been pounding on him all day. At lunch she had informed him he didn't know how to use a fork and knife properly. And that was just the beginning. He didn't speak properly. He didn't walk properly. He didn't dress properly. According to the lady, he didn't do anything properly. Sure did make a man want to prove to the prim little prude that there were a few things he could do *properly*.

"Let your voice be low and pleasant of tone and your enunciation distinct."

The brass lamps overhead rocked with the steady sway of the train, golden light drifting back and forth across her, touching her face, shimmering in her hair. Memory teased him: the memory of a woman lush and warm in his arms. He watched her lips, her English voice drifting over him, soft in tone, crisp and precise, each word carefully molded. She was the proper English lady. On the surface. But beneath that icy facade burned a fire that could consume a man.

"You must never interrupt a person who is talking. Never complete a sentence for them by stealing the words from their mouths. To do this is to demonstrate your lack of good breeding."

Heat trickled into his blood with the memory of her lips moving beneath his, her firm breast nestled against his chest, the sweet scent of her skin tingling his senses. Yet there was more than a kiss that teased his memory. There had been a look in her eyes, a warmth that beckoned to him, lured him like a man seeking shelter from a long winter storm. And foolish as it was, he wanted to see those flames flicker in her eyes, feel her warmth against his skin, bury himself in her fire.

"Never permit yourself to be coaxed into an argument while in society."

Lamplight touched the burgundy roses clustered at the shoulder of her sleeveless gown. He followed the slow sway of light as it brushed the pale skin of her shoulder, the curve of her neck, sliding like honey over the smooth expanse exposed by her heart-shaped neckline. During the day she was covered all the way up to her chin. But at night those proper gowns of hers dipped to give a man a tantalizing glimpse of feminine curves. In his mind he peeled the soft silk from her shoulders, exposing the pale curves of her breasts to the lamplight.

"The essence of mastering the art of conversation is to draw others out and aid them to shine. Be more anxious to listen than to hear the sound of your own voice."

Ash drew in his breath, trying to catch the scent of her skin. But the distance was too great. Unlike Hattie's perfume, he had to get close to sample the delicate fragrance of Lady Beth's skin. What would the lady do if he were to get close enough to draw her scent deep into his lungs? Close enough to taste her skin? Close enough to fill his hands with her breasts? He lowered his eyes, tracing the curve of her neck, his muscles growing tight with the lust pumping hard and hot in his loins.

"Mr. MacGregor?"

Ash glanced up, meeting the curiosity in her huge gray eyes with a lazy smile.

She frowned. "Is something wrong? You have a most peculiar expression on your face."

Nothing peculiar about a man in rut, he thought. Stupid, maybe. Strange; he never thought skinny old maids would be the type to burrow under his skin. But this one did. The truth was, unless he was willing to spend the rest of his life pretending to be something he wasn't, the lady was as far out of reach as a shining star. "I guess maybe I've had about all the etiquette I can handle for one day."

"Oh." She glanced down at the book. "I apologize. I hadn't realized it was getting so late. It's just that there is so much to learn, and so little time."

His stomach tightened at the thought of what would be expected of him once they reached England. "You mean there ain't much time before Trevelyan puts me on display for his friends?"

She glanced up, a single line forming between her arched brows. "Isn't. There *isn't* much time."

"Yeah. I got the idea." He gripped the smooth wooden arms of his chair. All day long, every time he had opened his mouth, the little lady had reminded him just how far apart their two worlds were. Truth was, they didn't even speak the same language. He felt the way he had after John MacGregor had rescued him from the massacre of his people—an alien in a world that held nothing but contempt for a young boy who didn't quite fit.

She closed the book and clasped her hands on the dark brown leather cover, her expression far too gentle. Dammit, she was looking at him as though he were a frightened boy who needed reassurance. "Marlow has no intention of putting you on display for anyone. But, you have to realize, once people learn of your return, you will cause quite a stir. There will be dinner parties in your honor, balls to attend. And I shouldn't be surprised if the queen wishes to meet you.''

He frowned, his apprehension a hard hand against his throat. "What queen?"

She looked surprised. "Her Majesty, Queen Victoria."

He stood and walked to the window behind his chair, stretching muscles grown tight with more than his desire for a pretty lady. The air in the narrow room had turned hot and thin. He couldn't breathe. He couldn't get enough air into his lungs. He grabbed handfuls of emerald velvet and threw open the drapes, golden tassels swaying with the sudden motion.

He threw open the window. The rhythm of wheels clacking against metal rails rushed through the window with the sharp scent of burning coal. Ash drew the pungent air into his lungs, searching for the inner balance that had sustained him all his life.

Silk rustled behind him, the sound crashing against his heightened senses. Although he didn't turn, he was aware of her every move. His skin tingled as she drew near, as though he stood bare in the rays of the sun.

She paused beside him, so close he could feel the warmth of her skin radiate through his white cotton shirt. After dinner he had discarded the coat he had bought to attend dinner at Shelby Radcliffe's. He had rolled up the sleeves of his shirt, winning a disapproving lift of her brows and the assurance that gentlemen did not go about half dressed. Still, he couldn't see much reason in getting all dressed up for dinner. Couldn't see why the old man and the lady changed clothes half a dozen times a day. Guess maybe it gave rich people a chance to show off all the clothes they owned.

He squeezed his hands into fists at his sides, expecting her to preach at him. Yet, she didn't look as though she intended to give him a lecture on how to rise from his chair, or open drapes, or hold his head, or breathe. From the corner of his eye he watched her, standing beside him, her face turned toward the window, as though the moonlight skipping across the dark shadows of trees was the most fascinating sight in the world.

"The day I was to be presented to the queen for the first time I couldn't keep down a bite. My knees were shaking so violently as I approached her, I was certain Her Majesty could hear my knees knocking. I thought I would tip over when I made my curtsy. I was certain I would make a complete fool of myself."

He glanced at her, his breath halting in his lungs when she looked up at him and smiled. Seems he'd been waiting all day for one of her smiles, for another chance to glimpse that warm glow she kept hidden deep beneath the ice. "How old were you?"

"Sixteen." She laughed, a soft ripple of sound that brought a smile to his lips. "And so terribly green."

He rested his shoulder on the window frame, turning to face her. Moonlight and lamplight kissed her cheeks, silver and gold paying homage to the sparkling jewel in their midst. A man could get real use to looking at her. "So, did you tip over?"

She shook her head. "I actually managed to get through the entire ordeal with nothing more than a dreadful headache to remind me of my horrible fit of nerves."

"It's not the same. I'm not sixteen. And I'm not some English marquess."

She smiled, her eyes filling with a mischievous light. "You didn't say *ain't* that time."

"I guess maybe you're a pretty good teacher."

She lowered her lashes with an honest modesty he had never seen in a woman. "Perhaps you're simply an excellent student."

Right now he was interested in teaching her a few things. He touched her cheek where the lamplight kissed her skin, absorbing the warmth of her beneath the golden light. Although she glanced up at him with surprise in her eyes, she didn't draw away from him, but stayed within his reach, allowing him the comfort of her warmth. And it was sweet, so damn sweet, pretending for a moment he wasn't alone with his fears.

He slid his thumb over the corner of her lips, her startled sigh warming his skin. Lust twisted like a serpent low in his belly, sinking fangs deep into his flesh, tempting him to take what he wanted from this woman. He slid his thumb over the plump curve of her lower lip. In her eyes he saw the shocked innocence of a woman who had never felt the slow slide of a man's body between her legs. And more.

Curiosity flickered with awakening desire in her beautiful eyes. The lady wanted answers to mysteries she was only just beginning to realize existed. Was that kiss they had shared really as potent as her memory? And what happened after a kiss? What secrets awaited her beyond that first nibble of forbidden fruit? Oh, yes, the lady was curious. Almost as curious as he was to taste her.

He slipped the tip of his thumb between her lips, a pale reflection of the way he wanted to touch her. The moist heat of her mouth teased the serpent in his belly. His blood thrummed through his veins, pounding like a fist in his loins. She made a sound low in her throat, the soft, plaintive sound of a small furry creature captured in the talons of a hawk.

God how he wanted her. Right here. Right now. With her back pressed against that narrow sofa where she had left her book of etiquette, her hair loose about her face, her long legs tight around his waist.

"What are you doing?" she asked, her voice carried on a warm whisper of breath brushing his hand.

It shocked him to find he had to swallow hard before he could use his voice. "Touching you."

"Oh," she whispered.

The lady had no idea how close he was to seducing her right out of that pretty silk dress. He had little doubt he could do it. The lady's innocence was no match for a man who had been turned over to the women at Miss Hattie's when he was thirteen. The ladies had used him well, teaching him how to pleasure them with more than simply the hard thrust of his body.

He knew the secrets of whores who craved tenderness where there was often only pain. They had showed him every delicious little recess of a woman's body. They had taught him the magic that could be conjured with his lips and tongue. They had shared the secret of lingering in all the right places.

Still, never in his life had he been the first to ease a woman over the threshold of innocence. In this he was as untried as the lady who stood like a doe in the lair of a mountain lion, trembling softly beneath his touch, frightened and enthralled, curious of what would come. He drew in his breath, catching a delicate thread of lavender drifting through the soot-filled air. Lady Beth wasn't just any woman. She'd expect some kind of commitment in exchange for a ride between her thighs. A commitment he couldn't make.

He dropped his hand. "It's late. You better get to bed," he said, his voice harsh from his hard-won restraint.

She stepped back, pressing her hand to her neck, the confusion in her eyes dissolving in the awakening flames of her anger. "Mr. MacGregor, I'm not a child who must be told when to go to bed."

If she had any idea how hard and fast his blood was pumping, she'd turn tail and run without looking back.

"And I'm not easily intimidated by your rather underhanded tactics," she said.

He frowned. "My underhanded tactics?"

"Kindly do not play the innocent. It doesn't suit you.

I realize you find it amusing to upset my composure, but it's hardly a gentlemanly thing to do.''

He smiled. ''Is that what I do when I touch you, Lady Beth? Do I upset your composure?''

''Yes. I find it quite unsettling to be touched in such a . . . a . . . familiar fashion. It's really quite unacceptable.''

''I see. You don't want my dirty hands on you.''

She met his hard glare with an icy resolve. ''A gentleman shows respect for a lady, Mr. MacGregor. He doesn't go about treating her as though she were a woman for hire.''

He leaned toward her. ''Seems to me you didn't start complaining until I *stopped* touching you.''

She lifted her chin, her nose an inch away from his. ''I can assure you, I don't find your primitive attempts at seduction at all enjoyable.''

''Lady, if I'd wanted to seduce you, you'd be on your back right now.''

She gasped. ''You really think much too highly of yourself, Mr. MacGregor.''

He forced his lips into a grin. ''I know women, Lady Beth. And I know when one is ripe for a tumble.''

She released her breath in a sharp exhalation that brushed his face with a damp heat that smelled of the hot cocoa she had been drinking a short while ago. ''You might have had all those unfortunate women at Hattie's drooling over your rather dubious male charms, but I can assure you, Mr. MacGregor, I want none of them.''

''That so?''

She smiled, her eyes shimmering with fury. ''That's correct. I find your tactics disturbing. Nothing more.''

He had half a mind to challenge her words. He fought the crazy urge to grab her and kiss her smug little mouth until she turned to warm honey in his arms. Lust stabbed his belly, a powerful ache begging for the sweet release he could find in her arms. Yet the look in her eyes kept the beast inside him at bay. She was filled with innocent fury and the fragile bravado of a delicate fawn facing a menacing lion. And just maybe he wasn't enough of a beast to destroy all that innocence. "Guess I've got a lot to learn about dealing with ladies."

"Yes. You do." She backed away from him, straight into a chair. She jumped, as though it had bitten her, then glanced at him, her chin held high in spite of her tattered dignity. "After breakfast we'll begin where we left off this evening."

He smiled, thinking of how much he'd love to pick up where they had left off. "See you in the morning."

"Good night."

He watched her go, fighting the primitive instincts of his aroused body. He stood for several minutes afterwards, staring at the door leading to the sleeping car, his body pounding with the blood she had turned to fire. The lady had a way of getting into his blood, in more ways than he wanted to admit. She awakened something inside him, something much more dangerous than lust.

Lust he understood.

Lust was safe.

Lust burned quick and hot and died when his body found release.

He had the uneasy feeling that the emotions this lady triggered inside him wouldn't die in a sudden blaze of passion. The feeling that the emotion awakening inside him would grow like a vine, curling around his heart, tying him up in knots he would never be able to cut loose. If he allowed her close. He didn't intend to let that happen, he thought as he left the parlor car.

A lamp was burning near the center of the corridor of the sleeping car, leaving both ends of the long car in shadows. Lady Beth's compartment was at the far end of the car from his. The old man had placed Ash as far from his ward as possible. Still, it wasn't far enough to banish thoughts of her. He opened his door, wondering how he was going to ease the pounding of his blood enough to sleep.

That was odd: The shade had been up when he left for dinner. Now it was drawn, blocking out the moonlight. Guess it was going to take a while to get used to servants messing around in his room.

A pale glow filtered into the compartment from the corridor, the faint light penetrating little more than a foot into the darkness. He stepped inside, reaching for the light near the door.

Something moved. Reflexes honed through years of tracking killers leapt inside him. Someone was there, in the shadows near the bed.

Chapter Twelve

Elizabeth didn't call for her maid to help her prepare for bed. It was late; Leah would be asleep. And Elizabeth was far too agitated to conceal her feelings. She snatched at the hairpins holding the mass of curls piled high at the back of her head. Oh, she wished she had never set eyes on the man! Never in her life had she met anyone so rude, so arrogant, so utterly heartless.

Her hair tumbled around her shoulders, falling to her waist. Her scalp tingled with the release of the weight. She dropped the hairpins in a tray on the vanity built into a wall of the compartment, the pins pinging against the white porcelain. He thought her amusing. She grabbed her silver-handled brush and began slashing at her hair. How dare he! He had toyed with her. Seduced her with a gentle touch, then delivered the blow; slapped her right across the face with his rejection.

She stared at her reflection in the mirror attached to the wall above the vanity, her gaze lingering on her lips. A curious thrill ran through her veins at the memory of the way he had touched her. She trembled at the thought of his thumb sliding past her lips. In a way she didn't quite understand how the touch of his thumb against her lips had seemed even more intimate than the brush of his lips had been. Almost as intimate as the sweet rhythm of his tongue in her mouth. She shook her head, dismissing her unfortunate reaction to the barbarian.

"Fool," she whispered.

The man was an uncivilized, unprincipled rogue. And she was an untutored, unsuspecting lamb where that lion was concerned. He teased her, and she trembled like a simpering idiot. Well, she learned quickly. If he thought he could toy with her, he was—

A noise slammed into her thoughts. She set the brush on the vanity and turned toward the door leading to the corridor outside her compartment. That had sounded like gunfire. What the devil was that barbarian up to?

Ash dove for the floor just as a shot cracked the silence of his compartment. Heat seared across his ribs. He hit the floor and rolled, pain knocking the air from his lungs.

A man ran past him, heading for the open door. Ash lashed out with his foot, hitting a leg. The man pitched forward, slamming to the carpet with a dull thud. Ash struggled to his feet. Before he could reach him, his assailant scrambled to his feet and dashed through the door.

Ash followed, running into the corridor. The man was headed for the far end of the corridor and the door leading to the dining car. Medium height. Sandy brown hair shaggy beneath a dark brown Stetson. Could have been one of a hundred men he knew.

The man turned near the end of the car, swaying with the train. His mouth was pulled into a tight line beneath a thick dark mustache, his eyes shadows beneath the brim of his hat. Ash had never seen him before. The stranger raised his gun, firing without taking aim. Ash ducked, slamming into the wall as the bullet whizzed past his head. Glass shattered behind him; the bullet had slammed into the glass panel in the door leading to the parlor. The assailant turned and ran.

Ash cursed under his breath. His own pistol and holster were wrapped in a suede bag, packed in a drawer in his sleeping compartment. No time to get it. Blood ran down his side in a warm, sticky stream as he ran after the assailant. The man threw open the door to the vestibule connecting the two cars.

A door to one of the sleeping compartments slid open a few feet in front of Ash, spilling golden light into the shadows. Elizabeth stepped into the corridor. She glanced at him, her eyes wide. "Mr. MacGreg . . ."

Ash swerved to avoid a collision, hitting the side of the car. Wood shuddered with the impact. A sharp pain flared in his shoulder. The man turned in the vestibule, raising his gun.

"Down!" Ash dove for Elizabeth. He tackled her, his forward motion sweeping her back into her compartment. He twisted as they fell, taking the brunt of the fall. He hit the carpet, flat on his back. She landed, her shoulder driving like a battering ram into his chest.

Air whooshed from his lungs. Bright splinters of light danced before his eyes.

"Oh my goodness," she whispered, twisting in his arms, ramming his wounded side with her elbow.

Ash groaned with the sudden pain. He closed his eyes, wishing he could curl into a tight ball. But that was impossible with a woman propped on his chest.

"Mr. MacGregor, I thought I heard gunfire. And here you are, knocking me to the floor. I really must insist on an explanation."

He opened his eyes, staring straight into hers. For three beats of his heart he forgot all about the man, who had probably managed to leap from the train by now. All he could do was stare at the woman perched like an indignant angel on his chest.

She had removed the pins from her hair. The silky tresses tumbled all around her face, pooling on his shoulders in a cascade of dark honey. Her breath brushed his face, falling soft and moist against his lips. She lay snuggled between his thighs, her heat bathing his loins.

"Mr. MacGregor, are you all right? Did you bump your head? You look a bit dazed."

He eased air into his lungs. "There was someone . . ."

"What the devil is happening?"

Hayward's deep voice bellowed through the small compartment. Ash looked past Elizabeth to where the duke stood in the doorway, an emerald silk dressing gown wrapped around him and a pearl-handled revolver in his hand. "There was someone in my compartment. A man with a gun."

"What?" Hayward glanced toward Ash's room, a bull looking for a fight. "Where is the blackguard?"

"A man with a gun?" Elizabeth drew away from Ash, sitting back on her heels between his legs. She gasped when she saw the blood on his shirt. "You've been shot!"

"It's just a scratch."

Hayward leaned over Elizabeth, staring down at Ash, his white brows knitted above the thin line of his nose. "Where is he?"

"He was headed for the dining car when"—Ash looked at Elizabeth— "Lady Beth decided to investigate all the commotion. He might still be on board."

Hayward nodded. "I'll search the train."

"Not without me." Ash struggled to his feet. The room swam before his eyes.

Elizabeth stood and grabbed his arm. "I must insist you stay here and let me tend to your wound. I always travel with all the essentials to tend to minor mishaps. Although I'm not entirely certain I would call a gunshot minor under any circumstances."

"Later." Ash looked at Hayward. "You know how to use that shooting iron?"

Hayward smiled. "I'm a crack shot."

"Targets?"

"Why, yes."

Ash held out his hand. "Better let me have it."

Hayward hesitated for a moment before turning over the weapon.

"Mr. MacGregor, I really must insist . . ." Elizabeth turned, following Ash toward the door. "Mr. Mac-Gregor!"

Ash hurried out of the room, brushing past Hayward, who followed him down the corridor.

"Mr. MacGregor," Elizabeth said, raising her voice as Ash ran down the corridor. "You shouldn't be running about while you're bleeding!"

Ash glanced back as he reached the door leading to the vestibule between the two cars. "Get back inside and lock your door."

She folded her hands at her waist. "I'm not a frightened little . . ."

"Lady, there's a killer on board. Get back inside and lock your damn door."

"You needn't swear." She sent Ash a frosty glance before closing her door.

Ash squeezed the brass door handle. "Is she always so bossy?"

Hayward grinned. "She has always been very . . . managing."

"*Managing* is the polite way of puttin' it, I guess." Ash glanced through the window, peering into the vestibule and the dining car, beyond the next door. Moonlight poured through the windows lining the length of the car, slanting across the polished sideboard, the round tables and chairs, the linen tablecloths glowing like a ghost in the dark. He couldn't see the man, but that didn't mean he wasn't hidden in the shadows, or lurking behind the bar at the far end of the car.

Ash glanced at the old man beside him. "I'd feel better if you went back to your room and let me handle this."

"And I'd feel better if I went with you."

Ash sighed, knowing that arguing with the duke would

be useless. "Stay behind me. And if I tell you to duck, don't waste time trying to see why, or you might get your head blown off. Understand?"

Hayward grinned. "Proceed, young man."

It took a little more than half an hour to search the rest of the train. They didn't find a trace of the man. By the time they returned to the sleeping car one side of Ash's shirt and trousers were soaked with blood. As the excitement of the chase drained away, so did his strength. His head pounded with the same rhythm as the pain throbbing in his side.

Hayward paused outside Elizabeth's compartment. "How do you suppose the blackguard got off a moving train?"

"We slowed down when we rounded that curve a few miles back. I guess he jumped then. Probably planned it that way."

Hayward rubbed his right eyebrow. "It isn't exactly the way I would have expected a burglar to behave."

Ash leaned back against the wall. "I'm not sure he was a burglar."

"What do you think he wanted?"

"Me. Dead."

Hayward stared at Ash in stunned silence. "Do you think it has anything to do with one of the men you've brought to justice?"

"Probably." Ash pressed his hand to the wound in his side, cringing at the sharp sting. "I guess I better take care of this little scratch, before it starts giving me big trouble."

"What about Elizabeth?"

Ash handed the revolver to the old man. "I've been taking care of myself a long time. I don't see any reason to change."

Hayward smiled. "I shall tell her."

*   *   *

Elizabeth paused in the corridor outside MacGregor's compartment, trying to calm the headlong racing of her heart. There it was again, that tingling excitement that sluiced through her every vein at the mere thought of seeing him again. Oh, he was the most infuriating, provoking . . . intriguing individual she had ever met. Now he was hurt. Bleeding. And too stubborn to accept her help.

She squeezed the smooth wooden box containing medicinal supplies to her chest, holding it like a shield as she prepared to do battle. She intended to help the man, whether he liked it or not.

She knocked on the door to his compartment and waited. No answer. Was he unconscious? She hesitated a moment before opening the door. The compartment was empty. The blue velvet counterpane covering the bed that was built into one of the walnut paneled walls was wrinkled, as though someone had been sitting there, waiting for his prey. She shivered at the realization that someone had actually been in here, waiting to kill Ash.

"Mr. MacGregor," she said, stepping into the compartment. "Are you all right?"

"I told Trevelyan I didn't need any help." MacGregor's deep voice thundered through the open door leading to the connecting dressing room.

She squeezed the box to her chest. "Yes. He told me as much."

"Get along to your own room, Lady Beth. I don't need your help."

"The wound must be properly tended." Elizabeth squared her shoulders and marched across the small room. "And I must say . . ."

Ash was standing in front of the porcelain bowl in his dressing room, wearing nothing except the soft golden glow of lamplight. She froze, as though she had suddenly come upon a wild animal by the side of a stream, staring, her breath trapped in her throat. Never in her life had she so much as glimpsed a man without his shirt.

The lamp over the basin poured golden light over his wide shoulders. With her gaze she followed the rivulet of light as it streamed down the sleek valley of his back and past his waist, where skin kissed by sunlight faded into taut, pale curves set on muscular legs.

Statues sculpted in Italian marble came to mind, those chiseled representations of male perfection she had dismissed as fantasies existing only in an artist's mind. Until now.

He shimmered in the golden light. The living, breathing personification of male power. She stared, every rule of polite society crumbling beneath the stunning sight of him standing there. A tremor started deep inside her, spiraling outward, trembling along her every nerve.

"Lady Beth."

His dark voice snagged her attention. She looked up at the mirror and straight into a pair of startling blue eyes. Eyes the pure blue of a summer sky. Eyes filled with far too much amusement. He knew she had been staring.

She pivoted, squeezing her box of remedies to her chest. There was no remedy for the embarrassment heating her cheeks. No cure for the terrible excitement he ignited inside her. No medicine to wash away the memory of him standing bathed in nothing more than lamplight.

"Mr. MacGregor, why didn't you tell me you were . . . you were, ah, not properly prepared to receive me?"

"As I recall, I told you to get along."

Elizabeth stiffened at the note of humor in his voice. "As I recall, I told you I would tend your wound."

Cloth rippled in the air behind her. It sounded like the soft flutter of a heavy cotton towel tumbling free of its folds. "I don't need help."

"You are a very stubborn man."

He released his breath in a long sigh. "I'd say we're about even on that score."

She marched to the bureau near the door. "I'm not stubborn," she said, setting her box on the smooth walnut top.

"And bulls don't have balls."

She gasped. She started to turn around to give him an icy glare but stopped herself, realizing she had already seen more of him than was proper or wise. "Mr. MacGregor, really. You mustn't go about using such profanity."

"I'll try to remember that." He drew in his breath, the shivering sound of a man who is weary to the bone. "Now, you get back to your room. I'll take care of this little scratch. I don't need . . ." His words evaporated in a sharp intake of air.

She wanted to run to him, but she hesitated, torn between concern for him and her own modesty. The brass lamp on the wall above the bureau cast her image against the smooth polished top of the bureau. She stared down at her frowning reflection, waiting for him to continue. "Mr. MacGregor?"

He hesitated a moment before he spoke. "Come to think of it, I . . . just might need . . ." He moaned, deep in his throat.

Chapter Thirteen

Elizabeth pivoted, her hair swirling around her shoulders. Ash was holding the frame of the door, his knuckles bleached as white as the towel he wore wrapped around his slim hips.

"Beth," he whispered, his knees dissolving beneath him.

"Oh, my!" Elizabeth lunged for him, throwing her arms around his lean waist as he sank to the floor. "Hold on to me." He wrapped his arms around her shoulders, leaning into her. "That's it."

He rested his brow against her head. "I'm . . . dizzy."

"I've got you. I won't let you fall." She struggled to steady him, staggering with him toward the bed. She clutched at his waist, her fingers brushing soft terry cloth. The towel slipped away beneath her nervous fingers, brushing her gown as it tumbled to the floor. She stared at the bed, refusing to acknowledge the fact that this man was naked against her. "That's it; let me lead. Oh, I'm sorry," she murmured as he bumped into the bureau.

He groaned deep in his throat.

"You're doing fine. Just a few more steps." She hit the side of the bed. "Easy. You're almost . . . oh, my. Careful!"

He pitched forward, taking her with him as he fell across the bed, his arms around her shoulders, hers still cinched around his waist. Elizabeth gasped as the solid weight of him fell across her. Blue velvet embraced her, goose down plumped around her, molding a soft nest for the man lying as naked as a newborn babe in her arms.

He lay still, his cheek against her hair, his lips near her neck, each soft breath a warm mist against her skin. The heat of his skin soaked through the burgundy silk of her gown and the soft white linen beneath, drenching her in his warmth. Her skin tingled. The beat of her heart flickered in the tips of her breasts, pulsing against the hard thrust of his chest.

For a moment the world outside this cocoon of male flesh and soft bedding disappeared. Slowly, as though she were easing her way through a darkened room, her senses absorbed the feel of him—naked skin a flame against silk, each place he touched her coming alive. His scent filled her every breath, that intriguing blend of rich leather and crisp lemon intoxicating her senses. The softness of his hair caressed her cheek, tempting her to turn her face into his silky mane.

She spread her fingers wide against his back, exploring the texture of his skin, the strength of the powerful muscles beneath. In dreams she had allowed herself the wicked pleasure of imagining a moment like this, when the most fascinating man in the world held her in his arms. In her dreams the man had always been Peyton. Only Peyton. A man who had been no more than a phantom. Until now.

He stirred, a soft moan escaping his lips as he lifted himself away from her, rising up on his elbow. "Did I hurt you?"

Elizabeth stared up into his eyes, trying to find enough breath to form a single word. But she couldn't. It was as though she were drowning. Perhaps she was. Drowning in the heat of sensation, sinking into a realm of emotion she had only glimpsed with this man. She stared into his eyes, watching as the fog of pain burned away beneath awakening flames in the startling blue depths, wondering if he would kiss her again.

Kiss me. She trembled with the danger of her thought, and the possibility her wish might be granted.

He touched her cheek, his long fingers trailing heat across her skin, smoothing the hair back from her face, caressing her neck just below her ear. His lashes tangled at the corners as he lowered his eyes. He studied her lips, his own parting on a soft exhalation of breath that touched her lips in a moist caress.

For a moment that stretched into eternity she lay perfectly still beneath him as the excitement expanded within her, tingling through her every vessel in a thrilling wave of pleasure. She waited, breathless, expectant, afraid any movement might shatter the spell spinning delicate threads around them.

He frowned, his hand curling into a fist above her shoulder. "You shouldn't be here."

No. She shouldn't be within a mile of this man. Not if she wanted to protect her heart. Not to mention her chastity. "If I hadn't come to help, you would have fallen flat on your face."

He smiled, a slow curving of finely molded lips that made her want to touch him, to capture that devilish grin beneath her fingertips. "Seems you got a point. Guess I should be grateful you're so stubborn."

Elizabeth pursed her lips. "I'm not stubborn."

"So I hear." He shifted above her, grimacing as he pressed his hand to his side.

"Are you bleeding again?"

"Yeah." He looked down at her gown, her skin growing warm beneath his lingering gaze. "I'm afraid I've ruined that pretty dress of yours."

"Don't give the gown another thought." She rested her hand on his shoulder. "Let me up. I need to see how badly you're wounded."

He hesitated, a frown tugging at his brow. "In case you haven't noticed, seems I lost my towel."

She had noticed.

"I ain't wearing anything."

"You *aren't* wearing anything."

"Yeah. So unless you want to expand your education even more tonight, you best close your eyes till I can pull this cover over me."

Heat prickled her cheeks as she acknowledged the blatant impropriety of their situation. "Of course."

She closed her eyes, resisting the wicked impulse to peek as he pulled away from her. The counterpane shifted beneath her as he tugged it from the foot of the bed; a moment later he informed her that it was all right to open her eyes. She sat up, looking at the man sitting beside her on the bed, dark blue velvet tossed over his lap, long legs poking out beneath the cloth. And above that strip of blue velvet . . .

Dark curls shaded his chest, spreading like an open fan across thick muscles, tapering to a narrow trail leading straight down into dark blue velvet. Something tightened low in her belly as she stared at him and imagined touching him, brushing her hand over those dark, starkly masculine curls.

"Lady Beth?"

Elizabeth flinched at the sound of his deep voice, like a sleepwalker coming awake with a start. "What?"

He lifted one dark brow, his eyes filling with a far-too-knowing light. "I thought you came here to tend to this," he said, lifting his hand away from the ragged wound in his side.

She cringed, realizing she had once again put her fascination with this man above his needs. "Of course."

She hurried across the compartment, retrieving his towel from the floor near the bureau before continuing to the dressing room. *Stay calm.* She must collect her wits, she thought, as she dragged a hand towel from the rack near the basin. She dampened the towel. Mr. MacGregor needed her help. This certainly wasn't the time to start acting like a fluttery spinster who had never been in the presence of a man. Even if the man happened to be as naked as Adam and as fascinating as forbidden fruit. Even if he set her pulse racing. Even if he was the one man she had waited a lifetime to meet.

She tossed the wet towel over her arm, along with the dry one he had once worn. She was not a child, she reminded herself as she gathered her box of medicinal supplies. Men had courted her in the past.

Dashing young men. Sophisticated. Worldly.

She turned to face MacGregor, her heart doing an odd tumble at the sight of him sitting there sheathed in a scrap of blue velvet. Strange; not one of those other men had ever added a single beat to her pulse.

"You can just leave the bandages," he said as she approached him. "I can take of it."

"Perhaps you can." She set the box on the counterpane beside him, along with the towels. "But, since I'm here, there is no need for you to do so."

He cocked one dark brow, looking at her as though he intended to argue.

"Don't be stubborn about this, Mr. MacGregor." She lifted the damp towel, hoping he wouldn't notice how her hand trembled. "Now, please remove your hand so I may cleanse the wound."

He shook his head, a smile curving his lips, as though he was surprised by her, and somehow amused. "Suit yourself." He lifted his hand, revealing the ugly red gash across his left side.

She stared at the wound, realizing how close the intruder had come to ending his life. A little to the left and the bullet would have entered his heart. In an instant he could have been taken away forever.

"You're looking a little pale. You aren't gonna faint, are you?"

Her back stiffened. "I assure you, I have never fainted in my life."

"That's real nice. Let's just hope you ain't gonna start now."

"*Aren't going* to start." Elizabeth drew in her breath. "And I assure you, I certainly will not."

He grinned. "If you say so."

Elizabeth set her jaw. Oh, the man was infuriating. If he thought she was some weak-kneed little ninny, she would simply have to prove him wrong. She swabbed the blood from his side, fighting to focus on the task before her, and not the fascinating sight of his wide, bare chest. Yet that intriguing landscape of smooth skin and dark male curls remained right there in the periphery, teasing her, tempting her to explore this fascinating territory.

She handed him the towel. "You might wish to cleanse your hand," she said, trying to keep her voice cool and efficient, in spite of the fact that she couldn't pull enough breath into her lungs.

"Thanks."

His deep voice brushed over her like warm, dark velvet. Her skin tingled in reply. What was it about this man that intrigued her like no other? She wasn't the type of woman to melt at the sight of a handsome face and a splendid body. At least she had never imagined she was. Until now.

He was not at all the type of man she had imagined Peyton would be, she thought, presenting an argument for her wayward emotions. He possessed none of the qualities she admired in a man.

She moistened a wad of cotton with alcohol. He was rude. Arrogant. Heartless. A mercenary only interested in money. Still, the mere thought of him made her pulse race, her skin tingle, her thoughts wander in directions no lady should ever tread. Why in the world did the man fascinate her as no man had ever done? Oh, the man was absolutely despicable. She pressed the cotton against the raw wound.

He sucked in his breath, his muscles tensing as the alcohol flooded his open wound.

Elizabeth cringed. "I suppose I should have warned you this would sting a bit."

"Yeah." He settled back against the bed. "Burns like whiskey in an open wound."

She glanced up at him, noticing the scar slashing a thin white path diagonally from one broad shoulder to the center of his chest. And there were other scars, faint traces of violence etched upon his body. Mementos of life lived in a savage land. "It would seem you have had more than one opportunity to experience the sting of alcohol in an open wound."

He shrugged. "A few scrapes here and there. Nothing much."

How could anyone dismiss such injuries so easily? She smoothed an herbal ointment over the gash, then pressed a pad of white linen against the wound. "Hold this in place, please."

He slipped his hand over the pad, his fingers brushing the back of her hand. The brief caress sent shivers tingling across her skin. She turned away from him, appalled at the shaking of her hands as she lifted a roll of linen bandage from the box.

"I never thought ladies went in much for patching up gunshots."

"I doubt many ladies have had the opportunity to do so." She slipped one end of the bandage over the pad beside his fingers, careful not to touch his hand. "Hold this, please."

He complied, shifting his fingers to grip the pad and the bandage. "So how is it you know all about taking care of them?"

"Fortunately, I know very little about gunshots." She drew the bandage over his chest, trying not to touch him any more than necessary. Yet it was impossible to ignore the warmth of his skin radiating against her fingers, the silky slide of those starkly masculine curls as she smoothed the bandage across his chest, the slow shift of thick muscles beneath smooth golden skin as he lifted his right arm to allow her to draw the bandage around his back.

She slipped her arm around him, smoothing the bandage across his back, her cheek a whisper from his neck. The exotic scent of him drifted with the heat of his skin, rising, bathing her face. She caught herself leaning closer, breathing deeper. All the while she was aware of him watching her, his lips tipped into a devilish grin, as though he knew exactly how her pulse was racing from simply being near him.

She really had to get a tight rein on her runaway emotions before she made a complete fool of herself with this man. Again.

"So, you don't know much about gunshots. But I doubt many fancy ladies know how to bandage a wound like you're doing right now."

"When I was a little girl I had the idea I might one day become a doctor." She pressed the end of the bandage to the center of his chest. "Hold this."

He did as she asked and more, sliding his hand over hers, holding her hand imprisoned between his warm palm and hard chest. All the moisture evaporated from her mouth. "So why didn't you become a doctor?"

Mischief sparkled in his eyes. The man knew exactly what he did to her, and he was teasing her. She eased her hand from beneath his, determined to regain some measure of her dignity. "I grew up, Mr. MacGregor. And I realized there are certain paths not open to everyone."

Ash frowned. "There's a lady doctor in Colorado

Springs. She came all the way from Boston. Real good doctor, too.''

She wrapped a piece of linen around his chest as she spoke. ''I suppose you had an opportunity to witness her abilities personally?''

''Yeah. She patched me up after one of the Strickland boys slashed me with a knife.''

The image of a knife slicing his smooth skin did something to her insides, set them shaking like leaves in a summer storm. When she thought of how blithely he had put his life at risk time and time again she wanted to scream. She tied the bandage, tugging on the linen harder than she had intended, dragging a soft moan from his lips. ''I'm sorry. I wanted to make certain it would stay in place.''

He grinned. ''You did a real fine job.''

She glanced away from him, busying herself with putting away the supplies. She had to get out of here, away from this man and the disturbing emotions he evoked within her. ''We should stop at the next town and have a doctor look at it.''

''No need. It's a scratch.''

''How can you say that?'' She turned to face him, appalled at the trembling that shook her entire body. ''You could have been killed tonight. And you act as though nothing at all happened.''

''In my line of work, a man gets used to it.''

''Why do you do it? Why do you go about chasing after criminals, risking your life for a few dollars?''

All the humor drained from his face as he held her look. A hard glitter replaced the teasing gleam in his eyes. ''I guess it's hard for someone from your world to understand. But a man like me doesn't have a lot of choices.''

''You could have taken work in a store.''

Ash laughed, a harsh, cynical sound that mocked her and everything in her world. ''I'm not the type to be caged in a store all day long, even if there was some store owner who would hire a half-breed gunslinger. There isn't.''

''There must have been some other alternative.''

''Yeah.'' He grinned, a chilling imitation of a smile that at times could be warmer than summer. ''I'm gonna take that money old man Trevelyan is paying me for this little masquerade and buy a prime piece of land just outside Stockton. Make a respectable living raising horses.''

She closed the lid of the box of medicinal supplies, fighting the urge to scream at him for his stubbornness. ''I don't understand you. Marlow is willing to give you the world and you turn your back on him.''

His lips drew into a tight line as he held her angry stare. ''No one is going to cage me.''

''No one is trying to cage you.''

''Like hell. You and Trevelyan want to turn me into something I *ain't*. You want to wrap me up in fancy clothes and fancy talk and parade me around like some trained puppy. Well, I'm going to play your game. For six months. Then I'm leaving, to live my life the way I want to live it.''

Elizabeth lifted the box, holding it against her chest, wishing it could shield her from the reality of this man and his callousness. ''Marlow has waited a lifetime for your return. Pity you aren't half the man he deserves as a grandson.''

Ash held her icy stare, seemingly relaxed, unconcerned with her insult. Yet there was an expression in his eyes, something more than simple anger, something that cut deeper and burned hotter. ''Seems you figured this Peyton for a real saint.''

''I expected him to have certain qualities you lack. Such as integrity and loyalty.''

''Guess I was a real disappointment to you.''

Elizabeth squeezed the medicine chest against her,

fighting the simple truth she couldn't deny. The only thing that disappointed her about this man was his stubborn refusal to accept his proper position in life. "My feelings on the matter are insignificant. I'm concerned only for Marlow."

"Is that so?"

"Of course."

"You mean you never wondered about this Peyton? You didn't have him all built up in your mind? Like some knight in shining armour."

She wanted to turn and run from this man and the truth he shouldn't know, yet somehow had discovered. "You're being quite ridiculous."

"Am I?"

"You certainly are."

He tilted his head, studying her, as though he could evaluate the expression in her eyes, the cast of her features, the tension in her muscles; as though each breath she took betrayed her thoughts. The seconds stretched between them, the silence filling up with the steady clack of steel wheels against the rails, the steady beat a distant echo of the blood pounding in her ears.

She should leave. Turn. Run. Hide. This man was far too perceptive, like a lion trained to seek the weakness of his prey. Her life experiences did not prepare her for him and the piercing scrutiny of his stunning eyes. Yet how could she leave without looking every bit as threatened as she felt?

"Tell me, Lady Beth. Why is it you never married? Were you waiting for Marlow's perfect grandson to come marching home?"

"Why I never married is none of your concern."

He smiled, one corner of his lips tipping upward in an arrogant grin. "Don't fret, Lady Beth; the real Peyton might be everything you hoped he'd be, instead of a no-account bounty hunter. Maybe one day you'll even get a chance to meet him.''

''I have met him. And he is a heartless rogue who cares only about himself.''

''If you're so sure I'm Peyton, why do you keep calling me Mr. MacGregor?''

''I have no doubt you are Peyton Trevelyan. And if you ever truly manage to live up to the integrity of that name, I shall be happy to address you properly.''

''Guess we're all lucky I won't be staying around long enough to disappoint you.''

She hugged the medicine chest against her, appalled by the tears welling in her eyes. It was all so terribly unfair. This man could be everything Marlow had ever wanted in a grandson; she was certain of it. Just as she was certain he could be the Peyton she had dreamed of. If he only tried. If he would only open his heart. ''One day I hope you come to realize how very precious family can be. I only hope it isn't too late.''

She turned and left him, before she humiliated herself by a display of weakness, retreating to the safety of her compartment. Yet there was no sanctuary against the emotions he stirred inside her. She sank to the bed, trembling with a frustration that came from wishing for things beyond her reach.

Ash closed his eyes. He listened to the rhythm of the wheels clacking against the rails. The soft swaying of the car should have been a cradle rocking him to sleep. Yet sleep was as elusive as peace of mind.

Moonlight and shadows cast by the telegraph poles planted beside the tracks cast a flickering pattern against the swirls of gold in the blue carpet covering the floor of his compartment. His sleepless state had little to do with the throbbing heat of the wound in his side. Elizabeth's words had stung far worse than the bullet that had seared his flesh.

The woman didn't know him. Yet she judged him, found him guilty of not living up to her lofty expectations. He didn't need her preaching to tell him how precious family was. He knew. And he knew how it cut deep inside when you lost someone you loved. It left a wound that never really healed, just stayed ragged and raw and aching.

She expected him to open himself up to that kind of pain again. She expected him to trust that crazy old man. She expected him to become something he wasn't, a fine English gentleman. A man who could saunter around her world and take what he wanted. And he wasn't about to try to fool himself. He wanted the lady.

He wanted her arms around him. He wanted to bury his face in all that silky, lavender-scented hair. Kiss her neck, her shoulder, her breasts. Discover the shape and feel and taste of every luscious inch of her. He imagined the feel of her long legs around his waist. His blood stirred at the erotic images coming to life in his mind. Blood surged low in his belly, awakening flesh hungry for the taste of her.

Damn fool!

He wasn't going to turn his life upside down to suit her. Even if she did feel like heaven in his arms. Even if she did turn his blood to fire with that intriguing blend of wide-eyed innocence and drowsy desire. Even if he did crave the sight of the affection he had glimpsed in her huge gray eyes. Affection for the man she wanted him to become, not the man he was.

To hell with her.

He didn't need her. He didn't need the old man and the counterfeit life he held out like a carrot to a hungry mule. He had a life of his own. A life no one could steal from him if they decided he wasn't exactly what they thought he should be. A life where he didn't have to watch his every word, his every move, his every thought. A life where a man could live with the freedom to be who he was.

Six months.

He could play their little game for six months, and then it was good-bye.

Chapter Fourteen

The last ten days had been the longest of her life. Elizabeth had spent every morning, afternoon, and most of each evening spouting rules, correcting grammar, teaching proper diction. All the while fighting to remain calm, detached, uninvolved with a man who could upset her composure with a grin.

She shifted on her chair, peeking over the edge of the novel she was reading to where Hayward and MacGregor were playing chess near the French doors leading to the upper deck of Hayward's private yacht. Since the second night of their journey, this chess match had become a nightly ritual for the two men. Hayward had taught his grandson the fundamentals of chess when Peyton was four. Elizabeth wondered if he now regretted repeating that lesson for MacGregor. The student was quickly outpacing the teacher.

In spite of her resolve to hold the man in utter contempt, she couldn't help but admire MacGregor. The man had a keen intellect. He absorbed all the rules she poured over him like a sponge sucking up water. He devoured the books in their floating library, like a starving man at a banquet. His knowledge of history and the classics expanded daily. *Ain't* had all but faded from his vocabulary. His diction became more precise with each passing day. He was becoming transformed before her eyes. Yet she knew it was merely the surface of the man. Beneath, he remained adamant in his belief that he didn't belong in England.

MacGregor faced the open French doors that looked out over the rolling waves of the Atlantic, his long legs stretched and crossed at the ankles, lounging as though he were on holiday in the country. Hayward, on the other hand, sat with one arm flat against the table, his right elbow planted near the few prisoners he had captured, rubbing his right eyebrow. He stared at the board as though the fate of his business empire rested on his next move.

Except for the fact that he had removed his coat and tie soon after dinner, a practice she still could not curtail, Mr. MacGregor looked very much a gentleman. His stark black trousers and shirts had been replaced by the elegant clothes that had been waiting for him in New York.

Elizabeth stared at MacGregor over the edge of her book, wishing she could put him out of her thoughts. She couldn't, of course. How could she, when even a glimpse of the man stole her breath away? Her infatuation had escalated into a debilitating disease. Yet it was obvious MacGregor was not plagued with the same malady.

Since that first night on the train he hadn't touched her. In fact, except for the necessary dialogue they maintained during their lessons, he ignored her. Elizabeth glanced away from him, appalled at the sting of tears in her eyes. It was silly, really, this horrible feeling of rejection. What did it matter if one infuriating man ignored her? She certainly wasn't going to dissolve into tears. He would find her dreadful display of hurt feelings much too amusing.

"Let's see you maneuver your way out of this, young man," Hayward said, leaning back in his chair.

MacGregor tilted his head, eyeing the chessboard for a moment before slipping his long fingers around his white queen. He slid the porcelain lady across the board. "Checkmate."

"Checkmate?" Hayward sat on the edge of his chair, staring at the board. He shook his head, a smile curving his lips. "Well done, my lad. Well done."

Ash glanced down at the board, his lips tipping into a smile. He actually looked pleased, as though he found pleasure in more than simply winning the match. Elizabeth stared at him, transfixed by the warmth unveiled by his smile.

"I do believe you could give Elizabeth a run for it. And she is a marvelous chess player." Hayward glanced toward her. "Why don't you come over here and give Peyton a real challenge?"

Elizabeth looked at Hayward over the edge of her book, the leather-bound volume trembling softly with the sudden rush of blood through her veins. She glanced at the man sitting across from her guardian. MacGregor was staring at her, his beautiful eyes narrowed, the fullness of his lips pressed into a tight line. It was obvious the last thing he wanted was to play chess with her, or any other game for that matter. Her chest tightened with the sad realization that the man who haunted her dreams found her utterly detestable.

"Come, my girl." Hayward stood and offered her his chair. "Show my grandson what it's like to face a gifted opponent."

MacGregor had the unfortunate ability to turn her brain to jelly. She doubted she could manage much of a match, even if the man looked willing to accept her as an opponent, which he didn't. "It's getting late. Perhaps another time."

"Late?" Hayward glanced at the grandfather clock standing against the wall near the spiral staircase leading to the dining room. "But it's not yet half past nine."

MacGregor lifted his queen from the board and stared down at the delicate porcelain. "Perhaps the lady is afraid of the challenge."

Elizabeth bristled at his words. If he thought she was a frightened little mouse, she would show him just how mistaken he was. She took the chair Hayward offered and tried to summon her scattered wits.

"I think I'll take a stroll around the deck. It's a nice evening." Hayward patted Elizabeth's shoulder. "Be merciless, my girl."

She glanced across the battlefield to her opponent, wishing her guardian didn't have the unfortunate habit of leaving her alone with the rogue. It wasn't that she was frightened of him; MacGregor had too much pride to try to force a woman into anything. Even if he wanted that woman, which in this case he didn't. It was simply that she felt so exposed when she was with him, as though he could look straight into her eyes and penetrate her every secret.

He rolled his queen between his thumb and forefinger, frowning as he looked across the board at her. "If you don't want to play, it's all right with me."

Elizabeth forced her lips into a smile she hoped looked less wooden than it felt. "I enjoy chess. Particularly with a challenging opponent."

He shrugged and began returning the pieces he had captured from Hayward. "We'll see how much of a challenge it is."

She couldn't be certain whether he meant his play or her own. She was only certain she wanted to win. She searched through the mush that her brain had became, trying to recall the fundamentals of a game she had been playing since she was five. In the first few moves, it became obvious, MacGregor did not have the same trouble concentrating that she did. Within half an hour he had her in check. Fifteen minutes later he had her kingdom. And, through it all, not a word passed between them.

She sat back in her chair, feeling edgy and stupid. She hadn't even been a challenge. He must think her a complete imbecile. Oh, she wanted to scream. "You play very well."

He shrugged. "Barbarians have always been pretty good at war."

She looked across the battlefield straight into his eyes. The ice in the blue depths made her shiver. Even though she had promised Hayward she would handle Mac-Gregor's tutoring, she wasn't at all certain she could continue this way. "Mr. MacGregor, we must talk."

He lifted one dark brow. "Must we?"

"Yes, we must." She clasped her hands in her lap to keep them from shaking. A cool breeze drifted through the open doors behind her. The salty air left a tang on her tongue as she drew in a fortifying breath. "I realize you haven't been satisfied with this arrangement from the beginning. I'm certain, if we discuss the situation with Marlow, he would understand and find another tutor for you."

Light from the brass-and-crystal chandelier above the table slipped golden fingers into his thick brown hair. The soft waves curled over the collar of his white linen shirt, coaxing wayward thoughts of smooth dark waves sliding through her fingers. "What's the matter, Lady Beth? Aren't you up to the challenge of turning a gunfighter into a gentleman?"

Was she? The man radiated power. He was like a flame, dominating the space around him, consuming all the air, until she couldn't breathe. She was definitely out of her element with him. "I doubt anyone could force you to become anything you didn't wish to become, Mr. MacGregor."

He nodded. "Guess that's true enough."

Simply being near him made her aware of things she usually never considered—the brush of her clothes against skin that tingled with excitement, the pulse of her blood fluttering in the tips of her breasts. Oh yes, she was definitely at a disadvantage with him. "I realize you don't have any desire to learn the proper behavior of an English gentleman.''

"Fancy ways don't make a man.''

"No. But proper manners are part of what keeps us separated from the beasts.''

His eyes narrowed as he stared at her. "Are you saying I'm no better than an animal?''

Oh dear, this wasn't going well. There was something about Ash MacGregor that stole all her composure. "I didn't mean to imply that you were a beast. Although at times your demeanor does put me in mind of a few creatures I've seen at the zoo.''

"Is that so?''

"Yes. One that comes to mind has a particularly nasty set of tusks protruding from his snout.''

"Look, lady, I never promised I'd enjoy your damn lessons.''

She lifted her chin. "You needn't swear.''

He leaned back in his chair, his blue eyes narrowed into an icy glare. "I never figured you were the type to quit something before it was done.''

"I never said I was quitting. I simply thought you might be more comfortable with someone else.''

"I doubt it. I've grown accustomed to your bossy ways. And I'm not real interested in getting used to someone else.''

"I seriously doubt we could find a tutor with enough courage to put up with your ferocious temper.''

He rested his arms against the table and leaned toward her. "I don't ever seem to frighten you.''

He was wrong; he frightened her more than she cared to admit. The heat curling upward inside her each time she was near him frightened her. The longing for him she couldn't suppress terrified her. "No, you don't frighten me at all.''

He searched her eyes as though looking for the truth

she was trying desperately to hide. "I guess that settles it. We're stuck with each other for the next six months."

Stuck with each other. Not exactly what she had hoped to hear. "So it seems."

MacGregor stood and eased his broad shoulders into a lazy roll that stretched the white linen of his shirt across his chest. "If you will excuse me, I want to look in on the horses before retiring."

He left without another glance at her, though she couldn't take her eyes from his departing figure. She watched as he strode through the open French doors, staring until he disappeared into the shadows, a solid chunk of regret pressing like a boulder against her heart. She was still staring into the moonlight when Hayward returned a few minutes later.

"Where is Peyton?" Hayward asked as he advanced toward her.

"He went to look in on the horses."

He paused beside her, studying the chessboard before he spoke. "It looks as though he got the better of you, my girl."

She stared at her few remaining soldiers, acknowledging the fact that MacGregor had been getting the better of her since the day she had met him. "He's very good."

"He's really quite remarkable, isn't he?" Hayward rocked back on his heels, grinning at her. "That rough-edged young man we met is all but gone. In a few more weeks, with just a little more polish, the lad will be able to step into society without causing a single raised eyebrow."

"He appears to have adapted beautifully."

"But you don't think he really has."

Elizabeth glanced up, meeting his perceptive gaze. "I think he's doing what he needs to fulfill his obligation for the next six months."

Hayward studied her for a moment, choosing his words

carefully before he spoke. "The air has a definite sting of electricity when the two of you are near. I get the impression you and Peyton have quarreled over something. It wouldn't, perhaps, be your fierce desire to protect me from being hurt, would it?"

Elizabeth folded her hands on her lap. "I must admit, I find his complete disregard for family quite vexing. You must know, I'm still not at all convinced he will choose to stay in England."

Hayward wiggled his eyebrows. "I intend to make certain he finds more reasons to stay than he does to leave."

The look in Hayward's eyes made her uncomfortable. She suspected he expected her to help convince MacGregor to stay, when she hadn't the least amount of influence with him. "He has lived his life as wild and untamed as a hawk. I'm afraid he will see our world as nothing more than a well-appointed cage."

"A cage?" Hayward frowned as he considered her words. "A cage. What nonsense. I can go where I choose, when I choose, with whom I choose. I have the means to live as I please. That young man doesn't realize what true freedom is. But I shall teach him."

Elizabeth smiled in light of his optimism, even though she found that commodity in short supply. "Perhaps."

"I shall make certain he learns all the very best a life of privilege has to offer. I shall make certain that young man makes his home at Chatswyck."

Elizabeth watched him leave, his step as light as a young boy's. She only wished she could protect him from the fall she suspected would come. But there was no protection for a heart given without reserve. She knew that. Her own defenses were threatened by that heartless rogue. Oh, sometimes she truly wished she had never glimpsed Ash MacGregor.

* * *

"I'll say one thing for Marlow; he knows how to travel."
Ash rubbed his hand along his horse's smooth neck,
glancing around the stable area. Wind Dancer shared the
floating stable with six other horses. A coach and a carriage were stored at one end of the stable area, near the
cabins set aside for Hayward's grooms. Both vehicles
were shiny black and a fancy crest was painted on the
doors of the coach. Apparently the duke liked to travel in
style, with his own horses, his own carriage, his own servants. "I don't guess he ever goes anywhere the way normal folks do."

Wind Dancer tossed his head, his long silvery mane
ruffling in the breeze drifting through the porthole behind
Ash. He nickered softly, bumping Ash's shoulder.

"Been caged up too long, haven't you, boy. You need
to stretch your legs. Feel the wind in your face. Well, so
do I." Ash pulled a carrot from his pocket and offered it
to the animal. He smiled as Wind Dancer nuzzled his
palm, a brush of velvet against his skin as the animal took
the treat. The musky scent of hay and straw and horses
filled his every breath. It was a comforting, something that
hadn't changed, even in this strange new world. "I feel
like I'm all wrapped up in chains. Every time I open my
mouth I have to think about what I'm saying and how
I'm saying it. I'll be glad when this is all over and we
can get our lives back to normal." Still, he wondered if
he could ever really go back to his old life again.

The door leading to the deck opened. Ash turned, his
muscles tensing in a moment of expectancy before Hayward stepped from the shadows into the glow of light
flowing from the three brass lamps suspended from the
beamed ceiling. Disappointment flickered inside of him,
coupled with a sudden surge of anger at his own weakness. Had he actually expected Beth to come walking
through that door? And if she had, what then? A tumble
in the hay? A furious ride between her soft white thighs?

Would that get the lady out of his thoughts, and the hell out of his dreams?

Ash rubbed the back of his neck, trying to ease his taut muscles. The woman had him as tight as a stretched bow-string. Every day pulled his nerves a little tighter. Each time she touched him—a brush of her arm against his, a graze of her skirts against his legs—desire poked a sharp stick at him. He was as randy as a stallion around a mare in season. And he hated his own stupidity for allowing the skinny little spinster to torture him this way.

"That's a fine-looking animal," Hayward said as he drew near.

Wind Dancer nickered, tossing his head as though he understood the words. Hayward rested his arms on the stall door, smiling as he studied the stallion. "Part Arabian?"

"His sire. I got him from a rancher near Durango. A few years back he brought a stud and half a dozen Arabian mares from Virginia." Ash slid a currycomb over the stallion's back. Not because the horse needed tending; he had no complaint with the way the grooms looked after the animals. But he needed some physical release for the tension inside him. "Aside from taking care of those fine Arabian ladies, he let that stud have his way with a pack of mustang mares. One of them was Wind Dancer's mama."

"I notice you didn't have him cut. Are you planning to use him for stud? Or do you simply enjoy the challenge of sitting atop a spirited mount?"

Ash grinned. "Both."

Hayward nodded, pride glowing in his dark blue eyes. Ash glanced away, uneasy with the warmth of affection he sensed radiating from the man. The affection wasn't his to claim. Or was it? For the past few days Ash's memory had been playing tricks with his head. Little things, like lifting a chess piece, triggered odd feelings of familiarity inside him. There were moments when he heard the old man's voice and was certain he remembered it from somewhere deep in his memory. At times he felt as though he was moving through a half-remembered dream.

"I would wager Julianna has a mare or two she would like to breed with this fine stallion when she sees him."

Ash glanced back at the old man. "Julianna?"

"Elizabeth's mother. She has a stable full of prize Arabians."

"I thought Lady Elizabeth's parents were dead."

"Her father died when she was a child of ten." He studied Ash, as though he was deciding the strategy of his next move in chess. "I had supposed she told you."

"She didn't. But then, the lady and I aren't exactly what you might call friends."

"Yes. I've noticed there's a bit of a chill in the air when the two of you are in the same room."

Ash only wished his blood would chill when he was near her. He stroked the currycomb along Wind Dancer's back, keeping his face turned away from the old man, concerned he might betray his conflicted emotions in an unguarded expression. Truth was, the lady had him all tied up in knots. One minute he was cursing the day he had first set eyes on her. The next he was thinking of ways to get her into his bed. "How is it you're her guardian if her mother is still alive?"

"Julianna is . . ." Hayward paused. "I'm afraid Julianna wasn't quite up to the task of continuing to care for Elizabeth."

Ash glanced at the old man, seeing the pain he had heard naked in Hayward's voice etched upon his face. "Is she ill?"

"Not in the way you might think." Hayward was quiet, staring past Ash to the darkness of the porthole, as though he was staring back over the years. "Julianna and Elizabeth came to live with us after Elizabeth's father and brothers were killed in the fire that destroyed the west wing of their home.''

Ash stared at Wind Dancer's smooth gray back, wanting to know more about the woman who taunted him day and night, yet afraid of the answers he might receive. He needed to keep her at a distance, and that was hard enough to do without knowing all about her.

Tonight it had taken every ounce of his will to keep his hands off her. When she had talked about turning him over to some other tutor he had wanted to grab her shoulders, yank her across the table, and kiss her sweet mouth until he chased every thought out of her pretty head. And that was just the beginning of what he wanted to do. ''How many brothers did she have?''

''Three. The oldest was eight. Alexander, Elizabeth's father, managed to get Julianna, Elizabeth, and his youngest son out of the house. He went back for the other boys.'' Hayward paused, his voice growing softer as he continued. ''He perished with his sons in the blaze. Philip, the youngest boy, died two days later of lung poisoning.''

Ash rested his hand against the warmth of Wind Dancer's withers. He rubbed his fingers into the rough horsehair, thinking of the gentle little girl who had lost nearly everything. It seemed he and Miss Prim and Proper had more in common than he had suspected.

''Both Elizabeth and Julianna had suffered from the smoke. Your grandmother and I were afraid, in the beginning, that their lungs had also been poisoned. It took some time, and a great deal of care, but the physical ailments eventually healed. Still, I'm afraid Julianna suffered wounds no one could mend. She has never been quite the same. You will understand when you meet her.''

''Guess it's been pretty hard on Lady Beth.''

''Yes. I'm afraid the accident stole her youth. She never really played the way little girls should. She was always much more concerned with looking after her mother. I'm afraid she looks after me and the duchess the same way. She is fiercely loyal. She would do anything to see us happy. If she believes anyone might harm us, she gets as angry as a tigress protecting her cubs.''

Ash glanced at the old man, seeing a glint of speculation in his eyes, as though he was evaluating an opponent's every move. He suspected Trevelyan had told him this story for a reason. ''I guess maybe you're hoping the lady and I can become friends.''

Hayward smiled. ''I suppose I thought if you knew a little more about her, you would understand her fierce loyalty to me and see her as less of a scold.''

Thinking of Lady Beth as a scold wasn't the problem; seeing her as one gorgeous temptation was far more to the heart of his problem.

''It would mean a great deal to me if the two of you could become friends,'' Hayward said, his voice low and soft.

Friends. It wasn't exactly what Ash had in mind when he thought of the lady. He ran his fingers over the smooth back of Wind Dancer's currycomb, careful to keep all emotion washed from his face. He wondered what the old man would think if he realized what Ash really wanted to do with little Miss Prim and Proper.

''From the time she was a small girl we would talk about you, and about Emory. I suppose it was my way of keeping both you and your father close to me.'' Hayward released his breath on a long sigh. ''I know it was my fault she became so interested in you, wondering what you would be like if she should ever meet you. I'm afraid she expected you to be a mirror image of Emory.''

Ash squeezed the metal handle of the currycomb. ''Guess I disappointed her.''

''Only in the sense of your reluctance to embrace your family.''

Ash held the old man's steady gaze. "I'm not sure I have a family."

Hayward nodded. "I understand how you feel. I'm asking you to understand how she feels."

"I suppose I can see her point."

"Then you will try to become friends?"

Ash had to admit he wasn't real anxious to continue this war raging between them. They were stuck with each other for the next six months; maybe they could strike a truce. "Guess that's up to the lady."

Chapter Fifteen

Elizabeth stood at the railing on the promenade deck outside her cabin. She stared out across the rolling dark waves, watching the moonlight gather and split against the water, silvery light shaping shimmering mirrors that shattered with the shifting waves. The ocean was far too restless to accept the moon's offering. Too wild. Too free. Untamable. Like the spirit of the man who haunted her every thought.

Strange, she had never in her dreams imagined Peyton would reject life as Lord Angelstone. Many of the men of her acquaintance would have committed any sin imaginable for a chance to wear that title. Wealth. Position. Power. All were within Ash MacGregor's reach. And he found it all sorely lacking. She released her breath in a long sigh, wondering what she could do to help change his mind.

"You look a thousand miles away."

Elizabeth flinched at the sound of that deep voice. She pivoted, her heart pounding at the sight of Ash Mac-Gregor standing a few feet away from her. "You startled me."

He smiled, a generous curve of his lips that made her realize just how much she had missed seeing it. "I seem to make a habit of that."

"Yes, you do." She smoothed her hand over her hair, wondering how much damage the wind had wrecked on her coiffure. She tried to coax a wayward curl back into the roll at her nape as she continued. "I'm not certain I've ever met anyone who could move as quietly as you do."

"Old habits." He walked toward her, each stride filled with the predatory grace she had come to expect from this man, and each footfall against the smooth oak planks as quiet as moonlight.

She braced her back against a thick steel pillar supporting the upper deck as he drew near, needing the solid support for legs that had turned to water. This behavior was ridiculous. She was hardly a naive little girl fresh out of the schoolroom. Still, all the scolding in the world couldn't add starch to her legs.

He rested his hands on the railing near her and stared out across the water, his expression thoughtful, as though he was contemplating the future waiting for him at the end of the journey. She traced the play of moonlight against his face, the pale light carving his features from the darkness, like an artist shaping white marble into sharp angles and curves, all designed to add a beat to a woman's unsuspecting heart.

He glanced at her and caught her staring. His lips tipped upward into a devilish grin. Moonlight revealed the glint of amusement in his eyes. "Marlow tells me we'll reach England sometime tonight."

She looked out across the water, avoiding his knowing look. The man was really the most infuriating creature she had ever met. "By tomorrow afternoon we'll be at Chatswyck."

"Anxious to be home?" he asked.

"Yes. It's always satisfying to come back home. Especially to a place as lovely as Chatswyck." She slanted him a glance. "It's a place most men would be proud to call home. At least if they had any sense."

He cocked one dark brow, his smile sliding into a lopsided grin. "Now, lady Beth, are you trying to say I don't have any sense?"

"I had entertained that thought."

He laughed softly, the dark sound sweeping over her, carried on the breeze. She resisted the urge to smile in return. She really didn't want to encourage him. He already thought she found him utterly fascinating.

"There's no denying you and I see things differently."

The wind tossed the wayward curl across her face. "You have a flair for understatement, Mr. MacGregor," she said, smoothing her hair back from her cheek.

"Still, I was wondering if we might try to be friends."

"Friends?" She turned toward him, wondering what mischief he had in mind. "I didn't think you intended to be around long enough to become friends with anyone."

He shrugged. "Six months."

"Hardly enough time to become friends."

"Would you prefer we remain enemies?"

"We aren't exactly enemies."

He shifted, facing her, resting his hip against the railing. "We step around each other like two cougars, each afraid the other one's going to pounce. What would you call it?"

She frowned. "A disagreement."

He lifted his brows. "It seems we share a flair for understatement."

She glanced back at the water; looking at him was simply too disturbing. To her utter chagrin, she found Ash more attractive each time she saw him.

"Why don't we just admit we're two headstrong people who have different ideas about how a man should live his life."

"That's obvious."

The breeze tugged at her hair, tossing the loose curl across her cheek. She didn't move to restrain it. Her entire attention was focused on the man standing beside her, so close she could feel his warmth reach her across the short space of moonlight shimmering between them.

"We're going to be together for the next six months. Maybe we should try to get along." He touched her cheek, his fingers sliding warmly across her skin as he swept the curl from her face.

She glanced at him, hoping her expression held the proper amount of icy indignation at his improper behavior, in spite of the fact that his touch left her trembling.

He tucked the loose strands behind her ear, immune to her scolding stare. The tips of his fingers lingered against the smooth skin behind her ear, sprinkling shivers across her skin. "Who knows, maybe we'd even find something we have in common."

Elizabeth pressed back against the pillar, escaping his gentle caress. Yet she couldn't escape the longing welling up inside her. She stared up into his eyes, fighting the lure of this man, the attraction that tugged at her in unexpected ways, coaxing her to lean into the heat of him, to slip her arms around him, to hold him until the world crumbled around them.

The breeze stirred his thick, dark mane, tempting her to smooth the silky strands back from his brow. *Tempting her.* The man was forever tempting her, drawing her toward the edge of a precipice.

He lowered his eyes, and for a moment he stared at her mouth. She resisted the urge to moisten her lips, sensing that it would invite his kiss. A kiss she had longed for every night since the day she had met him. A kiss that would lead her ever closer to her own destruction. "I'm certain your idea of friendship and mine are not the same, Mr. MacGregor."

He looked into her eyes, and she imagined she saw a bitter longing in the endless blue depths, a longing that mirrored the need aching deep in her soul. It must be her imagination, she assured herself; he didn't need anyone.

"And what exactly do you think a friend should be?"

Elizabeth lifted her chin, defying him to ridicule her sentiments. "Someone in whom you can confide your deepest secrets. Someone who is there when you need him, to share a laugh, to share a tear. Someone who understands your dreams and hopes they come true. Someone who wishes to share his life with you for more than a few months."

"You expect a great deal from friendship," he said, his deep voice low and soft on the cool breeze.

"Only what I'm willing to give."

He stared out across the water, his thoughts plunging into the dark, rolling waves. Elizabeth stared at his profile, each passing second pulling at her as she waited for a response, hoping for a change in him, fearing there was little chance of ever coaxing this beautiful, wild creature into her nice, tame world.

He drew in his breath, his shoulders rising beneath the white linen of his shirt. He glanced at her, all the longing gone from his eyes and in its place was something hard and determined. "Guess I don't have what you're looking for in a friend, Lady Beth."

Elizabeth held his bleak stare. The man had no right to make her feel so loathsome and selfish simply because she refused his offer of friendship. They couldn't be friends. The emotions he evoked inside her were far too powerful. Far too dangerous. She certainly had no intention of allowing him to play with her affections for a few months, then saunter off without so much as a single glance behind. She refused to become one of those pitiful spinsters who mourned her entire life the love that escaped her. "I suspect you're simply reluctant to give it."

He shrugged, dismissing the matter as though it meant nothing at all to him. "Suit yourself. If you don't want to be friends, there's nothing I can do about it."

Friends. Such an insignificant word in light of what she

had always wanted with this man. It left her feeling hollow in a place that should be filled with more than longing. They couldn't be enemies and neither could they be lovers. That left only the shadows in between, a place where desire yielded to far more tepid emotions. "Of course, I believe we should try to get along."

He tilted his head, looking at her with far too much icy disdain in his eyes. "You mean we should act like polite strangers."

Elizabeth clasped her trembling hands at her waist. "I mean we should try to be cordial. After all, I do intend to continue helping you adjust to your new situation."

He smiled, a cool curving of his lips that failed to touch the icy glitter in his stunning eyes. "Of course. We don't want to hold Marlow and the Trevelyan name up for ridicule."

She saw a glimmer of something in his eyes, a flicker of vulnerability hidden amid the stone walls of his defenses. He was a man walking into a world he didn't understand, a place where all the rules were different, where people were waiting to judge his every move, his every gesture, his every word. Was he frightened? Did he need some reassurance that he wasn't alone? "You're making tremendous progress."

"I don't have much choice, do I?"

She wanted to touch him, to slip her arms around him and hold him. But she had to keep her distance. It wasn't at all proper for a lady to throw herself at a gentleman. Especially if that gentleman wasn't a gentleman at all, but a man who would laugh at her silly infatuation with him. "Is it all so very distasteful? Being here, with Marlow." *With me.*

He was quiet for a moment, staring at the waves, the muscles in his cheek taut with the clenching of his jaw. "Every time I open my mouth I wonder if I'm going to say the right thing, say it the right way."

"It's only because everything is so new. And there is so much to think about. But you're going to be just fine. You've already managed to smooth most of your rough edges. Your ability to absorb all the details I've been throwing at you amazes me at times. You really have a keen intellect, when you aren't being stubborn."

He glanced at her, his eyes narrowed with suspicion. "Careful, Lady Beth, that sounded almost like a compliment."

She sensed that he needed a few compliments. He needed someone to assure him that he wasn't walking into a vipers' nest. "Yes, sometimes I rather shock myself with my own observations. For example, it's been quite some time since I formed the odd opinion you could actually manage anything your stubborn nature decided to accomplish."

He turned toward her, and for a moment her words actually seemed to have dented his armor. But the uncertainty in his eyes lasted only a moment before the hard mask of indifference once again slid into place. "Save your charity. I don't need my hand patted. I'm not a scared little kid."

She stared up into his beautiful eyes, wondering if there was any way to reach beyond the anger and bitterness she saw in the startling blue depths. "Apparently you don't need anyone."

"That's right. I've done just fine on my own."

"And that is precisely why we can't be friends. You see, friends need each other."

He nodded. "You don't want to be friends, that's fine with me."

Elizabeth pushed aside the hurt his words inflicted on her feelings. She sensed the fear behind the words, the reluctance to trust another human being with anything as precious as his own affection. "I hope you give yourself a chance. I hope you take it into your stubborn head to try to find your way back home.''

"I realize how much you want Peyton Trevelyan to come home. But I think you should know, even if by some twist of fate I turn out to be this guy, I doubt I'd ever feel at home in this fancy world of yours.''

"I'm not certain you even understand what it truly means to have a home.''

He looked away from her, barring her from looking into his eyes, from seeing the hurt she sensed dwelled deep inside him. "I know what it means to be an outsider. To have people look at you as though you're no better than dirt under their feet. And I don't ever want to feel that way again.''

She rested her hand on his arm, settling on this small contact when she wanted so very much to throw her arms around him and hold him. There was so much pain inside him, and she longed to ease it. The thick muscles of his upper arm tensed at her touch. He turned his icy glare on her, the one meant to scare away anyone who got too close to his secrets. She refused to turn away from him. "You need never be an outsider again. Give Marlow and the duchess a chance to become your family. Give yourself a chance to find your way back to them.''

He shook his head. "You don't understand.''

"Help me understand.''

He tipped back his head and stared up at the stars that burned bright holes in the dark fabric of the sky. "I'm not Peyton. Even if I was that boy who was lost twenty-three years ago, I'm not the Peyton Trevelyan that old man wants me to be. And I never will be.''

"How can you say that?''

He laughed, the dark sound bitter and filled with self-loathing. "All the rules you've been pumping into my head don't change who I am inside. You can't take someone like me, someone who has lived the way I have, and turn him into some kind of tame puppy.''

"Everything you've been through has only made you stronger. Perhaps too strong. You survived where others would have died. And in surviving you've built walls around you so that no one can hurt you. But until you let someone get close you will never be able to fill all the empty places deep in your soul."

He shook his head. "I've been on my own a long time. Maybe I don't need all those empty places filled. Maybe I'm just fine the way I am. Maybe I don't want to live in a place where people care more about how a man speaks than what he says."

"And maybe you're a coward." She turned away from him and marched toward her cabin. She had to get away from the stubborn beast before she ended up screaming at him.

He followed her. "Just what the hell did you mean by that?"

She pulled open her door and stepped inside, intending to stop the argument before it got rolling. "Good night."

"Oh no you don't." He grabbed the door when she tried to close it in his face. "We're gonna finish this right here and now."

A single lamp burned in her cabin, bathing his face with gold. He looked angry enough to strangle her. She lifted her chin, meeting his anger with a fair share of her own. "You're afraid you aren't quite good enough to be Peyton Trevelyan. Admit it."

"Like hell. Just because I don't give a damn about all your fancy rules and fancy ways doesn't mean I'm scared."

"You find fault with everything about polite society because you're afraid people will look down at you. Well, if you were truly a brave man, you would face everyone and show them you're every bit as good as any of them."

Fires flickered in his eyes. A muscle twitched in his cheek as he clenched and unclenched his jaw.

The rational part of her brain recognized the warning signs of his escalating anger and screamed, *Run!* But her own anger made her refuse to heed the warning. "If you were truly brave, you would find a way home, even if you had to claw your way to get there."

"I've had a belly full of clawing my way through life. I don't care to live someplace where a man is judged on how fancy his clothes are."

Frustration stiffened her every muscle. It was all she could manage to keep her voice level. "You're the most stubborn, arrogant . . ."

He grabbed her waist and hauled her upward until her toes dangled above the floor and she was nose to nose with the furious beast. He stared straight into her eyes, and for one terrifying beat of her heart she was certain he intended to toss her overboard.

"Witch," he whispered, before he slammed his mouth over hers.

Elizabeth's heart stopped, only to sprint into a dizzying pace with the next beat. She curled her hands into fists against his broad shoulders, stunned by the ferocity of his kiss. It was a bold, openmouthed assault that scorched her body all the way down to her toes.

He slanted his hot mouth across hers, threatening to sear her to ashes in the fire he ignited within her. He growled deep in his throat, a dark, primitive sound that triggered a tremor deep inside her. He slipped his powerful arms around her waist, holding her close against his body, melting her anger in the heat of a desire she couldn't deny.

His scent swirled through her senses, citrus and leather and man, more intoxicating than the finest brandy. It seemed a lifetime since she had felt the warm slide of his lips against hers, a lifetime filled with the ache of loneliness.

She slipped her arms around his neck, holding him,

kissing him back with all the force of her long pent-up emotions. He moaned at her wanton response. She had dreamed of a moment like this all her life. And with every dream the only man she had ever imagined holding her was Peyton.

He stepped into her cabin, his long legs brushing against her gown, and she found herself wishing she could feel the brush of his bare legs against hers. He closed the door with his foot, shutting out the world beyond this small room. The door closed with a thud that vibrated through her consciousness. That sound held such finality. As if to say—*your choice has been made, your bridges crossed, and there is no way to return.*

She should stop this. Now. Yet she couldn't bring herself to pull away from the warmth of his kisses. She tasted his need, recognized that it dwelled in a place where he allowed no one to enter. But she knew she had to try to reach him, even if it meant risking her heart and more.

He growled deep in his throat, desire scorching the tenderness of his kiss. She responded to his fierce demand, wanting him more than she had ever imagined wanting anything in her life. He was big and powerful and wounded in unseen ways. She wanted to heal him, to claim him, to keep him by her side until she drew her last breath.

He eased his fierce possession of her, allowing her to slide down the solid length of him until her feet touched the blue carpet. She clung to him, her arms around his neck, her body pressed against his hard frame, her lips against his mouth.

She had tried to dismiss this feeling she had for him as infatuation. Lust was simple to understand; it was that primitive kernel that remained deep inside each human being, a seed that could turn even a proper lady into a mindless fool. Something she had assumed was well and truly buried deep inside of her until she met him.

Now, with his arms around her and his lips warm against hers, she understood that lust was only part of what had haunted her every night in her lonely bed. Not lust alone had infected her blood, but something else. Something far more powerful than the needs of the flesh. Something that invaded every atom of her being. Something she had tried in vain to prevent. Something wonderful and far more frightening.

She slid her hands over his shoulders, absorbing his warmth, resenting the soft white linen that kept her from touching his skin. He slid his hands down her back, his fingertips grazing her buttons. Only when she felt the sapphire silk slip from her shoulders did she realize the full extent of that graze. He was undressing her.

"Tell me to stop, Beth." He spread the heat of his mouth across her cheek, her neck, lingering at the sensitive joining of her neck and shoulder. All the while his deft fingers were unfastening the laces of her corset, tugging at the tape on her petticoat, unraveling the layers of propriety. "Tell me."

In the small rational part of her brain that still functioned she recognized the need to end this before it got entirely out of hand. She should withdraw from this battle, retreat before it was too late. Yet, as hard as the proper, all-too-civilized part of her fought to form a protest, the wanton within her crushed any rebellion. She couldn't escape him, or the need for him she carried deep in her soul.

He touched her back, sliding his big, warm hand beneath the edge of her corset, massaging her back through the sheer silk of her chemise. He touched the pulse throbbing wildly in her neck with the tip of his tongue, then whispered against her skin, "Tell me now, before it's too late."

It had been too late the moment she had set eyes on him, and he knew it. He slid his lips over hers, sealing any protest she might have spoken with the heat of his mouth. His hands trembled as he slid the gown from her shoulders. She was stunned that she could move him this way. The heavy silk fell with a sigh in a puddle around her feet. Her corset and petticoats melted away from her body beneath the slow movement of his warm hands, settling around her ankles with a soft murmur of surrender.

He slid his arms around her waist, holding her as though he expected her to go running into the night like the lunatic she felt herself to be. Blue flames flickered in his eyes as he slid his fingertips over the swell of her breasts above the white lace of the low-cut neckline of her chemise. Pleasure spilled though her body, trembling along every nerve.

Slowly he pulled the pale pink ribbon nestled between her breasts, loosening the gathers. With the light touch of a magician he flicked open the three pearl buttons below the ribbon. She held her breath, trembling softly, as he slid one warm fingertip between her breasts, parting the soft silk, revealing the curves of her body.

A single sconce glowed on the wall behind him, sprinkling gold across the tips of his long black lashes. "I've wanted you since the first moment I saw you."

She managed a smile, even though her blood was singing in her ears. She felt anxious and eager. Impatient and afraid. All at the same time. "I rather thought you wanted to strangle me."

"You're the damndest female I've ever met." He slid his fingers into the coil of hair at her nape, cradling her skull. "One minute I want to strangle you, and the next . . ."

He tugged her toward him, capturing her lips beneath his. She groaned with the unexpected sensation of her breasts pressed against his powerful chest with nothing between them except the soft silk of her chemise and the warm linen of his shirt. Still, it seemed there were too many layers between them. She wanted the forbidden thrill of his skin bare against hers. And she was certain he could read every wicked thought that flitted though the muddle of her brain.

He slipped his hands over her hips and pulled her close, pressing the pulsing heat of his aroused male body against her belly. The heat of contact seeped through her skin, igniting flames that melted inhibition into a scorching streak of desire. A pulse flickered and throbbed low in her belly. Instinct answered the lure of him, fitting her body against his in a desire she couldn't even begin to understand. But he understood. He knew without words what she craved.

He dragged his lips across her cheek, down her neck, touching her skin with his tongue. "You're so damn beautiful."

She smiled at the harsh compliment, sighing softly as he nuzzled the skin beneath her ear. She had always imagined it would feel like this, being held by this man. Only this man.

He pulled the pins and combs from her hair, the heavy mass tumbling down her back. He slid his hands through the tangled waves, grazing her back with his fingertips. "You can't know how many times I've thought of doing this."

She ran her hands over his chest, smiling up into his handsome face. "As often as you've thought of strangling me?"

He smiled, his eyes filled with all the warmth she had craved these long lonely days. "It's at least a tie."

She tapped her fist against his chest. "How very flattering."

"Every time you'd start lecturing me, I'd strip you bare."

Her breasts tingled. "Wicked man."

"I thought I'd go crazy these past few days, with you

so near. Yet out of my reach.''

"I thought you didn't like me.''

"I wish I didn't.'' He slid his calloused palms over her shoulders, guiding the chemise down over her arms, baring her breasts. "I wish I could get you out of my head. Out of my blood.''

She tipped back her head, trembling with the intoxicating caress of his hands, of his dark velvety voice. He followed the slow slide of silk across her skin, kissing her, tasting her, swirling his tongue across skin that had grown hot and tingling. Still, she was unprepared for the first touch of his mouth against the sensitive tip of her breast. He drew the taut bud into his mouth, between his teeth, laved the aching flesh with his tongue. She gasped with the sudden sensation that spiraled out from her captured nipple, like ripples sent skittering across a lake by a strong gust of wind.

She sank her hands into his thick dark mane, arched against the strong arms around her back, offering her breasts to the scorching heat of his mouth. She moaned with the splendor of it, the overwhelming pleasure of having this man touch her so intimately.

When he lifted her in his arms and carried her to the bed she could only think of how right it all seemed. Inevitable. This moment had awaited her since the first instant she had set eyes on him. No, long before she had glimpsed his handsome face. Ever since she had daydreamed about a boy lost in a savage wilderness.

The sheets were cool against her bare back. The mattress sank with her weight, and the man pressing her back against the plump goose down. He kissed her, his warm lips over hers as his hands roamed over her skin, scattering sensation in his wake.

She gasped against his lips at the first touch of his hand between her thighs. He slid his fingers against the smooth silk of her drawers, seeking, finding the slit leading to the bare flesh beneath. She had never truly understood the ways a man touched a woman. Beneath his skillful touch, she realized that never in a hundred years could her innocent imagination have conjured the potency of reality.

He flowed down her body, kissing her with his lips, his tongue, nibbling at her breasts, awakening every nerve to shimmer with pleasure. She had dreamed of this moment of surrender before she had ever seen his face. She whispered his name, as she had whispered it a thousand times before.

He stiffened and drew back, dragging his mouth from her aching breast. She opened her eyes, staring up at him to see pain flicker across his features. He stepped back from her, as though he had been hit hard in the jaw. She lay with the damp imprint of his mouth against her bare flesh and stared at him, stunned by the sudden change in him.

Ice shimmered in his eyes, where before fires had burned. Lamplight revealed every nuance of a face that was carved into angry lines. She sat up and crossed her arms over her breasts, instinctively shielding herself against his anger. "What is it? What's wrong?"

A muscle flickered in his cheek. "The next time you decide to spread your legs for a man, you better know who he is."

She shivered at the icy fury that emanated from him. "I don't understand."

"Who the hell did you think was making love to you just now?"

She flinched at the harsh words. She stared at him, trying to make some sense of his anger. "You."

He closed the distance between them in two long strides. She raised her arm, instinctively warding off a blow.

He froze as if she had shot him. His expression shifted, hurt flickering through the anger that burned in his gaze.

"Do you really think I would hurt you?" he whispered.

She lowered her arm, stunned by the soft, aching sound of his voice. Somehow this had all taken a wrong turn, tilted into disaster. And she honestly had no idea what she had done. She gathered the sheet in her trembling hands and pulled it up to her chin. "At the moment you look angry enough to tear me to shreds."

He shook his head. "I've never struck a woman in my life. Guess it just shows how little you know about me."

"I don't understand what I did to make you so angry."

He hesitated, uncertainty flickering over his features, before his expression turned hard and unyielding. "I think it's best if we just leave it here."

She swallowed hard, pushing back the hurt. "And pretend nothing happened?"

He drew in his breath. "You got your innocence bruised a little bit tonight, sweetheart; that's all. Let's both admit it was a mistake and let it lay."

A mistake. The words struck her like the back of a hand across her cheek. She lifted her chin as she watched him go refusing to melt into tears. Even though she hadn't completely understood all the rules when she had delivered herself into the callused hands of Ash MacGregor, she was quick to learn. In her world, such passionate actions naturally led to marriage. In MacGregor's, such passion led to a grunt of satisfaction.

She offered love.

He offered lust.

She expected forever.

He expected moments.

The door closed with a soft click, the sound ripping through her like a knife. Infuriating rogue! If he wanted to pretend nothing had happened, then that was precisely what she would do. She certainly wouldn't go trailing after him like a lovesick schoolgirl. She certainly wouldn't allow him to destroy every shred of her dignity.

She swiped at her tears with trembling fingers. "Impossible beast!"

Ash prowled the ship after leaving Elizabeth, trying to purge the restlessness, trying to bury the memory of her soft and willing in his arms. It was useless. He paused by the railing outside his cabin and stared down at the restless churning of the sea, the rolling waves reflecting the turmoil in his gut. He had believed her. He had looked into those huge gray eyes and believed in the affection he imagined burning there.

He thought he knew women. He thought he could see right through every lie. But he didn't know ladies. They were a different breed all together. They could twist a man inside out and leave him aching.

Peyton.

She had betrayed herself in a single whisper. And with that betrayal she had plunged a knife into his heart. All the time he was holding her, kissing her, she had been thinking of Peyton. The man she wanted him to become. The fantasy she wanted him to bring to life. And what was worse than anything, a part of him wanted to crawl back to her, to beg for a crumb of the affection he had imagined he saw in her eyes.

He squeezed the smooth oak railing, trying not to think of her scent, the taste of her skin, the soft brush of her body against his. His blood stirred with memories he couldn't crush. She was a dream come true. But the dream didn't belong to him. Not really to him. Not unless he was willing to live a lie.

He couldn't do it.

It didn't work.

He didn't fit.

He lifted his face to the cool breeze and tried to draw a deep breath, but a solid weight of pain and regret pressed against his chest, compressing his lungs. It was better this way, he assured himself. Better to end it now, while he still had enough sense to see it couldn't work.

He didn't have a future in England. He belonged in the West, where a man could breathe without worrying that he wasn't doing it the way everyone thought he should be. He couldn't pretend to be something he wasn't. And he couldn't believe the lies he saw in her eyes. No matter how much he wished they were true.

Chapter Sixteen

Sunlight poured over Chatswyck Hall, turning stone walls to gold, glittering on hundreds of windows, transforming the place into something straight out of a fairy tale. Three stories high, with two massive wings sweeping out from a central block, the place was bigger than the Denver public library. Bigger than any house Ash had ever seen.

Ash stood on the gravel drive and stared. Yet it wasn't the huge, imposing beauty of the place that fixed his attention. It was something more. Something he couldn't quite name. The blood pounded in his veins. The roar of his pulse filled his ears, drowning the rustle of the wind through the tall oak and elm trees lining the long driveway. He stared at Marlow's country home without blinking, without breathing, his senses dulling and sharpening all in the same instant.

An odd feeling flickered inside him, a glimmer of familiarity, like a single firefly lighting for a brief moment in the depths of a forest. He reached for that flicker of memory, yet it eluded him. When Hayward touched his arm Ash flinched.

"Do you remember being here?" Hayward asked, his voice filled with the same expectancy shimmering in his eyes.

Ash took a tight grip on his emotions like the reins of a runaway horse. He wasn't certain why he had experienced this odd feeling of familiarity, but he sure as hell

211

wasn't ready to believe it had anything to do with ever having been here before. "No."

Hayward nodded, his face reflecting disappointment before his smile returned. He patted Ash's shoulder. "I'm sure it's only a matter of time before the memories return."

Ash glanced away from the hope in Hayward's eyes. It was a terrible thing, hope. It made you wish for things that couldn't be.

He looked at the woman standing by the coach a few feet away. Elizabeth was watching him, her expression cool and remote, as though she had tucked all her emotions away in a safe place. Still, her eyes reflected the iciness of her anger. She didn't take losing well. Neither did he. Even though he hated to admit it, he hadn't walked away a winner last night.

The few hours he had slept the night before had been filled with images of Beth—her hair spilling across white linen sheets, her bare breasts kissed with lamplight, rising and falling, inviting him with each soft breath. His waking hours were filled with an aching need to touch her, to take her in his arms, to sink into her fire.

He crushed the need rising within him like a stream feeding on a steady spring rain. He had learned a long time ago that you couldn't count on anyone being there when you needed them. Trust was something better kept to oneself. He wasn't about to start singing a different tune now. Even if he was having a hard time getting the woman off his mind. And an even harder time getting her out of his blood.

Ash allowed the old man to lead him up the wide stone steps leading to a pair of oak doors recessed beneath a stone arch, half listening as Hayward rambled on about the dukes of Marlow. From the history of the family Hayward had given him to read, Ash already knew the title of Duke of Marlow extended all the way back to 1654.

As he approached the massive front doors, he imagined those old dukes rolling in their graves at having a gunslinger masquerade as one of the family.

The door was opened by a tall, thin man, who welcomed them with the formality of an undertaker and the smile of an old friend. "It's good to have you back, Your Grace."

Hayward nodded. "Angelstone, this is Hedley. You used to run him ragged with your pranks. I remember once you actually filled his boots with molasses."

"Glad to meet you," Ash said, extending his hand. "Sorry about the molasses."

Hedley hesitated, staring at Ash's outstretched hand as though it were a rattlesnake about to bite. "Please, milord." He released Ash's hand a heartbeat after accepting his greeting. "Don't give it another thought."

Ash stepped back, feeling like a schoolboy standing in front of class wearing pants six inches too short. He glanced at Elizabeth, who stood a few feet away, near the white marble bust of a man that sat perched on a black marble pedestal. She was watching him, frowning, the look in her eyes confirming that he had just made a complete ass of himself.

He turned away from her, heat prickling his neck. How was he supposed to learn all the right and wrong things to do in a few weeks? Hell, there were a thousand little rules out there, all waiting to trip a man with the next step he took. And he didn't care much about being made a fool.

Although it was cool inside, the air pressed against him, too thick to draw into his lungs. The fancy white silk shirt he wore beneath his black coat stuck to his damp skin. He fought to keep his expression from revealing any of his anxiety. He'd be damned if he let the angry little Princess know just how nervous he felt.

He ventured farther into the house, glancing around the

huge entry hall. Paintings in gilt frames lined the dark wood paneling of the walls. A mural stretched across the ceiling two stories above him where mythical gods and goddesses reined in a celestial kingdom.

"Welcome home, Angelstone." Hayward squeezed Ash's arm, chuckling softly. "I've waited a long time to say that."

Never in his life had Ash realized that a house could make a man feel so insignificant. But that's how he felt—small and stupid and about as at home as a wolf at the opera.

A soft feminine gasp whispered through the huge hall. Ash turned, glancing at the white marble staircase at the far end of the hall. A woman stood poised on the bottom step, her hand resting on the gilt iron balustrade as though she needed support to stand. She was staring at Ash, her brown eyes wide, her lips parted, as though he were a phantom newly risen from the grave.

"Leona, my darling, look who is here." Hayward tugged on Ash's arm in his haste to introduce him to his duchess.

Leona didn't respond, but stood staring at Ash, her eyes filling with tears. His muscles tensed. He resisted the urge to turn, to march out of this place, to deny all the affection he saw in the woman's eyes. He wanted to scream at her, to shout at the top of his lungs, to remind them all that this was nothing but a game. An illusion. He was a fraud.

Leona lifted her hands as he drew near. Even with the height of the stair, she barely came to his chin. He took her slender hands in his, staring into her tear-filled dark eyes. Guilt wrapped around his throat like a noose. Guilt for not being what she expected of him. Guilt for not having the courage to tell her right here and now.

"You're home," she whispered.

Ash tried to swallow, but his mouth had turned as dry as dirt. He searched for words to deny the illusion she believed in, but the raw need in her eyes strangled his words before they could be spoken. There was time enough to tell her the truth of things, he assured himself. Time enough to shatter all her hopes.

"Emory? Is that you?"

Ash glanced up, looking for the source of that soft question. Sunlight spilled through the diamond-shaped panes of the tall window at the landing, casting a golden glow around the slender woman standing there. The sunlight tangled in hair that tumbled around her shoulders in unbound waves of pale yellow. He blinked against the sunlight, trying to focus on her face, seeing only shadows against the light.

"It *is* you," she said, her voice filling with excitement. She descended the stairs, gliding like an angel on a heavenly breeze, the pale pink silk of her gown rustling with each step.

Leona gripped his hands. Ash sensed the sudden tension in her as she stared at the woman moving toward them. As the woman stepped from the bright cascade of sunlight, he looked into a face more serene than any he had ever glimpsed, as though every human care had been carefully scrubbed from her soul.

"Emory." The woman touched his arm, a caress so soft he scarcely felt her touch through the layers of his coat and shirt. "It's been such a long time since you went away."

She appeared to come from another realm, too fragile to be of this world. Yet he suspected he already knew exactly who this woman was. He glanced away from the screne beauty of her face to the woman standing in the hall behind him. Elizabeth was watching them. Although she stood as still as a painting against the paneled wall, her eyes betrayed her humanity. The stormy gray depths were filled with a sorrow that made him want to take her in his arms and hold her close to his heart.

"Julianna, dear." Leona's voice dragged Ash's attention back to the women standing before him. "This is Emory's son, Peyton."

Julianna looked at Leona, as though she didn't quite understand the words. "His son? Emory has a son?"

Leona's smile was as gentle as one she might reserve for a small child. "Yes, dear. This is Peyton. Emory's son."

"But I didn't know Emory had a son." Julianna frowned, her expression growing frightened. "Why didn't I know?"

Leona touched Julianna's smooth cheek. "You simply forgot, my dear. That's all. Nothing to be concerned about."

"Oh." Julianna rubbed her silk-covered arms, as though she were cold. "I'm sorry. I forget things sometimes."

Ash smiled. "It's all right. We all forget things sometimes."

"You're very kind," Julianna whispered.

She seemed a child, he thought, looking down into her wide, gentle blue eyes, an innocent little girl who needed protecting from reality. The impression was heightened as he watched Elizabeth greet her mother. Elizabeth seemed a lifetime older than this fragile creature who had delivered her into this world.

Elizabeth glanced at him, her expression once again scrubbed clean of emotion. Yet, there was a defiance in her stance, a stiffness in her shoulders, a chilling challenge in her eyes that had not been there before. Ash accepted the reality of it all. It sang in the air with the melody of Julianna's childlike voice as she greeted Hayward. The tragic fire sixteen years ago had taken more than her father and brothers from Elizabeth. As he held her challenging stare, he resisted the urge to cross the distance between them. He wanted to hold her. In some way he didn't understand he wanted to protect Elizabeth, and at the same time take shelter in her arms. Yet he knew he couldn't cross that distance.

"Hedley, have a cold pitcher of lemonade sent to the blue drawing room." Leona slipped her arm through Ash's. "Oh, how you loved lemonade when you were a boy. We had thirty lemon trees planted in the greenhouses so you could have lemonade all year round."

"You planted thirty trees so I could have fresh lemonade?" Ash asked, his voice revealing his shock.

Leona looked surprised at the question. "Of course."

Thirty lemon trees for one little boy. This place didn't just look as if it had come straight out of a fairy tale; it had. It existed in some make-believe world, where a little boy had lived like a prince.

"After you've rested a bit from your journey we must take a tour of the house and grounds," Leona said. "You will be amazed at how little has changed since you went away."

Ash allowed her to lead him toward one of the two wide corridors leading from the main hall. His head pounded with the blood pumping through his veins. He looked down at the small woman walking beside him. Didn't she realize he was an imposter? He was a kid who lived in an alley with rats, not in a palace with thirty lemon trees.

If the duchess really knew what he was, if she had any idea of the things he had done, she wouldn't have her arm tucked through his. The fancy little lady wouldn't want him within a mile of this palace.

Her footsteps tapped against the polished oak parquet of the floor as Elizabeth followed Ash MacGregor down the long corridor leading to the blue drawing room. Leona and Hayward flanked MacGregor, chatting about the trip. At least Leona and Hayward were chatting; MacGregor was silent. In profile, she could see his frown as he looked around him, glancing at the paintings on the paneled walls, the seventeenth-century mahogany chairs and settees placed along each side of the wide hall.

The life of this house extended beyond two hundred years. Stones from the original Norman castle that had been built on this site by an ancestor of Hayward Trevelyan still shaped the walls of Chatswyck. Tradition pulsed from the heart of the grand old home. One would think any man would be proud to be part of this. But the man calling himself Ash MacGregor was hardly an ordinary man.

Stubborn American.

She simply couldn't understand why the man couldn't accept the truth of his heritage. The infuriating beast didn't even have the sense to realize he belonged in his own home. When she considered the possibility he might one day turn his back on his family she could scream. And she had to admit a large part of her indignation wasn't solely for Leona and Hayward. Part of her concern was for the pitiful fool who had managed to throw herself at the man last night.

After he had left her cabin she had spent much of the night trying to convince herself to despise the rogue. But the beast had managed to barge his way past all her defenses. He had made a lair in her heart and she had no immediate hope for evicting him. After her anger had cooled she had examined the situation with more objective eyes.

In his eyes, she had called him by another man's name at a time when a man doesn't want to think a woman has thoughts of another man. In spite of his angry departure, every feminine instinct she possessed told her Ash cared for her. If he hadn't any feelings for her, he would have taken her last night. He would have had her and walked away with a smile. Instead, he had walked away with a fully aroused body and a frown. He might not like it; he would fight against it; but he cared for her in more ways than he was willing to admit. She felt certain of it. Now all she had to do was convince him of it.

She was a practical woman. He intended to leave. She wanted him to stay. Unless she planned to live the rest of her days mourning his loss, she would have to find a way to wiggle her way past all the thorns of distrust and pride surrounding his castle. She would have to find a way to tame the beast living within, and make a home for herself in his well-guarded, stubborn heart. Without being torn to shreds in the endeavor.

A soft hand on her arm made her glance to the woman walking beside her. Julianna smiled at her daughter. "Peyton is very handsome, isn't he?"

Elizabeth stiffened, wondering if she was wearing her heart on her sleeve. "Is he? I hadn't really noticed."

"Haven't you? Well, he is quite handsome. He reminds me of Emory." Julianna paused to admire the fresh flowers rising from a blue-and-white delft vase sitting on a pedestal table against the wall. "I wonder why Emory didn't come with his son. It's been such a long time since I've seen him."

Elizabeth studied her mother, wondering how best to respond. Julianna knew of Emory's death, but as in so many other things, she chose to forget it. She lived in a world of her own creation, a world where nothing tragic could touch her. "Emory died several years ago," she said, risking the truth.

"Died?" Julianna caressed the leaves of a white lily, staring at the long, tapering petals for a moment before she continued. "No, you must be mistaken. I would know if Emory were dead. We're as close as brother and sister. I would know. I would remember. So you see, you really must be mistaken."

Elizabeth realized there was little chance her mother

would ever face reality. "There are times when we forget what we don't wish to remember."

Julianna closed her hand around the flower, as though she needed to hold tight to a lifeline. "I would remember if Emory were gone. I'm certain I would. Wouldn't I?"

Elizabeth stroked her mother's shoulder. "It's all right. There's no need to be frightened."

Julianna looked up at her daughter, her blue eyes wide with a fear that came from demons no one could see. "You were gone a long time. I wondered if you would ever come back."

Elizabeth smiled. "I told you it would take several weeks. Remember?"

"Yes. I remember." Julianna opened her hand. The crushed petals of the lily fell from her grasp, settling against the polished surface of the mahogany table where Julianna's face was reflected in the wood. "But sometimes I have dreams. I see faces. People I should know, but I don't remember. People who have gone away. And I'm afraid. I'm afraid you'll go away."

Elizabeth slipped her arm around Julianna's shoulders and held her close, feeling the trembling in her mother's slender form. "It's all right. There is no need to be afraid."

Julianna hugged Elizabeth, her slender arms wrapped around her daughter's waist. "You will always come back, won't you? You won't leave? You won't stay away?"

Elizabeth rested her cheek against her mother's head, breathing in the sweet scent of violets clinging to the soft yellow tresses. "I won't leave you."

Julianna squeezed her arms tighter around Elizabeth, as though she were afraid her daughter would disappear if she didn't hold her. "Promise?"

Elizabeth swallowed past the tight knot of regret squeezing her throat. "I promise."

"I know I can trust you. I know you would never break your promise to me."

"Never." She held Julianna, enduring an embrace that was painful in its intensity. When she felt Julianna relax she eased away from her mother. "Shall we catch up with the others?"

"Yes." Julianna fiddled with the crushed petals. "The azaleas are in bloom. You must show Peyton. I know he'll think it's lovely here. There is no place lovelier than Chatswyck."

Elizabeth knew her mother would never leave Chatswyck; it was the only place she felt safe. And she wondered if the man calling himself MacGregor would ever come to think of Chatswyck as his home.

"Here you are on your fifth birthday." Leona smiled down at the album of family photographs that lay open across her lap. "And that's Taffey, your first pony. You were so proud of him. Do you remember?"

Ash had to swallow to use his voice. "No."

"No?" Leona glanced up at him, her dark eyes filled with surprise. "Perhaps it's for the best. I'm afraid he passed on five years ago."

Ash sat on an elegant little sofa beside a duchess, fighting his urge to stand and pace like a caged animal. A man in his profession learned early to control his emotions, to keep his fear closely guarded. If he didn't, he ended up in a shallow grave. Still, this was different.

Leona touched his arm. She was staring down at a photograph of the entire family gathered in front of a tall Christmas tree. An angel stood on the top bough, so high the tips of her wings nearly touched the ceiling. *My little angel.* A woman's voice whispered in his memory. Deep inside he shivered.

"Your father held you up on his shoulders so you could place the angel on the top of the tree."

He looked past Leona, to a place near a corner of the room. "The tree stood there."

"Yes. It stands there every Christmas."

He glanced at Leona, startled that she had responded to words he hadn't even realized he had spoken.

Leona patted the fist he held against his thigh. "Oh, how you loved Christmas."

He stared at the photograph of Emory Trevelyan, trying to deny the resemblance they shared, a resemblance that became more clear with each passing photograph. Was it really possible the man in that photograph was his father?

"You were always the first one up on Christmas morning, running through the house, rousing everyone from their beds."

Ash studied the face of Peyton Trevelyan, trying desperately to remember his own face at that young age. He stared at the photograph of this young family, seeing the joy they shared captured forever in sepia impressed on paper. Had he once shared that joy?

Leona turned the page. It was blank. She slid her slender fingers slowly down the empty black paper as she spoke, her voice filled with a ragged edge of pain. "So many empty pages."

Young lives lost in a brutal land. A family ripped into shreds. Was it his family? His parents? His life? A cool breeze swept in through the open windows, stirring blue brocade drapes, brushing his face with the scent of freshly cut grass. Yet he could scarcely draw the fragrant air into his compressed lungs.

Leona looked up at him, her smile full of hope. "Now that you are home we shall fill those pages."

The affection in her eyes mocked him, taunted him, demanded more from him than he could give. "I think there's something you should know."

Leona lifted one finely arched white brow. "What is it, dear? You sound so terribly serious."

He stood and paced a few feet away from the fragile old woman. He looked to where Elizabeth sat beside Julianna on a matching sofa across from the duchess. Elizabeth was watching him. The icy anger he had lived with all morning and most of the afternoon was gone from her expression. Her eyes revealed the world to him—her anxiety, her hope, her demand for him to accept Leona and Hayward. Looking into her beautiful face, he caught himself wishing she wanted the man he was, instead of the man she wanted him to become.

"Peyton dear, what is it?" Leona asked.

Ash looked at Leona, steeling himself against the warmth in her dark eyes. "I'm not convinced I'm your grandson."

Leona frowned, glancing first to Hayward, who sat in a chair to her left, then back to Ash. "Not convinced? What nonsense is this?"

Ash wished he knew. He wished he could pry apart the truth from illusion. Even though he was afraid of what he might find. "I could be some prospector's son." Yet, even as he spoke the words, they rang with a hollow sound against his awakening memory.

"Prospector?" Leona looked as through she had taken a big bite of a persimmon. She glanced at Hayward. "Marlow, did the young man bump his head on the way here?"

Hayward gave her a sheepish grin. "Perhaps I should have mentioned his sentiments in one of my telegrams."

"Perhaps you should have." Leona pursed her lips, giving Ash a severe look. "My dear young man, I want no more of this nonsense. You are Peyton. You are back home. And that is the end of it."

What if he was Peyton? What then? How could he justify leaving this place, and the only family he had? The room was warm, getting warmer. He wanted to run. He wanted to get as far away from these people as he could.

But there was nowhere to hide from the memories awakening inside him. "I'm sorry. I realize how much you want me . . . I mean, your grandson, back. But the truth is, I've got doubts about being here in the first place."

Leona looked to her husband. "Marlow, are you certain he didn't bump his head?"

Ash felt as though he had smashed his skull open on a rock.

"He was shot, but he had this notion before that rather unfortunate incident," Hayward said.

"Shot?" Leona folded her hands on the album. "Would you mind telling me why someone shot my grandson?"

"Because he wanted to kill me. Because I'm a bounty hunter. A gunslinger. And I probably killed one of his kin." Ash clenched his hands into fists at his sides, feeling like mud left on the carpet. He couldn't be Peyton Trevelyan. He could never fit in this world. "Now maybe you can see why there *ain't* much chance I'm your grandson."

Chapter Seventeen

A cool breeze whispered through the open windows of the drawing room, carrying the soft music of oak and elm leaves dancing in the breeze into the stark quiet of the room. Elizabeth eased her tight fists open on her lap. Ash MacGregor stood in the center of the elegant room, a compelling fallen angel, defiant in his conviction that he did not belong in heaven.

He looked lost. And so very lonely. The man might not know the meaning of friendship, but he certainly needed a friend. In spite of her resolution to tame his heart, she recognized the risks involved. No matter how much she cared for him, no matter how certain she was of his own reluctant feelings toward her, becoming entangled with this man was dangerous. Especially after last night.

Her face grew warm with the memory of the taste of his mouth, the warm slide of his lips and tongue against her skin. And she had to admit that the heat of her blush did not reside in shame. She was hardly a child. She was a woman with normal, healthy needs. For all the stupidity of it, the simple, regrettable truth was that she was completely besotted with the man. In love. In lust. Insane.

Leona shifted her gaze from her defiant grandson to her husband, all the shock washed from her face by a will of iron. "Our grandson is a bounty hunter."

Hayward nodded. "It was in the Pinkerton report."

Leona waved away his words with a graceful sweep of

her hand. "I know it was in the report. I read it. I know all about his rather strange upbringing, including his dealings with a Miss Hattie. What I don't understand is why he still thinks of himself as a bounty hunter."

Hayward glanced up at Ash, then at Leona, a smile tipping one corner of his lips. "My darling duchess, I suppose you should ask him."

Leona stared up at MacGregor. "Well, young man? Please tell me why in the world you believe this nonsense about not being our grandson."

Ash frowned, his thick armor of defiance cracking beneath Leona's steady stare, revealing a glimpse of the uncertainty lurking beneath the proud mask. "There's no proof of who I am."

"No proof?" Leona drew her lips into a tight line. "All anyone need do is look at you to know you are Emory's son."

Ash shook his head. "It doesn't prove anything. There could be a hundred men out there who have a passing resemblance to your son."

"A hundred men?" Leona stared at Ash for a moment, then directed her indignant stare to her husband. "I must say I find this all rather disquieting. Marlow, say something to convince him to stop this nonsense."

Hayward shrugged, seemingly unconcerned. "Perhaps in time his memory will return."

"You don't remember who you are." Julianna toyed with the lace at the high neck of her pink silk gown as she gazed at Ash. "Sometimes I forget things too."

Ash glanced around the room. "I'm not sure there is anything to remember."

"You remembered where the Christmas tree was." Leona smiled, sure of her logic. "You can't deny that."

Ash shook his head. "Anyone could tell that from the photograph. It doesn't prove anything."

Leona lifted her hand, as if to silence him if he meant

to say more. "I must insist you stop this nonsense immediately. You are my grandson; that is an end to the matter. I will not have you going about disowning us."

"I'm sorry if this upsets you, but the truth is, I might not be your grandson."

Leona dismissed him with a wave of her hand. "Nonsense."

Elizabeth hesitated before entering the fray. Although the duchess looked as delicate as a rose petal, her spine was pure steel. Leona was kind, generous, and accustomed to getting exactly what she wanted. "I believe we should all keep in mind how very difficult this has been for Mr. MacGregor. Try to imagine what it must be like to suddenly find yourself thrust into a completely different society."

Ash looked at her, frowning, as though he didn't trust her attempt to champion his sentiments. In spite of the fact that she would dearly love to box his ears, Elizabeth understood how difficult this was for him. If they were ever going to have a chance to be together, she would have to help him find his way back home. No matter what the risks.

Leona looked at her, her head tilted at a regal angle. "My darling child, this has been difficult for all of us. Now, it is time for Peyton to take his proper place. We shall have no more of this nonsense."

Elizabeth shifted in her chair, uncomfortable with Leona's stern glare. The matter could not be settled as easily as the duchess wished. "Perhaps he doesn't know what his proper place is."

"I understand how you feel," Julianna said, gazing up at Ash. "You're confused."

Ash glanced at Julianna, then at Elizabeth, the look in his eyes betraying his anxiety. He turned, and Elizabeth thought he might escape the conflict churning in the room by walking out the door and never looking back. Instead, he walked to one of the windows and stared out at the gardens. She released the breath she had been holding. Perhaps he knew there would be no escape. Not until he knew the truth.

"Marlow, we must teach our grandson exactly who he is," Leona said. "I will not have Peyton going through life uncertain of his heritage."

Hayward rested his chin on his clasped hands, smiling at his duchess. "I agree."

"We must also arrange a proper tutor. Peyton must be confident. He cannot be so without training. His upbringing hardly provided him with the appropriate foundation."

Although he remained quiet, staring out at the gardens, Elizabeth sensed a tension within Ash. She could see it in the slight lifting of his broad shoulders and the flicker of a muscle at the corner of his lips. She could only suppose what this proud man must be feeling as Leona discussed his less than acceptable background.

"I've already arranged a proper tutor," Hayward said.

Elizabeth stiffened as she looked to her guardian. Resuming the role of tutor for the stubborn oaf wouldn't be easy after what had happened last night. Still, if she wanted him to stay—and she admitted there was no *if* about it—she would have to make him realize this was where he belonged.

Hayward grinned. "Elizabeth has agreed to teach Peyton all he needs to know about being Lord Angelstone. She and Peyton have been hard at work since we left Denver."

"Elizabeth?" Leona stared at her ward, her eyes wide with surprise. "My dear child, have you actually agreed to this?"

Elizabeth clasped her hands in her lap. "It was what Marlow wanted."

"I see." Leona glanced at her husband, a speculative

look entering her eyes. "Well, I must say I couldn't wish for a more capable teacher."

"I thought you would agree." Hayward rose and offered Elizabeth his hand. "It's still early, my girl. Why don't you and Peyton take a walk through the gardens, and discuss how best to proceed with his lessons. There is so much of Chatswyck he has yet to see."

Elizabeth looked at MacGregor as she rose from the sofa. He stood framed by blue brocade drapes. The sun spilled through the open window, painting his face with gold, illuminating every line of his frown—a portrait of potent masculinity captured in a dark mood.

"Make sure you show him the maze." Hayward looked at Ash. "You always loved the maze. You used to play in it for hours at a time."

Ash shrugged, as if none of it mattered. Yet, Elizabeth suspected his indifference was only a shield.

"I'm depending on you." Hayward squeezed her hand. "I know you won't let me down."

She managed a smile. "I shall do my best."

Hayward stood by one of the windows in the drawing room, watching Elizabeth and Peyton walk away from the house. They each kept to the edge of the path on opposite sides, allowing as much distance between them as the span of the brick-lined walkway would permit. Elizabeth stared at the hedge they were passing, apparently finding it as fascinating as Peyton found the sea horse fountain on the opposite side of the path. He intended to make certain they eventually had to look each other straight in the eye. He had a feeling they would both like what they would see.

"Marlow, do tell me why you thought it necessary to assign Elizabeth the difficult task of civilizing our grandson."

Hayward glanced over his shoulder to where his wife

was sitting on the Sheraton sofa. She sat on the edge of the blue brocade seat, her back rigid, her hands clasped on her lap. Her look conveyed the fact that she wasn't at all pleased. They were alone; Julianna had left shortly after Elizabeth and Peyton, to look after her horses. He met his wife's speculative stare with a grin. "I thought it might serve two purposes at once."

Leona nodded, the look in her eyes telling him she had already deduced his reasoning. "You're hoping those two young people will fall in love."

"You can't tell me you wouldn't be happy to see Elizabeth properly settled. With Peyton."

"When I think of all the young men who have attempted to coax her to the altar, I simply shake my head in wonder that she is still unwed."

Hayward glanced out the window, smiling as he watched Elizabeth and Peyton turn on the path leading toward Leona's azalea dell. He had stolen many a kiss from his wife amid the bright blossoms. "Perhaps Elizabeth has never found the right man."

"And you believe that rough-edged young man who refuses to acknowledge us as his grandparents might be the right man for her?"

"Perhaps." He grinned at her over his shoulder. "Would it please you if he were?"

Leona looked down at her hands, sliding her palms together slowly as she considered his question. "There isn't a day goes by I don't give thanks for bringing that lovely child into our lives. You know I would be more than pleased to see Elizabeth marry our grandson."

Hayward frowned. "Still, you have reservations."

She looked up at him, her brown eyes revealing the extent of her concern. "Did you notice the way he looks at her when he believes no one will notice?"

"He looks at her like a young man who is interested in a woman."

"He looks at her like a hungry tiger eyeing a tender lamb."

Hayward wiggled his eyebrows. "I've been known to look at you that way, my darling duchess."

She waved aside his words with an elegant hand. "This is different. Our grandson was not exactly raised to appreciate the finer sentiments of a lady. He is, as much as I hate to say it, hardly a gentleman. Is it appropriate to allow him to spend time alone with her?"

"Elizabeth is hardly a child fresh from the schoolroom, my sweet. And she is not some unsuspecting little country miss. From the time she entered society she has had a mob of suitors chasing after her skirts, and she has managed to keep every one of them in line."

"Not one of whom was raised by Indians." She lifted one brow. "And I don't need to remind you where else he received his upbringing."

Hayward was counting on his grandson's more primitive instincts. "If anything were to happen between them, we could always make certain Peyton did the right thing."

Leona stared at him a moment, her eyes growing wide with understanding. "Elizabeth is not a lamb to be staked out to lure a tiger into a cage."

"Of course she isn't. I love the girl like my own daughter." He leaned back against the window frame. "I can't help thinking we need to give Peyton every possible reason to stay. You do remember me saying he intends to stay only six months, don't you?"

"Yes, of course I remember."

"And you can't say you wouldn't like to see them wed."

Leona released her breath on a long sigh. "Yes, I would. But there is something very wild about him. It will take time to tame him."

Hayward crossed the distance between them and leaned over his duchess. "Love can work miracles, my dear."

He cupped her cheek in his hand. "Just look at how easily you tamed me."

She huffed. "You weren't exactly raised as a savage."

Hayward kissed the tip of her nose. "You'll see, my dear. Elizabeth will soon have our grandson eating out of the palm of her hand."

Elizabeth peeked at MacGregor from the corner of her eye. He was staring straight ahead, the muscles in his cheek bunched from clenching his jaw, his full lips pulled into a tight line. The man looked angry enough to snap off her head if she should say a wrong word. Well, there was little hope for it; she was definitely going to say something he didn't like. And the sooner she said it, the better.

She halted on the path. "Mr. MacGregor, we must talk."

He paused beside her, lifting one dark brow in question as he looked down at her. "Must we?"

"Yes, we must." She clasped her hands at her waist, trying her best to appear calm and unruffled, while her entire body quivered like a bowl of aspic. She gathered the tattered edges of her dignity and plunged into the speech she had rehearsed this morning. "Since Marlow would like me to continue as your tutor, I suggest we forget about last night and continue as before."

A cool breeze drifted through the leaves of a tall elm standing beside the path behind him. "You mean we should go back to stepping around each other like wary cougars?"

"I believe we can manage to be cordial."

"That's very *civilized* of you."

The man actually had the audacity to be angry with her. The infuriating beast! "What are the alternatives?"

He glanced away from her, staring at the azalea dell that spread like a colorful patchwork quilt across the emerald yawns. "That's the hell of it. There is no alternative."

There was no future, at least none he was willing to embrace. Stubborn oaf! She turned away from him, following the path as it rolled down a gentle slope toward the azaleas. She turned into the dell and paused amid the tall bushes.

White and pink and red blossoms swayed in the breeze, spilling a delicate fragrance into the air. There was a calm to be found in nature. A calm that came from listening to the rustle of leaves, the song of birds. She needed to find that calm. She needed to grasp hold the emotions that threatened to bolt each time he was near. Before she did something foolish. Again.

She studied the clusters of white flowers on the bush beside her, brushing her fingers across the soft petals, sensing rather than hearing his approach. His footsteps were silent against the brick-lined path, as silent as a hawk soaring across the sky.

His warmth brushed her arm as he paused beside her. "I didn't think you'd be willing to continue with our lessons after last night."

She was willing to continue with far too many lessons, she thought, keeping her gaze fixed on the flowers. "It means a great deal to Marlow and the duchess."

"No doubt about that. They don't want a rough-edged bounty hunter tarnishing the proud Trevelyan name."

Although his voice was gruff, she detected a hint of uncertainty in the dark sound. Yet she saw nothing beyond the harsh mask he presented to the world that betrayed his emotions. "They want you to feel comfortable in your own home."

A muscle flashed in his cheek as he clenched his jaw. "They want me to become someone I'm not."

She folded her hands at her waist, meeting the condemnation in his eyes with all the dignity she possessed. "You don't know them very well, or you would realize the most important thing in the world to them is your happiness.''

He shrugged. ''If you say so.''

Patience. It would do little good to throttle the man, no matter how satisfying it might seem. ''Last night was a mistake, as you so wisely pointed out. I believe I can manage to put the entire incident behind me. If you can.''

He studied her, his blues eyes probing hers, searching beyond the words she had spoken. ''I didn't figure you'd be so willing to forget last night.''

She would never forget last night. Still, she had no choice but to put the incident behind her. At least for the moment. Until she convinced the stubborn oaf he belonged right here at Chatswyck. ''As you said, it's for the best.''

A certain wariness entered his eyes. ''You're being very reasonable about all this.''

''Would you prefer someone else tutor you?'' She held her breath, hoping he would deny the offer she felt compelled to make.

''I'd prefer not to have any more rules pounded into my head.'' He stared past her left shoulder for a moment before he continued. ''Since that option isn't open, I'd just as soon not have to get acquainted with another teacher.''

She breathed again. ''The lessons are only to help make things easier for you.''

He laughed, a harsh sound on the cool breeze that revealed the uncertainty he had tried so hard to hide. ''There's nothing easy about it.''

''You must be feeling a bit overwhelmed by it all.''

''Overwhelmed.'' He glanced around the gardens and grounds of Chatswyck that spread as far as the eye could see. ''It's too easy a word for the way I'm feeling.''

She stared up at him, sensing the pain inside him, the turmoil, the need. Somewhere in the gardens a lark serenaded them, as though to say all would be well. Yet, she had her doubts. "Even though you don't care much for fancy ways, you really have learned a great deal in a short period of time."

"Yeah." He laughed softly. "I really showed how much I learned when I shook old Hedley's hand. Guess I'm lucky he didn't keel over from shock."

"There are still a few things you need to learn," she said softly.

He smiled. "Only a few?"

"Until you master the essentials."

"You mean until I stop scaring the servants."

"Something like that." She continued along the walkway, wending slowly through the azaleas, hoping she looked calm and composed in spite of the fact that her legs were shaking. Several minutes passed, the only sound between them the soft rustle of her gown and the ripple of flowers in the breeze.

From the south side of the azalea dell they entered the long tunnel of elm trees that led to the maze. She tried not to think of all the times she had walked this pathway and imagined Peyton by her side. That kind of thinking would only lead to disaster. Student and teacher: That was the only relationship they could have. At least as long as the stubborn beast refused to admit he belonged here.

"The fifth duke, Marlow's grandfather, had a passion for gardening. He had the maze planted when he was sixteen." She resumed the role of teacher, gesturing toward the maze rising in the distance at the end of the long living tunnel. "According to family history, he had it modeled after the maze at Hampton Court, adding a few twists of his own. It's considered a rather fine maze. Very difficult. I've known people to be lost in it for hours."

He paused on the brick-lined path beside her. She glanced up at him. He stood staring at the tall wall of yew at the end of the tunnel, as though he saw some specter rising from a tomb. Beneath the sun-kissed bronze of his cheeks, he had paled. He stood as though sculpted from marble, his face a study in shock.

She touched his arm, as careful as she might be if she had come upon a sleepwalker. "Is something wrong?"

He flinched at her gentle touch, as though he were surprised to find her there. As if he weren't even certain of her name.

"Are you all right?"

He didn't answer her question. Instead, he headed off toward the maze, running through the tunnel of elm trees as though he were late for some long-awaited appointment.

Chapter Eighteen

Ash halted a few feet from the entrance to the maze, his breath coming in ragged gasps. The unevenness of his breath had nothing to do with the energy he had expended to get to this place and everything to do with the reason he needed to reach the tall emerald walls. A reason that remained an indistinct feeling of recognition inside him.

A pair of knights carved from stone, perched on pedestals flanking the narrow entrance, guarded the living labyrinth. They stared down at him as he approached, swords drawn, the tips resting on the stone at their feet, as if judging his right to enter. He studied one chiseled face, then the other, testing the glimmer of memory that had burned through the shadows clouding the lost years of his childhood. It was all so familiar. As if he had stood here before, staring up into those faces.

He didn't take time to question the feelings. He wanted only to follow the thread of light wending through his memory. He wanted only to know the truth.

Emerald walls rose more than three feet above his head as he walked through the entrance. The sharp tang of evergreen wrapped around him. Six feet before him the wall of yew ended in an abrupt turn, leading him to the first intersection, and the first decision.

He turned without debate, following the thread of memory as though it were a string pinned to the towering walls of closely clipped yew. The thread of memory led him to the heart of the maze. There, in the center, gray stones shaped the walls of a small pavilion, fashioning a Norman castle nestled behind emerald defenses.

Ash stared up at the crenellated walls, a voice whispering in his memory. *I'm the king, sovereign of all I see.* A chill brushed across his skin. In his mind faces flickered, brief glimpses through a heavy mist. He closed his eyes, blocking out the tangible, searching for the memories still lost in the shadows of his mind.

"Is something wrong?"

He flinched at the sound of Elizabeth's soft voice. He pivoted. She was standing in the opening to the outer pathway, one slender hand poised against the wall of yew, the other clenched into a fist at her waist. Her eyes were wide and wary, as though she expected him to throw back his head and howl like a lunatic.

"Are you all right?" she asked, taking a tentative step toward him.

No. He wasn't all right. He was too damned confused to be all right. But she didn't need to know what he was feeling. No one needed to know. He drew in his breath, easing the constriction in his chest. "I'm fine."

She lifted one finely arched brow, her eyes revealing her doubts. "I don't believe I've ever seen anyone more anxious to see the maze."

He shrugged, hoping to dismiss his odd behavior. "Can't say I've ever seen a hedge maze where I come from."

She studied him, as though judging her next words carefully before she spoke. "Still, it isn't the first time you've seen this maze, is it?"

He turned away from her and the perceptive look in her beautiful eyes. He felt trapped suddenly, caged by more than ten-foot-high walls of closely knitted bushes. He had always believed his lost memories, if ever found, would lead him to a freedom of his soul. Now he wondered if they would lead him to a place where he didn't belong.

He threw open the oak door of the pavilion, the heavy portal swinging on well-oiled hinges. Sunlight followed him into a room almost as large as the drawing room in the big house, carving a wedge into the cool sanctuary. Sunlight assaulted the shutters at each of the four long windows carved into the walls, creeping through the cracks like a band of marauders, destroying the shadows within the stone walls. The invading light unveiled tapestries hung on the oak-paneled walls—ancient knights captured in heroic scenes from legends.

I'm the king, sovereign of all I see.

His footsteps fell silently against the mosaic tiles inlaid in the stone floor. He paused, staring down at the image captured in the wedge of sunlight spilling through the open door. The light glowed against gold and colored tiles that formed the figure of a knight on horseback slaying a dragon.

A dragon shall guard my treasure.

Ash shivered with the whisper of memory. He tried to suppress the glimmer of light inside him. He wasn't ready to face all the consequences should his suspicions prove fact. Yet the gate imprisoning his past had opened, and the memories were escaping through the narrow crack, spilling into his mind. There would be no escape from the truth.

He sensed her approach before he heard the soft tap of Elizabeth's footsteps against the smooth stones. The air altered when she was near, turned crackling and charged, like the coming of lightning. His body responded, his muscles tensing, blood pumping fast and hot into his belly.

Dammit! He wasn't a smooth-faced boy with the scent of his first woman in his nostrils. Why the hell was he getting hard just thinking about her? Why the hell did he awaken in the middle of the night with his blood pumping from dreams of making love to her? Why the hell couldn't he get the little temptress out of his mind?

It was damn stupid even thinking about her. He wasn't going to be trapped into staying in this gold-lined prison by anyone. It was nothing short of insanity to imagine making love to her.

He glanced at an oak chair that stood against the wall to his left, the duke's crest painted on the high arched back. Here he stood, the world's biggest fool. Because he wanted her. Right here. Right now. Naked and soft against his skin. He wanted to strip her bare, pull her down upon his lap, plunge into her woman's fire until every fear, every doubt crumbled to ashes inside him.

''You remember something about this place, don't you?''

Her soft English voice brushed against him. He stood staring at the cracks of light peeking through the slates of the wooden shutters across from him, fighting the urge inside him—the need to turn to her, to pull her close, to hold her until all this madness made sense.

What the hell was wrong with him? He didn't need her. He didn't need her false offers of affection. He didn't need anyone. He had been taking care of himself for a long time. He could get through this just fine on his own.

She remained where she was, standing behind him, so far away he could only imagine the warmth of her touching him. ''I've never seen anyone solve the puzzle of this maze so quickly. You came here as though you knew each twist and turn of the labyrinth.''

Ash drew in his breath and found himself trying to catch a trace of her fragrance on the cool air. ''Maybe I'm just good at puzzles.''

''Marlow said you used to play here as a boy. You remembered something,'' she said, her voice filled with certainty.

He turned to face her. The light behind her cast her face in shadows. Yet he knew what he would see there if the shadows lifted—a quiet demand for the truth. "I'm not sure what I remember. It's glimpses. Maybe it's nothing more than my imagination."

"And maybe it's your past awakening."

He felt as though the ground wasn't quite solid beneath him. He couldn't rely on what had once been substance. Everything was indistinct. Not quite real. "Maybe it is."

She moved toward him, cautious, unsure. As she left the bright light spilling through the doorway, her features became clear to him. She was looking up at him, speculation and excitement glowing in her eyes.

The sweet scent of lavender rose with the warmth of her skin, beckoning him, tempting him to press his lips against her smooth white neck and breathe her fragrance deep into his soul. He fought against the treacherous images rising in his mind—her breasts bare in the lamplight, nipples pink and taut, and so sweet against his tongue.

"What are you going to do when you discover you are Peyton Trevelyan?"

There were no doubts in her words or in her eyes. Her conviction of his identity was as solid as the rock shaping the walls around them, as potent as the lust pumping hard and fast through his veins. "I don't know."

"You must realize, this is where you belong."

"If I am Peyton Trevelyan, I might have belonged here once, a long time ago. But things change. I've changed." He looked straight into the depths of her eyes. "I'm not sure I could ever stay here. I'm not sure I could ever think of this place as my home. No matter who I am."

Her lips tightened. "You feel that way only because you aren't comfortable here. And you aren't comfortable because you don't know all the rules of this society."

"I know enough to wonder if a man like me could ever really feel free in this place."

She smiled, her eyes filled with a steely gleam of determination. "Perhaps you should wait until after you have acquired more knowledge to make your decision."

Some of the weight lifted from his chest as he looked down into her smiling face. Funny, when he was with her, he began to think anything was possible. "I guess we're going to find out just how good a teacher you are, Lady Beth."

"If you seriously put your mind to it, I have little doubt you can master all the intricacies of polite society in short order."

He studied the curve of her lips, remembering the taste of her mouth, fighting the urge to take her in his arms. He was a fool, a damn fool to even think about touching her. She was a *lady,* full of all the devious little ways ladies had for leading a man around by his nose.

Yet, he couldn't push the thoughts from his mind, the need from his belly, the images that lured him like a beggar to a feast. He touched her cheek, craving her softness, her warmth. Her lips parted on a soft sigh of surprise. But she didn't pull away from him. Perhaps she understood the need inside him, a need he had long ago buried so deeply he couldn't even name it. Still, he knew he needed this, touching her, absorbing her warmth.

Elizabeth knew it wasn't safe being with him. It wasn't safe opening herself to the storm of emotions she sensed inside this man. Her own emotions were far too vulnerable where he was concerned. Still, she couldn't turn her back on him. She couldn't ignore his need. He was too much a part of her.

She rested her hand on his chest, above the heart that had barred anyone who came too close. "You aren't alone, Ash. I'm here for you."

He closed his eyes, his expression growing tense, as if he were fighting inner demons. When he looked at her the full impact of his desire snatched the breath from her lungs. In his beautiful eyes she saw the turmoil of emotions he didn't bother to hide—pain and anguish and a longing so sharply defined she could feel it radiate from him.

The heat of his skin soaked through the linen of his shirt, seeping through her skin into her blood, where excitement flared along her every nerve. His scent curled around her, citrus and leather and man. She didn't try to mask her need for him. She didn't want to think of consequences. She only wanted to feel his arms around her, his lips against hers.

"I've never met anyone like you," he whispered, lowering his head.

"I've never met anyone like you." She lifted herself on her toes to meet his kiss.

He slid his arms around her, holding her close. Through the layers of their clothes her breasts snuggled softly against his hard chest. Yet she could feel only a hint of the hard thrust of his body through the layers of wool and silk and petticoats.

She looped her arms around his neck, slid her fingers into his hair, holding him, kissing him as though the world would come to an end if he pulled away from her.

Logic melted in the warmth of his kiss. Somewhere, in the muddle that became her brain, she wondered whether her dream could ever come true. Could a man like this, wild and savage, ever give his heart to a woman? Could she tame him?

"I need you," he whispered against her lips.

She trembled at his husky words. It was a start. A very encouraging beginning.

He slid his hands upward, along her back, grazing the silk-covered buttons running along her spine. A heartbeat later she felt the cool air touch the bared flesh above her camisole. My goodness, the man could unfasten buttons better than her maid. This was getting out of hand, escalating beyond the bounds of her better judgment. Again.

She sighed against his mouth as he slid his bare hand across her bare skin. *Stop him.* Yes, she really must stop him. She didn't want him to think every time he touched her she forgot every rule of proper decorum. But she couldn't find the words to end the bliss of his kiss.

He spread kisses across her jaw, slid his tongue down her neck, pausing where the throb of her pulse beat wildly beneath his lips. ''You can't know how much I want you.'' His lips brushed her bare shoulder.

He wanted her. It had to be more than lust, she assured herself. He cared for her. Perhaps he didn't love her. Not yet. But love would come. She had to believe he would one day give her his love.

For now, this was enough. For now, she wouldn't ask for more than the feel of his arms around her, his lips against her skin, his hands stripping away her gown. For now she would give him what he needed. And hope one day he could give her forever.

She lowered her arms, like some enchanted marionette, dancing to the tune of her master. The silk slipped over her breasts, her hips, rustling softly as it gathered around her ankles. She wanted his lips against her bare flesh. She wanted to touch him, the way she had dreamed of touching him.

She slid her hands up under his coat, slipped the dark gray wool from his shoulders. The elegantly tailored material stirred the air around them as it tumbled to the floor.

He pulled her back into his arms, as though he were afraid she might change her mind, turn away from him. Didn't he know she was a poor besotted fool? Hadn't he seen how fascinated she had been with him since the first moment she had met him? Didn't he realize she loved him with all her heart and soul? ''I love you, Ash.''

He trembled with her soft confession. "My beautiful princess," he whispered, sliding his lips over hers.

There would be no stopping this time. No second thoughts. Yet even as the thoughts formed in her head, he was freezing in her arms. He jerked his mouth away from hers. She opened her eyes and found him staring at the doorway. And then, through the blood pounding in her ears, she heard it too: footsteps on gravel.

She glanced over her shoulder in time to see Hayward step through the door. And he wasn't alone. A man and a woman stood just behind him—the vicar and his wife. Thoughts darted through the shock stunning her. She had been caught half naked with a man. Mrs. Backster was the biggest gossip in the county. Scandal! She had caused a scandal that would pull Marlow and the duchess down into the mire with her.

She looked at Hayward, expecting shock and outrage and finding neither. The old duke was staring at his ward and his grandson, yes, but he was smiling. Had the shock snapped his reason?

"Oh, my." The short, plump Mrs. Backster lifted her hand to her heart.

The vicar said nothing, only stared at Elizabeth with wide eyes. Ash pulled Elizabeth against his chest, protecting her from the glare of the intruders. But it was too late. They had both been pushed into a pit of humiliation and scandal. And there was no way out.

"The vicar and his wife wanted to meet you, Angelstone." Hayward sounded calm, as though his ward wasn't standing in the arms of his grandson dressed in her underthings. "I suppose this would be an excellent time to announce your engagement."

Engagement! Elizabeth gasped. She glanced up at Ash, who had stiffened against her. He was staring at Hayward, his eyes narrowed, his lips pulled into a tight line. She didn't need the power of divination to know he was furious at the situation. She supposed at the moment it really was too much to ask for the earth to open up and swallow her. Still, she closed her eyes and prayed for a miracle.

Chapter Nineteen

Elizabeth sat on a sofa in the blue drawing room, watching the duchess lift a porcelain teapot from the cart nearby. They were alone. Hayward had tucked the vicar and his gossipy wife in the green drawing room in the east wing. Although Elizabeth would dearly love to keep them under lock and key, she supposed there would come a time when Marlow would have to release them; people would miss them this Sunday. She had little doubt the entire county would learn about her indiscretion five minutes after Mrs. Backster walked out the front door. As for Ash, Hayward had taken him into the study. For a serious discussion. She glanced up at Leona as the duchess offered her a cup of tea.

Leona frowned. "You look as though you would like to hang yourself."

Elizabeth took the cup and saucer from Leona, using both of her shaky hands to steady the porcelain. "I can't believe I placed you and Marlow in the center of a scandal."

"Stop whipping yourself, child." Leona sat on the sofa beside her. "You aren't the first young woman to succumb to a beguiling male before the vows were spoken."

Elizabeth watched the duchess arrange her lavender skirt, easing out the wrinkles as though she hadn't another care in the world. "I'm the one who was charged with teaching him proper decorum. And what did I do? I threw myself into his arms. And what's worse, if I'm to be perfectly honest, I only regret being caught.''

Leona patted Elizabeth's arm. ''The Trevelyan men have always been potential disasters to women. Virility wrapped in a handsome package, coupled with a ruthless sense of purpose. Do you know, one of Marlow's uncles was even known as the Devil of Dartmoor?''

''Yes. I've heard the stories about him.'' Elizabeth sipped her tea, welcoming the whisper of fragrant steam against her face, the warmth upon her tongue. She hoped the sweet creamy liquid would help ease her frayed nerves. ''I should have known better. I'm not a child. I should have controlled the situation, instead of encouraging him to run wild. But he has such a way about him. I turn to jelly when he touches me.''

''My darling girl, even I was not immune to my Trevelyan male.''

Elizabeth stared at the duchess in disbelief. ''You can't mean to say, you and Marlow . . .''

Leona nodded her head.

''Before you were married?''

''It happened in the rose garden at my father's country house in Leichestershire.'' Leona stared through the open French doors into the garden beyond the terrace, where roses swayed in a cool breeze that brought a whisper of their perfume into the room. ''We planted the rose garden here as a tribute to that evening.''

Elizabeth looked out at the garden, knowing she would never look at those roses in the same way.

''Afterward, I wondered why my mother would allow me to go walking through the gardens with Marlow without a chaperone.'' Leona tilted her head to look at Elizabeth. ''On my wedding day she told me she had hoped that walk in the moonlight would be enough to 'reel him in.' ''

''She wanted you and Marlow to . . . become acquainted before you were married?''

Leona laughed softly. ''Very well acquainted. I've since come to realize she wasn't the first concerned parent to allow a young couple a little time alone to decide the issue. And she wasn't the last. Marlow told me this afternoon he had been using the same strategy with you and Peyton.''

Elizabeth sat back, stunned, as though she had been slapped. ''You can't mean . . . Marlow actually wanted this to happen?''

''Why do you suppose Marlow has been leaving you alone with that rugged young man who refuses to admit he is my grandson?''

''I'm not at all certain what you mean.''

''Marlow has always been a rather stubborn man. When he sets his mind to something he remains quite fixed on his objective until he has it.'' Leona folded her hands on her lap. ''He has his mind set on Peyton staying here in England with us, and he isn't above using you as bait to lure the tiger into a cage.''

The room tilted with the sudden impact of Leona's words. Elizabeth's vision dimmed, and her temples pounded with the rush of her blood.

''My dear, you must realize Marlow took the vicar and his wife to the maze this afternoon hoping he would catch you and Peyton in a suitably compromising situation.''

Elizabeth set the cup and saucer on the narrow table beside the sofa, careful not to tip the cup with her unsteady hands. ''I don't like to think of how he will react if Ash thinks for one moment what happened this afternoon was a trap.''

Leona patted her ward's knee. ''Don't worry, my darling, Marlow will handle everything. You will be married to that young man before the day is out.''

''So soon?''

''Marlow and I both feel it's best not to wait.''

For fear the bridegroom would disappear, Elizabeth thought. "Ash MacGregor is not a man who can be forced into anything."

Leona cast her a disapproving glance. "You really must become accustomed to addressing him by his proper name."

Elizabeth refrained from telling her the disaster that had occurred the one time she had used his proper name. "If Marlow tries to force him to marry me, I wouldn't be surprised if Peyton rides out of here and doesn't come back."

"You must stop talking such nonsense. You'll have yourself sick with worry."

"I don't see how I can possibly marry him until he realizes it is what he wants to do. It would be . . ."

Leona raised her hand, cutting off the words her ward might have spoken. "Peyton must have feelings for you, or that incident in the garden would not have happened this afternoon."

"I believe he cares for me. In fact, I'm quite certain of it. Even though he has never really said it, I feel it in my heart. But if he believes someone is forcing him to do anything, even it that thing is something he wants to do, he is stubborn enough to do exactly the opposite."

Leona blinked. "Darling, you're babbling."

"I know." Elizabeth stared down at her clasped hands. "I've been babbling like an idiot since the first day I met him."

"Be calm, my dear. Peyton will do what is right. We will make certain of it."

Elizabeth shook her head. "If he truly believes he is being forced into marrying me, I can't marry him."

Leona rested her hand on Elizabeth's arm. "You can, and you will."

"But . . ."

"My dear girl, think of the consequences. If Peyton

doesn't do right by you, if he doesn't marry you, not only will your reputation be ruined, but his as well."

Elizabeth squeezed her hands in her lap. "I hadn't thought of that."

"Well, think of it. It will be a difficult task as it is to make society accept my grandson as Angelstone. If they believe he is a scoundrel who goes about ruining innocent women, he won't be accepted by any decent member of society. He will be an outcast. Not to mention what will happen to Marlow and me for allowing such a travesty."

Elizabeth's breath had turned to lead. A scandal would make it even more difficult for Ash to feel at home here. He would leave. Marlow and the duchess would be devastated. "I've made a mess of things."

"No. You simply followed your heart." Leona placed her hand under Elizabeth's chin and forced the young woman to look into her eyes. "Everything will be all right, my child. Trust me."

Elizabeth wanted to believe her. The alternative was far too disturbing. The last thing in the world she wanted was marriage to a man who didn't want her. Even if she was madly in love with the beast.

"We'll hold the ceremony tonight." Leona tapped her fingertip against her chin. "But we really must hold a reception or party of some kind later."

Elizabeth frowned, thinking of her lion prowling the confines of a ballroom. "Much later."

"I was telling Marlow earlier this afternoon how important it is to introduce Peyton into society as soon as possible. Rumors are already spreading about him, thanks to Marlow's odious nephew."

Elizabeth stared at Leona. "What kind of rumors?"

"Nonsense about his upbringing with savages. Clayburne spent the better part of an afternoon last week trying to convince me I would be scalped in my bed should I allow that 'savage imposter' into my home." Leona drew up her shoulders. "Such a disagreeable man. I wonder at times if he is truly a Trevelyan."

Elizabeth squeezed her hands together in her lap. "He wants Marlow's title."

"Yes. And if we aren't careful, he could very well get it." Leona stared out into the rose garden. "If we don't manage to firmly establish Peyton as Marlow's heir, Clayburne could cause a great deal of trouble for him after Marlow is gone."

"Without solid proof of his identity, Peyton could spend years in court."

"Exactly." Leona drew in her breath. "It's important that we establish him with society as soon as possible. We must show everyone he is hardly the uncivilized savage Clayburne wants them to believe he is."

Elizabeth smoothed her damp palms together. "I'm afraid Peyton has a great deal to learn before he is ready for his debut."

Leona shook her head. "We don't have time. We need to introduce him to society on our terms. I believe we shall hold a ball."

"A ball?" Elizabeth stared at her guardian. "When?"

"Let's see." Leona tapped the tip of her forefinger against her chin. "We can have all the arrangements made in a fortnight. We can celebrate your marriage and introduce Peyton in one masterful stroke."

Elizabeth lost her breath. "That doesn't give us much time."

"We can't allow Clayburne time to do any more damage. Society must see Peyton is hardly a savage. It will be a small party here at Chatswyck. No more than three hundred people."

Elizabeth swallowed hard. "Three hundred people?"

"Just a small group of acquaintances. There will be dancing, dinner, cards." Leona waved his hand. "The usual nonsense that occurs at one of these things."

Three hundred people. A ball. Ash would be miserable. "He isn't ready."

Leona patted her arm. "He will be. I have complete faith in you."

Elizabeth wished she shared that faith. She had little more than a fortnight to polish all the rough edges. A handful of days to prevent any chance Ash would be humiliated. And if he was, she knew there was little hope of convincing him to stay at Chatswyck.

"Now, my dear. We must prepare for your wedding."

Ash leaned back in a leather chair in Hayward's study, watching the old man pour brandy from a crystal decanter into two snifters. Hayward wasn't reacting the way Ash assumed a man would after finding his ward half naked in the arms of a man. In fact, the old man had the look of a cat who has just managed to trap a mouse. Had he?

The crystal stopper slid into place with a soft ping. Hayward turned away from the mahogany liquor cabinet built into the wall behind the desk. He walked toward Ash with all the confidence of a king.

"Have a drink, my lad." Hayward offered Ash one of the glasses.

"You don't seem upset over what happened." Ash accepted the proffered glass, easing his fingers around the deeply cut bevels. "In fact, you look pleased."

"I must tell you, I've always hoped you and Elizabeth would one day meet and fall in love." He lifted his glass in a salute. "Here's to a long and prosperous marriage."

The heady scent of brandy curled through his nostrils, tempting him. Yet Ash refrained from joining in the toast. He couldn't shake the feeling he had been led right into a snare.

Hayward raised his brows in question. "Is something wrong, my lad?"

"I keep thinking how much of a coincidence it was,

you showing up with the vicar and his wife, catching us.''

"It was good we caught you when we did, and not a few minutes later.'' Hayward chuckled softly as he sat on the edge of the big claw-footed mahogany desk. ''That would really have been embarrassing.''

Ash sipped his brandy, allowing the potent liquor to ease the tightness in his throat. He kept thinking of all the events that had led up to the discovery in the maze. Hayward had suggested the maze. Elizabeth had complied. Could she have planned it along with her guardian?

She is fiercely loyal. She would do anything to see us happy. Hayward's words echoed in his mind. The old man had encouraged him to go to her last night, and again this afternoon. Was Beth willing to act the whore to trap him? Was she willing to hold him, to touch him, to make him believe she loved him, all out of a sense of duty to her guardian? His chest tightened with the possibility of her betrayal.

You aren't alone, Ash. I'm here for you. He had snatched at those words like a drowning man seeking a lifeline. He had believed in the affection in her eyes. He had allowed himself to think of a future in her arms.

I love you, Ash. Had it all been a lie? The more he thought of it, the more impossible her love for him seemed. She was a princess; she thought he was a half-civilized barbarian. Yet she had let him touch her. More, she had encouraged him, invited him, tempted him from the first moment they had met.

Beth.

God, he was a fool. He had made an ass of himself, pouring out his need for her. He was no better than that skinny eleven-year-old kid who had gone from door to door looking for work, hoping for a kind word, a gentle touch. Worse, this time he had lost his heart, offered it to her like the fool he was.

"Mrs. Backster is one of the worst gossips in the

county. Once we turn her lose, I'm afraid half the county will know about what happened here this afternoon.''

Ash stared down into his brandy, trying to corral his runaway emotions. These people had turned him inside out. Beth had ripped open his heart. He didn't intend to let her or any of them know how much he was hurting inside.

''I think it's best if we have the ceremony as soon as possible. I believe I can have all the necessary arrangements made by early this evening.''

''What if I don't intend to marry the lady?''

Hayward frowned. ''Not marry her?''

''That's right.''

Hayward studied Ash for a moment, all the amusement fading from his dark blue eyes. ''I assumed you cared for her.''

Ash squeezed the heavy crystal snifter. He cared too much. ''A man doesn't marry every woman he takes to bed.''

Hayward twisted the glass in his hand. ''Do you mean to tell me you think of Elizabeth as some common trollop, to be bedded and forgotten?''

Ash forced his lips into an arrogant smile. ''One woman is much the same as the next.''

Hayward's lips flattened into a tight line. ''Elizabeth is a gently bred lady. And a gentleman does not go about ruining innocent women.''

Ash held the old man's steely gaze. ''I never said I was a gentleman.''

Hayward slammed his glass on the desk, brandy spilling on the shiny wood. ''I realize you didn't have the proper upbringing, but you are a Trevelyan. And no Trevelyan man has ever ruined a lady's reputation.'' He paused, his white brows tugging together over his thin nose. ''Well, there was that incident in 1814, but even the Devil of Dartmoor married the lady in the end.''

"And that's what you've had planned from the beginning, isn't it? Marriage. That's why you chose Lady Beth for my tutor. You expected the half-civilized savage to take advantage of her, to ruin her reputation, to marry her and stay here for the rest of his life."

"You make it sound like a trap."

"Isn't that what it was?" Ash slid his thumb over a deep cut in the crystal, a shallow reflection of the wound Beth had carved across his heart. "When you realized I planned to return to America you and Beth decided on a way to make me stay."

Hayward shook his head. "Elizabeth would never have agreed to such a plan. Even if I had asked her to debase herself in such a wanton fashion."

"You said yourself, she would do anything to see you get what you want."

"My dear young man, I certainly never meant she would allow you to seduce her." Hayward leaned forward. "You have to believe the only reason Elizabeth allowed such liberties is because she is quite enamored of you."

Ash laughed, the sound bitter to his own ears. "The lady thinks I'm an uncivilized barbarian. The only reason she allowed me near her was to help you."

"Nonsense."

Was it? God, he wanted to believe she had only one reason to allow him to touch her. He wanted to believe every lovely lie that had tumbled from her lips. *I love you, Ash.* His chest constricted at the sweetness of the memory. But it just didn't make sense.

Beth was a lady. She admired gentlemen, with fancy ways. He was lucky if he made it through a meal without using the wrong fork. If not for Hayward's valet, he wouldn't know how to tie one of the fancy ties they wanted him to wear.

She was right about him, he *was* half civilized. And

here it showed. In this elegant palace, he couldn't escape his every shortcoming. She had to see that he would never be the man she wanted him to become.

The only reason that beautiful lady had allowed a savage beast to put his dirty hands on her was for the sake of Marlow and the duchess. She was willing to sacrifice herself for them. In a way he admired her loyalty. But it didn't change the fact that she had used him. She had played him for a fool. She had taken his heart in her delicate hands and crushed it.

"I've already sent a message to my solicitor. I'm certain all the arrangements can be made in a few hours. You and Elizabeth can be married this evening."

Married to a lady who could set his blood on fire with a touch. It was a dream. As long as he didn't think about the fact that the lady was a lying little . . . Ash swirled the brandy in his glass, watching sunlight dance in the amber liquid. "And if I say I'm not interested in marrying the lady, what then?"

Hayward released his breath in a long sigh. "Her reputation will be ruined. She will become an outcast of society. Women will whisper about her. Men will try to seduce her, but only to make her their mistress. In short, her life will become a living hell."

Ash squeezed the glass between his palms, trying to crush the protective instincts rising in her defense. "She should have thought of that before she set a trap for me."

"I realize there is little chance for me to make you believe she had no intention of trapping you. Since you leave me no choice, I must insist you do the right thing by my ward."

Ash met the old man's steady gaze. "You can't force me to marry her."

"No, I can't." He rested his hands on his thighs. "I'm certain it would make little impression on you to know your own reputation will be ruined by the act of seducing an innocent young woman and then abandoning her. You will be known as a man without honor. A blackguard who will not be allowed within twenty feet of an unmarried lady.''

The image Hayward painted chilled Ash's insides, but he refused to let the old man see how much he cared. ''I don't plan on staying, so it doesn't make much difference what the people here think.''

''I thought as much.'' Hayward pursed his lips. ''You leave me no choice. Should you decide to journey along this dishonorable path, I'll be forced to remove you from my will. And withdraw my original offer of sixty thousand dollars.''

Ash set his jaw. He didn't like being forced into a corner, even if he had already decided the only way out of the mess was to marry the woman. ''We had a deal.''

''You agreed to become Peyton Emory Hayward Trevelyan for six months. And I can assure you, my grandson would never do anything as dishonorable as abandon that lovely child to the gossipmongers.''

Ash stared down into his brandy, refusing to allow the old man to see the emotions clashing inside him. He was a wolf in a steel trap. The only way to escape was to chew off his leg. He could leave with his freedom in tact and Elizabeth's reputation in shreds. He could leave now, empty-handed.

He tried to think of the money. He tried to justify what he was about to do based solely on his own mercenary needs. Yet no matter how much he wanted to believe Elizabeth didn't matter to him, the picture of how her life would be if he didn't repair her reputation wasn't something he wanted to live with for the rest of his life. ''Looks like the lady has herself a husband.''

Hayward came to his feet and patted Ash's shoulder. ''I knew you would do the honorable thing. I'll take care of everything.''

Ash watched Marlow leave the room, his step filled with the spring of a young man. He would marry the little lady, all right. But little Miss Prim and Proper would soon come to regret it.

Chapter Twenty

Elizabeth paced the length of her new bedchamber. The duchess had insisted she spend her first night as the marchioness of Angelstone in the proper apartments, a grand connection of cavernous rooms on the second floor of the west wing, reserved for the marquess and marchioness. A trace of lemon oil mingled with the fresh rose-scented potpourri the maids had placed in the room. Everything had been dusted and cleaned and polished, made perfect for the newly married couple. The only thing missing was the marquess. He had, in fact, disappeared moments after speaking his vows in the chapel at Chatswyck five hours ago. The new marchioness was beginning to wish he had disappeared a few moments before she had managed to bind herself irrevocably to the beast.

She paused beside the huge canopied bed, which was easily ten foot square. The covers had been turned down, revealing smooth white sheets. This wasn't exactly the way she had imagined her wedding night. But then, very little of the day resembled the dream she had cherished of her wedding. She had imagined this would be the most special day in her life, a day when she would pledge her undying love to one special man.

She had never in her life seen a bridegroom looking more grim than Ash MacGregor. Not even Lord Nickleberry. Desperate for money, Nickleberry had married a plump American heiress who bore a striking resemblance to a pug. Yet even he had not managed to look quite so unhappy as Ash. Of course, Lord Nickleberry had been nearly unconscious with strong spirits. Ash didn't have that excuse.

Ash had stood beside her in the chapel like a stone monolith. He had left little doubt in the minds of the few people attending the ceremony exactly how unhappy he was with his bride. She clenched her hands into fists at her sides, fighting the sting of tears. Thanks to the flighty, gossipy Mrs. Backster, by now the entire county would know every detail of her hasty marriage, including MacGregor's icy demeanor and scorn for his bride.

"Beast!"

She swatted one of the swags falling from the canopy. She prowled the room, too restless to be still. Fury and humiliation and a pain she couldn't suppress kept her moving. One look at him and she had realized how trapped he felt. She had tried to explain her innocence before the ceremony. She had expected him to understand. She hadn't expected him to look at her as though he hated her.

It was obvious the man didn't want to accept his part in this mess. She supposed it was easier to believe she was the villain. She certainly hadn't been alone in making this tangle, but it looked as though she would be alone on her wedding night.

She grabbed two handfuls of blue and gold brocade and pulled open the drapes at one of the long sashed windows. A cool breeze heavy with the scent of damp grass brushed her face when she opened the heavy window. The room overlooked the serpentine hedges. Past the curving pattern of hedges, she could see the emerald green walls of the maze rising in the light of a half moon.

I need you.

Ash's words whispered in her memory. She leaned her shoulder against the casement, reliving those few moments with him in the maze. He cared for her; she sensed the truth of his feelings each time he touched her. Even though she suspected he would cut out his tongue before uttering those words again.

You can't know how much I want you.

She had to believe they could work through these difficulties. If he would only listen to her. If he would only try to see reason. If he would only realize how much she loved him. If not, if he turned away from her, she didn't know how she would survive.

This waiting was getting her nowhere. She couldn't stand here feeling sorry for herself. She had to find him. She turned away from the window and froze. The marquess had joined her.

Ash leaned back against the door leading to the withdrawing chamber between their two bedchambers. "You look surprised to see me, *Wife*. Were you expecting me to forego the wedding night festivities?"

Surprise was only one of the emotions surging through Elizabeth, along with the tingling excitement he always evoked in her. Dark, windblown waves tumbled wildly around his handsome face, the silky mane spilling over his collar. He had removed his coat, tie, and waistcoat. His shirt was open halfway down his chest, revealing golden skin and dark curls. His light gray pants and black boots were mud splattered. He looked wild, untamed, exquisitely male. She couldn't breathe.

His stunning blue eyes narrowed. "Were you hoping I'd forget to consummate the deal?"

Elizabeth clasped her hands at her waist. The stubborn oaf had decided she was the enemy. Well, she would simply have to make him see the truth, even if she had to pound it into his thick skull. "I was hoping your mood would have improved in the time you were away. But it seems you're still as amiable as a bear with a thorn in his paw."

Ash laughed softly. "What's wrong, princess? Not happy with your new husband?"

"I'm certainly not happy with being humiliated. You couldn't have done a better job of showing everyone how very repugnant you found the idea of marrying me." She hoped he couldn't hear the pain of her injured feelings in her voice.

He shrugged, either oblivious to her feelings or unconcerned with them. "You should have thought of the consequences when you decided to set your little trap."

She squeezed her hands together, fighting to maintain her composure when she wanted desperately to throw something at him. "I would never try to trap you. You must believe me."

"Must I?" He laughed, a harsh sound that grated her frayed nerves. "From where I'm standing, a man would have to be pretty damn stupid to trust anything you had to say."

He thought she was a liar. It was all she could do to keep from screaming. "I realize you will find this difficult to believe, but I've never been interested in subjecting myself to public ridicule. I can't think of a better way to ensure humiliation than to be found half undressed in a man's arms by Mrs. Backster."

"Marlow tells me she's one of the biggest gossips around." He gave her a hard look. "You sure know how to pick an audience."

"What you don't seem to be able to get through your rather thick skull is that I did not plan that little debacle this afternoon. I'm not suicidal enough to try to trap you into anything."

"Save the heartfelt speeches." He tugged his shirt from his trousers, flicking open the buttons as he continued. "You wanted to make sure I'd stick around for the old man and the duchess. So you decided marriage was the way to do it. You offer up your virginity, I pay for it with my freedom. That is, if you really are a virgin.''

''If I really . . .'' She stared at him, anger snatching her ability to speak for the space of a heartbeat. ''Why, you stupid, arrogant oaf! How dare you imply I'm the type of woman who would go about consorting with men!''

''You fell into my arms quick enough.''

''I'm insane. It's the only possible answer.''

One corner of his mouth twitched. He peeled off his shirt. Golden light from the wall sconce behind him spilled across his wide bare shoulders.

Elizabeth stared; she couldn't help herself. The infuriating brute was one of the most compelling men she had ever seen. Beautiful. Sculpted muscles, smooth skin, dark hair. Standing there half naked, he was simply devastating.

He tossed his shirt on the floor, like a barbarian coming home from a day of pillaging and plundering. Still, she had the uneasy feeling the pillaging had yet to begin. She drew herself up to her full height, ignoring the trembling in her legs. ''What are you doing?''

''I'm getting ready for bed.'' He sank into one of the upholstered armchairs near the hearth.

She watched him tug off one filthy boot, frowning as she realized his intent. He expected to come to her bed after riding around the countryside for the past five hours. She, on the other hand, had spent more than an hour preparing for her new husband, hoping to please him. Now she realized there would be no pleasing Ash MacGregor. It wasn't enough to humiliate her in public; he expected to humiliate her in private as well.

''Your rooms are down the hall.'' She pointed toward the door leading to the withdrawing chamber connecting their apartments.

''But my wife is in here.'' He dropped his boot on the Aubusson carpet, splattering mud across an intricate pattern of roses and urns set in stitches of blue and gold and ivory

"Your wife isn't interested in having anything to do with the stubborn, unreasonable oaf she married."

He tugged off his other boot. "I paid a high price for you. I intend to get my money's worth."

"I beg your pardon, *my lord*. From where I'm standing, it seems I'm the one who has paid a substantial price for my own stupidity in coming within a mile of you."

He smiled as he stripped off his socks. "Save the act; I'm not impressed."

She shivered beneath his lethal glare. How could anyone manage to turn a smile into something so cold and menacing? "I realize there is little I can say to convince you I'm not Delilah intent on chopping off your hair. But I . . ."

"You already chopped off my hair."

She frowned. "Perhaps I did. But I didn't attempt to trap you into marriage."

"I see." He grinned, his eyes cold. "You simply found me irresistible."

Heat crept into her cheeks. At the moment she was resisting the nearly irresistible urge to kick him.

He stood, his gaze never leaving her. Slowly, he began flicking open the buttons lining the front placket of his light gray trousers.

She knew the basics of male anatomy. Aside from what she had learned in medical texts, Leona had believed a woman going into Society should have more than merely a dim notion of the male animal. Before Elizabeth's first Season the duchess had instructed her ward on all she should expect from the male of the species. Her instructions had included details on what transpired between a man and a woman once they were wed. The duchess believed that knowledge was power.

Yet Elizabeth wasn't feeling very powerful at the mo-

ment. Every muscle in her body was as taut as an over-
stretched bowstring. She was, as much as she hated to
admit it, apprehensive and a bit afraid of what this powerful, angry male might do.

"Relax, princess," he said, as if he could read her
thoughts. "I paid too much for you to break you. I intend
to enjoy playing with my new toy."

He stripped away his trousers. The smooth white silk
of his drawers molded his slim hips, his muscular thighs.
The solid ridge of his male member pressed against the
silk, like a wild beast straining to be free. She swallowed
hard.

She had expected a great deal from marriage. Patience.
Affection. Passion. She had always imagined her husband
taking time with her, easing her over the threshold of
womanhood. She had imagined gentle hands and soft
kisses. She had imagined whispers of love and devotion.
From this man. Only this man.

He flicked open the three buttons at the top of his drawers. "I never had much call for these, except in the winter.
But I've discovered I like the feel of silk against my
skin." He stripped off his drawers. "Though not nearly
as much as I like the slide of a woman's skin against
mine."

Elizabeth didn't want to think of all the women he had
held naked in his arms. She didn't want to think of the
way she might compare in his eyes. In the past, many
men had called her beautiful. At this moment, none of
those sentiments mattered. She only cared about what this
man thought of her. This man, who stood in the soft light
of the wall sconces like a sculpture of some mythical
Greek deity brought to life.

In spite of the cool breeze whispering through the window behind her, the room had grown warm. A pulse flickered in the tips of her breasts and lower, in the most secret
part of her.

He tossed his undergarment on the floor, discarding the last shred of civilization. He was man, in all his primitive, potent glory. "I've never seen a nightgown that covered a woman all the way up to her chin. Very innocent."

She had hoped to wear a gossamer gown of silk and lace on her wedding night. But this was the prettiest of all she possessed. "I didn't have time to acquire my wedding trousseau."

"Take it off. I want to see what I paid for."

Elizabeth set her jaw at his harsh command. "I'm your wife. I will not be treated like a trollop."

"You sold yourself like a whore, expect to be treated like one."

He wanted to control her, to debase her, to show her how little she meant to him. She realized there would be no victory for either of them if she met his anger with her own. "I didn't plan for us to be caught this afternoon. If you could only manage to look past your stubborn anger, you would see the truth."

"Come on, princess. We both know the only reason you allowed me to touch you."

She caught a glimmer of pain beneath the anger burning in his eyes. He had been disparaged and vilified all his life. He expected nothing but disdain from *ladies*. Under the circumstances, there was little reason for him to believe her. But she had to try. "There is only one reason why I would allow such liberties from any man."

He tilted his head, gazing at her like a sleepy lion. "And what would that be?"

"I might be insane." She dropped all her defenses, risking her pride for a chance to win his trust. "But I'm also incurably in love with you."

Chapter Twenty-one

Ash flinched as her soft words jabbed him like a knife. The witch thought she could control him with his own bitter need for her. She was so beautiful. An indignant angel, dressed in white linen and lace from her chin to the bare toes peeking out from under the voluminous nightgown. A gorgeous schemer who could make him believe in miracles. And that was the reason he hated her. She had actually made him believe she loved him. "No more lies."

She stamped her foot. "Stubborn fool!"

It was time the beautiful witch learned how dangerous it could be to trap wild animals. He stalked her, slowly, allowing her a chance to contemplate what he would do when he reached her. Her eyes grew large. Fear flickered across her features, then died in a blaze of determination. The woman might be deceiving, but she sure as hell had steel in her spine.

He stepped close to her, so close he could feel her warmth radiate against his skin. So close the soft linen of her gown brushed the sensitive tip of his swelling shaft. He swallowed a moan of pleasure. Blood pounded inside him. Even now, as angry as he was with her, he wanted her more than he wanted his next breath. Still, the lady would see the beast she had trapped was not easily tamed. "Strip."

She placed her hand on his chest, her warm palm resting over the heart she had torn to shreds. "Ash, look past your anger. Give us a chance to make a real marriage."

He would not be manipulated by this heartless beauty. He gripped the lace-trimmed edges of her gown. With one powerful tug he ripped open the garment, popping pearl buttons from white linen and lace.

She stumbled back a step, stunned by the violence of his action. She plucked at a torn piece of lace at her neck. "Was that really necessary?"

He planted his hands on his hips and speared her with his iciest glare. "Let's get this straight, princess. I'm not about to believe anything you have to say. So don't waste your breath."

"I realize you haven't had much reason to trust people in the past, but I'm not in the habit of lying to anyone."

He slid his fingers down the flesh exposed by the ragged edges of her gown. Her lips parted on a startled sigh. Her eyes grew wide and wary. He spread his hand against her smooth skin, grazing the sides of her softly rounded breasts, smoothing downward over her sleek belly. A tremor rippled through her. His blood pounded. "I want you naked."

She frowned, studying him as though searching for chinks in his armor. He had the uneasy feeling she could see right through his anger, straight into his pain. He clenched his jaw. "Take it off or I'll rip it off you."

She shrugged her shoulders. "If that's what you want, Ash."

Through the smoldering anger in his brain, he heard the dangerous undercurrent in her soft voice. This woman never surrendered without a fight. Yet, here she was, easing the nightgown from her shoulders.

He watched, entranced by the the white linen gliding over her breasts, her belly, the long length of her legs. The nightgown tumbled to the floor with a soft sigh. Light from the brass and crystal lamp fixed to the oak paneling behind her glowed against her smooth skin. Her breasts rose and fell with each breath, pink nipples taut and tempting. She was far more beautiful than his memory had allowed him to believe. "You aren't putting up much of a fight."

"I don't want to fight with you." She drew her fingertip down the center of his chest. "I want to make love with you."

"Make love?" He laughed, a soft sound designed to mock her. "Save the sentiment, princess. I'm only interested in what's between your thighs."

"I'll be your whore if that's what you want, Ash." She slid her hands over his chest, spreading warmth across his skin. "But I'm not certain what I have to do. You'll have to teach me."

He slipped his hand between her thighs, trailed his fingers through feminine curls, cupping the mound of her woman's flesh. Her lips parted on a soft breath that brushed his chest. Her eyes grew wide. Warm honey drizzled against his palm. He slid his thumb over the damp feminine petals, pressed the nub he had long ago learned was the secret to a woman's pleasure. She gasped and gripped his bare shoulders, as though her legs would buckle if not for him.

He brushed his lips across hers, tasted one corner of her mouth with the tip of his tongue. "Your body knows how to act the whore, princess."

She looked up into his eyes. "If you hate me, why do you want to bed me?"

The look in her eyes spoke of love and need and longing so deep it could drown a man. All lies, he told himself. "Hattie once told me it's all a matter of pretending. All I have to do is pretend you're not a lying, deceiving little wench."

Elizabeth swallowed hard. For a moment he thought the silver mist shimmering in her eyes would turn to rain.

Yet she didn't cry. She lifted her chin and held his angry glare. "And all I have to do is pretend you will one day realize how much I love you."

Damn the witch! Damn her for making him want to believe all her lies. He grabbed her waist, his fingertips meeting at the small of her back. He dragged her against him, forcing the hard blade of his arousal against her belly. "Last night you didn't have any trouble pretending I was the man you've been carrying around in your head all these years."

"You're right, I used to dream of Peyton." She smoothed her hands down the taut muscles in his arms. "I used to imagine what he would look like, the sound of his voice, the touch of his hand. I suppose I've always been a little in love with him."

Ash couldn't deny the jealousy snaking through his belly. She wanted a gentleman. A fantasy. And she had married a beast instead. "Then this should be easy enough for you."

She shook her head. "It isn't easy, seeing only hatred in your eyes."

"Close your eyes," he said, keeping a steely edge to his voice.

"No." She rubbed her cheek against his chest above his heart. "This is a special night for me, even if it isn't for you. This is the night I will give myself body and soul into your keeping. I want to remember every detail of it."

God, her lies were so damn sweet. But he couldn't believe her. He refused to let her rip out his heart. Not again. He cupped her face between his palms, staring down into her beautiful, deceiving eyes. "You're good. A better actress than any of Hattie's gals."

"I know you don't believe me. But I want you to know, I love you more than I ever imagined loving that phantom who lived in my head."

Liar! "You talk too much. A good whore knows when to keep her mouth shut."

"Only a coward is afraid of the truth." She turned her head. Her warm breath brushed his skin as she pressed her lips against his wrist. "And I don't believe you're a coward, Ash."

"I'm not a fool either. You wouldn't know the truth if it spit in your eye."

"I know how I feel. I'm yours. Now and always."

Her soft words shivered through him. He fought against the weakness he hadn't realized resided inside him until he had met her.

The scent of her skin drifted through his senses, warm lavender kissed with an exotic spice that was hers alone. The light in her eyes drew him, like a wanderer seeking shelter in the night. Anger faded in that light. He caught himself leaning toward her, seeking the affection he imagined glowing in her eyes. She made him believe in all that affection. She made him believe a beast could find comfort in the arms of a princess. She made him a fool.

Never again.

With a force of will that had gotten him through hell, he crushed the tenderness rising inside him, the damn foolishness that would bring him to his knees before her. He dropped his hands from her face. He would prove he had only one use for her. Still, he felt the back of his neck prickle as she smiled up at him.

"When I first met you I thought you were the most dangerous man I had ever seen in my life." She slid her hands over his shoulders, as though she loved the feel of his skin. He shivered inside. "I wondered what it might be like to touch you like this. I actually imagined what you would look like without any clothes."

More lies, he assured himself. He stiffened as she leaned against him, soft breasts grazing his chest. He clenched his jaw, stifling a groan of pleasure as she rubbed her silken belly provocatively against his aroused flesh.

"I never imagined you would be this beautiful." Her silky voice poured over his skin with the soft brush of her cheek against his chest. "I love all the different textures of you. Smooth skin, silky curls. So warm. I adore the strength of you. The power of you."

This wasn't going according to plan. She was supposed to be frightened of the beast she had trapped. He closed his hands around her arms, intending to push her away. She pressed her lips to his chest, swirled her tongue across his nipple. Pleasure speared through him, shooting like lightning through his every nerve. He dropped back his head, unable to prevent a husky moan from rising in his tight throat.

"I came apart when you touched me like this last night." She slid her soft hands down his sides, over his hips. "Shattered into a thousand shimmering pieces. I never realized I could want anything as much as I want you."

Need beat like a hammer against his skull. Need pumped with every pulse of his heart. Need pounded in his belly.

He had never crawled in his life. Even when he was reduced to living in alleys and eating scraps he found in the garbage. He had never crawled. Yet, she had him by the neck and she was forcing him to his knees.

He leaned into her softness. He couldn't save himself from the fall. She was fire and he was wood, dry and eager for the flames. He had never in his life wanted a woman the way he wanted this one. Completely. He wanted to wrap himself in all that smooth, silken flesh and forget all the ugliness he had ever seen in this life. He could find no strength to resist her. Anger withered in the hot blaze of his rising passion.

"Damn you." He crushed her soft mouth beneath his.

In spite of the harsh tone of his voice, there was no anger in his kiss, only a desperate need that mirrored the longing deep inside her. Elizabeth moaned deep in her throat, stunned by the hunger blazing in this man. He lifted her in his arms, wrapping her in the warmth of his arms, pressing her with powerful muscles that shifted against her breast as he carried her to the bed.

The cool silk sheet touched her back. She tugged him down with her, pulling him close, savoring the heat of potent masculinity against her softness. She had dreamed of a moment like this from the first day he had stalked into her life. Now he was here, in her arms.

"Touch me, Beth," he whispered against her mouth. "I won't hurt you; I swear I won't hurt you."

His husky words rippled through her. She slid her hands across his shoulders, down his back, anxious to learn every inch of his body. His skin was hot satin stretched tautly over thick muscles that shifted beneath her touch. He was every fantasy she had ever dreamed.

She had risked her pride for this moment. And, as he pressed soft kisses across her cheek, she realized it was a small price to pay for the pleasure of holding him this way. A shudder rippled through her as he smoothed his callused hands over her skin. She slid her legs against his, wanting to touch him everywhere, rough masculine curls teasing her skin.

He spread kisses across her jaw, slid his tongue down her neck, pausing where the throb of her pulse beat wildly beneath his lips. She couldn't disguise the need for him that pounded in her blood. She didn't want to try.

He spread the warmth of his lips and tongue down her body, tasting her breasts, her ribs, her belly. He settled between her thighs, his dark hair against her pale skin. His moist, hot breath touched the core of her femininity, a warmth that shuddered deep inside her. He pressed his lips to the curls crowning her thighs in the most intimate of kisses.

She tipped back her head, a soft moan escaping her lips. How wicked he was. How incredibly delicious.

She slipped her hands into his dark hair, arched her hips toward him, responding in a wanton fashion that would have shocked her a few days ago. Propriety had no place in this bed. Only pleasure. A pleasure that swirled up inside her, sparkling like bubbles in a glass of champagne, until she shimmered with pleasure, shivered and shuddered and called his name.

He rubbed his cheek against her belly, soothing the shudders that rippled through her with his big hands gliding along her hips. "Do you want me, princess?"

She had wanted him since the first moment he had held her in his arms. She cupped his face in her hands. "I've never wanted any other man."

He surged upward, over her, covering her with the heat of his body. She trembled at the first touch of his hard shaft against her inner thigh. The answer to a mystery waiting to be solved was almost within her grasp.

He kissed her breasts. With his lips and tongue he lavished all of his attention on one incredibly sensitive nipple, and then the other. He slipped his hand between their bodies, touching her, finding the secret bud he had tortured with his lips and tongue, sending sensation sparking through her every nerve.

She arched against him, seeking the hardness that pressed against her and triggered a sweet deluge of warm feminine rain. He pressed against her, watching her face as he entered her body for the first time. She arched her head back, her lips parting as he eased into virginal sheath.

"You're so tight. So incredibly small." He lowered his head to taste her parted lips as he eased into her untried passage.

Tight femininity relaxed beneath his gentle prodding. He slipped deeper inside her, easing his way, coaxing innocence into surrender with a sweet stretch of his body into hers.

She felt the barrier give way the very instant he brought her past the threshold of her innocence. She tensed with the sharp sting of pain. He drank the soft moan from her lips as he filled her for the first time, and the glory of the moment seared her memory.

He grew still inside her. Through the fog of her mind she recognized the trembling in his muscles for what it was. He was holding back, giving her time to adjust to the feel of him inside her. She pressed her face into the damp curve of his neck, breathed in his scent. After a while she felt the pain recede into a dull ache. She moved against him, testing his length with a slow dip and arch of her hips, the pressure easing within her as her body accepted the thick length of him.

''Beth,'' he groaned.

He moved within her then, as though no longer able to restrain the beast inside him. Pain faded into a pleasure that surged with each furious beat of her heart. She moved beneath him, rising to meet his every thrust, meeting his passion with all the love she had for him.

It didn't matter who had conquered and who had surrendered. In that instant, as she arched and shuddered beneath him and the world shattered around her, she wanted nothing more than to live the last day of her life in his arms.

He eased into her arms. She slid her hand down his back, absorbing the damp heat of his skin. She smiled against the top of his head, dark waves tickling her chin. He lay as naked as a babe in her arms, his face turned into her shoulder, his weight pressing her down into the soft goose-down mattress. The heat of his body warmed her.

Although Leona had tried, all the explanations in the world could not have prepared Elizabeth for the shattering pleasure of making love with this man. There simply weren't any words to describe the splendor of it.

He cared for her, even if he refused to admit it. He had taken time with her. He had kissed and caressed her. He had taken her with gentleness and passion. These certainly weren't the actions of a man who hated a woman. And it wasn't simple lust either, she assured herself.

Lust would have driven him to ram into her with unbridled passion. Lust alone would never have permitted him to ease her through the difficult part. No, she was quite certain he cared for her. Now, if she could only get the brute to admit it.

He stirred, bracing himself on his forearms to look down into her face. She stared up into the stunning beauty of eyes the color of a clear morning sky. Turmoil swirled in those heavenly blue depths. A confusion that gave her hope.

She slid the tip of her forefinger over the smooth curve of his lower lip. "I've never in my life felt anything quite that . . . extraordinary."

He glanced away from her, as though he realized all his doubts were in his eyes. "It's not supposed to be very good for women the first time."

"You mean it gets better?"

He shrugged, as though none of this were important to him. "So I've heard. Can't say for sure. I've never been with a woman her first time."

"Truly? You've never been with a virgin before?"

He fixed her in an icy glare. "I'm not the type of man who goes around seducing virgins."

She smoothed her fingertip over the deep lines in his brow. "Except me."

He stiffened against her. "I didn't seduce you, princess."

"Without knowing it, you did." She slid her hands over his damp shoulders. "All you had to do was glance at me and I shivered inside. You touch me and my brain stops working. I've been fascinated with you since the first moment I saw you. So you see, just being you was enough to seduce me."

A dark shadow of doubt crossed his features. "I suppose you're going to tell me that's the reason you decided to set your little trap."

She frowned. "You can't mean to say you still think I'm a lying schemer."

"Guess it's a lot easier to believe than your falling in love with a 'half civilized barbarian'." He pulled away from her and climbed from the bed. "We'll both be better off if we don't try to make this marriage any more than it is."

She gathered the sheet against her breasts, watching him walk away from her. "And what exactly is this marriage to you, Ash?"

He tugged on his trousers, keeping his back to her. "You sold yourself as a whore. As far as I'm concerned, that's what you are. My whore. For as long as I want you."

Anger flickered with the frustration deep inside her. She wanted to scream. She wanted to grab him and hold him until all the anger melted inside him. Until she was certain he didn't mean any of the ugly things he said. "I might be insane, but I'm not stupid. And only a stupid woman would try to trap you into marriage."

He turned to her, his face carved into hard lines, his eyes glittering with barely suppressed rage. "I've had enough lies, princess."

Stubborn fool! She clutched the sheet against her breasts as he walked toward the door. "Where are you going? I'm not through discussing this with you."

He paused at the door leading to the withdrawing chamber. "I'm through with you. At least for tonight."

She lifted her chin. "You can forget about coming back until you're ready to listen to reason."

He stalked her, each stride filled with the powerful grace that was so much a part of him. "Get this straight, princess. You're mine." He cupped her cheeks in his hands. "I'll take you when I want you. Where I want you. For as long as I want you."

"If you think for one moment . . ."

He clamped his mouth over hers, devouring her protest in a deep, penetrating kiss that sent heat shooting through her veins. Too soon he was stepping away, leaving her dazed and hungry for all he could give. She sagged back against the pillow, staring up into his furious blue eyes.

"You're mine," he said, his voice low and husky.

She stared at him, watching him march across the room. He left, closing the door leading to the withdrawing chamber between their apartments with a soft click.

"Beast!" She fell back against the pillows, closing her eyes against the scalding tears. She had learned a long time ago that tears accomplished nothing. They couldn't mend wounds or make the pain go away. Tears simply left you feeling weak and empty. When they were dry you still had to face the rest of your life.

She drew in her breath, easing the tension in her chest, quieting her emotions. She had to look at this calmly. She had to find a way past the barricades he kept erecting between them. He thought she was a liar.

"Oh!" She thumped her fist against the soft mattress.

But he wanted her. Even in his anger he had taken her with gentleness. She had to believe he had feelings for her. Buried beneath anger now, but still there. Somehow she would tame the beast. She had to. She couldn't allow him to walk out of her life.

Chapter Twenty-two

Although last night Elizabeth had managed to convince herself she could tame her infuriating beast, her confidence waned with the moon. One look at his shuttered expression across the table at breakfast and she realized he hadn't softened his position. She was the enemy.

After agreeing to meet for his lesson in the drawing room at ten he had disappeared before she had finished her buttered scone, as if he couldn't stand to look at her. Well, he would have to look at her. They had fourteen days to prepare for his first exposure to polite society. Fourteen days to ensure that he didn't humiliate himself and destroy every possible chance she had of coaxing him home.

At half past ten she went searching for the inconsiderate brute. She tracked her husband to the great stone building that housed the horses, where the head groom informed her that His Lordship was in the paddock behind the stables. She marched through the long building, her footsteps clicking against the brick-lined floor. There were a few things his lordship needed to learn about common courtesy, she thought. And she was . . .

She froze on the pathway leading to the large paddock area. MacGregor wasn't alone. He stood in the center of the paddock, watching Julianna cantor around the ring atop his gray stallion. Her mother's laughter drifted on the cool morning breeze, as bright as the sunlight streaming

all around her and the man standing nearby, smiling up
at her. They looked so at ease together, friendly and
laughing, enjoying the simple pleasure of being together.
Her chest tightened with a gathering of longing and regret
she couldn't suppress. He never looked that way when he
was with her, Elizabeth thought. He was never relaxed.
Never happy.

Julianna waved when she saw her daughter. "Elizabeth!"

Ash glanced in Elizabeth's direction, his smile fading
when he saw her standing in the shade of a tall elm tree.
Elizabeth fought to keep the hurt from her expression. She
refused to allow him to know just how easily he could
prick her feelings. If he wanted to treat her with a chilly
restraint, so be it. She would not make a complete fool
of herself for the sake of one infuriating male. Now all
she had to do was convince herself of it.

Julianna halted the horse beside Ash. He placed his bare
hands around the pale blue wool covering her mother's
small waist. Julianna didn't seem to mind having him lift
her from the saddle and place her lightly on the ground.
Apparently Ash wished to ignore the rules she had taught
him about helping a lady alight from a horse.

"Isn't he marvelous!" Julianna slipped her arm
through Ash's as she walked toward her daughter.

Her mother obviously couldn't see past the man's handsome facade.

"So powerful." Julianna smiled up at Ash. "And yet
so very gentle."

Elizabeth glared at the rogue. Did he manage to beguile
every female he met?

Julianna patted Ash's arm. "He'll make an excellent
stud."

Elizabeth blinked. "Pardon me?"

Julianna turned her innocent blue eyes toward her
daughter. "Peyton and I have been discussing which of

my mares we should breed with Wind Dancer.''

"Wind Dancer?'' Elizabeth whispered. Horses. Her mother had been discussing horses.

Ash's lips flattened into a tight line. "What's wrong, princess? Don't you think Wind Dancer is good enough to serve as a stud for one of your mother's mares?''

She looked up into the cold blue depths of his eyes and wondered how she always managed to tweak this man's anger. "I'm certain if my mother believes he will make an excellent stud, he will.''

He narrowed those icy eyes. She steeled herself, expecting him to say something nasty in reply. He chose instead to look away from her, glancing back toward the house, as though he wanted only to ignore her.

Elizabeth swallowed hard, pushing back the tight knot of pain rising in her throat. They might be making progress as far as his studies were concerned, but their own relationship was another matter entirely. It was all she could do to keep from screaming at him. She wanted to pound on his chest until his frozen heart cracked open wide enough to allow her inside.

"We thought we'd take a ride this morning.'' Julianna seemed completely oblivious to the dangerous undercurrents swirling around the man standing beside her and her daughter. "Would you like to come?''

They were going for a ride. Ash had intended to leave her stewing in the drawing room while he rode off and enjoyed the morning. Oh, she wanted to kick the man. "I'm afraid I have other business to attend to this morning.'' She pinned the rogue in an icy glare. "I rather thought you had a prior engagement as well.''

He shrugged. "It's a beautiful morning. I didn't feel like spending it locked up inside.''

Did he think she wanted to spend her every waking moment trying to pound proper decorum into his thick head? "The party is in a few days. And there is still a great deal to cover."

Ash nodded. "Guess our ride will have to wait."

"Oh." Julianna pulled her lips into a pout. "I was looking forward to riding Wind Dancer."

He smiled down at Julianna with a gentleness that made Elizabeth's heart squeeze painfully in her chest.

"Take him," Ash said.

Julianna pressed her hand to her neck. "Do you mean it?"

Ash nodded. "He knows you now. You shouldn't have any trouble with him."

"I'll take good care of him." Julianna patted his chest before she turned and walked back toward the paddock, leaving her daughter alone with Ash.

Elizabeth looked up at the rogue, hiding her hurt behind a mask of icy disdain. "I suppose you thought it would be amusing to leave me sitting around waiting for you to return from your morning ride."

He gave her a hard look, his eyes as cold as the chill creeping up her spine. "Julianna suggested the ride just before you arrived. I intended to tell you about it."

"After you returned?"

"Before we left." The breeze tossed a thick wave over his brow. "I figured the proper thing to do was to invite you to come along."

The proper thing. Her heart ached with the sharp prick of his words. "How very thoughtful of you."

He shrugged, as though he didn't care what she thought. "I figured you'd choose sitting around lecturing over taking a good hard ride in the sunshine."

Did he think she enjoyed playing the role of task master? "I happen to enjoy riding."

He lifted one dark brow. "If you say so."

"I shouldn't need to remind you the party is a week from Friday."

"And there are still a hundred things left to drive into my head." He turned away from her and started walking back toward the house. "Guess we better get started."

She hesitated for a moment before following him down the path. He had no right to make her feel like the warden in a prison. He had no right to make her feel selfish and petty and boring. She knew far too well how vicious the members of polite society could be. They would be looking for every flaw in the man who would be presented to them as the long lost Lord Angelstone. And she intended to make certain they didn't find any.

If she had anything to do with it, the man would not be humiliated. Even if he could be a beast. Even if he did think her a nuisance. Even if he did have the most unfortunate ability to tear her heart into shreds.

She caught up with him. "I thought we would begin with a tour of Chatswyck."

He didn't look at her. "Doesn't matter to me."

She only wished it didn't matter to her. She only wished she could force him out of her heart. But she couldn't. Her only hope was to make him see he had a place here. He had been born here, as had his father, his grandfather, his great grandfather, and every duke since 1673. He was part of a long line of men and women who had lived here, loved here, raised their families here. She had to make him see, this was his home.

Morning sunlight flowed through the skylights overhead, illuminating the portraits that lined the walls of one of the long passageways of Chatswyck. Yet Ash scarcely noticed the men and women encased in elaborately carved frames. His thoughts were focused inward, to that place of doubts lurking deep inside him. He wanted to believe they had all made a mistake. He wanted to believe he wasn't really the old man's grandson. It would make everything easier.

Every moment he spent here chipped mortar from the wall holding back his memories. This place, everything he saw, was far too familiar to dismiss the very real possibility that he had lived here before. Was he Peyton?

"Family portraits line this hall and the next. On these walls and throughout Chatswyck, you can find a portrait of every duke and duchess of Marlow since the title was created in 1654," Elizabeth said.

He glanced at the woman walking beside him. His wife. His chest tightened with a longing he couldn't deny. She was staring straight ahead, her chin held at a damn-the-world angle. She looked icy and angry and so damn beautiful his heart ached. It was better this way, he assured himself. Better to endure her anger than to allow her to twist him into knots with her dainty little hands.

He filled his lungs to capacity, fighting the tension he had felt since coming to this place. Strange that the only time he had felt at home was when he had lain in her arms. For those few moments he had known contentment. *Happiness.* He had imagined brief glimpses of happiness in his past, yet nothing had prepared him for the pure joy of losing himself in her warm embrace. For one exquisite moment in time he had imagined belonging to someone else. And it was all a lie.

Her gown rustled softly as Elizabeth walked beside him, the pale blue wool brushing against her petticoats, reminding him of everything he would find if he peeled away all the layers of wool and linen—softly rounded breasts, pink nipples that grew taut and sweet beneath his tongue, sleek femininity turning to warm honey against his mouth. He tried to crush the memories rising with heat inside him to no avail. The woman burned like a fever in his blood.

She led him down the wide hall, pointing out the paintings of people who might have been his ancestors, oblivious to the fact that she stood beside a man who was at the moment mentally unfastening the hooks lining the back of her gown. He didn't want to think about ancestors; he wanted to take her in his arms and hold her, as much as he wanted to deny his attraction to her.

Mentally he shook himself, fighting his need for her, the longing that wrapped like chains around him and drew him toward disaster. It was better to keep his distance from her, no matter how much he wanted her. He couldn't look in her eyes and trust the affection he saw there. She would do anything to keep him here, for Marlow and the duchess.

He followed her down an adjoining corridor that was just as long and just as elegant as the portrait gallery. If they lined up all the corridors in this place, they'd stretch from Denver to New York. Did Marlow and the duchess really use all of these rooms? Damn, a man could get lost and wander around here for a month.

"This is the library." Elizabeth stepped into one of the rooms lining the long passageway. A soft sound whispered through the room as she turned a switch near the door. Gold and crystal fixtures attached to the oak-paneled walls sparked to life, glowing with incandescent light.

Ash stood for a moment on the threshold, staring into the room, feeling like a starving beggar who has been invited into a bakery. Books stretched the length of the room, two stories high and about a mile long.

"It was the first duke's Long Gallery, until 1815, when it was turned into a library. The sixth duke, George William, decided the original library was much too small to contain his passion for books, so he had the gallery transformed. There is also an ante-library, adjacent to this

_owed her as she strolled past book-lined _ked around, wondering what treasures _ _ the leather covers. He could take years just working his way through the library. But he didn't have years.

She paused near a glass-fronted cabinet built into one of the walls. "Emory's collection of rare manuscripts is kept here."

Ash stared through the glass at the thick leather-bound volumes standing on polished shelves. One of the books on the middle shelf was open. Light glimmered on the gold framing the pages. An intricate border of figures and flowers surrounded words etched in flowing script. A painting of a street scene in medieval Venice graced the center of the page. The colors of the illustrations shimmered like gems. "Guess maybe I can see where a man would take pleasure in collecting old books after all."

"Yes." Her gown rustled as she moved away from him. She paused in front of a painting that hung on the wall beside the collection of manuscripts. "This portrait was made the year after Rebecca became the marchioness of Angelstone."

Ash looked up at the portrait, unprepared for the impact of emotion that struck him. An angel smiled down at him from a frame of gilded wood. She stood in a rose garden, her dark blue gown standing out amid blossoms of red and white and pink, her eyes the same shade of blue as the sky above her. Unbound waves of pale yellow tumbled around her shoulders. The soft waves framed a face that might have graced the pages of a fairy tale, or haunted a young boy's dreams.

Memories flickered inside him—the brush of a rose against his cheek—soft laughter rippling on a warm summer day. He closed his eyes, chasing that wisp of memory. "Roses were her favorite flowers," he whispered.

"Were they?"

He glanced down at Elizabeth, startled by the sound of her voice. "What?"

"You said roses were her favorite flo

ment shimmered in her eyes. "You remembered something, didn't you?"

"Maybe. But maybe I thought roses were her favorite flowers because she's standing in a rose garden."

"I don't believe that." She crossed the room, pausing at the painting hung directly across from Rebecca. "This was painted when Emory was a year younger than you are now. Take a good look at him."

The photographs Ash had seen of Emory Trevelyan had failed to fully define the man. The painter, with his palette of oils, had rendered an image so lifelike it seemed the man might step through the frame of gilded wood and join them. Emory was smiling, just a curve of finely molded lips that lent his handsome face a hint of devilry. Yet it was the eyes that commanded attention. The dark brown eyes were filled with the good-natured humor of a man who possessed all he needed from this world.

"You can't deny the resemblance. You look a great deal like your father."

Little rogue. You're going to grow up to be as handsome as your father. And every bit as filled with mischief. The words slipped through the cracks of the walls containing his memories. A feminine voice so soft, so sweet. A voice that told stories of faraway places. A voice that whispered to a young boy at night, until he fell asleep beneath the soft stroking of her hand. Ash shivered with the memory.

"You see the resemblance, don't you?" she asked, her voice edged with excitement.

He didn't look at her. He couldn't, because his eyes ___ted with tears. He stared up at the portrait of ___lyan, seeing the same sharply defined fea-___ him in mirrors. They might have been ___ looking at the face of his father? ___eth whispered. ___y pushing down the emotion that threatened to overwhelm him. "I'm not sure what I remember."

"What was it just now? You remembered something; I could see it in your face."

"Glimpses." He stared at Emory Trevelyan's smiling face. "Images that could be nothing more than my imagination."

She released her breath in a frustrated sigh. "Is it really so difficult to admit you are Peyton Trevelyan?"

He laughed, the sound bitter to his own ears. All his life he had been looking for a place where he could belong. He always figured if he found his family, that search would come to an end. Now, he might be standing in his father's house, and he realized he belonged here about as much as Lady Beth belonged at Miss Hattie's.

"I don't understand you. You have the chance to reclaim your life and you resist."

He looked down into the anger in her gray eyes and tried to find a way to make her see the impossibility of him ever coming back home. "After John MacGregor died I had nowhere to go. I lived on the streets, in alleys, until one day I found this big building where they kept books. John had taught me to read, and so I thought that big building was paradise."

Ash turned, gazing up at the rows of books lining the shelves of the second-story gallery, testing the old wounds carved deep inside him. Even now, after so many years, the pain was still there, dull and dark, like a scab crusted over a jagged wound. "The librarian threw me out. He didn't want a dirty half-breed in the place. But I found a window in the back. Every night I would sneak inside and hide until everyone had gone home. Every night I'd read until I fell asleep beside the bookshelves. I used to pretend that big building with all the books was my home."

She touched his arm, and he was stunned to find the light brush of her hand upon his sleeve made his chest tighten. "You've come home."

"Have I?" He looked down into the endless depths of her eyes, wishing he could believe her, wishing he could somehow erase the life he had lived up until this moment, forget all the ugliness that had shaped him into a man who didn't belong within an ocean of this palace. "I'm not sure I could ever belong in this place. There have been too many years between the boy who lived here and the man I've become."

She studied him, and he had the uncomfortable feeling she could look straight through him, as though he were made of glass, his feelings on display. "I don't believe you're a man who would allow his past to limit his future. If you want something with all your heart, nothing will keep you from obtaining it."

He stared down into her eyes, knowing for certain the one thing in his life he wanted—her love. He wanted to believe her. He wanted to believe the flames that flared between them were real. Yet, he knew better than to trust her, or anyone here. He knew how much she wanted him to become Peyton in every sense. "I know better than to believe I can conquer the world."

"Society is a much smaller task, Ash. I have no doubt you can conquer it." Her smile filled her eyes with warmth, like sunlight touching an early morning sky.

He touched her, craving her warmth, drawing his knuckles lightly across the curve of her cheek. Her lips parted on a startled sigh. He saw uncertainty in her eyes, and an awakening desire. So sweet. So very tempting.

"Come home, Ash," she whispered. "Come back to your family."

Family. The word rippled with longing deep inside him. All his life he had yearned for a place to call home, a family to call his own. But how could a man who had lived the way he had ever become the man she expected him to be? "I might be Peyton. Then again, I might not.

No matter which way it comes out, I can't promise I'm going to stay.''

"Your home is here. Chatswyck is more than stone and glass and wood. It's hundreds of years of tradition. It's a legacy, like a torch passed from one generation to the next. You are Marlow's grandson. Without you, his torch will die.''

He stared up at the portrait of Emory Trevelyan, a weight of regret pressing against his heart. "I'm not even sure I am his grandson.''

"Aren't you?''

He rubbed the taut muscles in his neck. "It would be better for everyone if I'm not Peyton.''

All the hope in her eyes melted in the sudden fire of her anger. "How can you say that? How can you look at Marlow and the duchess and think it's for the best if Peyton remains lost to them?''

"He *is* lost. I can't be the grandson they want me to be. I can't erase all the years and all the things that have happened to make me who I am. I can't live here.''

She turned away from him. Her gown swished, echoing the anger and frustration he sensed building inside her. He forced his own frustration into a tight corner of his heart. He wanted her, in every way a man could want a woman. And she wanted another man. A man with his face, but not his soul.

She paused beside a table that had bookshelves built beneath the round top. She stared down at the smooth mahogany for a long moment, as though collecting her thoughts. Finally she turned to face him, her beautiful face hard with determination. "You can't decide this now. You haven't given Marlow and the duchess a chance. You haven't given yourself a chance.''

He shook his head. "Don't pin any hopes on me becoming the man you've been carrying around in your head.''

She lifted her chin. "One can only hope you come to learn to appreciate your family. Otherwise, what you call yourself is really of no importance."

As far as this woman was concerned, Ash MacGregor was no better than mud on the bottom of her shoes. Oh, at times she liked him well enough, as long as she could look at him and see the man she'd been carrying around in her head all these years. A man who didn't exist. It was time she realized just how far apart he was from Peyton Trevelyan.

"You have such devotion to Marlow and the duchess." Enough devotion to lure a beast into a trap. "It's awe-inspiring."

Her eyes grew wide and wary. "I think we should continue with our tour."

He followed her to the door. When she opened it he slammed it shut with his hand. "I have a better idea."

She glanced over her shoulder, staring up into his eyes, color rising in her cheeks with the realization he saw dawning in her eyes. "You can't be serious. Not here." Her voice rose to a soft squeak. "Not now."

He was serious, more serious than he wanted to admit. He rested his hands against the dark polished oak on either side of her shoulders, trapping her against the door. "I want you. Right here. Right now."

She moistened her lips, a quick slide of the tip of her tongue that left a tempting sheen. She squeezed the brass door handle. "If you insist on doing this, we should go to my room."

"I insist." He tried to tell himself that he wanted only to humiliate her, to teach her a lesson—never tease a wild animal, never trap one, never break his heart. Yet he knew anger was only a small part of what he felt for this woman. He slipped his arm around her waist, drew her against him, pushing his hips into the soft folds of her gown. "And your room is too damn far away."

Her breath escaped in a startled sigh as he pressed his lips to the smooth skin beneath her ear. "Someone could come in."

"Well-trained servants always knock," he whispered. He breathed her scent into his lungs, savoring the fragrance of lavender and woman. He ran his hands upward, over warm wool, skimming her ribs, sliding his hands over the curves of her breasts. "And there are only well-trained servants at Chatswyck."

She trembled beneath his hands. "Ash, we shouldn't."

He slid his fingers over her nipples, feeling the soft buds grow taut beneath the layers of wool and linen. "I want you, princess."

She dropped her head back against his shoulder. "You want to humiliate me for what you think I've done," she said, her voice smoky with desire.

He nipped her earlobe. She whimpered low in her throat. "You trapped the beast, princess. Now you have to deal with him."

"Stubborn brute," she whispered, the words lacking their usual sting.

He grabbed her shoulders and turned her, pressing her back against the solid oak door. "Where's the fight in you, princess?"

She slid her arms around his neck. Warmth glowed in her eyes, desire edged with the sweet fire of affection. "I'm not your enemy, Ash," she whispered, rising up on her toes. She pressed her lips to his, kissing him, slanting her mouth across his, turning anger to need, hunger to desperation.

Damn her! For making him want her. For making him crave the warmth he imagined in her eyes. For looking so sincere when all she offered was counterfeit devotion. He dragged her skirts up around her waist. She dropped her head back against the door as he slid his hand between her thighs. Smooth silk warm from her body brushed his hand. He sought the silky curls beneath, sliding past the slit in her drawers. A few soft strokes turned her hot and slick as melted butter against his hand.

No matter what lies might have passed her lips, this was real. She wanted him. She moaned, arching into his hand, the supple shift of her body lifting her breasts into his hard chest. Pleasure surged within him, filling him, flooding every vessel.

He pressed soft kisses across the warm satin of her cheek. It seemed he had been waiting a lifetime to teach his pretty schoolmarm a lesson in the pleasure to be found in impropriety.

He flipped open the buttons of his trousers. She glanced down, her breath catching with a soft gasp. He was already hard for her. His arousal pressed against the silk of his drawers, straining to reach her. In three rapid beats of his heart he unfastened the buttons of his drawers.

"Ash," she whispered, as he grasped her hips, his fingers digging into the soft skin beneath sheer silk.

"Wrap your legs around my waist," he said, his voice harsh with need.

She complied, sliding her long legs around his waist. He groaned as damp curls teased across his hardened flesh. She pushed against him, lush in her feminine arousal, sweetly wanton.

He thrust upward, sinking into her fire, reveling in the soft gasp of pleasure escaping her lips. Need drove him into her. A weakness he couldn't deny. Still, he tried.

He snatched at the illusion of lust as her body welcomed the hard thrust of his. Yet, the illusion melted with the rise of pleasure. It melted in the heat of her feminine fire.

The door rattled with each thrust of his body into hers, pounding out the ancient rhythm, like a pagan drum celebrating this primitive dance. She tipped back her head, moaning her soft song of release, her body shuddering around his, the soft contractions dragging him from all conscious thought. He surrendered, delivering a part of himself into her keeping, his body convulsing with the pleasure that surged through his every nerve.

A long shuddering sigh escaped her lips as he collapsed against her, pinning her against the oak door. She held him with her arms and her legs, as though she never intended to release him. And deep inside he wished she never would.

"You wicked, wicked man," she whispered, her lips brushing his brow. "Is there any wonder I couldn't resist you?"

He pulled back to look into her eyes, searching for a trace of betrayal beneath the soft words. "Beautiful schemer. Is there any reason I should believe a word you say?"

She slid her fingers across his left temple, into his damp waves. "Because I don't lie. And I find it most vexing to continually be forced to defend my honor."

"Save it for someone else, princess."

Anger flickered in her eyes. "I swear, one of these days you'll be on your knees, begging me to forgive you."

He feared that day would come. He withdrew from the heat of her, fighting back a groan as the cool air touched his damp flesh. He slipped his hands from her hips, allowing her feet to slide to the floor, her petticoats and gown falling into place with a soft rustle. She looked every inch the lady, her gown hiding the stains of their lovemaking. A lady who played the whore better than any woman he had every known. Was it all a lie?

He turned away from her, straightening his clothes, trying to straighten his tangled emotions. It was then he heard a soft rap on the door.

Chapter Twenty-three

Elizabeth flinched at the soft rap. She pressed her back against the door, her heart pounding at the untimely interruption. Ash didn't look the least concerned about the intrusion. He was straightening his starched white cravat, as nonchalant as a man who had been doing nothing more than leafing through a book. No one could tell he had recently made love to his wife against the very door someone was now knocking upon, she assured herself. She smoothed her fingers over her hair. "How do I look?"

Ash grinned. "Your cheeks are pink. Your lips are red. And there is a sparkle in your eyes. I'd say you look like a woman who has just been thoroughly tumbled."

She sucked air between her teeth, resisting the urge to box his ears. She dug her heels into the carpet, pushing back against the door when the intruder tried to open it.

"Elizabeth," a deep male voice rumbled through the oak. "Is something wrong?"

She bit her lower lip. Of all the people to be on the opposite side, Dwight Trevelyan was the last she wanted to see at the moment. The handsome rogue would know. He would take one look at her and know what she had been doing a moment ago.

Dwight jiggled the door handle. "Elizabeth."

Ash leaned back against a round table, obviously enjoying her embarrassment. "I think you'd better let him in, princess, before he knocks down the door."

Elizabeth drew in her breath, acknowledging the inevitable. She molded her lips into a smile and opened the door. Dwight stood in the hall, frowning down at her. "What a surprise!"

"I'm sure it is." Dwight surveyed her, drawing his perceptive blue gaze from the top of her head to the tips of her black shoes peeking out from beneath her gown. "You look none the worse for wear."

Heat crept into her cheeks. She shifted on her feet, painfully aware of the moisture clinging to her drawers. "I'm not at all certain what you mean."

Dwight winked at her. "I could hear the door banging all the way down the hall."

She pursed her lips. "A gentleman would not have noticed."

"How you wound me." The sparkle in Dwight's blue eyes betrayed the humor beneath the guise of wounded pride. "After all, I did wait until after the door had stopped shaking."

"A true knight."

Dwight glanced past her, studying Ash before he spoke. "This must be the man who stole you away from me."

Elizabeth shook her head. She had known the man most of her life, and aside from his usual teasing Dwight had never been serious about taking her hand in marriage. She doubted he was serious about any woman. "As if marriage had ever entered your head. You're having too much fun acting the role of eligible bachelor to even think of settling for one woman."

Dwight grinned. "But if I were in the market for a wife, you would top my list."

"How flattering."

Dwight pressed his hand across his heart. "Alas, my lady, I had thought you would wait for me to end my feckless ways."

"I pity any woman who is waiting for you to mend

your ways.'' She slipped her arm through Dwight's and
turned toward Ash. He was watching her, his eyes narrowed into icy slits, his face pulled into tight lines. A thrill
rippled through her. He was jealous. She knew enough
about men to recognize when one of the species has laid
claim to a female, and Ash was showing all the signs of
having placed his brand on her.

She gave Dwight one of her warmest smiles. Let the
beast stew in his own jealous juices. ''Allow me to introduce you. Angelstone, this is your cousin, Lord Dwight
Trevelyan, Viscount Wickham. He is the eldest son of
Marlow's nephew Bertram, who is the Earl of Clayburne.''

Dwight glanced from Ash to the portrait of Emory and
back again. ''You really have risen from the dead.''

''So it seems,'' Ash said, watching the fair-haired man
like a lion wary of the intruder in his midst.

''I must say, it's been a long time since you and I
played together, Angelstone.'' Dwight sauntered across
the room, tall and slender, every move filled with ele-
gance. He paused at one of the windows, staring out into
the gardens. ''As I recall, the maze was always your favorite place. We had some prodigious battles. Of course,
you were always claiming the castle, even though I was
older by a year. You always had to be king.''

Ash frowned, troubled by Dwight's words. Did they
trigger any memories for him? Elizabeth wondered.

Ash felt a shaking deep inside him, in that place where
doubts lurked with the missing memories. He had the odd
sense of standing in a blackened cave, where any step he
took might lead him to a killing fall. *A dragon shall guard
my treasure.* The memory teased him, a flickering light
that vanished when he reached for it. His skin grew moist
beneath his clothes.

Dwight turned to face him. "Is it true? Were you really raised by Indians?"

"The Cheyenne saved my life."

Dwight lifted one golden brow, his blue eyes filled with skepticism. "I've never heard of savages saving a white man's life before."

"It just might be that you don't really know much about the Cheyenne," Ash said, keeping the irritation from his voice.

Dwight frowned. "There really isn't much to know about them, is there? They are little better than animals. Slaughtering innocent men and women. Including your parents."

"The Cheyenne fought to protect their land from those who would steal it, and with the land their very way of life. When it was clear the white men had come to stay they wanted only peace, a chance to live on the small parcels of land granted them. The whites would not allow it. The government kept breaking treaties, kept stealing more and more of what belonged to the People, until there was nothing left."

Dwight rubbed his chin. "You speak as though you side with the savages."

"How would you feel if your home, your family, all you held dear were threatened by invaders?" Ash asked.

Dwight fixed Ash with a cool stare. "I would protect what was mine, of course."

Ash had faced enough dangerous men to know when he was looking into the eyes of a man who would fight when his back was to the wall. "Then perhaps you have more in common with the Cheyenne than you realize."

Dwight considered this a moment, then laughed. "I do recall a few ladies telling me I was a heartless villain."

"Only a few?" Elizabeth asked.

Dwight pressed his hand to his heart. "Ah, milady, I fear my reckless ways are the legacy of a broken heart.

One only you can mend. But it seems I tarried a moment too long in my lonely bachelor ways." He glanced at Ash. "You wasted little time claiming the lady as your own."

Ash saw Elizabeth stiffen. She looked at him, her eyes wide and wary. *You really couldn't have done a better job of showing everyone how very repugnant you found the idea of marrying me*—her words whispered in his memory.

Obviously the lady thought he intended to make a farce of their union in public, as any self-respecting barbarian would. He molded his lips into a smile. He preferred to conduct this war in private. "I couldn't resist her. One look at her and I was captivated."

She stared at him. Ash had the impression she was holding her breath, waiting for the slap she thought would follow the soft words.

"Yes. I do understand what you mean." Dwight smiled down at the woman standing beside him, his expression betraying the longing beneath the teasing facade. "She's very special."

Another heart Elizabeth had captured in her silken web. Ash couldn't help wondering what had kept her from marrying the handsome young aristocrat. As much as he wanted to deny it, he couldn't crush the jealousy coiling in his heart.

His chest tightened as Ash watched his wife smile and chat with this polished young man. God, he was a fool. He was a dangerous beast who didn't belong in a pretty cage. He didn't intend to become a freak on display in a sideshow. He wouldn't be trapped in this palace, no matter how tempting the lure might be.

"I've been charged with bringing you back to the drawing room." Dwight squeezed Elizabeth's hand. "Father is here, anxious to meet the newly resurrected Angelstone. But perhaps you would like to take a few moments to freshen up a bit."

Elizabeth glanced at Ash. "Yes, I think that would be an excellent idea."

Ash set his jaw. He wasn't sure how well he could play the role of Peyton Trevelyan. And he didn't care much for the fact that he didn't have a choice.

It was too soon to expose Ash to Bertram, Elizabeth thought. She stirred a strawberry through the clotted cream on her plate and peeked at Ash through her lashes. She didn't want him to think she was watching him. He would think she was waiting for him to make a mistake. And he would be right.

As much as she enjoyed Dwight's company, Elizabeth wished he and his overbearing father had not stayed for refreshments. It was far safer to keep Ash secluded until she was certain he wouldn't threaten to snap someone's neck. Society didn't take well to men who went about threatening violence. And Bertram had every reason to hope society shunned Ash.

"I understand you have no memory of your life before you came to live with a pack of savages," Bertram said.

Elizabeth glanced at the slender dark-haired man sitting in a wing-back chair across from her. Bertram was a disagreeable bore at best. Ambitious. Pompous. Arrogant. Every time he was here she had the unpleasant feeling he was watching Hayward, calculating the number of years he would have to wait before assuming the title. It didn't take much dissembling to realize he was trying to provoke Ash.

"My memory is clouded," Ash said, his dark voice betraying none of his emotion.

Elizabeth looked at Ash, noting the narrowing of his eyes. Although he appeared every inch the gentleman, dressed in an elegantly tailored dark gray coat and trousers, he also looked . . . dangerous.

Sunlight slanted through the windows behind him,

searching for him, slipping into the thick dark waves that tumbled over his collar. She couldn't dismiss the thought that Ash was like a lion attending afternoon tea. Beneath the elegantly tailored facade lurked a man who was scarcely civilized. A man who could lash out and strike should someone say or do something he didn't like. A man who would make love to his wife against a library door. She tingled with the wicked memory.

"In all this time you had no inkling of your actual identity?" Bertram asked.

Ash pinned Bertram in a cold stare that any man with a shred of sense would not ignore. "None."

"Now that we have him home, I expect those clouds to lift." Hayward smiled at his grandson.

Ash didn't return the smile. He didn't move but sat staring at Bertram. Oh, dear, she really didn't like that look in his eyes. Elizabeth swallowed hard, forcing a nibble of strawberries and cream past the knot of apprehension in her throat. She stared at Ash, silently willing him to remain calm. They didn't need to deliver any ammunition into Bertram's slimy hands.

Bertram dabbed his linen napkin against his lips. "I suppose the loss of memory is really very convenient."

Ash stretched his hand flat against his thigh. "I never found it convenient."

"No?" Bertram stared at Ash for a moment. "But here you are, without a single inkling of your name, or your home, or your family, even though you were five when the tragedies occurred. It's rather convenient that no one can question you on anything that might have happened to Peyton before he left on that fateful journey."

Leona rested her hand on Ash's arm, a gesture that seemed both protective and restraining. "What he does and doesn't remember is of no consequence, Clayburne. He is home. That is all that matters."

"So you don't remember anything?" Dwight asked.

"Including the day I pushed you into the river and you nearly drowned?"

Ash glanced at his cousin, as though meeting a challenge. It was clear he expected further attacks. "I'm afraid not."

Dwight gave him a wide, mischievous grin. "In that case, as I recall, I was nowhere near you when the incident occurred."

Elizabeth could have hugged Dwight for diverting the conversation to safer ground. "Are there any other crimes we should know about?" she asked, hoping to keep them in safe territory.

Dwight considered this a moment, a look of exaggerated concentration on his handsome face. "No. I'm afraid my life has been dreadfully dull. Most monks have actually lived a much more exciting life than I."

Elizabeth was certain more than a few women would disagree. She smiled at the incorrigible rake, wondering how a man as seriously unlikable as Bertram Trevelyan could possibly have produced a son as endearingly feckless as Dwight.

"Odd, isn't it?" Bertram asked, gripping his evil intent like a terrier with a bone. "I believe most people can recall something of their childhood. Especially from the age of five."

Elizabeth clamped together her teeth to keep from screaming.

Ash didn't flinch beneath Bertram's speculative stare. "Do they?"

"Why, yes. Certainly." Bertram stirred his tea, circling the cup three times, then resting the spoon against his saucer. "I can remember many things from childhood, including incidents when I was four or five."

Hayward looked at his nephew with a warning in his eyes. "Most people are not subjected to such traumatic experiences at the tender age of five."

"True." Bertram sipped his tea.

Elizabeth released the breath she had been holding.

"Still, one would think you would at the very least remember your name," Bertram said. "It's really almost beyond belief to think someone could lose all his memories."

The man's tenacity was almost beyond belief. As much as she would like to see the arrogant bore dangling by his shirt collar, she prayed Ash kept his temper under control.

"Find it strange if you like," Ash said, his voice far too smooth for the turbulent look in his eyes, "but, the truth is, I don't remember."

Bertram lifted his brows. "So you say."

"Are you calling me a liar?" Ash asked, his voice never rising above a polite tone.

Silence spread like a chilling fog throughout the room. Elizabeth was aware of the others, frozen where they sat, as though each feared any movement might unleash the anger simmering in Ash MacGregor's eyes. She held her breath, staring at Ash, willing him to restrain the beast inside him. It simply would not do to strangle Bertram, no matter how much she wanted to perform that service herself.

Bertram smiled, a tight twisting of his lips that left his voice filled with disdain. "I'm simply saying it's difficult to understand."

"I think it's easy to understand." Elizabeth ignored the annoyed look Bertram cast in her direction. "A child witnesses the death of his parents. He is taken in by people who give him a new name, a new culture, a completely different way of life. In essence they obliterate everything he is. I believe it would be quite astonishing if he didn't lose his own identity."

"Quite true. Well put, my dear." Leona glared at Bertram. "I should think anyone of intelligence could understand why my grandson cannot remember his past, Clayburne.''

Bertram shifted in his chair beneath Leona's censuring gaze. He concentrated on his tea, lifting his spoon, stirring the liquid in his ivory cup, abandoning the battle under the strength of superior forces. Yet Elizabeth knew it wasn't the end of the war.

''That is one of the most disagreeable men I have ever met,'' Leona said, after Bertram and Dwight had left the drawing room.

''Yes, indeed,'' Hayward murmured. ''Although I must say, our grandson managed to keep him in his proper place.''

Ash eased his hand open against his thigh. He couldn't remember the last time he had more wanted to plant his fist in a man's face than he had with Marlow's nephew. Yet he had refused to allow the man to goad him to anger. He suspected that was what the arrogant aristocrat had wanted, a display of rage from the half-civilized imposter. Even though he knew it would have felt damn good to knock Bertram into the next county, it felt even better to know he could beat the man at his own game.

He glanced at Elizabeth, hoping to see some glimmer of respect in her eyes, hating himself for needing it. She was watching him. When he met her eye she smiled. A smile that touched him as surely as a soft caress on his cheek. It was all he could do to keep from touching her.

''He wanted to provoke you, my lad; I'm certain of it.'' Hayward rose from his chair. He paced the length of the room, pivoting at the white marble hearth. ''I believe he would like nothing better than to have you seen in a bad light. Possibly even discredit you.''

''Why?'' Ash asked. ''What's this guy got to lose by Peyton coming back to life?''

Hayward opened his arms. ''Chatswyck. He is next in

line to inherit should something happen to you.''

''I don't guess I blame him much,'' Ash said. ''Some stranger shows up one day, ready to claim what's his.''

''You're hardly a stranger.'' Leona folded her hands on her lap. ''Even if you do have the unfortunate penchant for refusing to acknowledge your own grandparents.''

Ash cringed inwardly at her condemning stare. She didn't realize it was better for everyone if he didn't stay.

''Unfortunately I have no doubt Clayburne intends to do everything he can to keep you from claiming what belongs to you. He all but told me so before we came into the drawing room,'' Hayward said.

Ash curled his hand into a fist on his thigh. ''There's not much sense in causing trouble with him. Since I don't plan on staying.''

Leona shook her head. ''Really, dear, I do wish you would stop saying that.''

Elizabeth stared at him, determination glowing like polished steel in her gray eyes. There were no doubts in her eyes. The lady intended to turn him into Peyton, if it was the last thing she did. Pity she didn't give a damn about the man he really was.

''You may not want to live here,'' Hayward said. ''I can only hope you come to change your mind. Regardless, you are my heir. All that is left of your father. You shall inherit my title, whether you decide to go back to America or stay where you belong. It doesn't matter. You are my grandson.''

There was so much here Ash didn't understand, but the look in Hayward's eyes wasn't one of them. He understood that determination, that bitter desperation. He recognized it for what it was—the last attempt to hold tightly to the son he had lost. And he found no argument within him to fight that need, only doubts that he could ever be the man his grandfather wanted him to be.

''Now, then.'' Hayward rested his hand on the smooth

mantel. "Since I don't care to be haunted in my grave by the knowledge that my nephew is dragging my only grandson through the courts, we must find a way to prove your identity."

"Pity you didn't pass along your birthmark, Marlow." Leona glanced at Ash. "But, as I recall, you didn't inherit that little strawberry mark on your bottom."

Ash's cheek warmed with the thought of how well the duchess knew him. "No, ma'am, I don't have a brand burned on my bottom."

Hayward smiled at Ash. "I believe the best course of action is to introduce you to society as soon as possible. By the time I pass on I want you firmly established as Peyton."

Ash refrained from telling the old man a hundred years wouldn't be enough time to turn him into Peyton.

Elizabeth rose from her chair. "If you will excuse us, there is a great deal your grandson needs to learn before the party."

Ice trickled into his blood. He had a little less than two weeks to learn every rule that might trip a man. A handful of days before he faced his first real chance to make a complete fool of himself.

Chapter Twenty-four

Elizabeth leaned back in the big white marble tub in her private bathroom, sighing as the warm, scented water lapped around her collarbone. Steam curled around her face, fragrant with the scent of lavender, soft as a lover's caress. A few days ago she wouldn't have known the softness of that caress. Yet her entire life had been altered, irrevocably changed by one maddening male.

Every muscle in her body was stiff from the tension of being near Ash MacGregor. The man was the most infuriating creature on the face of the earth. He mocked her every attempt to turn him into a respectable gentleman, to reach past his defenses. He ridiculed her unfortunate affection for him.

Stubborn beast!

He hadn't humiliated her in front of Dwight; he had, in fact, played the role of devoted husband quite well. And the jealousy was real. Unfortunately, so was the anger. Ash thought she had betrayed him, and he intended to make her pay. She understood his thinking, even if she found it appalling. From his point of view she was the enemy.

She rubbed the tight muscles in her shoulders. The man had actually commanded her to appear in his room this evening. *I want you in my bed by ten. And I want you naked.* Excitement curled in her belly. Her breasts tingled with the memory of his hands on her skin. Still, she refused to go running like a besotted lunatic into his arms.

His Lordship would soon realize Her Ladyship was not about to dance to his tune. A cold shiver skittered across her wet skin as she wondered what the beast would do when he realized she had defied him. It didn't matter what he tried, she assured herself; he would not win this war. She was his wife, not his slave. She intended to teach him that lesson if she had to pound it into his rather thick skull.

"It seems you have a problem telling time."

The dark sound of Ash's voice echoed on the marble-lined walls. Elizabeth glanced toward the door, her heart sprinting into a dizzying pace when she saw him. He was standing with one broad shoulder propped against the door frame, his dark hair falling in damp waves over his brow, one hand shoved into the pocket of the sapphire blue silk dressing gown she had chosen for him in New York.

At the time she had imagined the rich color would heighten the incredible beauty of his eyes. She hadn't truly realized how the soft silk would drape on his broad shoulders, or outline the sleek lines of his legs. She hadn't realized the wrapped style would fall open across his chest, revealing the hollow of his neck and an intriguing vee of dark skin and masculine hair. The steamy air pressed against her, growing hotter with each beat of her heart.

Ash smiled, a predatory glitter in his eyes. "It's half past ten, princess."

"And your *wife* is taking her bath." She turned away from him, hoping to look calm and unaffected by the compelling male in her midst. She rubbed her sponge across a cake of lavender-scented soap as she continued. "I've had quite a vexing day, trying to help a stubborn, ungrateful brute adjust to his new home."

He laughed softly, the deep sounds brushing against the unyielding walls, curling back around her, as if one hearing of the mocking tones wasn't enough. "Poor princess, locked in battle with the terrible beast. Are you licking your wounds?"

She shot him a chilly glance. "I'm enjoying my bath. At least I was, until you intruded upon my privacy. Afterwards, I intend to curl up in bed with a novel and try to forget I ever met you."

"I have a much more interesting proposal." Sapphire silk flowed around his long legs as he moved toward her, carrying the box of chocolates she had ordered for him from London.

She scrubbed the sponge upward along her left arm, spreading fragrant white lather, hoping he wouldn't notice the way her hand trembled with her surging pulse. "I'm quite certain I don't care to hear any of your suggestions. At least not until you're ready to treat me as your wife, and not some slave you purchased at auction."

He tugged open the sash cinched around his lean waist. "If you sell yourself like a whore, can you expect to be treated as anything else?"

"I might be insane enough to lose my heart to a stubborn beast, but I'm not so insane as to trap that beast into marriage." She splashed water across her soapy arm, trying not to notice the way the sapphire silk parted along the center of his body, revealing an intriguing amount of male flesh. Still, given the fact he was standing directly beside the tub, it was impossible not to notice the rising swell of his male member.

Her skin, already flushed from the warmth of the water, grew hotter, so hot she felt a melting within her, in that place of mystery only he had ever claimed. She dunked her sponge in the water. "Of course it's much easier for you to believe I'm the one at fault. That way you aren't obliged to try to fashion this marriage into something more than the farce you seem intent on making it."

He stripped the dressing gown from his shoulders and

tossed it on the rosewood armchair near the white marble lavatory. She glanced up at him; she couldn't prevent it. His raw male beauty demanded her attention.

Light from the wall sconces shimmered gold in the steamy air that closed around him in a loving embrace. Steam kissed the smooth curves of his broad bare shoulders. Golden light glistened in the dark curls shading his wide chest. Those silky dark curls tapered into a thin line across the plane of his tautly muscled belly. The water lapping against her skin was transformed into tongues of fire stroking her.

"I find it easier to believe you roped me into marriage, hoping to help Marlow and the duchess, than I do believing Miss Prim and Proper would stoop low enough to fall in love with a half-civilized savage."

She turned to face him as he knelt beside the tub, looking straight into his cool blue eyes. Behind the harsh mask she sensed a man in need of everything she had to give him. If he would only open up enough to trust her. "I did mention I was insane."

One corner of his mouth twitched, but he crushed the smile before it could transform his arrogant grin into genuine warmth. He slid the tip of his forefinger along her collarbone, scattering shivers in his wake. "You're in love with me. That's what you want me to believe?"

She moistened her lips, tasting the fragrant steam on her tongue. "I must say, a woman gets a bit vexed with having to say it time and time again to a man who refuses to admit the smallest affection for her."

"And that's what you want, isn't it, princess?" He tossed the lid from the box of chocolates on top of his dressing gown. "You want me curled in the palm of your hand. So infatuated with my beautiful wife that I can't see straight."

"No." She pressed her hand against his chest, above the solid thud of a heart beating in time with hers. "I want you to see the truth that's right before you.''

His eyes revealed the turmoil inside him. He glanced away from her, staring down at the chocolates he held in his hand. ''Hedley said these came from you. Were these a peace offering from the princess to the savage?''

''I wanted you to know we have very fine chocolates here in England. Every bit as good as those in America.''

He fixed her in a steady stare. ''More reasons for me to stay, is that it?''

''More reasons to make you realize you can be happy here.''

He slid his hand around her neck, his long fingers cradling her nape. ''And if I asked you to come live with me on a ranch in California, what would you say?''

She stared at him, stunned by the question. ''I would ask you why on earth you want to leave your home.''

''It makes me wonder just who you are in love with, Peyton Trevelyan or Ash MacGregor? Who is it, princess?''

She frowned. ''You are one in the same.''

He shook his head. ''Ash MacGregor belongs on a ranch raising horses. Not in this fancy palace.''

''But you're remembering things. You know in your heart you are Peyton.''

A muscle flashed in his smooth cheek as he clenched his jaw. ''I told you before; no matter what, I don't plan on staying here.''

She stared into the cool depths of his blue eyes and saw that he meant every ridiculous word. ''I can't believe you would simply turn your back on Marlow and the duchess.''

He smoothed his damp thumb over the skin beneath her ear. ''I can't be something I'm not.''

''But you are Peyton.''

He slipped his hand from her neck. ''Guess that answers my question.''

Looking into the cool depths of his eyes, she realized she had taken a big step backward in her quest to win his trust. "Why is it so wrong of me to want to call you by your real name?"

He set the chocolates on the chair nearby. "It's more than a name, princess."

"Yes, it is more. It's learning to accept your family. It's deciding to take your proper place in life."

He plucked a chocolate from the box. She leaned back against the tub, watching him, tingling with curiosity at what he would do with that piece of chocolate.

"One of these days I'll show you what I like to do with melted chocolate. But this will do for now." A lazy smile curved his lips as he drew the solid dark nugget over her lips, sweeping the sweet taste over her mouth. "Open up for me."

She parted her lips, allowing him to slide the chocolate into her mouth. He teased her with the rich confection, dipping it against her tongue, withdrawing, sliding the chocolate slowly between her lips, dipping inside again.

"Lick it." He held the chocolate above her lips, forcing her to reach upward for the lush morsel.

She tilted back her head, giving herself over to the erotic game. She flicked her tongue over the chocolate, licking his finger, tasting the salt of his skin mingling with the sweet confection. A pulse flickered in the tips of her breasts and lower, in that most secret place, a sweet pain throbbing with each beat of her heart.

He slipped the chocolate into her mouth, then lowered his mouth to hers. She parted her lips, welcoming the slow plunge of his tongue into her mouth.

"Humm, delicious," he whispered against her lips.

He reached across her, his hair-roughened arm brushing the slope of her breasts as he lifted the cake of lavender soap from the gold holder near her shoulder. He rubbed the soap between his hands, releasing the sweet scent of lavender into the steamy air. He touched her, letting his warm, soapy fingers glide across her slick shoulders. "There are a few things you need to learn, princess. Like who the man is you married."

A sigh escaped her lips at the silky slide of his hand against her flesh. "I know who I married. But I wonder if he knows."

Anger blazed in his eyes, but his gentle touch betrayed other emotions. He leaned toward her, his full lips flattened into an angry line. "You talk too much."

She parted her lips in welcome as he slanted his hard mouth over hers, meeting anger with tenderness. Anger was useless against him. Her only chance to gentle the beast lay in surrender. And, as he slid his big soapy hand over her breasts, she acknowledged a very real benefit found in this particular surrender.

He captured her nipple between his thumb and forefinger, squeezing until the wet peak grew hard and tingling. She moaned against his mouth and grasped his bare shoulders, her wet hands moving sleekly across his smooth skin.

"Do you like this, princess?" He rolled the tight bud between his fingers, sending sensation splintering through her in shimmering sparks.

She pressed her hand over his, holding him against her aching flesh. "I love the feel of your hands on my skin."

"You're so damn beautiful." His mouth traveled over her cheek, down her neck, nipping the sensitive joining of her neck and shoulder.

"So are you," she whispered, stroking her hand down the sleek muscles of his back.

He slid his hand over her ribs, down across her belly. Beneath the heat of the water he found her feminine mound. He teased her, sliding his fingers lightly over the curls, barely touching her. She arched her hips, pressing wantonly against him, seeking the pleasure only he could grant her.

"So sleek." He rubbed his cheek against her wet shoulder as he parted the sweetly swollen petals of her secret place. He found the bud where sensation flared and stroked it, the water oiling his fingers.

She tipped her hips, lifting into his hand. Water lapped over her breasts with each soft movement of her hips. Pleasure pulsed through her, bubbling and surging until her soft sobs echoed from the white marble walls.

Before the last shudder of pleasure rocked her body, he was lifting her from the water, lifting her against the smooth heat of his skin. Silky curls teased her breasts. She snuggled against him, wrapping her arms around his neck, nuzzling the warm skin beneath his ear.

"What are you doing?" she whispered as he let her legs slide from his arm.

"Setting you on your feet, princess."

She didn't like that. She had expected him to take her to bed, to finish what he had so masterfully begun. To leave her this way was much too underhanded, even for her beast. Her feet touched the cool marble floor. She swayed, her shaky legs threatening to buckle beneath her. But he was there to steady her.

"I thought you wanted me in bed," she said, beyond caring about her own wanton behavior. "Naked."

He kissed the tip of her nose. "Can't leave you all wet. You might catch cold."

"Not when you're near." She slid her hands over his shoulders.

Flames danced in the blue depths of his eyes. "Touch me, princess."

His husky words rippled with longing. She moved her hands across his chest, trailing her fingers over silky curls, touching the intriguing nubs of his dark male nipples, smiling as he sucked in his breath.

She hesitated only an instant before she brushed her fingertips over the tip of his hardened sex, dragging a soft growl from his lips. He was an amazing collection of textures, warm velvet stretched over steel. The powerful organ stirred at her touch, as if seeking each gentle caress from her fingers, and she felt her own heat stirring.

"That's nice, princess." He slipped a towel around her. He rubbed her back, her bottom, her thighs, the friction a delicious tease against her sensitive skin. All the while he was kissing her, licking beads of moisture from her breasts, her belly, nipping her skin, as though he wanted to devour her. He dropped to one knee before her.

She stared down at him. In some remote corner of her mind she wondered if this was nothing more than a dream, a wicked, erotic dream where a handsome knight pays tribute to his lady. But the sensations skittering along her nerves were far too potent to exist in some ethereal plane.

He pressed his lips against her, breathing hotly against the wet curls at the joining of her thighs. She gripped his shoulders. She tossed back her head, wanting to scream, hearing only a whimper echoing back from the marble walls. As the pleasure surged once more inside her, he stood and swept her into his powerful arms. He carried her through her dressing room, into her bedroom, to her bed.

"Do you want me, princess?" he asked, as he laid her down upon the silk sheets.

She smoothed her hands over his cheeks. "Now and always."

He came to her, sliding inside with one thrust of his hips. She gasped with pleasure and moved against him, meeting each fluid motion of his body into hers, taking him deep inside, allowing him to retreat only to draw him back again. She absorbed the luscious feel of his body sliding against hers, reveling in the different textures— smooth skin, silky curls, corded muscles.

She slanted her mouth over his, savoring his deep, penetrating kisses, glorying in the plunge and withdrawal of his tongue in time to the rhythm of his hips flexing against hers. Then all thoughts were swept away in the storm of pleasure ripping through her. She lifted into his last wild thrust, feeling the pleasure shudder through his body as her own trembled and shattered around him.

She held him long after the last shudder rippled through her. She held him, afraid he might leave her alone and hungry for his arms around her. She held him, hoping he would shield her from the loneliness that haunted her.

He gently withdrew from her, and when she refused to release her hold around his neck he didn't protest. Instead, he rolled to his side, taking her with him. He wrapped his sleek body around her, drew the sheet over them, and held her, seemingly content to stay in her bed.

She lay quietly in his arms, afraid to speak, loath to destroy the delicate peace that had settled around them. There would be time enough for lectures and arguments. Time enough to convince her beloved beast that this was right where he belonged.

Chapter Twenty-five

With each passing day Ash become more and more certain his head would explode with all the rules Elizabeth pounded into his brain. Every day she lectured and prodded and pounded, trying to transform him into Peyton. Every night she became an enchanting temptress in his arms—wild, sweetly wanton, as hungry for him as he was for her. Every night he succumbed to the temptation of her, making love to her, hoping to purge her from his blood. But the more he had her, the more he wanted her.

Every night he allowed the illusion of her love to wrap around him, to draw him into a realm where nothing else mattered but the feel of her arms around him. Never before in his life had he known a contentment as powerful as the happiness that came from holding her.

He felt like a stallion sniffing after a mare in season as he followed her into a huge room on the third floor of the house. Desire pounded through his veins. His need for her coiled around his heart, like a tether, drawing him toward her.

"You spent a great deal of time here when you were a boy," Elizabeth said, pausing beside a big mahogany desk across from the windows.

He strolled across the schoolroom, glancing around, hoping she wouldn't notice the tension that had his gut tied into knots. A long table stood at the far end of the

318

room. Early morning sunlight spilled through the mullioned windows, splashing squares of gold across an old battlefield spread across the table.

He paused on the fringe of the battle, staring down at the landscape of hills and valleys that stood on the table. Soldiers in blue marched from one side of the table to engage the soldiers dressed in red who were camped on the other side.

A few of the trees that dotted the landscape had broken branches. He slid his fingertip across a scar in the ground, where an enthusiastic child had dragged a soldier across the moss and paint, revealing the wooden platform beneath. He lifted one of the soldiers, staring down at the intricate carving. He had never seen toy soldiers with such detail. He turned the wooden soldier in his hand, touching a place where the paint had been chipped from his blue coat.

It's all right, son. You can't fight a war without causing some damage. The words whispered in his memory, and with the memory came a shivering deep inside.

"Do you remember anything?" Elizabeth asked.

He glanced over his shoulder at her, seeing the expectancy in her huge gray eyes. "That's why you decided to hold our lesson in here this morning. You were hoping I'd remember something."

"I thought it might help. Everything is as it was the last day Peyton played here." She brushed her fingertips over the top of the desk, the polished wood glowing reddish gold in the sunlight. "The room has been kept the same. This was your tutor's desk. And that was yours." She gestured toward a small version of the mahogany desk placed near the windows. "The wall covering, the furniture, everything is the same style that was here when you were a child. You must remember something."

He rubbed his thumb over the rifle the wooden soldier held, resenting the insistence in her voice, her need to turn him into the Peyton Trevelyan she carried around in her head. He needed her in ways he didn't want to understand, and he hated the weakness inside him that craved her acceptance.

"You spent a great deal of time in this room." She prowled past the mahogany and brass bookcases across from the windows, the shelves filled with toys and books. Narrow stripes of white ran down pale yellow silk covering the walls from the ceiling to the mahogany paneling that rose three feet from the floor along the other walls. "Do you remember being here before?"

How could he answer? How could he explain that odd feeling deep inside him? Everything seemed familiar, as though he had seen this place in a dream. In the past few days his memory had been ambushing him. He would turn a corner and an image would flash in his mind. At first he had been able to dismiss the memories; he figured his mind was planting images from scraps of what he had seen since coming here. Faces from oil paintings. Images based on stories and hopes. In time he realized he couldn't hide behind that defense. He had to face the truth.

Elizabeth paused behind the sofa that sat with a pair of wing-backed chairs near the carved mahogany mantel. She ran her fingers over the curved back of the sofa, moving her fingertips across the pale yellow and white pinstripes in the silk covering the sofa. "Emory and Rebecca would come and watch you play."

"Peyton was five years old when he left here. I'm not sure how much anyone can really remember from that age."

"You have to try." Elizabeth crossed the room, pausing before a bookcase filled with toys that hadn't felt the hand of a child in twenty-three years. "Does anything look familiar?"

He stared at the collection of toys on the shelves—wooden carriages, carved wooden horses, stuffed animals, wooden rifles. Everything for the amusement of a little prince. "Nothing."

Sunlight glinted on the blades of ice skates as she lifted them and held them up for him to see. "You loved skating."

He shook his head and turned away from her. He set the soldier back on the field of battle. He had seen war in all its bloody glory. He had seen his Cheyenne father raise his hands in peace when the army had ridden into his village. He had watched as a soldier lifted his rifle and he had watched the horrible truth that followed. One moment he had been standing beside Ash, the next Lightning Walker was on the ground, his face ripped away by a bullet.

Ash had seen women and children butchered for no other reason than the color of their skin. He had come within a whisper of his own death. How could that boy be the same little prince who had played in this room?

Yet he couldn't deny the truth that whispered inside his head. Deep down he knew this place had once been his home.

"I'm certain it's merely a matter of time before your memory returns."

He glanced over his shoulder. The heart he had often been accused of not having squeezed painfully in his chest as he looked at her. She stood near the desk. Sunlight flowed around her, slipping into the curls piled high on her head, spinning pure gold from the honey brown tresses. It glowed on her features, and for a moment, as he looked into her eyes, it seemed all the light emanated from her.

She was all the gentleness that had been missing from his life, all the warmth, all the affection. But none of it was for him. "If my memories do return, do you think that will magically transform me into the Peyton Trevelyan you expect me to be?"

She frowned, a line forming between her delicately arched brows. ''You can't deny that you're beginning to remember things.''

''What if I am?'' He stared down at the battlefield. ''What if I was the boy who lived here twenty-three years ago? What real difference would it make in who I am today?''

''It would remove your doubts,'' she said with all the confidence in the world.

''Only about who I was. Not about who I am.''

''You're Peyton Trevelyan. You belong here, with your family. You're just too stubborn to admit it.''

He turned to face her. ''Maybe you're too damn stubborn to see I don't belong here, no matter what my name might be.''

Her eyes flashed like silver lightning. ''If you would stop finding reasons for not belonging here, you might get it through your thick head that this is your home.''

He stalked her, unchaining the beast deep inside him. The lady needed to see just what kind of predator she was facing. She needed to see she had no business trying to shape him into some tame housecat.

Her eyes grew wide. He could almost hear the argument raging in her head, a sane voice screaming for her to turn tail and run for the hills. He narrowed his eyes, a warning he wanted her to heed. She should run. She should get as far away from him as she could, while she still had the chance.

Warning bells chimed in Elizabeth's head. She had the uneasy feeling she had just poked a stick at an angry lion. He stalked her, blue eyes narrowed, full lips drawn into a tight line. A sensible woman would pick up her skirts and run for the safety of her room. She didn't budge. He would see she wasn't easily cowed. He kept coming, a slow prowl that sent excitement rippling along her every nerve.

"Look, lady, I ain't one of your fancy gentlemen." He leaned toward her. "No matter what the hell my name might be. It doesn't change who I am."

She leaned back against the desk, trying to avoid the heat of his body. His warmth invaded the layers of her clothes, simmering across her breasts, her belly, scorching her defenses. Desire drizzled into her blood. She lifted her chin, refusing to cower beneath the fury flaming in his eyes or surrender to her own foolish need. There were issues that needed to be resolved. "Even a lion has a home and a family."

"His own kind."

"You were born here. Your family is here."

"I'll never be the fancy gentleman everyone here expects me to be."

She held his angry glare. "No one is expecting you to be anything you aren't."

"Like hell they aren't." He slipped his hand around the nape of her neck, his long fingers curling beneath her ear.

She trembled at his touch, remembering the caress of his hands on her bare skin. He made love to her every night, pretending it was nothing more than lust. He wanted her to feel like a prostitute serving a customer.

Yet no matter what he said, or how much he pretended not to care, he revealed his feelings for her in every touch, every kiss, every potent thrust of his hard body. He might not love her, at least not yet. But he wanted her. And he wanted her to feel desire for him each time he took her. It was all he would accept from her.

"You've been pounding on me since the first day we met, trying to shape me into the man you've got in your head."

"No. I've only been trying to help you find your way

back home.'' She sensed the need deep inside him, the longing for affection he wouldn't admit he wanted. He scorned her each time she professed her love for him. But some of the hard edges had worn away beneath her constant pounding. If it was the last thing she did, she would find some way to gentle the beast she had married.

His warm breath brushed her cheek. ''If you knew half the things I've done, you'd be praying I'd climb onto the next ship and get far away from this place as fast as I can.''

She wanted to throw her arms around his neck and kiss his hard, angry mouth until some of the bitterness melted away from him. ''You only did what you had to do to survive.''

One corner of his mouth twitched. ''All that ugliness doesn't go away. It's still there, under the fancy clothes and fancy manners.''

''If you weren't so stubborn, you'd see . . .''

He slammed his mouth over hers. He pushed between her thighs, trapping her against the desk, forcing her to feel the potent masculinity through the layers of her clothes. Yet the wanton in her wanted more. His mouth opened over hers, taking what she would so gladly give. But there was no demand for surrender in his kiss. She felt his anger, his misguided need to frighten her, perhaps to show her he was well beyond redemption. Still, in that savage kiss she tasted the need beyond the pain and anger.

He was dangerous. He could shred her heart with one swipe of his claws. She should remain passive beneath the assault. She should show him she wasn't afraid of the beast in him. Yet she could no more deny the need she sensed in him than she could deny her own need to hold him. She slid his hands across his shoulders, but he was already pulling away from her.

He stared down at her, his breath coming in ragged

puffs that touched her mouth with the warm scent of coffee. His voice was harsh and strained when he spoke. "This is what I am. And all the fancy clothes and fancy manners won't change me."

"I don't want to change the man you are inside," she said softly.

He cupped her face in his hands, and in his eyes she saw the ugly wounds scrawled across his soul. "You want a man who doesn't exist."

"I want a man who is brave enough to risk his pride to find his way home."

He shook his head. "The boy who lived here died when he was five years old."

She rested her hand on his chest, over the heart she hoped to tame. "No he didn't. He took a different path in life, a much more difficult path. But he is here now, back home, where he belongs."

"Take a good look at me."

She couldn't take her eyes from him. He was compelling, a beautiful deity cast from Olympus, doomed to wander in an alien world. She saw pain and tragedy in his eyes, and a need for things he didn't think he wanted.

"I'm not the man you've been carrying around in your head for the past twenty years. I'm not some piece of clay you've been molding." He brushed the back of his fingers across her cheek. "I'm the same man you met at Miss Hattie's. Maybe I speak a little better, and I don't use my knife to eat my peas, but inside I'm still the same. And no matter how hard you pound on me, no matter how much you want me to be someone else, I'll never be Peyton Trevelyan. I'll never fit into your world."

"If you would only give yourself a chance, you could be anything you want."

He smiled, but his eyes remained troubled. "Don't you mean anything *you* want?"

He was everything she wanted. She looked up into his

eyes, realizing all her feelings for him were naked in her eyes. "Isn't there anything in my world that you want?"

His expression turned hard, as though he were crushing all the softness she had found inside him. "No matter how much I want you in my bed, I can't pretend to be something I'm not."

His words pricked her heart. Was she fooling herself? Did he only want her in the most primitive of ways? "Is that all you want from me?"

He stared down at her, his features set in hard lines, emotions churning in the depths of his incredible eyes. She ached to touch him, to slip her arms around him and hold him until all the sadness and pain disappeared. Yet she sensed he would only push her away from him.

"I'm afraid I want more than you're willing to give, princess," he said, his voice soft and filled with a poignant longing.

She fought back her tears. "I'm willing to give you anything you need."

He closed his eyes, his shoulders sagging as if beneath a great weight. "As long as I'm willing to become Lord Angelstone, the perfect English gentleman."

She touched his arm, her fingers closing around the thick muscles of his forearm. "Ash, come home."

He took a step back, breaking free of her touch. He stood for a moment, half turned from her, glaring down at the carpet, his jaw clenched, his lips tight with strain. "It isn't that easy. I can't be trapped and caged by anyone."

"I never tried to trap you. I never would."

He looked at her, searching her eyes for the truth she wanted him to believe. She could see the doubts he had about her. He hadn't quite decided whether she was a siren tempting him to disaster or a child obsessed with a fantasy. She needed to prove she was neither.

"Nothing else matters in this world except family,

friends, someone special to give our affection to. Nothing else.'' She took heart in the turmoil in his eyes, the need swimming in the endless blue depths. In her heart she knew he needed more than he was willing to admit. And she was willing to give him everything. If the stubborn oaf would only see reason.

Chapter Twenty-six

Ash turned away from her, fighting the lure of her, and his own weakness. If he let her, she would have him on his knees, begging for scraps of her affection. He couldn't step into that trap. He stalked to the windows, welcoming the rush of cool air sweet with the mingled scents of the gardens. "And what about all the lessons? What about all the lectures on how to walk and talk and think? I got the impression they were pretty damn important to you."

"I hardly see where lessons on proper decorum and your refusal to recognize your family have anything in common. The lessons are only to help you feel more at ease in society."

The third-story window provided an excellent view of the kingdom of Chatswyck. Emerald lawns dotted with fountains and reflecting pools, twisting shrubbery, and flower gardens rolled away from the palace. He had crossed an ocean and discovered a new world. A place where a small boy had been pampered and spoiled and loved. A place waiting for the return of a sovereign. *I'm the king, sovereign of all I see.* Only that little boy had grown up to be a peasant.

She didn't understand that it was more than scraping away the rough edges that showed. It was altering the man inside. He belonged in the West. He couldn't live his life worrying about every word he spoke and every move he made.

Her gown rustled softly as she moved toward him. "Marlow and the duchess care for you. I care for you. How can you keep turning away from us?"

He curled his fist against the window frame and fixed his gaze on the walls of yew shaping the maze, rising in a corner of the gardens. "Would it be any better if I pretended I was going to stay?"

"No." She was quiet for a moment, and when she spoke her voice was soft with a sadness she couldn't disguise. "It will only be better when you realize how important a home and family can be."

Ash closed his eyes, resisting the urge to turn to her. He wanted her. Now and always. He knew how important a family and home were. He had lived a lifetime searching, wondering if one day he would find his family, if one day he might have a home. A farm. A ranch. Someplace where he could prop up his feet on the back porch and listen to the crickets at night. Not a palace, where even the servants looked at him as though he were a freak.

She released her breath in a long shuddering sigh. "Since this is getting us nowhere, I suggest we do what we can to prepare you for the party."

Her skirts swished as she marched away from him. Without looking he knew she had paused beside the desk. He imagined she had assumed her schoolmarm pose. He could feel the insistence of her stare bore into his back. Still, he refused to face her. He couldn't be certain his feelings were carefully masked.

"It's very important for you to wear gloves at all times during the evening," she said, her voice once more crisp with propriety. "Except, of course, at dinner. Under no circumstances should you remove your gloves before dancing with a lady."

Anxiety coiled into a tight fist in his gut when he thought of what would be expected of him tomorrow night. "My bare hands might send her into a fit of the vapors?"

"Your bare hands would soil her gloves and quite possibly the bodice of her gown."

"If I don't dance with anyone, I guess there won't be a problem."

"It's a ball. The main entertainment will be dancing. You really must dance."

He must dance. He must try not to frighten anyone by unsheathing his claws. "You mean to say married men go around dancing with other women?"

"Your status as a married man will not exempt you from dancing with other women. Of course, you must be careful not to confine your attentions to any one lady. You might excite comment."

There was only one lady he wanted. He glanced over his shoulder and found her standing by the desk, exactly as he had imagined. The pretty schoolmarm. Strange, how this odd little female managed to put a flicker of fire in his blood even when she looked cold enough to freeze a man with a glance.

He grinned, deliberately inciting her anger. He could deal with anger; it was all the other emotions that threatened to push him over the edge. "You mean, if I see a pretty woman, I can't spend all my time with her?"

She lifted her chin, her eyes glittering with fury. "Only if you wish to humiliate me, your grandparents, and yourself."

"Guess I'll be obliged to spend the night by your side," he said, attempting to sound bored with the prospect.

She drew in her breath, and he could almost hear her counting silently, snatching that icy control to her chest like a shield. "It's considered bad form for married couples to spend the evening in each other's company."

The blood pounded in his belly as he thought of the

company he would like to be keeping with her at this very moment. A single curl had tumbled from its mooring pins. The silky strands slid over her shoulder, shimmering like gold in the sunlight, drawing his gaze to the soft rise and fall of her breasts. Heat whispered across his skin. Need nipped at his loins.

She cleared her throat. "You must not dance more than two dances with any lady in the same evening. Otherwise people will think you are paying far too much attention to her."

He leaned back against the wall. "I don't see why I have to dance with anyone."

She fiddled with the cameo pinned to the lace beneath her chin. "People will think you're a complete clod if you don't dance at least half the dances."

"I should have realized the people here would judge a man by something as silly as dancing."

She stared at him, and he had the uncomfortable feeling she could look straight through him. "You don't know how to dance."

His back stiffened at the quiet assessment. She might have stripped him bare and passed judgment on the quality of his masculinity. "I've never had much call to learn."

She nodded. "I should have realized."

In other words, he didn't have any other social skills, why the hell would he know how to dance? He forced himself to hold her direct gaze, refusing to let her see how backward he felt.

"Wait here," she said. "I'll be right back."

He watched her leave, uneasy at what she might have in mind. When she returned a few minutes later she was carrying a shiny wooden box.

"The duchess and Marlow won't be back until this afternoon. Since I can't teach you to dance and play the piano at the same time, this will have to do." She set the box on the desk and lifted the lid. The sparkling strains of a waltz drifted from the box, each bright note stabbing in his gut.

"It's very old." She smiled down at the music box. "My great-grandfather, the marquess of Blackthorne, gave it to my great-grandmother in 1812. It was the first waltz they ever danced to."

She stared down at the box, her beautiful face solemn, almost tragic, as though she were thinking of someone or something that had died. Was she thinking of the man she would like to be waltzing with to this sweet old tune? Was she wishing he was someone else? Someone who already knew how to dance with her. Someone who already knew all the right things to say and do. Someone who belonged here.

In the time it took for her to close the lid and wind the small golden key at the bottom of the box, she had washed all the tragic longing from her face. She was once again the teacher, all prim and proper and ready to instruct the imbecile she had for a pupil. He set his jaw.

"You should always give your partner proper support, with your right arm around your partner's waist. You hold her right hand in your left. Like this." She put her right arm out in front of her at waist level, as though taking hold of a phantom partner. She lifted her left arm, demonstrating the way he should hold a lady's hand. "The dance is in three quarter time."

He crossed his arms over his chest, watching as she glided through the golden columns of sunlight spilling into the room, holding her phantom partner, her gown sweeping over the gold urns and white flowers stitched into the woolen carpet. It didn't seem so difficult, he assured himself, listening as she explained each step. Still, when she motioned for him to join her near the desk, he couldn't dislodge the lead ball in his gut.

He lifted his hands as he walked toward her. "I'm not wearing gloves."

She lifted her bare hands. "We'll have to pretend. Put your right arm around my waist."

He slipped his arm around her waist, rested his hand against the warm silk of her gown, and tried not to remember how soft she was beneath all the layers. She stiffened in his arms, and he wondered if she too were fighting memories.

She lifted the lid of the music box, releasing the melody of the old waltz. She stared at his shoulder as she directed his steps. He followed her, feeling like an ox trying to make his way through a parlor without knocking over anything. And then it happened. His great clumsy foot came down hard on her dainty little toes. He cringed as she gasped with pain.

"Sorry," he said, breaking away from her. "Look, maybe no one will notice if I don't dance."

She leaned back against the desk, easing her injured toes under her skirt. "I'm afraid they're going to notice everything about you."

They would peel away the thin mask of civilized gentleman and see the beast beneath. "I forgot, I'm the entertainment. The dancing bear performing in the sideshow."

She closed the lid on the now quiet music box, all the notes spent. "This is hardly a sideshow," she said softly.

"If you say so."

She glanced up at him. "Do you intend to give up, before you've even given this a good try?"

He frowned. "Maybe we should quit before you end up with broken toes."

"I assure you, I've had my toes trodden on before." She cranked the key in the music box, lifted the lid, and offered him her hand. "Shall we try again?"

A challenge glittered like silver in her eyes. He took

her in his arms. "Don't say I didn't warn you."

Her lips flattened into a tight line. "Step back with your left foot."

He complied, following the insistent prodding of her hand on his shoulder. Her instructions pounded against his ears, quietly demanding that he learn another lesson in proper decorum. Still, as his clumsy feet began to adapt to the steps and the soft rhythm of her voice penetrated his skull, he realized this was one lesson that wasn't so bad. The notes slowed and faded as the music box wound down. She picked up the tune, humming softly, emphasizing the rhythm.

"That's it." She smiled up at him. "You're doing beautifully."

The warmth of her smile curled around him. He swirled around the room with her, her skirts brushing against his legs with a soft rustle that triggered images in his head—her gown soft beneath his hands, the soft silk pooling around her feet. He flexed his hand against her waist. The warm silk taunted him. He craved the warm slide of his hand against flesh smoother than silk. He wanted to taste her, savor the heat of her skin against his tongue.

He lowered his eyes, watching the soft rise and fall of her breasts beneath apple green silk. She was covered all the way up to her chin, but in his mind he saw her the way she slept in his arms every night. Soft and bare. Her nipples taut and pink, glistening from his hot, wet kisses.

A tremor rippled through her and into him. Her next step came down hard on his toes. "Sorry," she murmured, pulling back in his arms.

He held her when she would have broken free of his embrace. He met her confused stare without trying to disguise the hunger inside him. This is what he was—a beast who wanted to devour her luscious body. Right here. Right now.

Yet the beast stood like stone beneath her confused

gaze, muscles rigid while his senses came alive with her.
Lavender rose with the heat of her body, drifting around
him, the fragrance made richer with the scent of her skin.
Morning sunlight bathed her features, gilding the soft
fringe of curls falling over her brow, exposing the small
perfections of her face. It seemed strange that he had ever
looked at her and not imagined her one of the most beautiful women he had ever seen.

The beast stirred inside him, howling his ravenous need
for this woman. Still, he might have chained the beast if
she hadn't chosen that moment to touch him. She moved
her hand along his shoulder, touched the nape of his neck
with the warmth of her bare fingers.

Control made brittle through the long days of wanting
her snapped like dried kindling. He pulled her close
against him, snatching her up off the floor and into his
arms. He clamped his mouth over hers, sealing in any
protest she might have uttered. Yet there was no protest
in her.

She threw her arms around his neck, meeting the harsh
demand of his kiss with a hunger that melted the strength
from his legs. He staggered back, straight into the desk.
She slid down the length of him, pressing him back onto
the desk. He groaned with the exquisite torture of her soft
body brushing his hardened frame. He ran his hands upward along the slim curve of her back, flicking open silk-
covered buttons.

Her hands roamed over his shoulders, his chest, as
though she couldn't get enough of him. Her fingertips
scraped his skin as she dug into the edges of his shirt.
Before he realized what she had in mind, she yanked open
his shirt, buttons popping from soft cotton.

He dropped back his head, gasping for a steadying
breath. She was fire, licking over his chest with her lips
and tongue, her hands tugging at the buttons lining the
placket of his trousers, consuming him in a passion that

threatened to devour him body and soul. He pushed her gown from her shoulders. The silk swished to the floor. He turned with her in his arms. She spilled back across the desk, dragging him down into her softness.

He had dreamed of a moment like this from the first day she had barged into his life. Each time she had lectured him on the proper rules of society he had imagined her naked and willing beneath him. Now she was his.

He kissed her, pressing his lips to her sweet mouth, sighing inwardly at her warm response. He shoved her petticoats up around her waist, his hunger too impatient to deal with all the intricacies of ribbons and laces. He slid his hand across the silk covering her belly, seeking the slit in her drawers, finding the breach. His fingers slipped into silky curls. Soft feminine petals parted beneath his touch.

She moaned against his mouth, pushing against his hand, seeking the pleasure he had taught her to demand. He tasted the soft skin of her neck, her shoulder, breathing in her fragrance. He dragged down her chemise over the lush curves of her breasts. Taut, pink nipples lifted to him, luring him.

He brushed his cheek against the soft curves, tasted the smooth valley between. She stirred beneath his caresses, sliding her long legs against his. He trailed kisses upward along one lush breast, finding the peak, taking the tight bud into his mouth. She gasped, grabbing his shoulders, as he suckled like a babe at her breast.

She tugged at the buttons on his drawers, where he strained against silk. "Blast it," she murmured, impatient with the task.

He groaned as she tugged on the barrier, shredding buttons from silk. She closed her warm hand around his aroused flesh, dragging a moan from his lips. She led him to the sleek heat of her tight sheath. He plunged into her fire, abandoning himself in the conflagration. She rose to meet him, taking his length, arching away, drawing back to receive him time and time again, until the pleasure raged out of control, until she shook and shuddered and cried out with the shattering power of her release. In that instant of total abandon he joined her, spilling his essence into her, knowing with every fiber of his being that it could never feel this way with another woman.

He surrendered to the lush demand of her embrace, burying his face against the smooth curve of her neck. The fragrance of her skin swirled though his senses, innocent lavender spiced by the lush scent of their lovemaking. Her long legs squeezed his waist, her arms curved in tight possession around his neck, trapping him in her tender snare. Yet he couldn't find the strength to resist.

She stroked her hand across his head, slid her fingers into the thick waves at his nape. "It's shocking, really, the way you have completely destroyed my sense of propriety."

He lifted himself above her. She looked tousled and pretty, color high on her cheeks, her lips soft and red from his kisses. "This is what I am, Beth. A man who has so little sense of propriety he makes love to his wife on a desk, in the middle of the morning."

She smoothed the tip of her finger down the length of his chest, from the hollow of his collarbone to the indentation of his navel. Shivers skittered across his skin at the provocative touch. "I would wager there are more than a few women who would trade their very proper husbands for a man who has a spark of passion in his blood."

She didn't seem to mind. She honestly looked as though she were contented with her beast of a husband. The world tilted when he looked in her eyes and realized this beautiful princess might actually be in love with him.

He eased away from her as the cool breeze licked over skin made warm and wet from her body. He turned away and straightened his clothes as best he could with half the buttons missing on his shirt and drawers. When he turned to face her she was sitting on the edge of the desk, dressed in her lacy petticoats and drawers, her corset pushing her bare breasts up over the crimped edge of the white silk chemise drooping from her pale shoulders. Completely at ease with her own state of undress, she watched him with a cat-in-the-cream smile on her pretty lips.

He lifted her gown from the floor. There were things they needed to discuss, and unless she got dressed— soon—his mind wouldn't be worth a penny. "Better get dressed before someone comes in and finds you that way."

"Well-trained servants always knock." She tugged the chemise back over her bare breasts and slid from the desk. She eased her arms over her head, her breasts lifting with the sinuous stretch. "I do like the way you look at me when I'm not dressed. It makes me feel very . . . pretty."

She was too damn pretty for his own good. He helped her into her gown, fumbling over the buttons lining her spine.

"You're much quicker at undressing women than you are at dressing them," she said softly.

He clenched his jaw, certain she knew how she could turn his entire world upside down. "Never had much call to go around dressing a woman."

She glanced over her shoulder as he was fastening the hook at the top of her gown, smiling at him in that soft way that made his insides grow hot and melting. "You do the undressing very well."

He stepped away from her, hoping the distance would help him think. Was this strange female in love with him? It was going to take a while to believe that. But if she was . . . God, if she was . . . "We might never be able to prove who I am. Have you thought of that? After the old man dies Clayburne could waltz in here and take everything.'' How would she feel about her husband then? he wondered.

She smiled, her eyes filled with a confidence he couldn't share. ''Marlow is going to be around for quite some time. When he does pass on you will be firmly established as Lord Angelstone.''

He was shaking inside, the way he had the first time he had faced a man in a gunfight. ''If Clayburne takes the issue to court, there's a good chance they will decide in favor of a man like him, rather than a man like me. You could find yourself married to a man without a name. How would you feel then, princess?''

A frown stole some of the bravado from her expression. He clenched his hands at his sides, watching her as she walked to the bookcases and paused before the array of old toys. He told himself it didn't matter what she thought of him. Yet he couldn't stop the shaking deep inside.

She lifted a stuffed rabbit in an emerald green suit from a shelf. She stroked the long gray ears, staring into the small button-eyed face as she spoke. ''I thought you were a man who would fight for what belonged to him.''

She wanted him, as long as the title and Chatswyck came along with him. He tried to draw a breath but couldn't force air past the tightness in his throat. He tried to form his lips into a mocking grin, but even that was beyond him. ''I think I've had enough lessons for one day.''

He left her, before he betrayed every weakness of his foolish heart.

Chapter Twenty-seven

Where was he?

Ash had ridden away from Chatswyck that morning after abandoning her in the schoolroom. He had returned in time for dinner, yet he had contributed nothing to the dinner conversation. He had answered questions directed to him with the barest of replies. He had disappeared soon after dinner, retiring to his chamber as though he wanted nothing at all to do with anyone.

Elizabeth had waited for him to come to her bedroom, as he came to her every evening. At midnight she had given up hope. Two minutes after midnight she had barged into his bedroom, intending to show her infuriating husband that he could not dismiss her so easily. If he was not happy with her, he could very well discuss it with her. If he was simply in a black mood, he would have to allow her to attempt to alter it. She would not be barred from the castle. But the beast wasn't in his lair.

She sank to the window seat in his room. Before meeting Ash she had deluded herself into thinking she had a fairly strong grasp of the male mind. Since meeting him she had realized she was as naive as a schoolgirl.

What was he thinking? Had he simply decided to withdraw from her completely? Did he intend to turn his back on her and sail back to America as though she didn't exist? Well, he would have to deal with her first. She wasn't about to let him get away from her without a fight.

Every time she looked at him she sensed that he needed her. When he made love to her, she actually convinced herself he cared for her. She also sensed he despised the need within him. If he had it his way, he would keep her at arm's length.

Arrogant, stubborn man!

A cool breeze heavy with the scent of damp grass brushed her face. Light from a plump, generous moon spilled across the curving body of the serpentine hedges. It gathered in a shimmering pool of silver in the pond near the maze. From the advantage of his second-story window, she could see the crenellated roof of the pavilion at the heart of the maze. The gray stones glowed like a ghost in the moonlight. A phantom from the past. Those stone walls had triggered memories in Ash; she was certain of it. Just as she was certain memories were the key to convincing him to stay.

Elizabeth stiffened as a figure emerged from the tunnel of elms leading from the azalea dell to the maze. A tall, broad-shouldered man stood for a moment staring up at the stone knights guarding the entrance to the labyrinth before he passed through the entrance. Her missing husband.

"What are you looking for, my beguiling beast?" she whispered. "A piece of your past?"

Perhaps she should allow him to explore on his own. Even as the thought formed she was coming to her feet. He might not want to admit he needed help finding his way back home, but he did. And she was going to give it to him, even if she had to fight him to do it.

A cool breeze rippled the hem of her blue satin dressing gown as she hurried along the path leading to the maze. Her heart crept upward in her chest, pounding at the base of her throat, as she approached the pavilion at the heart of the maze. The door was open, spilling a golden wedge of light into the night. She hesitated a moment, wrestling with doubt, before entering the lion's lair.

A single wall sconce cast flickering light against the oak paneling, spilling the scent of burning oil into the large room. Ash stood with his back to the door, staring at the floor. Light from the lamp embraced him, slipping gold into the dark waves that curled against the collar of his white shirt.

She paused on the threshold, feeling like a trespasser prying once more into this man's life. Still, she knew it was necessary. She had to find a way to drag him back home, back into her arms.

"Didn't anyone ever tell you it's dangerous for pretty women to go walking alone through the woods at night, princess?" he asked, without turning to face her.

She curled her toes inside her satin slippers. "How did you know it was me?"

He glanced over his shoulder, a deep line carved between the dark wings of his brows. "I could feel you."

The husky sound of his voice sent excitement quivering through her. "There is something about this place that's bothering you. Something that has triggered your memories. That's why you came here this evening. Isn't it?"

He glanced down at the floor. "I don't know what I'm remembering. I'm not sure what's real and what's just my imagination."

"I know it must all be terribly difficult, trying to sort through your past, trying to reconcile it with the present. I don't know why you can't admit you could use some help in getting through all this confusion."

He stared down at the mosaic of St. George slaying the dragon. She wondered if he would ever conquer his own demons. "Why are you here?"

She took a step into the room, but that was as far as her courage would take her. "I saw you from your bedroom window."

He glanced at her, his expression revealing his surprise. "*My* bedroom window?"

She clasped her hands. "I waited for you until midnight. Then I decided to storm the castle gate."

He turned to face her. He looked straight into her eyes, as though searching for something he desperately needed. "After what happened this morning I didn't think you would want me to come to your room tonight."

She took a step toward him. "I want you. Now and always."

He glanced down at the mosaic inlaid upon the floor. "Do you, princess?"

"I wish I didn't. I find this all rather vexing. We're married, yet I keep wanting to ask your intentions toward me. At the same time, I'm not sure I want to know what they are. When we make love I convince myself you really do care for me. But perhaps you don't care any more for me than you do for any woman who has warmed your bed. You have a rather annoying habit of keeping me off balance."

He glanced at her. "I'm not trying to."

"And here I thought you rather enjoyed torturing me this way."

He drew in his breath. "I realize I've been difficult."

She rolled her eyes toward heaven. "A bear with a thorn in his paw is difficult. You've been impossible. At times, I truly think I'm insane to be so besotted with you."

A smile touched a corner of his lips. "Besotted?"

She nodded. "You see what I mean? I must be insane."

"Beth," he whispered, his voice soft with longing.

He took a tentative step toward her. She rushed across the distance. And he welcomed her, opening his arms, drawing her close against his chest. She wrapped her arms around his waist, pressing her cheek against his chest, where his heart beat to a furious rhythm, echoing her own.

His scent swirled around her, citrus and leather and man. She inhaled deeply.

He stroked her unbound hair, sliding his palm down her back. "You deserve so much more than a man like me."

She lifted her head and looked up into his eyes. Light from the wall sconce glittered in the stunning depths, revealing every doubt he had about himself. "You're the man I want."

His expression tightened with a grimace of pain. "You deserve a man who knows all the right things to do and say. A gentleman who won't make you nervous every time you meet someone in public. A man who won't shame you in this fancy world of yours."

She ached for this man. He had known so much suffering in his life, yet he had grown straight and strong and proud. "Never think you're less of a man because of what you've been through, Ash. Never."

He shook his head. "I managed to carve out some respect back in Denver. But nothing I learned there makes any sense here."

With her fingertip she traced the lush curve of his lower lip. "All the rules of proper behavior don't make a man. You could have become an outlaw. You could have died in the streets. But you didn't. Because you're strong and honest and good. Those qualities make a man, no matter where he lives."

"People here judge a man by the way he talks, the way he wears his clothes."

"You wear your clothes very well." She smiled up at him, hoping to lighten his mood. "Although I have to admit, I prefer you in far less than you're wearing at the moment."

He smoothed his fingertips over the curve of her jaw, sliding heat across her skin. "I always suspected you were a lusty wench under all that prim and proper starch."

"And I always suspected you were a gentleman, some-where deep beneath that gruff facade of yours."

He rested against her, his breath falling soft and warm against her lips, flavored with the heady scent of brandy. "I'm going to do my best, princess. I'm going to try to live up to all those expectations everyone has for Peyton."

His words spoken in that husky voice caught at her heart. Her throat tightened with emotion. She closed her eyes on a silent prayer of thanks. "That's all I've ever wanted, my darling. Your best is more than I'll ever need."

"I hope you're right. Tomorrow night will be a trial by fire." He gripped her shoulders, holding her far enough away to look down into her eyes. "I hope you won't be disappointed, princess."

She looked up into his wonderful eyes and prayed everything went well for him tomorrow night. She had the uneasy feeling her entire future hung in the balance. "You'll see. Tomorrow night you will have society eating out of the palm of your hand."

He grinned. "I'll settle for getting through the evening without making a fool of myself."

"I have faith in you."

He rubbed his thumbs against the blue satin of her robe, his fingers tight against her shoulders. "I'm not a man who's good at words, Beth. But I know how I feel. And I want you as my wife."

She stared up at him, not quite believing the words she had longed to hear. "I've never wanted to marry a man until I met you."

"I can't promise I'll stay. I don't know if I can."

"Ash, you can . . ."

He pressed a fingertip against her lips. "I need to know if you'll come with me if things don't work out here."

She stepped back. "You want me to go to America? To live there?"

He frowned. "Why is that any more strange than you asking me to live here?"

She turned away from him, needing a few moments to pull together the wits he had managed to scatter with a few words. She stared at a tapestry of King Arthur drawing Excalibur from the stone. "This is your home."

"No, princess," he said softly. "This is *your* home."

She turned to face him, searching his features for some sign of softness. He stood stiff and hard and firm in a conviction in opposition to her own. "You're right. This is my home. I've lived here most of my life. Marlow and the duchess are as much my family as they are yours."

"And I've lived most of my life in the west. I need a place where I can breathe without worrying about how I'm doing it. I don't know if I can survive here."

She crossed the distance between them. "Ash, give yourself time. You can't expect to feel at home here in a few days."

"I can't say time will change anything, princess. I can't promise I'll stay." He cupped her cheek in his hand. "Will you come with me?"

"There's so much to think about."

His fingers tensed against her face. "There's only one thing. Do you want to be with me?"

She looked up into the turmoil in his eyes and saw the raw need in him. "Of course I want to be with you. I love you."

He stared into her eyes, a man who had known nothing of affection in this world, looking for the truth of it in her eyes. "Do you mean it, princess?"

She rested her hand on his chest, above his heart, feeling the fury of his emotions throb beneath her palm. "Yes, of course I mean it. If you weren't so stubborn, you would have realized it a long time ago."

He cradled her face between his hands, as though she were a fine piece of porcelain he was afraid of breaking.

"Guess it's going to take a while to get used to the idea."

He looked so vulnerable, she wanted to hold him. But there were things that needed to be settled between them. "Ash, I wish it were as simple as me deciding to live with you in America. But it isn't."

A certain wariness entered his eyes. "What are you getting at?"

"There are other people involved. Marlow and the duchess. My mother."

He dropped his hands to his sides. "There comes a time when a woman has to make a choice, princess. To marry and live with her husband, or stay with her folks. You have to make the choice."

"This is different. My mother needs special care. I can't turn my back on her."

He nodded. "We'll take her with us."

She stepped back, putting some space between them in the hope of plowing through her muddled thoughts. "Mother won't even leave Chatswyck to visit London. I doubt I could ever convince her to journey to America."

"I understand." He stared at her, and she could see him rebuilding the barriers between them.

She curled her hands into fists at her sides, fighting the urge to scream. "No. I don't think you do."

"You're willing to be my wife as long as I stay here."

"And you're willing to be my husband as long as I go with you to America."

He parted his lips as if to argue but thought better of it. He turned away from her and stalked to the far side of the room. He paused beside the oak chair that stood against the wall, staring down at the duke's crest emblazoned in gold and red on the carved back.

She gave him a few moments before she joined him there. "Ash, won't you give yourself a chance to find your way home?"

His shoulders lifted with a deep intake of breath. He

kept his face lowered, his gaze fixed on the chair. "I'm not sure I belong here."

"You were born here. Your family is here. No matter what you think right now, you do belong here."

"Open those pretty gray eyes, sweetheart. Take a real good look at me, and you'll see why I have my doubts."

She slipped her arms around his waist and pressed her cheek against his chest. "You can do anything you put your mind to, my darling. Anything at all."

He slipped his arms around her and held her close. "I'll try, princess."

It would be all right, she assured herself. Ash would conquer society tomorrow night. He had to. She had the horrible feeling it was the only chance they had.

Chapter Twenty-eight

Ash sat behind a huge mahogany desk in Hayward's study, looking at the duke over three stacks of bound reports piled two feet high on the desk.

"Since there isn't anything for us to do until the party this evening except stay out of the way, I thought it would be an excellent opportunity to expand your education in a different direction." Hayward tapped his forefinger against one of the ledgers. "Although you could have a steward run all of your business affairs, I believe a wise man knows what is happening with his investments."

Ash refrained from telling him a wise man wouldn't be trying to turn a gunslinger into a businessman.

"A few years ago the earl of Clarington was nearly ruined by a dishonest business agent." Hayward lifted his brows. "A man should always know the sources of his income and have a good idea how they are faring, if not all the details."

Ash stared at the stacks of reports, feeling like an ant facing a hike up Pikes Peak. How the hell was he going to make sense of any of it? He didn't know the first thing about running a general store; how the hell could he even think about running a business empire?

"Your father loved all the intricacies of business. He looked at each concern as though it were a chess piece to be moved about a board." Hayward glanced up at the painting hanging on the wall across from his desk. "He was so very good at it."

Incandescent lights in brass and crystal fixtures attached to the mahogany-paneled walls chased away the gloom of a chilly gray morning. The soft glow from the lamps fell upon the portrait of a young family captured in vibrant oils. Emory stood beside a blue velvet chair, his hand resting on the high back, near Rebecca's golden head. Peyton stood on the other side of his mother, one small hand on the arm of her chair, smiling with all the innocent confidence of a young prince.

That boy would have grown to stand proudly beside his father in business, in life. He would have mastered this world and everything in it. Yet something happened along the way. The boy had grown into a man who stumbled through this fancy palace like a court jester. His chest constricted as Ash thought of everything that had been lost.

Hayward cleared his throat, his voice husky when he spoke. "You'll find yearly reports regarding our concerns in America for the last twenty-five years in these stacks."

Ash glanced up at the old man, seeing the pain that would never completely leave him.

Hayward smiled. "I thought you would like to start with the American holdings before learning about our British and colonial investments. That way you will have some idea of what is what when we start discussing business with Radcliffe this morning."

A month ago Shelby Radcliffe wouldn't have glanced at Ash on the street. And here the man was, making a trip from Denver all the way to England, to discuss business with Ash, to help his newly discovered "cousin" enter society.

"If there is anything you want to see in detail, the records are kept in the west tower," Hayward said.

His learning the business meant a great deal to the old

man. And somehow Ash knew it would have meant a great deal to the young man who had been killed along with his beautiful wife. Ash thought of his own beautiful wife. Was it wrong to ask her to leave her home to come live with him? "I'll do my best to make sense of it all," he said, realizing he meant much more than the reports stacked in front of him.

Hayward smiled. "Your best effort is all I ask of you, my lad."

What if his best effort still wasn't good enough? Ash wondered. What if he never lived up to the expectations he saw in Hayward's eyes? What if he was nothing but an embarrassment to the Trevelyan name? Wouldn't it be better for everyone if he left? And if he left, would Beth come with him?

"If you should need me, I'll be puttering about in the green houses," Hayward said.

Ash watched the old man walk toward the door. The responsibilities of Peyton Trevelyan rested like an iron yoke across his shoulders. So many years had passed. Years that should have been filled with all the proper training for becoming the man his father and grandfather and all of those noble men and women who lined the portrait gallery expected him to be. Years that had separated him from this place and these people until he didn't feel a connection any longer. Years that couldn't be erased.

Hayward paused near the door. He turned around and stared at the painting of Emory and his family. "The ring. Emory's emerald signet ring. That's it!"

Ash glanced up at the ring his father was wearing in the painting, the same ring Hayward had offered him in Denver. "What about it?"

Hayward turned to look at Ash, excitement shimmering on his face. "Emory gave you a ring just like his on your fifth birthday."

Ash shook his head. "He gave a five-year-old a fancy ring like that?"

Hayward seemed confused by the question. "Yes, of course. Unfortunately, you did something with it the day you left for your trip to America."

"I was five. I probably swallowed the thing."

Hayward shook his head. "I don't believe so."

Ash refrained from telling the old man he hadn't been serious.

"Now, as I recall, Emory had been telling you stories about pirates at sea. It was just before you were to sail for America." Hayward rubbed his chin. "You decided to hide your ring for safekeeping until you came back home. We've never been able to find it."

Ash frowned. "What are you getting at?"

"If you could remember where it was, we could use it as proof of your identity."

"It's a nice plan, but I don't even remember the ring."

"Hmmm, yes, I'm afraid that does prove a problem." Hayward released his breath in a long sigh. "Well, let's hope you do remember. I'm certain the more you learn about the life you were meant to live, the more your memories will return. And one day I hope you'll decide you want to wear your father's ring, my lad."

Ash glanced away from the old man. "I can't make any promises about staying."

"I'm certain you will do what's right."

Hayward's words echoed in Ash's mind long after the old man left the room. What the hell was the right thing to do? Somewhere along the way everything had blurred until he wasn't sure who he was and where he belonged.

He grabbed a bound volume from the stack of reports. He had to see whether he could find the man everyone said he was.

After an hour of plowing through the reports he had to admit they really weren't difficult to understand. The yearly reports were presented with the basic information of each investment, companies involved, partners, profits, losses. Two hours into the stacks, he found the investments his father had made with Shelby Radcliffe.

It was strange to realize he owned a piece of the businesses that had built that huge house on Brown's Bluff. Banking, mining, railroads. All profitable, with the exception of a silver mine Shelby had purchased back in 1865, the year he had moved to Denver. The year Emory had agreed to finance the venture. If he hadn't become involved with that mining operation, Emory and Rebecca might never have taken the trip to Colorado. They might be alive today.

Ash closed the book, his throat tightening with regret. He looked up at the portrait of a man, a woman, and a child. *My family.* He closed his eyes against the slow burn of tears. He had grieved for them before ever remembering their faces. Now he remembered. And he mourned their loss, as well as his own. For as truly as Emory and Rebecca had died that day twenty-three years ago, so had Peyton.

"I see Marlow has you busy," Bertram said, from the threshold of the room.

Ash tensed as he watched the arrogant aristocrat saunter toward him. "If you're looking for Marlow, I believe you'll find him in one of the green houses."

Bertram ignored the subtle invitation to leave. He lifted a bound report from one of the stacks in front of Ash. "Getting a feel for all the responsibilities that come with the title?" he asked, flipping through the pages.

"It's important for a man to know what is happening with his investments."

Bertram lifted his dark brows. "I was under the impression you were somewhat reluctant about accepting your position here. I thought you had doubts about whether or not you were Peyton."

Ash had learned a long time ago not to betray a weakness to an enemy. And he had no doubt Bertram was the enemy. "Marlow doesn't have any doubts."

Bertram closed the book. "I'm really quite amazed that Marlow is willing to present you to society without proof of your identity. This ball tonight is a terrible idea. He puts not only you in an awkward position but himself as well. I'm afraid people are beginning to question his competency."

If people were questioning the duke's ability to reason, Ash knew who was planting the seeds of doubt. He folded his hands on the desk, meeting Bertram's snide look with a direct glare. "There's nothing wrong with Marlow's mind."

"Not everyone shares your opinion." Bertram put down the book on the stack in front of Ash. "It's possible, after Marlow passes on, that your right to assume his title will be questioned in court."

"I suppose you don't have any idea who might bring up the issue."

Bertram smiled, one corner of his thin mustache lifting higher than the other. "Without proof of your identity, you could very well find yourself out in the cold."

If the bastard wasn't careful, he'd find himself on his ass, nursing a bloody nose. Ash fought the anger rising inside him. A gentleman did not allow his fists do his talking. "If you have a point to make, make it."

"It's really quite simple." Bertram rubbed his fingertip over the gold letters tooled on the leather cover of the bound report. "I want you to leave."

"You want Marlow's title."

Bertram inclined his head, looking at Ash down the length of his Roman nose. "I intend to have the title, one way or another. I'll do what is necessary."

Ash held Bertram's gaze, meeting the man's attempt at

intimidation with an icy calm that had served him well over the years.

Bertram shifted on his feet. "Although I'm quite confident the courts will see fit to bestow the title and everything that goes with it on me after Marlow's death, I would prefer to avoid bringing our family squabble to public attention. I'm willing to make you an offer."

Ash leaned back in his chair, responding only with a smile.

Bertram's tongue flicked between his lips. "I'm willing to pay you one hundred thousand American dollars if you will go back to America and forget you ever heard the name Trevelyan."

It was a great deal of money to do something Ash had already considered doing. Still, he didn't like Bertram's methods, his motives, or the man. Ash glanced past Bertram, looking up at the portrait of Emory Trevelyan. His father deserved better than a son who would throw away his name. He deserved more than Ash knew how to give.

"You don't belong here," Bertram said, his voice as smooth as snake oil. "With a hundred thousand dollars you can go back to America and live like a king."

Ash looked at Bertram, noting the glitter of expectation in his dark eyes. "Get out of here."

Bertram's nostrils flared. "No one speaks to me that way."

Ash rose from his chair. "I told you to get out. Now go, while you're still able to walk."

Bertram smiled smugly. "You wouldn't dare touch me."

Ash came around the desk, stalking the earl in slow strides, giving the man a chance to turn and run.

Bertram backed away from the desk. "I warn you, keep your filthy hands off me."

Ash twisted his hands in Bertram's lapels, the soft wool twisting around his fingers. "If you do anything to hurt

that old man and the duchess, I swear you'll pay for it.''
He released Bertram's coat with a hard shove. "Now get
the hell out of here.''

Bertram stumbled back, toward the door. He stared at
Ash, his eyes wild with rage. "You're nothing but a half-
civilized savage. If you think for one moment I'll allow
you to take what is mine, you're mistaken. I'll make certain you never assume the title.''

"I believe my grandson asked you to leave, Clayburne,'' Hayward said.

He was standing just inside the entrance and he wasn't
alone. Heat prickled his cheeks when Ash realized both
Hayward and Shelby Radcliffe had witnessed the altercation.

Bertram marched across the room, pausing when he
reached his uncle. "You can't really mean to release that
young savage on society?'' he asked, straightening his
coat.

Hayward smiled, allowing Bertram a moment to stew
before he responded. "That young man is my grandson,
Clayburne. And no one is going to take away his legacy.
No one. Including you.''

Bertram smoothed his hand over his thinning hair. "I'm
only trying to protect you and the duchess.''

"We both know what you're trying to do.'' Hayward
gestured toward the door. "Now run along. We have work
to do.''

Bertram glanced back at Ash, his dark eyes narrowed.
He left without another word, but Ash knew it wasn't
over. Men like Bertram didn't give up without a fight.
And that fight was usually dirty. He had little doubt he
would have to watch his back where Bertram was concerned.

Hayward closed the door and smiled at Shelby. "I'm
afraid my nephew isn't willing to bow out gracefully. For
the past twenty-three years he's been waiting for me to

take my last breath. Now he's faced with a much younger obstacle.''

"I understand.'' Shelby gave Ash a sympathetic smile. "I imagine your arrival has stirred up more than a few hornets.''

"Guess it has,'' Ash said, keeping the tension from his voice, even though it wrapped like barbed wire around his chest.

Hayward patted Ash's back. "Not to worry. We can handle Clayburne.''

Could he? Ash wondered. Could he tackle the earl on his own terms? Could he look society straight in the eye and tell them he belonged here?

"You're making progress, Marlow. The last time I saw this young man, he refused to even admit he was your grandson.'' Shelby rested his hand on the back of a coffee-colored wing-back chair near the desk. "Has coming back home helped restore your memory?''

Ash met Shelby's direct look, sensing the uneasiness beneath the smile. It was clear Shelby wasn't sure how to approach his cousin. "Looks that way.''

"Every day he remembers more,'' Hayward said. "In time all of his doubts about who he is will vanish.''

"That's wonderful,'' Shelby said. "It seems I have another partner.''

Hayward smiled at Ash. "I have no doubt he will be every bit as shrewd at business as his father was.''

Ash sank to the edge of the desk. He was tired. So damn tired. Tired of fighting to remember every rule of proper society. Tired of searching through his memory, trying to find answers that weren't there. Tired of trying to be something he wasn't.

He reached deep inside himself, seeking the balance that had sustained him all his life and finding it damaged. He needed Beth. He needed her arms around him, lending balance to a world tilted off its axis. He needed her, and hated the weakness that brought the need.

Instincts finely honed through years of living by his wits screamed for him to escape, to leave this place while he still had some shred of dignity. Yet he couldn't. Not yet.

For the first time in his life there were other lives entwined with his. People who expected the best he had to give. Ghosts and shadows haunting him from portraits and memories. A boy who had once played within these walls. A woman who had given him her innocence and love. Could he find his way back home?

"Promise me." Julianna squeezed Elizabeth's forearm. "You must promise me."

Elizabeth smothered her feelings, forcing anxiety and frustration into a dark corner of her heart. She forced her lips into a smile she hoped would seem reassuring, in spite of her own doubts. "I promise."

Julianna eased her hand from her daughter's arm, staring down for a moment at the red marks her fingers had branded across Elizabeth's skin before she spoke. "I must change for tea. It's getting late. The overnight guests will be arriving soon."

The sun had refused to emerge all day from its refuge behind a wall of gray clouds. Elizabeth pulled a cashmere shawl more tightly around her shoulders, trying to chase away the chill that had seeped into her blood.

Julianna rose from the stone bench she had shared with Elizabeth. "Are you coming?"

"I've already changed."

Julianna hesitated, staring down at her daughter, bunching the skirt of her cinnamon riding habit in her hands. "You are coming in for tea?"

"I want to sit here for a while. I'll be in for tea."

Julianna nodded. "I'll see you later."

Elizabeth remained on the stone bench near the sea-horse fountain in the south garden, watching her mother. Julianna walked toward the house, clutching her skirt, her boots tapping on the brick-lined path.

Elizabeth turned away, staring at the silvery plumes of water spouting upward from the mouths of a pair of stone sea horses, wondering how she might repair the damaged threads of her life. The discussion with her mother had been a mistake. She had suspected the impossibility of what she had proposed. Yet she had needed to know. Now that certainty pressed against her chest.

"You look as though your best friend has just been swept out to sea."

Elizabeth flinched at the sound of Dwight's deep voice. She glanced up and found him watching her from a few feet away, a frown etched on his handsome face. "What are you doing here?"

He crossed the distance between them, each step filled with a fluid grace. "Is that any way to greet one of your most ardent admirers?"

She managed a smile. "I didn't say I wasn't pleased to see you. I'm simply surprised."

He didn't wait for an invitation to sit beside her on the bench. His warmth radiated against her, but it couldn't chase away the chill inside. "Your dark mood wouldn't have anything to do with my father's visit this morning. Would it?"

She frowned. "Your father was here?"

"Apparently he had a bit of a row with Angelstone. I don't believe I've ever seen Father as angry as he was when he returned home from here." Dwight brushed his hand over the ears of a topiary rabbit growing beside the bench. "I didn't think Father would take losing the title well. But I'm afraid he won't be content until he finds some way to be rid of Angelstone."

Elizabeth glanced at him. "What do you think he'll do?"

Dwight shook his head. "He's already spent a fair amount of time spreading rumors about the prodigal. I doubt there is a house in London not aware of the fact that Angelstone was raised by Indians. I'm afraid people have started calling him '*Lord Savage.*' "

"Lord Savage?"

Dwight nodded. "It's rather colorful, don't you think?"

That was all she needed—another reason for Ash to feel an outsider in his own home. "I hope no one calls him that within his hearing."

He grinned at her, his blue eyes sparkling with mischief. "Are you afraid he might scalp them?"

She frowned. "This isn't amusing. Your cousin is faced with the rather daunting task of entering society."

"And society is breathless with anticipation. Everyone wants a glimpse of Lord Savage, the marquess who was raised by bloodthirsty savages."

"He isn't some freak to be put on display."

He lifted his brows in mock surprise. "No?"

She fixed him in a stern glare. "No."

He peeled a leaf from the topiary bush. "Well, no, I don't believe he is. But you have to admit, it isn't an everyday occurrence."

"It's all we can do to make him feel comfortable without someone going about labeling him with some derogatory name."

He studied her for a moment. "It sounds as though there might be trouble in paradise."

Elizabeth glanced away from his perceptive gaze, staring at the fountain. "I only wish to make certain Peyton feels comfortable, that's all. He has had a difficult time of it."

"From what I hear, you've had a difficult time with him."

She shot him a glance. "What have you heard?"

He glanced down at his hands, slowly wrapping the leaf

around the tip of his forefinger, releasing a sharp, tangy scent. "There is no secret your marriage was a bit hasty. I have to admit, the news hit me like a fist to the jaw."

He kept his gaze on the leaf, his profile carved sharply against the background of the serpentine hedge rising in the distance, revealing the hard set of his jaw. He had often teased her about marrying him one day, but until this moment she had always assumed there was nothing behind the light banter. "I don't know what you've heard, but I'm quite content to be his wife."

He lifted his head, studying her before he spoke. "You don't look content."

She pulled her shawl closer around her shoulders. "He isn't certain he will stay at Chatswyck. He might return to America. If he does, he wants me to go with him."

His eyes grew wide. "Good gad, he wants to take you to live in America?"

She nodded. "I don't know what I'm going to do."

He turned on the bench and took both of her hands in his warm grasp. "Don't tell me you're even considering going with him?"

"I have considered it." She stared at the fountain, where water spouted upward from the mouths of the twin stone sea horses. Silvery plumes stretched for the sky, only to tumble and splash in a wide stone basin. "I mentioned the possibility to Mother just before you arrived. She was very upset. Frightened I was going to leave her. The only way I could calm her was to promise I would stay."

He squeezed her hands. "There you see; it's impossible. You simply cannot leave."

"I shouldn't even have mentioned it to her. I know how upset she got when the duchess and I coaxed her to go with us to London two years ago. We scarcely arrived at St. James Place when Mother started trembling. By dinner she was whimpering like a child." A heaviness pressed against her chest—the realization that her alternatives were few and far between. "I can't abandon her. She won't leave Chatswyck. And I'm not certain I can convince Peyton to stay. It's a horrible tangle."

"Any man who would walk away from you doesn't deserve to be your husband."

She smiled, in spite of the heaviness pressing against her heart. "You've always been a good friend."

He pressed his lips against her brow, his breath a warm sigh against her skin. "I'll always be here for you, milady."

Tears misted her eyes at the tenderness in his touch. "Thank you."

The tenderness of the moment wasn't lost on Ash. He stood near a window in the library, staring out at the south garden, where his wife sat with his cousin. A woman didn't meet her lover in the middle of the afternoon, in plain view of the house, he assured himself. He felt a certainty in his bones that Elizabeth hadn't taken a lover. Still, he couldn't kill the serpent of jealousy coiling around his heart. Dwight was the type of man the lady deserved. He fit into her life better than Ash could ever dream of doing.

Ash stiffened as Shelby joined him at the window. He saw a frown touch Shelby's brow, noting the look of speculation in his dark eyes when he looked at Ash.

"I'm certain they're only friends," Shelby said, resting his hand on Ash's shoulder.

Ash set his jaw. He didn't care for anyone speculating about his wife's relationship with the handsome aristocrat, even if it was entirely innocent.

"What's this?" Hayward left his place behind the desk and moved to Ash's side.

Ash forced his lips into a smile he didn't feel. "Wickham has arrived a little early."

"I see." Hayward stared out into the garden as Elizabeth and Dwight walked along the path leading to the house. "Nothing to be concerned about from that quarter, my lad. Dwight might be a bit upset about losing out to you, with the title and Elizabeth slipping through his fingers, but I'm certain Elizabeth never took any of his marriage proposals seriously."

"Marriage proposals?" Ash asked.

Hayward nodded. "You know how these things are."

Ash suspected he knew exactly how things were with Dwight. The man had lost a woman and a title to someone who had risen from the dead. Ash doubted the young aristocrat had any friendly sentiments for his long-lost cousin. And he couldn't help wondering if everyone would be better off if Ash simply disappeared.

Hayward glanced at the walnut longcase clock standing in one corner of the room. "It's just about time for tea. I suggest we give all this talk of business a rest and join the ladies in the drawing room. The guests who will be staying overnight will be upon us before we know it."

The last thing Ash wanted to do right now was sit in the drawing room, sipping tea and watching Dwight entertain everyone with his wit and charm. Compared to his cousin, Ash was a great lumbering ox. Still, he allowed Hayward to usher him out of the room. He had never backed down from a challenge in his life and he didn't intend to start now.

Julianna was standing in the hall outside the study, staring down at a blue-and-white porcelain bowl that sat on a polished mahogany table against the far wall. She looked up when the men entered the hall, her blue gaze fixing on Ash.

The hair on the back of Ash's neck prickled as Julianna approached him. She had a wild look in her eyes, as though she was holding back a scream.

"May I speak with you?" she asked, gripping his coat sleeve.

Ash glanced at Hayward. The old man was frowning, as though he too sensed the barely restrained emotions in this small woman. Still, he nodded to Ash and left with Shelby, escaping into the drawing room down the hall.

Julianna stared up at Ash, her eyes overly bright. "I thought you were my friend," she whispered.

"Julianna, what's wrong?"

She twisted the dark gray wool of his coat sleeve. "You want to take her away from here. You want to take my daughter away from me."

He stared at her, realization seeping like ice water into his veins. "Beth talked to you about coming with us to America, didn't she?"

Julianna pressed her clenched fist to her mouth, whimpering against her fingers. "You can't take her away from me. I won't let you take her."

"We need to talk about this," he said, keeping his voice soft, hoping to calm her.

"Promise me you won't take her away." Julianna squeezed his coat sleeve. "Promise me."

Ash stared down into her wide, terrified eyes. She was balancing on a narrow ledge, inches from tumbling into hell. If he made one wrong move, she would fall. "I promise."

"Do you mean it?" she asked, her voice as high and thin as a frightened child's.

He rested his hand on her narrow shoulder, feeling his own alternatives dissolving in the light of her need. "Don't worry. I won't take her away from you."

Chapter Twenty-nine

There was no need to be nervous, Elizabeth assured herself. Ash was doing just fine. She tilted her head, looking past the shoulder of her partner, Lord Stephen Danbury, watching the marquess of Angelstone swirl across the dance floor with Lady Susannah Kerridge. Ash moved with a confidence and powerful grace few men in the room could claim. No one would suspect she had taught him the steps to the waltz only yesterday.

Still, she didn't care much for the look on Susannah's face. The fair-haired young woman was staring at Ash's shoulder, her lips drawn tight, her cheeks washed of color. Why, she actually looked frightened.

"It looks as though you've managed to tame Lord Savage," Danbury said. "He looks positively civilized."

"He *is* civilized." Elizabeth looked up at Danbury's round face. "And I really wish you wouldn't refer to him by that dreadful name."

Danbury smiled, his green eyes filling with humor. "I wouldn't mind the name. It's rather dashing. Gives a man an air of danger."

Ash didn't need anything to give him an air of danger. He managed quite well on his own. She was certain Danbury wouldn't mind being fixed with the title of Lord Savage because he hadn't been raised under the same circumstances as Ash had been. It was an amusing name for a staid young aristocrat who had never done an exciting thing in his life. Ash, on the other hand, would find it humiliating. "I doubt Angelstone will find it amusing if someone refers to him by that unfortunate name."

Danbury's eyes glittered. His voice was filled with excitement as he spoke. "Tell me, do you think he'll resort to violence? Fisticuffs, perhaps?"

The man was actually hoping for a brawl. "I think he shall think you and anyone else who calls him Lord Savage exceedingly rude."

Danbury glanced toward Ash and Susannah. "The Kerridge girl looks as though she's afraid Lord Savage is going to take a bite out of her."

Elizabeth was certain they had Bertram to thank for Susannah's fear. Her face was as white as her gown. And the lady's uneasiness had not been missed by her partner. Although his face was wiped clean of emotion, Elizabeth could see his tension in the tight line of his lips, the angry glitter in his eyes. At the moment she would dearly love to shake Susannah Kerridge until the girl's teeth rattled.

As Danbury swirled her around the floor, she noticed Bertram standing with three other men near one of the open French doors leading to the gardens. Bertram was staring at the dance floor, frowning as though he wasn't at all pleased with what he saw. After what Dwight had told her this afternoon she was amazed Bertram had had the nerve to attend the party. She only hoped he didn't cause any more trouble.

She turned her head, finding Ash in the crowd swirling around the dance floor. As the orchestra in the minstrels' gallery played the last shivering notes of the waltz, Susannah stepped back from Ash. So quickly she collided into the gentleman behind her. The nitwit of a girl glanced up at Ash, hesitating a moment before accepting the arm he offered her. She kept as much distance as possible from him as she allowed Ash to escort her from the floor in proper fashion. At least he was displaying proper decorum, Elizabeth thought. She certainly couldn't say the same for Susannah.

The Kerridge girl was as skittish as a mare trapped in a corral with a cougar, Ash thought, as he approached the sofa where Susannah's grandmother, Lady Marjorie Pickwell, was waiting. But then, Susannah had probably never before been obliged to dance with a man everyone was calling Lord Savage behind his back. He wouldn't be surprised if the little mouse expected him to bite her. He glanced at her pale profile, resisting the urge to bare his teeth and growl.

Half the people here were waiting for some slip on the part of the half-civilized savage in their midst. The other half were hoping for a brawl. They were expecting a scene, some grotesque breach of etiquette made by the imposter. He could see it in their faces as they stood at a distance and stared at him, as though he were a freak in a sideshow.

He had half a mind to oblige them, to give them a reason for the fear and revulsion in their eyes, to send them all scurrying back to London like a pack of rats. Still, some measure of pride kept him from performing for this glittering gathering.

Susannah scurried away from him, taking refuge with her chaperone. He forced his lips into a smile. He needed some air. He needed a few moments when he wasn't concentrating on every move he made.

Lady Marjorie peered at him through the lorgnette she wore on a satin ribbon attached to the bodice of her purple satin gown. "I must say, you do look a great deal like your father."

"So I've been told." She had made the same remark when he had come to claim her mouse of a granddaughter for the dance the duchess had insisted he request from the girl.

"Looking at you, I would never have guessed you were raised by bloodthirsty savages."

He was at the end of his tether, about to break away and smash something. Still, he managed to keep his voice low and calm as he spoke. "I wasn't."

Lady Marjorie frowned. "I was led to believe you were raised by Indians."

"The Cheyenne are hardly bloodthirsty savages," Ash said softly.

Lady Marjorie lifted one white brow. "I would hardly consider them civilized, considering all the people they have slaughtered."

Ash crushed the anger rising inside him. He didn't intend to entertain the audience by performing like the savage they thought him. "In all the time I was with them I never knew them to enter into any kind of warfare."

Marjorie looked puzzled. "But wasn't it Indians who killed your mother and father?"

"No," Ash said. "It wasn't."

"It wasn't?" Marjorie asked. "But, I'm quite certain Marlow told me it was Indians."

Ash frowned, realizing he had responded with a conviction that had no basis in fact. At least not a fact he remembered. Yet, for some reason, he felt certain Indians had not ambushed his father's coach. "I'm certain it wasn't."

"Interesting." Marjorie studied him for a moment, as though he were a rare species brought back from the jungle. "Did they teach you to scalp people?"

Ash pinned the nosy old biddy in a chilling glare. "If they had, Lady Marjorie, you would be the first to know."

Lady Marjorie dropped her lorgnette. She stared up at him with wide eyes, her thin lips parted in shock. Susannah eased behind the sofa, as though she expected to be pounced on.

"Do excuse me." Ash turned and nearly collided with Shelby Radcliffe.

"Sorry." Shelby stepped back. "I didn't mean to get in your way."

Ash nodded. "No harm done."

Shelby fell into step beside him as Ash headed for the nearest door leading to the gardens. "How are you enjoying your first taste of English society?"

Ash clenched his jaw. "It's a little bitter."

Shelby chuckled softly. "I know what you mean. It takes some time to get accustomed to it."

Could he get accustomed to it? Did he have a choice? Ash glanced around the crowded room, looking for Beth. He noticed Bertram making his way through the crowd a few yards away, heading straight for him. He glared at the man. Bertram halted in his tracks. One corner of his mustache twitched, once, twice, three times, before the earl pivoted and walked in the opposite direction.

"I believe you're going to have trouble with Lord Clayburne," Shelby said. "It's hard to say what a man will do when he is faced with losing a fortune."

"I've faced men more dangerous than Bertram Trevelyan." Ash noticed Beth on the edge of the dance floor with two men, one of whom was Dwight. That fact did nothing to lighten his mood. "Excuse me. I need some air."

Shelby smiled. "I understand."

Ash escaped through one of the open French doors, crossing the stone terrace without a pause in his stride. He took a deep breath of the damp night air, cleansing the mingled scents of perfume and cologne from his nostrils with the crisp fragrance of freshly cut grass. The sound of music and conversation followed him, chasing him along the brick-lined path wending through the gardens, fading as he approached the living walls of the maze.

He hadn't intended to come here. Wasn't really sure why he had. Yet this place drew him like a siren's call. He paused at the entrance, staring up at the twin knights guarding the emerald realm. The moon peeked out from behind a cloud, spilling silver across the granite faces, spinning stone into ghosts that haunted him.

Images flashed in his mind, fragments from a childhood shattered long ago. A dragon spitting fire. Blood spilled beneath the tip of a silver sword. *A dragon shall guard my treasure.* He shivered with the memory. The same images had been haunting him for days, each time he looked at the maze.

His instincts prickled. He sensed movement behind him. Before he could turn, something struck the back of his head. Pain flared with a suddenness that snatched the strength from his limbs. He pitched forward, tumbling into the dark pool opening up to swallow him.

Oil lamps atop wrought-iron posts lined the path stretching through the long tunnel of elms leading to the maze. Flames flickered behind polished glass, lighting her way, as Elizabeth hurried along the path. She hoped Ash was sequestered in the maze. From the look on his face when he had left the ballroom, he might have decided to take his horse and ride away from this place, never looking back.

She wasn't at all certain what she would say to him. She could tell him that members of polite society were in general a dull lot. She would of course tell him he must ignore them. In time they would lose interest in "*Lord Savage.*" She only hoped they hadn't already made him eager to turn his back on the whole lot of them, including his wife. She had to find some way to convince him to stay. It was her only chance to be with him.

Her heart pounded like a fist against the wall of her chest as she approached the maze and sought the first words she would say to him. There was so much at stake.

A thread of smoke swirled in the cool evening breeze, filling her nostrils with the scent of burning wood. Smoke curled in a dark ribbon upward from the center of the maze. Something was burning at the heart of the maze. She hurried along the twisting pathways, wondering if Ash had come here. He might not be anywhere near this place, she told herself.

She froze as she stepped from the sheltering yew into the heart of the maze. A bright orange glow blazed at the long windows of the pavilion. Smoke and heat poured from the open door.

Memories ignited of another place, another time. A fire that had ripped her life to shreds. She could feel the heat on her cheeks, taste the smoke on her tongue, hear the terrible screams of her brothers. For a moment she couldn't move, too terrified to breathe. A single thought pulled her from the dark memories: Ash could be in there.

With a force of will, she dragged her feet toward the burning structure. She crouched, looking below the smoke that coiled and slithered like a fat serpent through the door. The fire fed on the air in a loud, sucking whoosh. Smoke collected in a growing black cloud against the ceiling. Flames licked from a broken chair upward along one wall, devouring the tapestries, flicking serpents' tongues against the ceiling. In the bright orange glow she saw a man lying facedown on the floor.

"Ash," she whispered. She hesitated only a moment before plunging into the inferno.

Her eyes stung and filled with water, blinding her. In the back of her mind she thought of the silk of her gown; one spark could set it ablaze. Still, she pressed on through the smoke, raising her handkerchief to her mouth and nose, fighting against the acid stench. She dropped to her knees beside Ash, blinking back the water in her eyes.

"Ash!" She grabbed his shoulder, shook him. He

didn't stir. She tugged on his shoulder, rolled him to his back. His head lulled on the mosaic beneath him, his eyes closed, his lips parted.

Heat pressed against her, embracing her with demon arms. The flames roared like an angry dragon. Pieces of burning tapestry dropped to the floor, hissing against the stones. They didn't have much time.

She hooked her hands beneath his shoulders and pulled. She staggered with the heat, dragging him across the stones, coughing as the smoke filled her nostrils and seared her throat. She closed her eyes against the smoke, staggering backward, holding her breath, dragging him.

At last she felt the cool air on her back. She kept moving, dragging him across the gravel path until she bumped against a tall wall of yew. The strength melted from her limbs. She crumpled to her knees, coughing, gulping at the cool air. Tears fell from her eyes as she blinked and tried to clear the oily film from her vision.

Ash lay on the gravel in front of her, deathly still. Gently, she eased his head and shoulders onto her lap. "Ash," she said, her scorched throat strangling her voice to a whisper that was drowned in the roar of the fire.

She pressed her hand against his chest, above his heart. A slow, steady beat throbbed beneath her palm. "Thank God."

She flinched at a loud crash. Sparks skittered through the open door, spitting across the gravel. She clutched Ash close to her. Flames shot upward toward the sky. In her mind she saw her father standing on a third-floor balcony, with her brothers on either side of him.

Flames danced like frenzied demons in the room behind them. Smoke billowed around them, the devil's arms reaching for them. Her mother's screams filled the air.

Elizabeth hadn't screamed. She hadn't the air in her lungs to scream. She had stared in mute horror, watching the slow tumble of her father and brothers as the balcony gave way.

She cupped Ash's face in her hands. "You have to be all right, do you hear me? You have to wake up. We must get away from here. The entire maze could burn."

Light glowed on his face, revealing his parted lips, the stillness of his black lashes against his cheeks. He showed no signs of awakening. If his lungs had filled with smoke . . . she refused to finish the thought. She could run for help. But by the time they returned the maze could be completely engulfed in flame.

She drew air into her lungs, came to her feet, and grabbed his shoulders. She dragged Ash into the dark pathway, fighting her cumbersome skirts. She had gone only a few steps when she heard the first shouts of alarm. People had noticed the fire from the ballroom. A few moments later Hayward, along with Dwight and two other men, found her in the twisted labyrinth.

"What the devil happened?" Hayward asked, crouching beside Ash.

"Are you all right?" Dwight slipped his arm around her shoulders, steadying her.

"He needs help." She leaned against Dwight. "We have to get him to the house."

Sharp, piercing screams shattered the cool air. Elizabeth shuddered in Dwight's embrace. "Mother," she whispered.

Chapter Thirty

A blacksmith was inside Ash's head, using his skull as an anvil. The relentless pounding throbbed behind his eyes, echoed against his temples, ricocheted off the back of his head. Ash watched his grandfather, trying to follow Hayward as he paced back and forth beside Ash's bed. But he was getting dizzy watching, and the sights were much prettier when he lowered his gaze.

Elizabeth sat beside his bed, holding his hand as though to do so would prevent him from drowning. Her hair had tumbled from the elegant coils that had been piled high at the back of her head. The thick honey-colored tresses cascaded around her shoulders in wild waves. A single streak of soot marred her right cheek. The pale blue silk of her gown was stained by smoke and blood. Still, he had never thought she looked more beautiful than she did at that moment.

The lady had risked her life to save him. She had plunged into a burning building to pull him out. When he thought of how easily that silk gown could have caught fire his blood turned as cold as a mountain stream.

Hayward pivoted at the foot of the bed and continued back in the opposite direction, a floorboard beneath the thick Aubusson carpet creaking with his restless footsteps. "I never thought Clayburne would go this far."

Ash glanced at the duke. "I got hit from behind," he said, his throat raw from the smoke he had swallowed. "I

374

can't be certain it was Clayburne.''

Hayward paused behind Elizabeth's chair. ''Who else wanted to see my grandson dead?''

''I can think of a few men. Although none of them are on this side of the Atlantic,'' Ash said.

Hayward gripped the carved back of Elizabeth's chair. ''I swear, I'll see him in chains.''

Ash shook his head. He gasped at the splinters of pain shooting through his temples from the slight movement. ''We need proof.''

''You need to be still.'' Elizabeth smoothed a wrinkle in the shoulder of the silk nightshirt she had purchased for him in New York, before she had discovered he never wore anything to bed. She looked up at Hayward. ''I shouldn't need to remind you that the doctor said he has a concussion. He needs rest.''

Rest sounded damn good at the moment, Ash thought, as long as the lady curled up beside him. His entire body ached.

Hayward gave Ash a sheepish grin. ''I believe she is telling me I should go away and let you get some sleep.''

Ash grinned at his wife. ''She's a bossy little thing.''

Hayward nodded, his eyes glittering with humor. ''A true tyrant.''

Elizabeth lifted one delicately arched brow. ''You haven't seen me at my best. I'm a true Wellington when it comes to managing a sickroom.'' She pointed toward the door. ''Now, march.''

''Aye, sir.'' Hayward laid his hand on Ash's shoulder. ''Glad you're still with us, my lad.''

A tight knot formed in his throat as Ash looked up into the wealth of affection glowing in the old man's eyes. All his life he had wanted a family. Now it was his, if he had the courage to take it.

He watched the old man leave, his thoughts lingering on all the arguments Elizabeth had presented since the first day she had stormed into his life. *Nothing else matters in this world, except family, friends, someone special to give our affection to. Nothing else.* What about pride? What about respect? A man had to feel he could walk through life without people whispering about him.

"I hope you don't mind that I chased him away. You need rest." Elizabeth smoothed the hair back from his brow, her fingers grazing lightly against his skin. "I intend to make certain you get well."

"You took quite a risk this evening." He brushed his hand over a dark stain on the pale silk covering her thigh—traces of blood from where she had cradled his cracked head on her lap. "You could have been killed."

"It was awful. Seeing you in there. The fire . . ." She shuddered, releasing her breath in a shaky sigh. "There wasn't any time to go for help."

He stared at the dark red smears on that pale silk, searching for words that might tell her how he felt. Yet every word seemed insignificant in light of what she had done for him. Tonight. In all the days since he had met her. "What made you come looking for me? Were you going to scold me for leaving the party?"

She smiled. "I intended to tell you how proud I was of you."

The room tilted with her soft words. The woman had the damndest way of tipping his world upside down.

She lifted his hand in her warm grasp. "I saw you leave. You didn't look as though you were enjoying the party."

"I got tired of being stared at as though I were a freak. I left before I gave them a good reason to call me 'Lord Savage.' "

She crinkled her nose. "You heard."

"Several people managed to say it loud enough for me to hear. I think they were hoping I would get angry, jump on the nearest table, and pound my fists against my chest.''

She squeezed his hand. ''You must realize they live dreadfully dull lives. Members of the upper class are always looking for some type of diversion. In time they will grow weary of the novelty of it all. Danbury even told me he wished they would call him 'Lord Savage,' as if that freckle-faced young man could ever do anything exciting enough to warrant such a title. Why, Marlow even had an uncle everyone called the Devil of Dartmoor. I'm told he absolutely reveled in that moniker.''

Ash realized what she was doing. He forced his lips into a smile. ''Guess I should be flattered, is that it?''

''You are the marquess of Angelstone; you should not care what those horrible people say. It only shows they need lessons in proper decorum.'' She rubbed his hand between hers, frowning. ''You've shown them all you're far more civilized than they are. Your manners are impeccable. Not a man at the party is more of a gentleman than you.''

The soft words were more precious to him than a trunk full of gold. ''Guess I have to thank my teacher.''

''You can thank me properly when you get back your strength.'' She brushed her lips across his mouth.

The heat of her sigh pierced him, searing through his blood like a flaming arrow, headed straight for the powder keg in his loins. He wanted to take her in his arms and hold her. But the demon blacksmith in his head pounded him back against the pillows when he tried to rise.

She pressed her hand against his shoulder, the warmth of her palm seeping through the sapphire silk. ''You need rest. Close your eyes,'' she said softly. ''Forget about all this unpleasantness. Concentrate only on getting well.''

He moistened his dry lips, wishing he had the eloquence of the gentleman she deserved. ''Thank you,'' he whispered, hating the inadequacy of the simple words.

She smoothed her hand over his cheek, lamplight glittering in the silvery mist filling her eyes. "I'm thankful I was there in time."

He turned his pounding head and pressed his lips against her wrist. Beneath the bitter scent of smoke he caught a trace of lavender lingering against her skin, like hope dwelling in the shadows. When the pounding in his head stopped he would show her just how grateful he was.

Elizabeth glanced at the door at a sharp rapping on the solid oak. At her invitation, Hedley entered the room.

"Her Grace asks that you join her in Lady Julianna's chamber, milady. It seems the doctor is having a problem calming Her Ladyship. She keeps calling for you."

Elizabeth looked at Ash, her lips parted, her eyes filled with indecision. "The fire was quite a shock to Mother. I'm afraid it brought back too many horrible memories."

Ash squeezed her hand. "Go to her. I'll be all right."

She brushed her lips over his. "I'll be back as soon as I can."

Ash watched her leave, the sweetness of her kiss lingering on his lips. He stood at a crossroads in his life. One path led to Chatswyck, to Elizabeth, to his family. If he chose that path, he could have everything he had ever wanted, as long as he was willing to pay the price—his pride. If he chose to live here, he would be Lord Savage. A freak. A man who would always be pointed at and whispered about. If he left, he left behind his heart.

He closed his eyes, surrendering to the hellish pounding in his head. He felt as shaky as a newborn colt. Just as weak. Just as vulnerable.

Rest. He needed to get back his strength. He needed to figure out who wanted him dead. But most of all, he had to have a clear enough head to make the most difficult decision in his life.

He was just slipping over the edge of slumber when he heard a floorboard squeak beside the bed. He glanced up, fighting to focus his blurry eyes. He caught a glimpse of a white silk pillow case before someone forced the pillow over his face.

Ash surged upward, reaching for the killer. Shards of light flickered behind his lids. His head pounded with pain. Strong hands forced him back against the bed. Ash struggled, digging his fingers into soft wool and the taut muscles of his assassin's forearms. The hands holding the pillow pushed harder, forcing Ash deeper into the soft goose-down pillow beneath his head.

He was drowning in goose down. His lungs, still raw from smoke, screamed for air. He fought for breath, trying to drag air into his burning lungs, sucking soft silk into his mouth instead. He clawed the arms holding him down, but his strength was ebbing.

Darkness wrapped chilly arms around him, dragging him down into a black well. He thought of Beth, imagined he heard her voice before darkness engulfed him.

It took one shattering beat of her heart for Elizabeth to take in the horror of the scene before her. A dark-haired man was leaning over Ash, smothering him with a pillow.

"Take your hands off him!" Elizabeth shouted, darting across the floor like a tigress after prey.

The assassin started at her voice. He glanced over his shoulder, his expression revealing his horror as he saw her. She scarcely had time to register the assassin's identity before she launched herself at the man. She latched her hands around his arm and pulled, trying to tear him away.

He came away from the bed, stumbling like a drunkard. The pillow dangled from his trembling hands. He stared at her as though she were a ghost risen from the dead.

"Ash!" Elizabeth sank to the edge of the bed. His lips were parted, his eyes closed. He didn't seem to be breathing.

"Is he dead?" the assassin asked, his voice a harsh whisper.

"Breathe." She cupped Ash's cheeks in her hands. "You have to breathe."

"I didn't want to kill him. I didn't have a choice."

The words swirled in her head, but she couldn't make sense of them. She couldn't try. Nothing made sense. Ash was dead. "No!"

"I couldn't take the chance he would tell everyone what happened." A floorboard near the bed creaked. "And now you'll tell everyone I did this."

Elizabeth gasped as he whipped his hands around her neck.

"I can't let you tell anyone." He dragged her off the bed. "I'm sorry."

She struggled in his grasp, digging her fingers into his arms. He squeezed, pressing his fingertips against her throat. Bright pinpoints of light danced before her watering eyes. Blood pounded in her ears. She couldn't breathe. With every ounce of strength she could muster she rammed her elbows into his chest. His breath escaped in a whoosh of brandy-soaked air. She twisted, breaking free of his stunned grasp.

She gulped at the air, staggering toward the door. She needed help, but when she tried to scream, her voice was only a harsh whisper.

"I can't let you tell them!" He grabbed her arm and yanked her back against his chest. "You understand." He clamped his arm around her neck. "I can't let you tell anyone. I'm sorry."

"They'll know it's you." She ground out the words against the tight pressure of his arm against her throat.

"No, they won't." He tightened his arm against her neck. "No one will know. No one except you."

Pitiful whimpering sounds filled her ears, and she realized the noise came from her own lips. The room darkened. She struggled against him. But he was too strong.

The assassin flinched against her, a low groan escaping his lips. He released her and she stumbled a few steps, catching the back of a chair when her legs would have bucked beneath her. She stood braced against the tall wing-backed chair, digging her fingers into the silk brocade, gulping at the air like a landed trout, her head sagging between her shoulders. She had to get away from him.

Through the pounding in her head she was aware of someone moving toward her. She tried to run toward the door, but he stopped her, gripping her upper arm. She lashed out, hitting him squarely in the jaw with her clenched fist. He groaned. She twisted free and staggered for the door.

"You've got one hell of a right, princess."

Elizabeth froze. That harsh whisper was very familiar. She peeked over her shoulder. Ash was standing a few feet away, rubbing his jaw. The man who had tried to kill both of them lay facedown on the carpet near the foot of the bed. A jade figurine of a dragon that usually sat on the table near the bed lay on the floor nearby.

"Don't tell me, I know." Ash grinned at her. "I startled you. Right?"

"Ash!" She staggered toward him, tottering as though she had imbibed one too many brandies.

He opened his arms, catching her against him, holding her close. "Thank God you're all right."

"I was afraid he had killed you." She locked her arms around his waist.

"I gave him a good crack on the head for his trouble. I only hope his head pounds as much as mine does when he wakes up."

"Why did he do this?" she asked, her cheek pressed against his chest. "Why did he want to kill you?"

He pressed his lips to her hair. "I don't know, princess. Guess we'll have to ask him."

Chapter Thirty-one

Ash sat beside Elizabeth on a leather sofa in the study, staring at the man who had tried to murder him. Shelby Radcliffe sat in a leather chair near the desk, his head bowed, his wrists bound together with manacles. Hayward sat on the edge of his desk, his face growing pale as he listened to Shelby's soft confession.

"Emory found out about the money I had taken from the company." Shelby glanced up at Hayward. "I hadn't meant to steal it. But I needed cash. I was overextended. I would have paid it back."

"Why didn't you ask my son for a loan?" Hayward asked.

Shelby smiled. "That's what Emory asked me the night before he left Denver. He said he could no longer trust me. Even though he wasn't going to press charges, he was going to pull out of the mining venture. He didn't want to remain business associates."

Ash curled his hand into a fist against his thigh, his fingers sliding against the smooth black wool of his trousers. He was shaking deep inside, where memories dwelled in shadows.

Shelby wiped the back of his bound hands over his eyes. "I didn't want to kill him. I didn't want to hurt anyone. Not Emory, or Rebecca. God, I didn't want to hurt Rebecca. But she knew everything."

Images flashed in Ash's memory—his father falling

back against the leather coach seat, blood spilling from a wound in his chest. His mother's screams pierced the shadows in his mind. *She was pulling on him, pushing him out the door of the coach. Run, Peyton! She dragged him toward the woods. Another shot. She gasped and then she was falling. Run, Peyton! Run into the woods!*

Elizabeth rested her hand on his arm, as though she realized the horrible images flooding his mind. The warmth of her hand seeped through the white linen of his shirt, fighting the chill in his blood.

"I couldn't let Emory pull out of the mining venture," Shelby said. "Without his financial support I would have lost everything."

Hayward closed his eyes. "So you killed them. You killed my son and my daughter-in-law."

Ash dragged air into his tight lungs. Moisture beaded on his upper lip. He stared at Shelby, fighting the need to strangle the man with his bare hands.

"Were you responsible for the man on the train outside of Denver?" Hayward asked.

"I hired him to kill Peyton." Shelby looked at Ash, tears streaming down his cheeks. "I'm sorry. I'm so sorry. I didn't mean to hurt anyone. But I couldn't take the chance you would remember me from that morning on the trail."

Ash swallowed hard, forcing down the bile burning a path upward in his throat. "I never saw your face."

"Oh, God!" Shelby closed his eyes, his face twisting into a mask of pain. "You didn't know."

"If you had left my grandson alone, we never would have realized you were a cold-blooded murderer." Hayward glanced at the constable standing near the door. "You can take him now."

For a long time after Shelby and the constable had gone no one spoke. Finally Hayward looked at Ash, his eyes glittering with unshed tears. "All of this time I was doing business with the man who murdered my family. Thank heaven you survived.''

Ash stood, his head pounding with the sudden movement.

Elizabeth came to her feet and gripped his arm. "Are you all right?''

He looked down into her beautiful face, touched the bruises on her neck, and felt his eyes burn with tears. "I need a few minutes alone. All right?''

Uncertainty and fear flickered in her eyes, but she managed a smile for him. "I'll be here, when you need me.''

He left the study, needing to put the last of his doubts to rest. After taking a knife from the butler's pantry he made his way to the maze, pausing for only a moment to glance up at the stone guards before entering the labyrinth. Early morning mist swirled the scent of ashes as he made his way to the heart of the maze.

The stone walls of the pavilion had protected the thick walls of yew. The pavilion stood as it had for a hundred years; battered, blackened, but it had survived. He paused on the threshold, staring into the blackened interior. Boards from the roof lay in twisted heaps across the stone floor. Shreds of tapestries were burnt and twisted against the charred walls. Yet a single tapestry had survived. The colorful threads depicting Arthur drawing the sword from the stone had been darkened by the smoke, but not beyond redemption.

He pushed rubble aside with his foot, lifted away debris, until he uncovered the mosaic inlaid in the center of the room. Memories flickered inside him. He crouched beside the dragon. *A dragon shall guard my treasure.*

He slipped the knife along the edge of stone shaping the dragon's chest, where the thick silver sword of St. George had pierced the emerald skin, spilling the beast's blood. His heart crept upward in his chest as he found a ridge in the stone.

Slowly he eased the stone upward with the knife and his fingertips. He set the stone aside and stared down at a small leather bag nestled in the hiding place beneath the dragon, his heart pounding.

After Elizabeth bathed and changed she checked on her mother. She expected Julianna to be sleeping at this early hour, especially after the terrible night she had suffered. Instead, her mother was sitting in an upholstered armchair near the window, gazing at an album of photographs resting in her lap.

Julianna looked up as Elizabeth approached her. Morning light glistened on the tears brimming in her eyes. "I've been looking at photographs. Come, look."

Elizabeth leaned over her mother's shoulder, gazing down at the photograph pressed against the black page. It was her family at Christmas. The last Christmas they had ever shared.

"It's been such a long time since I've seen their faces." Julianna brushed her fingers over the faces preserved in shades of brown on the paper. A tall, handsome dark-haired man stood beside his wife in front of a tall Christmas tree. His daughter stood on his right, and his three handsome sons sat on the floor in front of them. "They were so beautiful."

Elizabeth rested her hand on her mother's shoulder. "You remember," she said, emotion catching in her throat.

Julianna nodded, fresh tears spilling from her eyes. "Last night. The smell of smoke. The orange glow of flames in the night. I remembered," she said, her voice dissolving in a sob.

"It's all right." Elizabeth slipped her arm around her mother's slender shoulders. She rested her cheek against Julianna's unbound hair.

Julianna dabbed at her eyes with a lace-trimmed handkerchief. ''I feel as though a part of me has been locked away in a dark cell for so many years. So many years. I saw them in dreams, but I never let them come near me. It hurt so much. I thought I would die from the pain if I let the memories near me.''

''I know. It hurts when I remember too. But I don't want to forget Father or my brothers.'' She knelt beside her mother's chair. ''Memories are all I have of them.''

Julianna stared down at the photograph. ''Your father would brush my hair every night before we retired. He had such gentle hands.''

Elizabeth fought against the tears, but they fell in spite of her best effort. She wanted to be strong for her mother. She had to be strong. Yet the memories conspired with her fears for her own husband. She could lose Ash.

Julianna cupped her daughter's face in her hands. ''My darling child, how difficult this all must have been for you. And I wasn't here for you. Not really here.''

''I'm sorry,'' Elizabeth whispered. ''I don't mean to upset you.''

Julianna swept her thumbs over her daughter's cheeks, wiping away the tears. ''You've always been my brave little girl. I don't know what I would have done without you.''

Elizabeth smiled in spite of the tears she couldn't prevent. ''I love you, Mother.''

Julianna pressed her lips to Elizabeth's brow. ''I swear to God, I'll never abandon you again.''

Elizabeth stayed with her mother most of the morning, looking at photographs, sharing memories of mischievous boys and a gentle man, of picnics and sleigh rides and walks in the park. When she left Julianna's room Elizabeth knew her mother had taken the first step toward healing the ragged wounds a fire had scrawled across her soul. She only prayed she could find a way to help heal Ash's wounds.

*   *   *

Ash sat in the window seat of his bedroom. The afternoon sun had burned away the clouds and mist of the morning. Golden light spilled across the curving body of the hedges and gathered in a shimmering pool of gold in the pond near the maze. He stared at the crenellated walls of the pavilion at the heart of the maze, welcoming the memories spilling into his mind.

"You should be in bed," Elizabeth said as she entered the room. "And here you are, up and about, not even dressed for bed."

Warmth curled around him when he looked at her and saw her smile. The lady had a smile that could light up an entire room, or a heart that had lived too long in shadows. "I couldn't sleep."

She settled beside him on the plump cushions, her rose-colored gown rustling softly. Sunlight touched her face, gilding the tips of her dark lashes, kissing her moist lips. The golden light slipped over her unbound hair, streaming in rivulets down the thick honey-colored waves that tumbled to her waist.

He wished he could capture her in this moment. He wished he could dab paint to canvas and preserve forever the way she looked right now. Yet he wasn't an artist. He would have to settle for painting her image across his heart.

She tilted her head to look at him, her hair slipping over one shoulder. "Marlow is going to have the pavilion restored."

"I'm glad. There are a lot of memories pinned to that small castle." He looked down at the small leather bag that lay across his palm, his chest growing tight with bittersweet memories. "I remember Father would don a silver helmet and do battle with me in the maze. We would fight to the death with wooden swords. He always allowed me to win. Mother would meet us in the pavilion after the battle, with cakes and lemonade.''

She rested her hand on his arm. ''They loved you very much.''

Ash nodded, taking time to ease the tightness in his throat before he spoke. ''Mother was going to have another baby. They told me about it a few days before we left Denver. They said, I was going to have a little brother or sister. I remember thinking how happy they were.''

She squeezed his arm. ''Coming here, regaining your childhood memories, must be like losing your parents all over again.''

The memories had brought pain, but with the pain had come a sense of peace. He knew who he was. And for the first time in his adult life he knew where he belonged. He held the bag out to her, holding the leather string cinching the top, allowing the small pouch to dangle from his fingers.

She frowned. ''What is it?''

''Something I buried a long time ago. I found it, under the dragon in the pavilion.''

She stared at the small pouch. ''What's in it?''

''I was waiting for you before I opened it.'' He drew a deep breath, drawing the delicate fragrance of lavender into his lungs. ''If I remember correctly, this it the proof Marlow has been hoping for.''

She pressed her left hand to the base of her neck. ''Please open it.''

He tugged on the ends of the pouch, easing open the leather. ''Put out your hand.''

She hesitated, crinkling her nose. ''There isn't anything crawling in there. Is there?''

He glanced into the bag, his chest tightening with the realization of what this moment meant. ''I think it's safe enough.''

She extended her hand, cupping her palm to catch the contents of the bag as he spilled it into her hand. A ring tumbled into her palm. A thick band of gold glowing in the sunlight.

"Oh, my." She lifted the ring, turned it, allowing golden light to twist and shimmer on a single square-cut emerald embedded in the center of the Trevelyan crest carved into the gold. "Your ring," she said, her voice barely above a whisper.

He took the ring from her trembling fingers. He stared into the emerald, his vision blurring with the mist rising in his eyes. "I was afraid pirates would steal it if I took it with me to America. So I buried it beneath the dragon in my castle."

She laughed. "Clayburne will howl when he sees this."

He smiled when he thought of the arrogant aristocrat. "I suppose there will be a few people disappointed to learn Lord Savage is undeniably Peyton Trevelyan."

"There can be no more doubts about who you were," she said softly. "Do you still have doubts?"

He looked up from the ring. She was looking at him in that soft way that made his heart melt. Yet there were questions in her eyes. Doubts and fears he had placed there. He lifted his hand, showing her another ring, this one on the third finger of his left hand, the gold glowing in the sunlight, the emerald winking as if it had a secret to tell. "The day before we left Denver, Marlow offered me this. It belonged to my father. I didn't want it. I didn't think it belonged to me."

She slipped her hand around his. She kept her eyes lowered, staring at the ring as she spoke, as though she were afraid to see what might be in his eyes. "There have been a great many things you haven't wanted."

His chest tightened when he thought of all the pain he had caused his grandparents and the woman he loved. "Marlow said the ring would be waiting for me when I was ready."

"You're ready to accept the ring." She glanced up at

him, her expression revealing a hesitant expectancy. "Are you ready to come home? To stay?"

"In the past few days I've come to realize that home isn't a place. Home is a feeling, a sense of belonging. I might not be sure about a great many things in this life, but I'm sure of one thing." He lifted their clasped hands and pressed his lips to her fingers. "I belong with you. No matter where that is. You are my home."

Tears glittered like silver in her eyes. "It's about time you figured that out, Ash MacGregor."

He slipped the small ring onto the little finger of her left hand, next to her wedding band. "It's about time you learn the proper way to address your husband."

She lifted one finely arched brow, the sparkle of humor in her misty eyes spoiling the stern look. "And what might that be? Lord and Master?"

He kissed the tip of her nose. "I think Peyton will do just fine."

"Actually, I've become rather fond of the name Lord Savage. Is that all right with you?" She gave him a mischievous grin, but he sensed something more serious beneath her lighthearted banter. She was asking him, in her own subtle way, if he would ever feel comfortable in this place.

"If you don't mind being married to Lord Savage, I guess I don't give a damn what anyone else says."

She made a soft sound deep in her throat, a little sob that caught at his heart. She threw her arms around his neck and held him, as though she were afraid someone would tear him away from her. "I love you, Peyton Emory Hayward Trevelyan, Lord Angelstone, Lord Savage, lord of my heart."

He held her close against the heart she owned. "I don't know what I did good enough to deserve you, but I'm not going to question my luck." He rubbed his lips against her neck, inhaling the sweet fragrance of her skin. "I love you, Beth. Now and always."

Epilogue

Chatswyck, 1898

Peyton left a stack of correspondence in the study to join his family in the blue drawing room. He paused beneath the arched entry, taking a moment to watch them. Hayward sat by the hearth, playing chess with his eight-year-old great-grandson, Emory Hayward Peyton Trevelyan.

"Let's see you maneuver your way out of this, young man," Hayward said, leaning back in his chair.

Emory tilted his dark head, eyeing the chess board for a moment before moving his white queen. "Check."

"Check?" Hayward rested his elbow on the table, studying the board a moment before grinning at the boy. "Well done, my lad. Well done. But you don't have me yet."

Life was a circle, Peyton thought. A circle completed by the joining of hands, one family member to the next. Warmth curled around his heart when he thought of his own place in the circle.

Peyton's six-year-old daughter, Rebecca, sat on a sofa between her grandmother and great-grandmother, her golden curls plump upon her narrow shoulders, watching as the ladies tried to teach her how to place perfect stitches in a sampler.

"That's it, sweetheart," Julianna said, rubbing her granddaughter's shoulder. "That is a perfect little daisy."

391

Peyton's three-year-old son, Alexander Jonathan, sat on the carpet near his mother's chair, making chugging noises as he scooted a wooden train across the blue and gold carpet.

A tall evergreen sat in one corner of the room, its graceful branches filled with ornaments and ribbons, spilling the fresh scent of pine into the air. Christmas was two days away, yet Peyton could think of no other present he needed except the people in this room.

Snow fell outside the big room, drifting past the long French doors, etching frosty patterns on the mullioned windowpanes. A fire crackled on the hearth, casting warmth and light into the room. But the fire paled when Elizabeth smiled at him. All the warmth and light in his world was concentrated in that smile. She stood, laid the novel she had been reading on the seat of her chair, and crossed the room to join him.

"You look like a king surveying his realm," she whispered, slipping her arms around his waist.

He rubbed his hands down her back, absorbing her warmth through the soft merino wool of her gown, craving the sleek silk of her skin. "Just a man, princess. A man thankful for his home and family."

She raised herself up on her toes and kissed his lips, a soft brush of warmth that left him hungry for more. "There is a fresh box of chocolates waiting for you in your bedroom. I don't believe anyone would notice if we slipped away for a few hours to enjoy them."

He slipped his arm around her slim waist and led her into the hall. "You know, I have a particular passion for melted chocolate."

She gave him a wicked smile. "It's one of the reasons I married you, my darling Lord Savage."

Author's Note

I hope you enjoyed spending time with Ash and Elizabeth.
I had a great deal of fun watching the sparks fly when
they came together.

A few years ago I had the pleasure of touring Scotland.
I took one look at the Scottish Highlands and knew I
would one day write a book set in that beautiful country.
In *MacLaren's Bride,* I invite you to journey with me to
the Scotland of 1816, where you'll meet a handsome Scottish Highlander and his lady.

Alec MacLaren, Earl of Dunleith, never dreamed he
would one day kidnap a woman and force her into marriage. But that is exactly what his father's old friend, Sir
Robert Drummond, has asked him to do. It seems Robert's estranged daughter, Margaret, is about to commit the
grave mistake of marrying an English fortune hunter.
Honor compels the handsome war hero to comply with
Sir Robert's outrageous request. He never expects to find
everything he has been looking for in this inconvenient
marriage to his tempestuous, half-English bride. Still,
Alec must teach his wary bride how to trust again before
they can claim a love as bold as the Highlands.

I love to hear from readers. Please enclose a self-addressed stamped envelope with your letter.

Debra Dier
P.O. Box 584
Glen Carbon, Illinois 62034-0584

Bestselling Author Of *Shadow Of The Storm*

To Devlin McCain, she is a fool who is chasing after moonbeams, a spoiled rich girl who thinks her money can buy anything. But beneath her maddening facade burns a blistering sensuality he is powerless to resist, and he will journey to the ends of the earth to claim her.

To Kate Whitmore, he is an overpowering brute who treats women like chattel, an unscrupulous scoundrel who values gold above all else. Yet try as she might, she cannot deny the irresistible allure of his dangerous virility.

Hard-edged realist and passionate idealist, Devlin and Kate plunge into the Brazilian jungle, searching for the answer to an age-old mystery and a magnificent love that will bind them together forever.

_3583-9 $4.99 US/$5.99 CAN

Dorchester Publishing Co., Inc.
65 Commerce Road
Stamford, CT 06902

Please add $1.75 for shipping and handling for the first book and $.50 for each book thereafter. NY, NYC, PA and CT residents, please add appropriate sales tax. No cash, stamps, or C.O.D.s. All orders shipped within 6 weeks via postal service book rate. Canadian orders require $2.00 extra postage and must be paid in U.S. dollars through a U.S. banking facility.

Name _____

Address _____

City _____ State _____ Zip _____

I have enclosed $_____ in payment for the checked book(s).

Payment **must** accompany all orders. ☐ Please send a free catalog.

DON'T MISS THESE LEISURE HISTORICAL ROMANCES— *LOVE STORIES FOR ALL TIME.*

Love A Rebel, Love A Rogue by Shirl Henke. The Blackthorne men—one highborn, one half-caste—are bound by blood, but torn apart by choice. Caught between them, two sensuous women long for more than stolen moments of wondrous splendor. But as the lovers are swept from Savannah's ballrooms to Revolutionary War battlefields, they learn that the faithful heart can overcome even the fortunes of war.

_3673-8 $4.99 US/$5.99 CAN

Deceptions & Dreams by Debra Dier. Sarah Van Horne can outwit any scoundrel who tries to cheat her in business. But she is no match for the dangerously handsome burglar she catches in her New York City town house. She knows she ought to send the suave rogue to the rock pile for life, but one kiss from his scorching lips makes her a prisoner of desire.

_3674-6 $4.99 US/$5.99 CAN

The Roselynde Chronicles: Gilliane by Roberta Gellis. After marrying a man she abhors, Gilliane becomes the helpless prisoner—and dazzling prize—of her husband's most dangerous foe, Adam Lemagne. But in the arms of her handsome captor, Gilliane succumbs to his sweet seduction and willingly surrenders her yearning heart in a stormy quest for unending love. Classic Medieval romance.

_3675-4 $5.99 US/$6.99 CAN

Dorchester Publishing Co., Inc.
65 Commerce Road
Stamford, CT 06902

Please add $1.75 for shipping and handling for the first book and $.50 for each book thereafter. NY, NYC, PA and CT residents, please add appropriate sales tax. No cash, stamps, or C.O.D.s. All orders shipped within 6 weeks via postal service book rate. Canadian orders require $2.00 extra postage and must be paid in U.S. dollars through a U.S. banking facility.

Name_____

Address_____

City _____ State_____Zip_____

I have enclosed $_____in payment for the checked book(s).
Payment <u>must</u> accompany all orders.□ Please send a free catalog.

SHADOW of the STORM
DEBRA DIER

Bestselling author of *Surrender the Dream*

Although Ian Tremayne is the man to whom she willingly surrendered her innocence, Sabrina O'Neill vows revenge on him after a bitter misunderstanding. Risking a daring masquerade, Sabrina plunges into the glittering world of New York high society, determined to make the handsome yankee pay. But the virile Tremayne is more than ready for the challenge. Together, they enter a high-stakes game of deadly illusion and sizzling desire that might shatter Sabrina's well-crafted fascade—and leave both their lives in ruin.

_3492-1 $4.50 US/$5.50 CAN

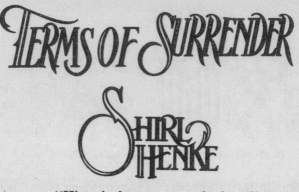

Terms of Surrender

Shirl Henke

"Historical romance at its best!"
—Romantic Times

Devilishly handsome Rhys Davies owns half of Starlight, Colorado, within weeks of riding into town. But there is one "property" he'll give all the rest to possess, because Victoria Laughton—the glacially beautiful daughter of Starlight's first family—detests Rhys's flamboyant arrogance. And she hates her own unladylike response to his compelling masculinity even more. To win the lady, Rhys will have to wager his very life, hoping that the devil does, indeed, look after his own.

_3424-7 $4.99 US/$5.99 CAN